Dedication

I dedicate this book to Troy and Gene. Two men who have always accepted the crazy, weird and often abrasive person I am, but who have had to fight to be accepted by the world despite being the most loving, kind people anyone could hope to know.

Acknowledgements

My heartfelt thanks to Tim, Sara, Sian, Anke and my husband, without whom I would have crawled under the table and covered my head. Even as a writer, there aren't words enough to express the depth of my gratitude for the help and support you gave me.

SHATTERED GLASS
BY
DANI ALEXANDER

Chapter One

Fucking Bunny Slippers

Colorado's Finest Diner was ugly. I had an excess of time to study it in the two hours I waited for my no-show informant. Brown booths. Yellowed walls and floors. Yellowed tables, for that matter. The window on my right displayed beat-up Fords and Volkswagens that were roasting on pavement and swimming in refracting light. The inhabitants of the diner were more interesting. Teenagers mostly, snacking on fries and chicken fingers. Baubles bounced from their eyebrows and black-painted lips while they chatted energetically. My gaze hopped from one table to the next. With all the boisterous laughter and the rapid fingers texting, it was the quiet, methodical busboy who caught and held my eye. He was wearing bunny slippers.

Dingy pink and brown ears languished against aged linoleum, making a soft sh-sh sound as the man gathered used dinnerware and placed them in a tub at his hip. Curious about the wearer, I skipped over the ripped pajama bottoms and stained tank top, to his face. My breath caught.

Model beautiful, with thick red hair and millions of freckles, the man was as incongruous to the setting as those endearing slippers.

"Gaines says he'll get Alvarado there," Detective Luis Martinez relayed into the cell phone tucked against my ear.

"Uh huh," I replied. Vice busts weren't that interesting right now. Bunny Slippers was pierced. Lots of places. Little rings, nipple high, were outlined under his tank top and the ones in his ears and eyebrow glinted. I immediately began to speculate where else he was pierced.

"Glass?" Luis huffed into my ear. "Glass, get your head in the game."

Blue eyes. No, not just blue, blue like glacial waters, like romantic poems, like heavens and moonstones. Cornflower blue. And—

Blue like romantic poems? What the ever-living fuck? I turned away quickly and tried to concentrate on Luis's voice.

"What? Oh." I gave my head a shake, scattering the strange thoughts. "If Gaines says Alvarado will be there, we go with that. My guy is a no-show. Gaines is all we have now." I hoped that was the response Luis was waiting for because Bunny Slippers was coming my way, and I lost all ability to think.

"Can I take that for ya?" He had a deep drawl. Not Texas, like my mother, but perhaps Alabama or Georgia. I was so wrapped up in the voice that it took a moment to follow the long, slim finger pointing across the table at my syrup-filled plate. My attention snapped back to the busboy.

Up close Bunny Slippers was even more gorgeous, and older than I'd originally assumed. Freckles dusted his skin from forehead to fingers. A colorful tattoo of the god Hermes covered the right arm from shoulder to elbow. A busboy with an interest in mythology?

"Glass?" Luis growled.

My brain had left the building. "Huh?" I replied brilliantly, to the busboy, not to Luis. I could barely hear Luis. Cold blue eyes. That was all I could concentrate on. Cold but captivating. I had always thought freckles went with innocence, but there was nothing innocent about those eyes.

"Glass? *¡Carajo!* Glass!"

What was someone who looked that good, doing working as a busboy in a place this ugly?

"GLASS!" Luis blasted into the phone, a stream of Spanish invectives following the shout.

The yell snapped me out of my daze. "What the fuck, Luis? Someone is talking to me here. Settle your dick down." Great, I had now acknowledged that while I knew slippers-boy was speaking to me, I had just been staring at him. The slight smirk spreading across the man's perfect lips told me he had noticed the gawping, too.

With considerable effort, I flicked a glance to the plate, knowing there was a question in there somewhere.

"Your plate?" The busboy motioned once more, this time leaning across the table. The scent of tobacco, soap and cinnamon made my mind go blank again. I closed my eyes and inhaled, unconsciously lifting a hand to brush my knuckle on the underside of the man's reaching arm.

Apparently this was an awesome time to not only discover I had a bunny slipper fetish, but to violate someone's arm in public. Some *guy's* arm.

"Yeah," I said stiffly, dragging my offending appendages into my lap before they did something stupid, like tweak a nipple ring. Luckily, the guy hadn't noticed the knuckle-assault, or else he was choosing to ignore it. *Please let it be the former.*

I felt twelve again, those nervous flutters in my stomach appearing for the first time since I had let Mitzi Baylor tongue kiss me in eighth grade. Okay, *let* is probably the wrong word. More like forced her tongue into my mouth while I tried to protect my tonsils from unexpected removal. The memory was enough to jar me back into reality a second time. I checked my phone. Luis had hung up. With a sigh, I tucked the cell into my pocket. I'd deal with Luis at work Monday.

Bunny Slippers had long since grabbed my plate and was making his way back to the kitchen without a single backwards glance. He hipped the swinging door and disappeared into the back. It was only then that I managed to exhale.

Get a grip, idiot. This is a bad time to ogle teenagers.

Is there ever a good time to ogle teenage boys?

All these weird thoughts were giving me a headache. The guy was just interesting. That was all. Like spotting an exotic flower in a field of—

I really needed to stop thinking like my eleven-year-old poetry-writing cousin. Actually, I just needed to leave. Stop thinking about this and leave. After paying the bill, I slid sunglasses over my eyes and pushed out into the summer sun.

Little beads of sweat popped up on the bridge of my nose, tempting me to remove the offending eyewear. But the light bouncing off my side mirror convinced me that dealing with irritating sweat was better than being blind.

Colorado heat didn't blast so much as bake. It was a deceiving warmth, slowly building like a preheating oven and just as dry. The other trick of summer in the Mile High City of Denver— breezes. They moved lackadaisically, intermittently dying out and then ambling back, providing little in the way of their supposed function: cooling. By the time I had walked across the small parking lot and opened the door to my Jag, my hair was hot enough to fry an egg, and I dearly wished to be wearing shorts rather than full length khakis. I pinched the fabric of my cotton shirt and waved it while the single breeze that rolled through offered only a tumbling brown paper bag and no relief from the warmth. Across the street, a bank marquee announced the date and today's temperature: ninety-seven degrees.

Ignition on, A/C maxed, I left the door open while waiting for the air to cool. Maybe another breeze would surprise me and suck the staleness from the car. Sitting half-in, half-out, I heard the door opening in the alley beside the restaurant. I saw him in the rearview first, then swiveled in my seat to check the back window.

Bunny Slippers leaned against the wall, dragging a foot up to brace behind him and cupping his hand over his face. I fixated on the tattoo marking the web of his fingers, my pulse jumping. When the hand dropped to his side, he took a long drag of his cigarette. His mouth puckering and blowing a cloud of smoke toward the sky was sufficiently erotic enough to ignore the nag of the tattoo and focus on his lips.

I hated smoking. The smell alone was enough to nauseate me. But right then, more than anything, I wanted to be that cigarette.

I was unsettled by an onslaught of unbidden fantasies, which ranged from pressing my lips against the guy's neck to grinding our hips together. I wasn't sure how long I watched him, but I knew it was long enough for my neck to cramp. Sweat accumulated under my glasses, spreading to my forehead and upper lip and eventually dripping down my temple. The cool air blowing from the car created a stark contrast to the heat outside, but I wasn't at all sure it was what made me shiver.

His head swiveled slowly against the wall, turning to my Jag. No smirk this time, but those eyes were no less beautiful for being empty. The pit of my stomach clenched.

I had seen that look before—abuse victims, prostitutes, dealers, pimps, they all carried it. Grief, sudden and powerful, poured over me in waves, making me avert my eyes. Broken boy, was all I could think. Broken people were dangerous. I swung my legs in and slammed the driver's door, backing quickly out of parking spot. It took every ounce of my will to avoid glancing into the rearview mirror as I pulled onto the street.

I aimed the Jag downtown where my tuxedo was getting fitted.

The tuxedo you're getting married in, Austin. The tuxedo you're marrying Angelica in, Austin, I reminded myself.

Not a Cock Sucking Fixation

Downtown was a maze of cross streets which, like slippers-boy, were incongruous with the rest of their surroundings. While most streets across Denver ran vertically and parallel to each other, some cruel genius decided to build downtown streets diagonally. Although I had lived in the city all of my adult life and had been made to study every street when I had patrolled as a rookie, downtown still remained the most frustrating area to navigate. I usually ended up making at least one wrong turn. And since the streets alternated one-way, whenever I missed one, I had to drive a few extra blocks to get back on track; which meant running into a gazillion traffic lights and waiting for the Light Rail trolleys or shuttle buses to pass. Which also meant that today I was later than I otherwise would've been, and I had to call my fiancée.

"Mm, you're late. What have you been up to?" Angelica's soft voice, filled with amusement, was about the only thing that could make me smile right now.

"Ogling young, pretty boys in diners," I replied. As predicted, she laughed.

"Long as it's not pretty girls." Static told me she had covered the mouthpiece. "Jeffrey wants to know how long it'll be until you get here?"

"If I can find a parking spot, and a street that doesn't lead one way to hell? Maybe fifteen minutes."

"You said that an hour ago," she reminded me.

"I'm downtown now. Looking for a parking spot."

I flipped off a street sign that didn't conform to my need to go right, earning a glare from a misunderstanding motorist who yelled, "Cocksucker!" as I passed. I briefly considered rolling down my window and explaining that I was not, in fact, a cocksucker; that it was just that one fantasy. And besides, I was fairly sure I had a bunny slipper fetish, not a cock sucking fixation. That seemed like a lot of information to impart in the second and a half we had before he pulled ahead of me, so I let it slide.

The fact that I was more comfortable owning up to the slippers thing and not the cocksucker thing was mildly disturbing. I'd rather have a footwear fetish than a sudden attraction to penises? Yeah, that sounded about right.

"Just park anywhere. You can afford the ticket." Angelica had no logic when it came to money. Her idea made complete sense to her. Paying for a ticket was infinitely easier than finding a legal parking spot. And as a trust fund baby, I could just as easily pay it. The only problem was that downtown also enjoyed a healthy respect for tow trucks. And no one was going to tow away my beloved Arturo—so named after my training officer.

"I see an open lot. Be there in fifteen. Love you." I hung up after hearing her reply in kind and then pulled into a garage parking structure. After parking and paying, I walked the half block to the 16th Street Pedestrian Mall.

The mall stretched, coincidentally, sixteen blocks, straight down into the heart of the business district. Large granite sidewalks extended six feet out on either side of the shuttle bus lanes. Restaurants, office buildings, outdoor cafés, street vendors, shopping centers and upscale boutiques huddled together on each block. The tailor was at the far end of the mall—not a long walk, but, with the crowds, an annoying one.

The only vehicles allowed on the two-lane road between the sidewalks were police cars, vendor trucks and environmentally friendly shuttle buses. Otherwise, the mall was strictly foot traffic. On weekdays, it teemed with businessmen and women, as well as tourists. In the evenings and on weekends, suburbanites bustled past street performers and the homeless. Almost half of the dirty outstretched hands belonged to teenagers. They were the ones that I had difficulty ignoring. Especially today, with the image of that broken boy still haunting my conscience. My gaze kept wandering down to feet, checking for bunny slippers.

I jammed whatever bills and change I had into their hats or hands, until, when I ran out of cash, I had to jump on the overstuffed shuttle. The shuttle wasn't air conditioned, so I arrived at the tailor shop baked and glazed with sweat like the main dish at a luau. Angelica was too engrossed in a gold tie to notice my disheveled appearance.

Pricks and Bunnies

Angelica was, as always, elegant and beautiful. Her brown hair fell into soft waves at her shoulders, and her summer halter dress glowed bright with white polka dots.

"Austin, I'm rethinking the gold," she said when the bell over the door announced my arrival. Her lips were pursed in deliberation as she held up the gold tie with a navy print, tapping her patent high-heeled shoe against the marble floor.

Grateful for something new to think about, I pushed the weirdness of redhead fantasies out of my head and gave my attention to Angelica. Propping an elbow on a nearby shelf, I rested my chin in my hand, basking in the air conditioning. "We could make a rainbow of all the colors you've run through, Angel."

Her lips pursed for a moment then slowly curved upward. "Bit political," her hand waved, "But I'd go with that. We could have a gay wedding. Rainbow suits and ties? Jessica would be pleased." She regarded the ceiling in contemplation. Only her teasing smile gave away she wasn't serious.

"I refuse to make such a suit, mademoiselle!" Jeffrey, of Jeffrey's Custom Tailor, was a small man with long pointed nose, frizzy grey hair and a constantly furrowed brow. Though that last descriptor might be due to our presence, rather than a permanent state. Not that I could blame the tailor. With each of our six visits, Angelica decided on a different style or color. So far, poor Jeffrey had been commissioned for three different suits: one black, one brown, and most recently, one navy; as well as two tuxedos.

"I don't really think she wants a rainbow suit," I reassured him, hiding my grin. To Angelica I raised an eyebrow. "Is your sister gay now? I'm losing track of her sexuality. One week bi, one week straight. It changes faster than our wedding colors, and that's saying something. What are they now, by the way?"

"I don't know. I think she's still testing the waters. She told mom she was going to Pridefest and ride a Harley naked with some woman called..." She tapped her perfectly manicured nail against a pile of shirts, "I don't actually remember what she was called. Something that sent mom into fits because it was definitely female." Putting down the gold tie, Angelica held up a grey cravat dotted with dark flecks for my inspection. "Navy and silver? Can we see that navy suit again, Jeffrey?"

"Great. I wouldn't even need Jeffrey. I could just wear my dress uniform." Jeffrey threw me a look bordering on murderous and stomped to the back room. Actually, wearing my dress uniform would have been preferable. The idea of wearing another tuxedo for any occasion made my skin itch.

"Mm. You are yummy when you wear your costume."

"Uniform," I corrected with a rueful grin and chuckle.

"Whatever," she replied airily and laid the grey tie atop a stack of white button-down shirts. She didn't mean to be flippant about my job; she was just preoccupied with wedding planning.

"Exactly," I said. "Whatever you want."

"You're not helpful," she said and shook her head, smiling absently.

"Because I want to live to see twenty-seven. You're on the wrong side of crazy with this wedding planning."

"Pah," Angelica huffed. "You're exaggerating."

I really wasn't. Angelica was one of the kindest and most uncomplicated women I knew; but since she'd started planning this wedding, I was a little afraid. And I dealt with drug dealers and crack whores for a living.

She had fired the caterers when they didn't "condescend to make a buffet style dessert table". The florist had quit after Angelica had said she wanted the roses to match the bridesmaids' dresses, and then promptly changed the wedding colors two days later. She had asked me to tell Mark, one of my groomsmen, to wear heels because he was shorter than all the bridesmaids. I refused and she blamed me for all of the bridesmaids wearing ballet slippers.

Later she would apologize and promise to do better. We forgave her because, in all honesty, the girl who apologized was "our Angelica", not the crazy bride.

Angelica was the barracuda lawyer to whom I could send troubled kids and expect her to defend them vigorously from prosecution. She routinely tried to cook dinner and laughed harder than I when it ended up smelling like an outhouse. She dropped her head and snored loudly when I talked about sports. She burped and watched Saturday morning cartoons.

Angelica was not flakey or indecisive. Until she had to pick chiffon or silk, or roses or chrysanthemums.

Truth be told, I didn't recognize her during wedding planning. So I preferred to steer clear of it.

"Should I stay for another fitting, or have we determined my uniform will work? Or maybe the navy suit he already made?" I asked. Jeffrey, carrying said suit, was approaching us. The sound that echoed in his throat conjured up images of choking cats.

"We're going with the navy suit," Angelica decided with a perfunctory nod and wrinkled her nose at the bundle the tailor held. "Oh, not that one, Jeffrey, the one with the mandarin collar," she clarified.

The strangling cat sound erupted as a screech. "That was black, mademoiselle. Not navy!" I stifled a grin.

"Mm. Oh, Jeffrey, calm down. It's basically the same suit, just in navy." She patted his wiry hair and walked toward the back rooms. Jeffrey's face was red enough to sub as a police light. "Don't disappear, Austin," Angelica called over her shoulder. I watched the way her ass moved under the halter dress. "And stop leering. It's unnerving poor Jeffrey."

"Wouldn't dream of leaving." Or of stopping my leering. "But I'm reasonably sure you're the one unnerving him." The little man made another choked sound and tensed so hard he shook. Being fitted for another suit while a pin-wielding Jeffrey was in the apoplectic throes of agony, officially made me a masochist. By the end of the day I'd have enough pricks to prove it.

I should stop thinking about pricks. And bunnies. And pricks fucking bunn—

"Please, I beg of you, stop her, Monsieur Glass," The tailor's nervous eyes twitched from Angelica at the back of the shop, to me. I couldn't blame him for his plea; she was now investigating a beige suit jacket. "I haven't completed one suit!"

"Now, now, Jeffrey, eight more weeks and we'll both be put out of our tailoring misery."

Douchebag of the Year Award

Two hours later, Angelica twined her fingers with mine as we walked toward my car. We would split up for the day before arriving there, as she had "things to do that would only annoy you, Austin." The wedding colors had been officially changed to navy and silver; though by the next week I expected them to be red and gold, or even pink and black. I was relaxed enough that my mind wandered back to slippers-boy as we moved quietly through the mall. Which relegated me to Biggest Asshole on the Planet.

I needed to stop thinking about it. *Him.* I felt like such a jerk. Especially since I was so lucky to be with her.

"Austin?" Angelica prodded me out of my musings. "What *are* you thinking about?"

I offered a guilty smile at her furrowed brow. "How lucky I am," I said, touching her hand to my lips while wiggling my brows.

She laughed musically and leaned into my arm. The bump was too soft for any effect other than to cause me to look at her. I winced when I compared her tanned shoulder to freckled skin. I was a bastard. Angelica was beautiful, both inside and out, and to compare her to some grungy man-child was Grade-A douchbaggery.

"My dress came in today," Angelica sighed blissfully, her green eyes glazing over. Unbidden, I pictured eyes the color of the sky.

"Can I come in your dress today?" My brows waggled again, earning another bright laugh from her.

"Mm. Maybe later this week. Oh, and don't forget we have the gala next Sunday." We stopped at a nearby hotel, using their taxi stand to get her a ride home. With a quick kiss and a gentle wave, she climbed into the first cab that pulled up and they drove off.

Continuing the Douchebag of the Year theme, I walked the half block, got into Arturo and drove thirty blocks out of my way to pass slipper-boy's diner.

I honestly had no idea why I was there, or why I couldn't keep my mind off him. *Him.* I even had to keep reminding myself it *was* a him. Not a her. No breasts. And, I guessed, no vagina. Definitely a him. And my fantasies were filling with images of *his* mouth on naked things of mine.

Naked things. With a guy. Naked things with a guy. Surreal.

I sat outside for half an hour with those words buzzing in my ear, before giving myself a mental slap and driving home. I resolved to forget about Bunny Slippers.

A block later the resolve crumbled as I began picturing those slippers' ears flopping around with the guy's feet in the air while I pounded into—

Jesus! Okay, that's just disturbing.

We Played Football Together, They Can't Be Gay

Back at my apartment, I sat at the computer and shuffled through websites. The moment I found myself downloading the wrong kind of porn, I figured I should go out. I needed to get my mind off sex. It was nearly an impossible feat, so I settled for keeping my mind off sex with a *guy*. Seriously. What the fuck?

I wasn't gay. You don't go twenty-six years before the gay gene suddenly just kicks in. It didn't work like that. I was sure of it. Not that I knew that much about being gay. I had one friend with same-sex orientation, and Dana hadn't spoken to me since I asked her to describe her honeymoon in graphic detail—and then made vibrator noises. Actually, I would have called Dana anyway, but she was out of town until the end of the month.

Obviously Angelica's sister came to mind. But Jessica had about as much figured out as I did. And if she was a lesbian, well, I probably would be less interested in that aspect of gay life than my current dilemma. I decided to call my best friend.

When I was in eighth grade, I used a self-timing camera to take nude pictures of myself in various stages of erection. I then exchanged my biology teacher's slides with the images. The teacher, in a state of panic, kept rapidly pressing the 'next' button. It was like a pornographic flip-book. That was the last straw in a very heavy pile of straws. I was expelled, and I ended up transferring mid-year from boarding school to a public school near home.

In retrospect, I probably shouldn't have included my grinning face in the pictures. With a thumbs up next to my penis.

Having spent the previous years at an overseas coed Catholic preparatory school, I had no idea how to cope with students who were not rich and privileged. I went from being one of sixty students to one of fifteen hundred plus. On my first day of class, I wore my former school uniform: tie, blazer, tan pants, button-down shirt. I don't remember much except dark lockers and so many wedgies that even at age twenty-six I couldn't see a thong without cringing.

By the end of the day, a sophomore named David Buchanan had rescued me and taken me under his wing. We had been getting in trouble ever since.

Dave was now married, and his wife was pregnant with their fourth child. He was the first person I went to when the world confused me. Which it often did. "Do you know any gay guys?" I asked when he picked up the phone.

"Why? Are you switching teams?" I heard the low chuckle on the other end.

"I'm not sure. Maybe," I answered sincerely. He laughed again, because that's what everyone did when I told the truth. It was a little disconcerting.

"Yeah, I know some gay guys. And you do, too."

"I know some gay guys?" News to me.

"Jake and Terry."

"They're not gay," I argued.

"Yeah? You better tell them to stop sleeping together, then."

"We played football with Jake and Terry," I maintained. "They can't be gay." They were also cops, like us. I was sure I didn't know any gay cops. The stationhouse didn't have the most gay friendly atmosphere.

The silence on the other end was either him covering the phone to laugh, or him waiting for me not to be stupid. Usually it was the latter.

"This for a case?" There was a hint of amusement in his voice. I pulled the phone away and studied it, unsure of how to answer that question.

"No. I need to know about ass-sex." Dave choked, ended up in a coughing fit and, from the clunk on the other side, I guessed he must have dropped the phone. I grinned, having already figured that would be his response. When the coughing had subsided, I attempted to change the subject—before he took me seriously. "How's Marta?"

"Beautiful," he answered.

"Am I still banned from Sunday night dinners?" Marta was Swedish, tall, and always pregnant. But I should have asked David if she was pregnant that last time I saw her, because Marta was also a very large woman—rotund, my grandfather would have said. And I was very congratulatory.

"Next time, ask me first. She was barely three weeks along. Not showing at all." This sent us both into nervous laughter. Not only because we were ashamed. If she heard us laughing about it, she'd stop making those awesome Swedish brownies.

"I plan on it. Give my love to the rugrats. And tell her if it's a boy, she should name him Austin."

"I'll skip that recommendation. You're not at the top of her favorite people list."

"Tell her I'm sorry." *Again.* I sighed.

"Send her a pair of baby sneakers. She goes nuts for baby things."

"She'll have them by Friday," I promised.

"Gotta go," he replied, and in the background I heard screaming which sounded like their two year old, Petra.

"Go," I laughed.

After we hung up I considered calling Terry or Jake, but I needed a game plan first. I didn't really want another set of friends banning me from their houses—or house. I really should have asked Dave if they lived together. Terry's cell was programmed into my phone. I made a mental note to call. Later. Tomorrow. Next month. Or January.

On another note, now that I thought about it, I seemed to get banned from a lot of friends' homes.

Tapping my fingers against the computer desk, I considered what to do next. I was avoiding the computer because of the gay porn, avoiding Angelica because I was guilty of wanting to watch gay porn, and avoiding my friends because I had to ask them about gay porn—or being gay, same difference. I could have called my father, but it would be too tempting to piss him off by telling him I might be gay. Which I wasn't.

I settled on a beer and ESPN.

By the time I crawled into bed, I refused to acknowledge the last few minutes of beating off while watching the Duke/Notre Dame lacrosse match. I rolled over and forced myself to go over my Sunday routine of workouts, sports bars and what to do in the absence of my normal Sunday dinner at Dave's.

Chapter Two

Denial. How fucking works it?

Sunday morning I opened my eyes and immediately went into denial.

I was not gay. I was engaged. To a woman. I wasn't gay. And I backed up my denial with some sound reasoning.

First, I masturbated to images of women. I fantasized about women. Sure, there were men *in* my fantasies, but they were always doing women. Everyone did that. There were never solo men in my fantasies. Or my porn—discounting the previous night's anomaly. Therefore, I wasn't gay.

Second, people didn't suddenly wake up gay. Being gay wasn't like changing eye colors; you couldn't just get contacts and "Whammo!"—gayness. Point two for me. Not gay.

Third, I had sex with women. Six women, in fact, since I graduated from high school. I had even been engaged to women before Angelica—who I'd been with for three years now. A man didn't date a woman in her mid-thirties without realizing commitment was going to be on the table—very prominently, lit up with flashing lights, stacked above everything else, on the table. If I was that eager to get into a committed relationship with a woman—point three in the 'not gay' column.

And finally, being gay would seriously piss off my dad. Something I enjoyed immensely. The fact that I was debating if I could possibly be gay, and not driving over there to watch him keel over in shock as I announced it—another tick for 'not gay'.

That settled that, then.

"I'm not gay," I told my ceiling.

Taking a deep breath, I crawled out of bed and grabbed a pair of track pants. After getting dressed, I tried to avoid all internal discussions and zoned out watching ESPN while running on the treadmill. That plan was shot to shit the moment I turned on the TV.

There was no way gay men watched as much ESPN as I did—another check to the 'not gay' column. My confidence was returning; that made five ticks in column 'not gay', zero ticks for column 'gay'. I felt immeasurably better. Until I entered the shower.

Why were men, who weren't me, figuring in my fantasies at all? That was the first question that popped up in my mind. My subconscious, not-so-covertly, slipped into my head, *You've cheated on every woman you've been with.*

Yes, but with other women, I answered it.

Because you didn't want to get married, it said.

The relationships weren't working.

Shut up.

I didn't even need my subconscious to argue why the relationships weren't working: Sex.

It had never been exactly perfect. I had never felt that burning sensation in my stomach when I was around women or when I met someone new. But I was twenty-six. Kids got that feeling, not adults.

Mitzi. That was the last time I had felt that sensation. She was a girl.

That was your first kiss, though, and twenty-some other kids were watching.

Stop thinking about this! Easy to say, impossible to do.

That wasn't the last time, now that I was thinking about what-I-wasn't-supposed-to-be-thinking-about. I paused in the middle of soaping up my chest.

It *wasn't* Mitzi. It was Jesse Chambroy, and I had been fourteen. I exhaled sharply and collapsed against the tile wall. After standing under the spray, in shock, for a good ten minutes, I climbed out of the shower, carefully, and braced my hands against the counter top, dripping onto my bathmat. I stared up into the mirror. My stunned brown eyes staring back at me.

Jesse Chambroy, the captain of the varsity football team. Muscled jock who'd had a smile like Tom Cruise. How could I have forgotten that? How could I have forgotten *him*?

Austin or Alex or Idiot

"I'm not gay." That wasn't what I *meant* to say. At least not so bluntly. It had just become a mantra as I drove across town. Repeated over and over so many times that, by the time I stood in the diner, confronted once again by this visceral attraction to a perfect stranger, the words tumbled out.

"Congratulations. Would you like a medal?" Bunny Slippers asked.

"I already have a medal. For bravery, not for being gay. I think you made me gay."

"I *made* you gay?" He set down the napkin he was holding. "Is that better or worse than the person who made you stupid?""

"Worse," I answered automatically. Then I computed what he said. Ouch. "I have a degree."

"What are pointless and obtuse bits of information, Alex?"

"Austin," I corrected.

"Right now, you're Alex."

"What?" This conversation wasn't going at all like I planned.

"This is Jeopardy, right? You give all the answers, I tell you the questions?"

"You're confusing," I answered. Confusing and beautiful. Jesus. So beautiful. His eyes were bright and angry, framed by thick copper lashes. Another white t-shirt wrapped itself tightly against his chest and stomach, showing off his lean body. I might have drooled.

Bunny Slippers watched my appraisal for at least a full minute before clasping his hands and resting them on the table. "You stand in the doorway, clothes sticking to you like you just got out of the shower and didn't dry off." I hadn't dried off actually. "Your hair is wet like it's been raining, but it's near ninety outside. You glare at me for a good ten minutes before you come over. Sit across from me in *my* booth, without an invitation. Don't introduce yourself. Don't say hello. You announce you're not gay, but that I made you gay, and *I* am confusing *you?*"

Well, when he said it like that. "I'm not gay. You just made me *think* I was gay," I clarified. I was frustrated and needed answers. Somehow I figured he had them. Logic: not one of my finer points today. Considering the last twenty-four hours of intense internal debate, I thought it understandable that I was being confusing, and feeling confused. I just wanted to stop thinking about him. Then I could go back to being not gay.

He let out an annoyed breath, blinked and grabbed another set of silverware from the tub to his left. "Go away, little boy," he said as he rolled the utensils up into a paper napkin.

Teenager calling me little boy. Ouch again. I pulled a napkin from the stack and fiddled with it. "I might need to kiss you."

He grabbed the napkin from my hand. "Because you assume *I'm* gay." Once again, this conversation was not going where I thought it should, or where I needed it to go. I had just assumed he was gay. Or, well, I hadn't actually thought about his side of things at all. I just wanted these new feelings and thoughts to coalesce into something that made sense.

"I don't think anything is wrong with being gay. I even have friends who are gay." Now I did, anyway. Yesterday I had *a* friend who was gay, until I talked to Dave.

"Why are you here then? You expecting me to fix it? Something you don't even think is wrong in the first place?"

"Not fix it." *Yes, fix it.* "Just, people don't discover they're gay at twenty-six."

"People have found out at fifty they were gay," he pointed out, concentrating on his work. I wanted to take that tub of silverware and toss it through the plate-glass window, so he could give this crisis the attention it deserved.

"Yeah, but those are repress—" Oh. I rubbed the bridge of my nose and then gave him what I thought was my most sincere smile. "I have no reason to repress it. I really, really don't think there's anything wrong with being gay. In fact, if I were gay, I'd probably take out an ad. It would piss my dad off. I live to do that. There's even a motto to that effect tattooed on my ass." *Wanna see?*

"Listen, Alex—"

"Austin."

"Austin, Alex, *Idiot*. Whatever. I don't care. Not about your name, not about your gayness or not gayness, not about your parents or your friends. I don't care about you perio—" I leaned across the table and parked my lips a hair's breadth from his. Bunny Slippers took a shuddering breath mid-sentence as his eyes blinked to my mouth, and then his lips parted. I wanted to take advantage of that, but the fucking table was busy cock-blocking me.

By the time I maneuvered close enough for our mouths to meet, he was glaring at me and pulling away.

Then he flicked my nose hard enough to make my eyes water.

"Ow! Shit." I sat back down, rubbing the stinging skin and watched him slide out of the booth. He disappeared behind the kitchen doors without so much as a 'fuck off.' Not that I would have done anything even if he had stuck around. The fact that I had tried to kiss him at all had stunned me into a motionless blob. I had wanted that kiss. I had wanted to kiss a guy. Badly. Then another thought leapt into my head before I had the opportunity to weasel my way back into denial.

Why had I gone directly to gay? Not bisexual. Not a passing interest in someone of the same sex. Straight—so to speak—to gay. Do not pass go. Do not collect $200. Gay.

I wandered out into the parking lot in a daze, sat in my Jag, staring ahead. Cars zoomed past. I began counting them in order to avoid thinking. It didn't work. I drove home thinking about it, thought about it while eating dinner, through another ESPN marathon, when ordering a truckload of baby stuff for Marta online. And when I climbed into bed, it was still the only thing I was thinking about.

What would Monday be like at the station with this new found information? Would I suddenly start checking out guys? Would someone see something different about me?

I still had no answers when I fell asleep, just one more question. What about Angelica?

Booyah!

My tie flapped behind me. My dress shirt soaked with sweat under my suit jacket. "Suspect heading north on Josephine, crossing 19th. Over," I huffed into the radio. Blood pounded in my ears while I panted each breath. My shoes lifted off the sidewalk as I twisted, dodging pedestrians and hopping over parked cars.

I was gaining ground, pushing myself to go faster when Prisc Alvarado stumbled into the intersection ahead of me. The toes of my shoes nearly collided with his sneakered heels before I leaped onto his back, both of us falling in a heap.

Alvarado's elbow smashed into my ribcage as he threw his head back. I jerked away just in time to stop him from smashing my nose into my brain. "Fucking," I panted, "stay," huff, "still, asshole."

Digging my knee into his ass, I scooted it up to the small of his back, fingers wedged into his neck. I pushed his face into the cement while reaching for my cuffs, trying to see what I was doing while sweat blurred my vision. My hundred and seventy pounds of muscle fought every inch of his two hundred plus pounds. Adrenalin at an all-time high, I laughed euphorically while slipping the steel over Alvarado's wrists. Two patrolmen pulled up and rushed over to assist. I jumped off my suspect once he was cuffed and did a small victory dance, still panting merrily.

"What was that, thirteen blocks?" I looked to both uniformed men for an answer.

"Seventeen," Fitzpatrick answered with a chuckle, lifting the suspect onto his feet.

Officers Kelly Fitzpatrick and Jason Dillon were affectionately known as Mick and Dick. The names derived from some very serious racial stereotyping in Mick's case. And Dick? Dick resembled a walking penis. Not that either of them complained. Dick, a tall, skinny, dark-skinned man with all of seven hairs on his head, clearly won in the nickname department, as far as I was concerned. Mick, by contrast, had a full head of salt and pepper hair and was built like a truck.

"Booyah!" I pumped a fist to my hip, wearing my goofiest grin. This was a good collar, and I was going to milk it.

Luis pulled our unmarked piece-of-shit (read: police issued car) to the curb beside the patrol car and got out shaking his head. The two patrolmen led our suspect to their vehicle. Then Luis smacked me upside the head.

"Knock that shit off," he said, nodding at my dance of triumph. My dance halted, but my grin didn't fade.

"Fucking cracker," Alvarado hissed as he was shoved into the patrol car.

"Aw, that's discrimination, right there." I feigned hurt. "See, I see you as scumbag first, Alvarado. Or dick-cheese. Scum-sucking pedophile. Asshole. The fact that you're Hispanic doesn't even factor into it." I aimed my stupid grin at Luis.

"Lawyer," Alvarado spat as the door slammed shut.

Well, shit.

"Nice bust, kid." Luis laughed. My grin widened at the compliment.

Still high from my Superpowers of Awesomeness, I pushed off the sidewalk and slid across the hood of our car on my back, landing neatly on the other side. The heat from the car's metal hood clung to my suit. "Let's catch some more bad guys."

Throwing open the passenger door, I flopped in the seat, pulling the door shut.

Luis stayed outside, talking to Fitzpatrick and waving happily at Alvarado, who was probably giving us the finger. I scrambled out of my suit jacket and prayed for air conditioning.

"You kids today," Luis commented as he slipped into the driver's seat. Neither of us mentioned the way my hands shook as they drummed against my knee. "See what you did? Now we have to go and fill out goddamn paperwork for the rest of the afternoon."

We turned to each other and chuckled. After a six-hour stakeout and then a manic chase, we were both counting on some mind-numbing paperwork.

At fifty-four, and two hundred and thirty pounds, there weren't many foot pursuits that ended in arrests for Luis. Which was, I assumed, why they had paired us. Well, that, and the fact that he had the highest closure rate in Vice and Homicide combined, and I needed experience. But, while I was the rookie detective, I could hold my own—especially in situations like today, when one of our arrestees threw himself out the open patio doors and booked it down the street.

In the world of dirtbags, Prisc Alvarado was aiming to be the king. Like most seasoned criminals, Alvarado's arrest record began small with petty theft, dealing and pandering. It was as a pimp where he found his calling. His arrest, we hoped, would severely slow the expansion of his growing human trafficking business. The case of a lifetime in a city not known for high profile organized crime. It was a good day for Luis and me. Hell, it was a good day for humanity.

"We gotta go back to that dirtbag's house and watch them complete the search," Luis told me.

"What's it look like?"

"It looks like one of Vice's biggest busts in three years." He laughed, lighting a cigarette and rolling down the window. I grimaced and rolled mine down, too. To reiterate, I hated smoking. And much as I liked Luis, I didn't want to be *his* cigarette. With an extra thirty pounds around his middle, he was definitely no Bunny Slippers.

And now, of course, I was thinking about him.

Luis did a one-eighty, and we were both silent as we headed back to Alvarado's house. I got lost in thoughts about freckles and hostile youths, while trying to hold my head out the window and avoid the smell of smoke. Luis, I presumed from the silence, was contemplating the mounds of paperwork we were going to be doing until late tonight.

"You bringing Angelica by this Sunday?" Luis said.

"Sunday?"

"Yeah. The barbeque."

I regarded him blankly for a second and then remembered that he'd invited us to a cookout a few weeks ago. We always had a good time with Luis and his family. But I hadn't seen my fiancée in two days, since the tux fitting, and I didn't relish the thought of talking to her anytime soon. My stomach knotted just thinking about it. Better to not think about it. Always better to not think about it.

"Can't do, sorry. Parents having a fundraiser. Just found out the Chief'll be there." I waggled my brows.

"Kissing some ass, then?"

"Whatever it takes," I replied. Luis knew about my FBI plans. Everyone in the division knew. "Kissing ass, sucking cock." I blanched at the words as I said them. I had been trying to not to think about that very thing all day. My stare settled outside my window where rolling green lawns sparkled with sprinklers.

Now I was thinking about jizz.

"Hey, you don't need to kiss ass, kid." I didn't mind the nickname, though it was condescending. He could've called me a lot worse than 'kid'.

Way back when I started the force, I got a lot of flak from the other officers. My family was rich—*I* was rich. A lot of the guys assumed, rightly or not, that being a cop was just some flakey rich kid's rebellion. I was going to college at night back then. My days were spent on patrol. I joined the police force early so I could get the required experience before I applied with the Federal Bureau of Investigation. Rich kid joining the police force for kicks? That was bad. Rich kid using the police force for his own ambitions? That, other cops could understand, even if they didn't approve of it. Ambition meant that I was going to work my ass off. And I did.

"I gotta kiss ass, Luis. You know it, and I know it. My record's good, but when the hiring freeze is over, applications are going to pile high. I want mine to rise to the top." I batted my lashes at him, adding in an affected feminine voice, "Like lovely clotted cream." This earned me another swat to the head.

Whatever. I still felt on top of the world, even though I was going to spend the rest of my shift doing nothing but cataloging evidence and filing paperwork.

We left the station around midnight, exhausted, but still on a high from our bust. Although Alvarado had lawyered up, we had good evidence: Mexican passports and I.D.s; pictures of men, women and children along with names and ages; paperwork on various warehouses in the city and a hefty sum of cash. I waved goodnight to Luis, fully intending to head home and sleep—or, more likely, blackout. But once out on the road my car seemed to steer on its own.

Neutral Schmeutral

Throughout my crazy day, I had failed to keep my mind off Bunny Slippers, but at least they were neutral thoughts. Was he a college student, working as a busboy to pay his tuition? Did he live at home, or in a dorm? What did he taste like?

Maybe not so neutral.

This obsession was terrifying. I couldn't go one hour without thinking about him. I was sick of thinking about it. My sexuality shouldn't be an issue at twenty-six. I had to do something. To prove...Prove what? I didn't know. My answer was inside the diner; I had somehow convinced myself of that much.

The thought of even possibly being gay terrified me. I worked hard to prove myself on the force, and soon I'd have enough experience as a detective to apply to the FBI. Law enforcement careers weren't particularly conducive to being gay. *And fuck it, I'm not gay. Goddammit.*

I'm bunny-slipper-sexual?

Not gay, but there I was, sitting in my car, parked in the diner's lot, watching the alley through my rearview mirror. My stomach twisted at the thought of seeing him. It was becoming more and more difficult to swallow with the knot in my throat. And I had barely thought about Angelica all day.

"You're an asshat, Austin," I said to myself.

Shit. Hell. Damn.

Go home. Call Angelica. Or go to a shoe store and buy the boy some loafers.

I switched the car on and prepared to pull out. The dashboard clock blinked at me. I had been sitting here three hours arguing with myself over whether to go in or go home.

Three hours.

Oh, Christ. This was getting creepy.

Reaching for the stick shift, I got ready to pull out. The side door to the restaurant opened.

I froze as the lighter illuminated his cheek and lips. He took a long drag, billowing smoke out into the night. My heart beat erratically. I sat there, same position as last time, same neck ache, same inability to leave. He was about fifteen feet from my Jag. Fifteen bunny-slippered feet.

Even this late, the parking lot was full of battered cars, probably from club-goers getting a last meal before passing out. But mine was the only car idling. Which was why I wasn't surprised when Bunny Slippers propped his shoulder against the wall, cocking his head slightly as he looked toward my car. My breath halted. I was sure he couldn't see me through the darkened windows, but somehow, it felt like he was seeing right into my slipper-obsessed soul.

The bunny slippers, a different pair—and how many did he have, for fuck's sake?—appeared under the street lights as he walked toward my car, cigarette flicking from his fingers and bouncing across the pavement. I followed the trail of red sparks until they burned out. "Fuck," I whispered.

I stared in horrified fascination as he made his way to the passenger side door. My pulse jumped at each tap of his knuckles against the window. It took several seconds to decide whether to roll it down or just unlock the door. I chose the latter.

Pulling his apron off over his head, Bunny slippers climbed in the passenger seat and shut the door. Scents—his scents—filled the car: tobacco, soap, and something herbal that reminded me of my college girlfriend's incense. I detected cinnamon and sugar as well, and I wondered if he had been baking.

"Hey," I said lamely. I didn't know what else to add. *I just want to get to know you? Buy you loafers?* The longer I sat, the faster my heart worked. *Say something. Say something. Say some*—"How was your day?"

"Who gives a fuck?" His voice was as cold as his glare. Not that coldness detracted from his beauty; quite the opposite. It only complemented the sharp angles of his face.

I didn't know how to respond to his aggressive declaration, and apparently he wasn't adding anything else to the conversation, so the two of us sat in silence.

I guess I thought he'd give a fuck. He had, after all, climbed into my car. Though now he seemed to be debating whether to leave or talk or, well, judging by the way his fingers were opening and closing on the door handle, there was some debate about something. I was about to ask him to coffee—because I was the lamest guy *ever*—when he spoke up.

"Fifty bucks for a blow, twenty for hand. You don't touch me or kiss me. And I don't fuck. Payment up front. Got it?" His head tilted, those dead eyes watching me like he could give two shits whether I took the offer or left it.

I should have expected it. Shit, I was a vice cop, I should have fucking expected it. But the thought hadn't even crossed my mind. And the clenching ache in my gut was ten times worse because of my ridiculous idealism. I blamed those damn slippers.

Of course, I couldn't take him up on it.

But Jesus, I wanted to.

Our eyes met as I heard myself ask, "How much to touch you?" *Jesus Christ. What the hell am I doing?* A giant sign in my head kept flashing: "Career ending! Career ending!" in bright neon red.

I knew what I was doing, though, and I just had to take the risk. Him touching me could leave doubts. But if I willingly put my hands on another man, and I enjoyed it, then some of my questions would be answered. I *needed* this debate resolved to function normally again. And better with a whore than some random stranger who could get attached. Or with whom I could get attached.

His shoulders dropped for a second and then tensed. He set his jaw and chewed his lower lip. He was calm. By contrast I was a mess. My nails dug into my thighs, my breathing heavy and clipped, and I couldn't stop staring at him. Was he gauging my desperation? It had to be obvious just how desperate I was. The sad part was, it wasn't even desperation to fuck him. Well, it was and it wasn't. It was more than that.

"Two hundred." He turned to the scenery outside my window.

"Do you want to wait here while I go to an ATM?" Did I actually just say that? I was oddly excited, vaguely nauseated and terrified. I didn't even know how old he was.

And...I kept staring at his feet. What would his reaction be if I offered to buy him sneakers? Big, ugly, pink-checkered sneakers. The kind of footwear that even I couldn't find attractive.

Bunny Slippers reached behind him and pulled the safety belt across his chest. I mentally laughed at the gesture. For all he knew, I could be taking him off to murder him, and he was putting his seatbelt on, making it easier to hold him hostage.

Wrapping my arm around the back of his headrest, I twisted to check my blind spots and pulled out of the parking lot. I kept my hand on his seat while I drove. Delicious sprouts of auburn hair almost touched my skin. Almost. If I just stretched my finger...

Think of something to say, Austin. Nothing came to mind except that flashing sign that kept changing its marquee. FBI career over! Arrested! Underage Prostitute! Prostitute! Male Prostitute!

Half a block away, I pulled into an ATM kiosk and emptied five hundred dollars from my account; all the while I tried to talk myself out of, and into, this insane plan to pay someone, a *guy*, for sex.

Not sex. You're not having sex with him.

I practically fell into the driver's seat, fumbling with the cash and my seatbelt as I shut the door. Bunny Slippers continued to stare out my window. He hadn't looked at me once since we left the restaurant parking lot. After separating two hundred from the stack of bills, I handed them to him with trembling fingers. "Here, two hundred," I rasped. He tucked the money into what I was just now noticing were jeans, not pajama bottoms. I exhaled in relief. At least I hadn't been checking out what he was wearing.

I slipped the remaining three hundred into my wallet, and without another word I drove toward home. "Do you need to go back to work?" Great, *now* my voice had to quiver? My heart tried to burst through my chest. My palms were slick with sweat. I was a wreck, propelled back into my teenage years by someone who was probably a teenager himself.

"Eventually," he spat out. He seemed unconcerned about our destination, just sitting and staring at the houses as they went by. He was so hostile. I had no idea what the fuck I was doing.

I was a moderately attractive guy—in the wholesome, frat boy way. Nothing exotic—brown hair, brown eyes, and tanned skin. I was attractive. I got plenty of offers. So why was I paying some kid for— And, Jesus, it wasn't even to screw him.

Risking career over paying a hustler for not having sex with you. Brilliant, Austin.

You fail at prostitution.

I wove through town, driving as fitfully as my heart beat. It was a miracle I didn't get pulled over. Bunny Slippers said nothing, no matter how badly I drove. I tried to come up with something to say, anything, to fill the awkward silence.

"What's your name?"

"What do you want it to be?" he asked acerbically, not bothering to acknowledge me with more than words.

"Bunny Slippers," I said, trying for a smile that I hoped wasn't a leer. It probably was a leer, though. I was so hard my cock was aching.

"What the f—" He sighed, eyes rolling in his head. "Peter," he ground out through clenched teeth. My heart jumped as the corners of his lips twitched. Was that the truth? I hoped it was. Not because the name had any significance, but because I didn't want him playing a part for me. I wanted to believe he was real. My naïveté was ridiculous. I was only assigned to Vice six months ago, but I'd been on the force for eight years. Boys like Peter were hard-edged and dangerous. If the captain could see me, he would boot me off the force for being an idealistic jackass—and possibly for statutory rape.

Oh yeah, and solicitation, Austin. Don't forget that career-ending solicitation part, Austin. Penal code 18—7—202: Solicitation for prostitution. Otherwise known as: Your-Fucked-Career.

"How old are you?" I finally asked.

The withering scowl he gave was uplifting. At least it wasn't inscrutable. "How old do you want me to be?"

I laughed. "I walked into that."

"Whatever."

"Does open hostility work well in your profession?" I flashed my most charming grin. He stared back at me, blank.

"You're not paying me for conversation." It was hard to tell, while trying to drive and study him, but I thought I saw his lips twitch again.

"I assumed it was part of the package." I threw another layer of charm into my smile.

"Does naïve and clueless work in your profession?"

Five blocks passed in silence. "Twenty-four," I said, pulling onto my street. I laughed as his brows curled in confusion. "How old I want you to be."

"Tough shit. I'm twenty." Some of my nausea disappeared.

"Home sweet home," I announced.

My apartment building had been converted from an old Victorian home. I owned it, loved it, treated it with the kindness it deserved. The main house contained six units and there was an old, detached carriage house around back. The flower garden was bisected by a path to the side gate, and a row of bushes lined the stairs that led to the entrance. Peter followed me up the front stairs and along the path behind the main house to the carriage house—my carriage house. I had refurbished it into a two-story apartment. It was my pride and joy.

On Angelica's recommendation, I had hired the best interior designers and decorators, and it showed in the expensive contemporary brown and cream designs. Of course it was the stupidest idea ever to bring a hustler here, where there were so many pawn-able items.

Jesus H. Christ. I am a fucking idiot.

Once inside, Peter said nothing about how awesome the apartment was, and I was a little perturbed. But, then again, he only seemed to vacillate between hostile and apathetic; I wasn't sure I wanted his opinion.

Hours of stalking—er, sitting—in my hot car had enhanced the loveliness of my natural scent. Plus I was nervous—like this was a first date. There were sweat marks all around my clothes. "I'm going to take a shower upstairs. There's one down here, too. In there." I pointed to the right, where a hallway led to the guest bedroom and bathroom. "Try not to steal anything." I was joking but, then again, I wasn't. I didn't realize that the words might be offensive—*were* offensive—until they slipped out.

Whatever. He was a whore. Right?

"I'll try my best. But just in case I find a fence willing to open his own personal Pottery Barn, leave the keys to the Jag so I can load it up," he tossed back caustically.

My jaw fell. Was that a joke? I was about to ask him, but the words collapsed in my throat as he pulled his shirt over his head. I caught the rippled muscles and slope of his back before he disappeared down the hall.

My mouth went dry. I started hoping he'd rob me or beat me. At least that would break this...whatever it was. Obsession? I nearly ran upstairs to take a shower.

It wasn't until I stood under the shower spray that I remembered Angelica. Guilt made me press my forehead against the white tiles. Then the stream of questions and doubts surfaced again. My job. My fiancée. My job. A prostitute. A male prostitute. My fucking *job*. What, what, *what* was I doing?

Nothing. I was going to do nothing. Talk. I'd talk to him. Nothing more. This was just a phase.

Walking into the bedroom, towel wrapped around my waist, I pretended not to stare at Peter as he reclined on my bed in nothing but his well-worn jeans. His hair was wet and straggly, with strands plastered against his forehead and cheek. He was exquisite.

Shit.

Without thinking, I grabbed jeans and a pair of boxers from the dresser and pulled them on under my towel. Because naturally people put clothes on *after* hiring a prostitute. I did a mental facepalm.

"Time's tickin'" Peter drawled, blank eyes casually checking me out as he propped himself up on his elbows. His body was incredible. I needed something to wipe the drool from my lips.

I couldn't remember being this attracted to anyone—male or female. And Peter was most definitely male. I couldn't even claim that he had a single feminine quality. He was leanly muscled and had a faint six-pack—the sort of stomach that I barely managed with daily rigorous workouts. His skin was pale with a healthy pink undertone. And freckles dotted his stomach, more sparsely than they did his arms, nose and cheeks. I wanted to kiss each one. It would take me hours.

"How much time did I buy?" Apparently nonchalance wasn't an option with a dry throat and trembling voice. My blood grew warm, my pulse sprinting through my veins and my stomach careened down from unfathomable heights.

"An hour," he replied.

Retrieving my wallet from my discarded khakis, my eyes widened in surprise. The other three hundred dollars were still tucked into the leather pocket. Huh. The pants were completely visible on the floor. He saw me put the money in my wallet earlier. It would have taken seconds to find the wallet, pocket the money and get out of here. What would I have done, report him? What kind of whore didn't steal money?

"Come here," I ordered softly. He hesitated and stretched up like a cat. His bare feet made soft sticky sounds on my hardwood floor as he padded over to stand in front of me. He was my height, five feet eleven, or maybe a little taller—it was tough to say. But it made it easier to fall into those blue, blue eyes.

Taking his hand, I placed the last of my money into his palm, catching his fingers as they clenched around the bills. He lifted his chin. "I still don't fuck."

I reached out to touch his lips. He jerked his hand from mine. "How much to kiss you?" *Oh Jesus God, what the fuck am I doing?*

Finally something besides hostility and vacancy in the slight widening of his eyes. Fear? It was gone before I could to analyze it. "You don't have enough money," he answered, tongue flicking out to wet his lips.

I stepped closer, cupping his jaw gently in my palm, my thumb pulling lightly at his chin until his mouth parted. His breath warmed my thumb. "A thousand? Two? Four? Ten?" I'd pay more. I'd pay anything. I wanted to know. Needed to know. Did men turn me on? Was I gay?

As hard as his eyes were, his body was responding—skin flushing, breath quickening. His pulse jumped slightly against the skin on his neck. Whether he was reacting to my offer of money or the way I trailed my thumb across his bottom lip, I wasn't sure.

"There isn't enough money." He flashed his hand in front my nose, opening his palm and releasing the cash to feather-drop into a mess at my feet.

I ignored the crumpled paper, concentrating instead on the rough and soft surfaces of his skin as my fingers traced his cheek and neck. "Two hundred to touch you, only fifty to have my dick in your mouth, but no amount can buy one kiss?"

"The extra is for a blow job? Fine." He reached for my pants, but I stayed his fingers.

"Quit acting like a child," I sighed. "I don't want to have sex with you."

"Fucking liar." He cupped my crotch—my very strained, very hard, very responsive crotch.

"Okay, I'll rephrase. I don't want to have sex with you *right now*." Maybe never. And not for money, I added silently. There was only so much hostility I could take. But there were those small flashes of…something. Every once in a while, they showed through his sharp comments, and I was hooked. "Two hundred to touch you for an hour. Three hundred more for you to stay and…talk with me for the night." I nearly asked how much to keep the bunny slippers on. This conversation was ridiculous. I so failed with whores.

"Something seriously wrong with you," he whispered as my fingers slid from his chin to the dip in his throat.

"Yeah. Yeah, I'm coming to that conclusion, too." As much as he pretended to feel nothing, when my hand pressed against his smooth chest, his heart hammered against it. I was absolutely enraptured by the way he trembled, the goose bumps popping up beneath my delicate exploration of his stomach.

His skin was warm, and softer than I'd imagined, though the muscles were tight just beneath the surface. Each place my fingers trailed a muscle twitched. I licked my lips and brushed them against his shoulder. He tasted of sweat, and a grain of sugar caught on my tongue. "Beautiful."

His body tensed, only to tremble again like a plucked bow string. When I pulled my head back, his eyes were focused on my hand grazing his hip; his lips parted, his skin flushed, and his breath grew sharper with each tiny exhale.

This was too intimate. Maybe more intimate than sex. I drew my hand back and pushed it through my hair.

What are you doing? This is insane. Truly insane.

I had no idea who he was. I wasn't even sure if he had been lying about his age or name. My job, my life, my everything could be torn away thanks to this one little indiscretion. The whole situation just seemed more and more fucked up

Yet, I couldn't help being a little satisfied. I had at least part of my answer. I liked touching him. Still, this was too fucked up to continue.

"You want me to take you home or to the diner?"

His head whipped up. "I'm not giving the money back," he said.

For some reason, that made me laugh. "Keep it." Grabbing my keys off the dresser, I slipped into sandals and threw a shirt over my head. Peter still hadn't moved by the time I was dressed.

He eyed the floor, hands tucked into his pockets. I was astonished to see him smiling. Not a sweet, or even humorous smile; it was just a sad little curl of his lips, and it made him appear so vulnerable. And, like every other emotion I'd seen—besides hostility, which wasn't even really an emotion so much as it was a state of being—this one disappeared quickly. "Whatever." He pushed past me, and I heard his soft footsteps down the stairs.

I followed him with the intent to drive him back. Halfway down the stairs, the front door slammed.

I checked to see if he was waiting by the car, but the area was empty, so I went back inside. Once undressed, I climbed into bed. Exhausted, frustrated and anxious, sleep took hours to find me. I didn't even spare a passing thought about Angelica.

Chapter Three

Theme Of The Day: Prostitutes

Tuesday I was so tired that I confused my orange juice with milk and used the OJ to make scrambled eggs. I didn't even notice until I was chewing. Too groggy to care, I ate it all anyway. It tasted like sweaty feet. Three cups of coffee later, the taste was finally out of my mouth, and the caffeine woke me up enough that I could get dressed and drive to work without nodding off.

I arrived at work thirty minutes late and in an expensive, but rumpled, brown suit. The only positive about working while being this tired was that I couldn't dwell on last night and my epic failure at paying for, but not screwing, a prostitute.

"You look like shit," Luis noted as I took my seat at the desk across from him. His suit wasn't much better than mine in the wrinkled department, and the whole thing probably cost him less than my tie. I had a feeling he'd bought his blue blazer sometime in the 80's, and the trousers a decade before that—back when maroon polyester had actually been in style.

"And you look like the love child of Barney Miller and Archie Bunker." It was as much wit as I could summon in my state. "What's on for today?"

"Gaines has poofed." Great. Our new informant was now our new problem.

I groaned and sized up the inviting surface of my desk. I wanted to lay my cheek against the wood and sleep until everything requiring a functioning brain went away. I didn't have patience for an idiot like Gaines.

Him 'poofing' meant he was going underground, probably because he was vying to take over Alvarado's operations—a common reason why snitches snitched on their business partners. The only other reason why he might disappear was that he had been outed as a snitch. Either way, Luis and I would be spending the day questioning whores and pimps and the rest of society's dregs in order to find him before Alvarado made bail.

"Can we shoot him?" I asked. That earlier feeling of wanting to press my face against the desk returned. I went with it. "Didn't that whore—whatshername? We busted her last month. Said Gaines was her baby's daddy," I mumbled into the desktop.

"Are you making out with that desk?"

"Well, my boyfriend keeps refusing to."

Luis stopped typing on his computer. A few seconds later he said, "Rhonda Pendergrass."

"Think his name is Peter."

"The whore?"

"My boyfriend." Well, yes, the whore.

"Right," Luis said, ignoring my statement. No one took me seriously. "Well the whore's name is Rhonda Pendergrass. She rents a house on 27th and Gay—don't say it—lord street."

"I wasn't going to say a word," I lied, standing up and going to the break room to snatch a cup of coffee from the machine. It tasted like mud squeezed off a sweaty foot (my second foray into that food group today). I deliberated on if Peter had sweaty feet. At least I knew I could stand the taste if he did.

What was with me and feet all the sudden?

Peter had been right about one thing. There was something *seriously* wrong with me.

I followed Luis to the car and settled into the passenger seat, leaning my temple against the window. The car dipped as Luis climbed into the driver's side, but I didn't lift my head from the glass until the car got moving.

"You need a nap, kid?" Luis asked.

"I was thinking more along the lines of hibernation," I said, taking a sip, or rather, chewing the coffee as it oozed into my mouth. Blessed caffeine. Who cared about the taste? Or texture, for that matter.

"Late night with Angelica?"

"A male prostitute."

"Named Peter."

"Why not Peter?"

"You should watch what you say. One day someone's is going to take you seriously."

I doubted it. They never had before. And this conversation wasn't nearly as absurd as some of the others. Luis still didn't believe I went to Paris that one night.

"I think I need to ask him on a date," I said. I knew I was pushing it, but I was trying to gauge his response as clandestinely as possible while at the same time getting myself to say it—admit it.

"The prostitute?"

"He wouldn't be one on the date."

"Peter."

"Unless you've come up with a better name?"

"Nah. A date with Peter the prostitute. Sounds like a plan. Be sure to bring flowers."

"I was thinking condoms. But, your idea sounds more romantic."

"Romance with the male prostitute, now?"

"It's a little judgmental to assume they don't like romance, Luis."

"Is he jealous of the boyfriend?"

"He *is* the boyfriend." I paused. "Maybe."

"I'm going to change the subject now," Luis said slowly. His careful glance at my hand told me that I was not imagining the uneasiness in his voice.

"Sounds like a plan," I said, echoing his earlier statement. The coffee cup shook in my unsteady fingers.

Luckily, we pulled up to Rhonda's ranch style house a minute later, saving us from coming up with a pretense of conversation. The theme of the day was prostitutes.

We Tested Negative For Hepatitis

If I were casting a commercial on the dangers of methamphetamine use, Rhonda Pendergrass would star in it.

Before meth destroyed her teeth, skin and figure, Rhonda had been a willowy blonde with a come-hither smile; she used to flash it at me as if it could dazzle me enough to keep from arresting her. These days she was still blond, but her hair was greasy. I counted four teeth in various stages of decay, and the dull green of her eyes reminded me of rancid pond water. Her body, encased in a pair of too-tight shorts and tube top, made me worry about bones popping through her scab-smattered skin. She also had five mixed-age children ranging from two-to-nine years old, all of them staring through me with vacant eyes. Additionally unsettling was recalling from her rap sheet that she was only twenty-three.

Since entering her house my main objective had been to leave it, and not just because of the stench of unwashed flesh; I was calling social services the instant we left.

"He ain't here. I don't know where he is," Rhonda stated when Luis asked about Gaines. "He don't come round 'til beginning of the month, when my check come in." Her welfare check. The one she most likely used to buy more meth instead of feeding those kids.

We stood by the front door, at the far end of a brown carpeted living room. The kids sat or crawled on the floor and the holey sofa a few feet away. The pair of preschool-aged twins watched a fuzzy television while a girl about five or six, with a bushel of awesomely bouncy curls, was de-stuffing the cushions. The oldest boy, tall and olive-skinned with angry brown eyes, grabbed a drug pipe from one of the toddlers, who appeared to be using the bulbous end to soothe his gums. I couldn't help myself; I walked a few steps inside the house, took the pipe, and slipped it into my coat pocket before returning to my position by the door at Luis's side. I tried to avoid eye-contact of any kind with the kids after that.

"Why don't you go ahead and write down a list of his numbers and places he'd go," Luis said, holding out his notepad and pencil to her. "Friends. Relatives. Anyone or anyplace you can think of."

"I don't know his friends." She ignored the tablet, crossed her arms and scratched her elbow. I winced and unconsciously took a step back as a scab pulled off and blood bubbled out.

"Do you think going downtown might help you remember a couple of his friends?" I said. "While social services comes and gets your kids? Wonder how big your check would be with them in foster care." My threat produced a more cooperative Rhonda. She grabbed the pad and commenced scribbling an info-dump on it.

Except for the TV, the whole house was silent while Rhonda scrawled on the notepad. Likewise, aside from a few small actions, the kids had barely moved since we had arrived. The ones not in diapers were wearing jeans with massive stains. The curly haired girl wore a threadbare dress over hers. I'd heard foster homes were bad, but they had to be better than what these kids were living in.

And then the whole situation, the kid's emotionless eyes, the mother's profession, the rank stench of tobacco—all of it made me think of Peter.

This was his future, looking forty at the age of twenty-three with nothing but a string of arrests and lovers who would either steal his money or pimp him out. The sad part was that I had been a cop long enough to know it was probably too late for him. One glimpse of Rhonda's bony clavicle and I decided I was going to try and change the trajectory of Peter's life.

"He visit them boys on the Platte," Rhonda said, meaning the Platte River which ran through the city. Certain underpasses in the warehouse district near the river were notorious for hooker traffic of the 'different' kind: young boys, transvestites, transsexuals. The kind of people less wary about cops because cops were busy with the drug trade and the sea of hookers working on the main street. "He be there three, four times a night before Prisc. Now his boy in jail, he probably go back and shake down them boys for quick cash. They don't make no fuss." She handed the pad to Luis. I leaned over to see her writing. Every 'i' had a heart over it.

We left with a list of names and places to check out, most of which would probably not be worth our time.

The very second I stepped foot outside, I took a cleansing breath and pressed my cell phone to my ear. Luis said nothing as I contacted the Division of Child Welfare Services on our way across the street to the car. I took his silence as approval.

"I want to wait until they get here," I told him once we were seated in the car.

Luis's brown skin dotted with sweat within seconds. "Could be hours," he said before switching on the car just long enough to roll the windows down and light a cigarette.

"If we had arrested her, we could have put the kids in custody immediately," I pointed out, leaning toward my open window and waving the smoke out.

He wasn't going to argue the point. We both knew arresting her would have been a mistake. If we had arrested her, she would have clammed up; she wouldn't have had anything left to lose.

"An hour," Luis said and maneuvered out of his blazer. I did the same, throwing both our coats across the seat divider.

"Or until the social worker comes."

"An hour."

"Or—"

"One. Hour."

Our wait turned out to be a lot less. But it wasn't social services that got our asses moving.

Twenty-five minutes into becoming two slabs of broiled cop-steak, Prisc Alvarado parked in front of Rhonda's house.

The fact that he was out on bail so soon set my hackles up. "Why do they even call it a justice system? They should call it a motel with mildly restrictive checkout requirements."

"Lawyers," Luis grunted in response.

Alvarado jogged up the path and rang her bell. There was an animated conversation in which Rhonda shook her head a few times, arms flailing with fingers clutching a cell phone. Two seconds later, she dialed a number and spoke into the phone. When she hung up, she said something to Alvarado, something that lit a fire under his ass. He rushed back to his car.

"Hour's up," Luis said, twisting the car on and making a U-turn to follow Alvarado's black SUV.

"This is why you should always listen to my instincts," I grinned. "If we'd left earlier…"

"Your instincts? As in the 4th Street Deli?"

"Hey, we both tested negative for hepatitis."

"The 'strange' looking guys at the grocery store on Racine Street?"

"Stopped a robbery, didn't we?"

"I got shot."

"You got *grazed*," I corrected. "Are you hormonal or something?"

"You ever say that to Angelica?"

"Do you see me still breathing? Yes? There's your answer." I didn't want to think about Angelica. The guilt and recrimination wouldn't help with the case. I needed to focus on work.

"Where's he going?"

I twisted and grabbed my suit jacket, slipping it on and adjusting my holster. "Obviously somewhere import—" My words died as Alvarado swung his car left into the lot of the restaurant where Peter worked.

Oh, Shit. Oh, Shit. Have I Mentioned: Oh, Shit!?

The parking lot of Colorado's Finest Diner was uncharacteristically empty for three in the afternoon. I expected it to be just as crowded as ever, but apparently Tuesdays were slow.

Alvarado had parked in a spot less than three strides from the front door, before disappearing inside the restaurant. Luis and I pulled in a minute later. The flashing "Career Ending Now" sign reappeared.

"This is Joe Dench's place," Luis murmured, turning the car off and settling back in his seat. "Where you waited for the no-show?"

"Yeah," I croaked, watching the side door with trepidation. My stomach tightened and twisted.

Retired Detective Joe Dench was, from what I heard, a soft-hearted schmuck no one figured would last a year in Vice. And they were right. He lasted twenty-seven instead. Nearly four years ago he abruptly retired at age fifty-six, bought the diner and then not-so-quickly keeled over of a heart attack three years and eight months later. I only knew of him from Luis, who made comparisons of him and me. According to Vice legend, Joe Dench was a bleeding heart who had too soft a spot for street kids.

Luis had backed into the parking spot at the far corner of the lot, sandwiching us between a minivan on the left and an older model sedan on our right. I avoided glancing at the sedan, since it was exactly where I had parked last night. We could only see the cash register and first four booths from our vantage point, but the side door and alley were in full view. Directly across from the side door was a retainer wall, with dumpsters huddled against the far end. Peter stepped outside with two large black bundles, which he tossed in the trash containers.

"And that's Joe's kid," Luis said with a nod, just as Alvarado followed Peter out and jammed a cell phone into Peter's chest and spitting words at him.

"Huh?" I said intelligently.

"Foster kid. Took in him and two other kids, about four years ago. They all used to hustle under the bridge. Coincidence Alvarado's here looking for Gaines?"

Lovely.

"Now that I think about it," Luis continued, "there was talk that Dench and Alvarado had 'history'." He air quoted the last word.

I sat there and watched the heated exchange, deliberately not clenching my fists as Peter slapped away Alvarado's pointing hand. They were toe-to-toe, giving the impression they were going to come to blows, when something far more disturbing happened.

Prisc's palm roped around Peter's neck and pulled him into a hard kiss.

"Now that is interesting," Luis said. I tried not to do something ridiculous—like growl. I was only partially mollified when Peter pushed Alvarado away.

To feel the first stirrings of jealousy was shocking. Especially since I didn't have *any* relationship with Peter. Besides, I had plenty of other problems without adding possessive feelings for a whore to the list. I had never been a jealous guy, which might explain why it had always been easy for me to cheat. Every one of my relationships had ended because of my philandering. Angelica was the first and, so far, the only person who had ever been able to curb that particular vice.

"I said no!" Peter shouted. He backed up to the retainer wall, tactically lighting a cigarette to maintain the distance between himself and Alvarado. It worked. Alvarado retreated to the opposite wall, still muttering something in a voice too low to carry our way. Good thing he did, too, because we would have had to intervene if things had gotten physical, which would have meant giving away our position and the fact that we were tailing Alvarado.

And it would have meant me giving away a lot more personally.

"Please tell me how the fuck that asshole got released this fast?" I was more terrified than angry, but my words were filled with so much heat that I hoped Luis couldn't hear the quiver in them.

"Even murderers get bail, let alone glorified pimps. Alvarado's star is rising. Lots of cash for fancy lawyers." Luis blew a long stream of smoke into the car after he lit up. I couldn't summon the will to wave it away, so I settled for a cough full of fucking-stop-smoking meaning.

"Asshole lawyers," I muttered, my imagination conjuring a very satisfying picture of shooting Alvarado in the face with my Taser. And then shooting his lawyer.

The conversation between Alvarado and Peter continued out of earshot, with Peter rebuffing several attempts at affection—a hand swatted away from Peter's cheek, a hard shove when Alvarado moved in closer. Most of the 'discussion' was one-sided, with Peter answering nonverbally so often that I figured he could find work as a bobble head.

Luis pointed his cigarette at the pair. "Doesn't seem to be about Gai—" He was interrupted by his cell phone ringing. "Martinez," he answered. "When? … Where?" He started the car while I frowned at him. "Nah. Keep him there." After clicking the phone off, he gave a relieved puff of air. "They got Gaines."

"When? Where?" Today was apparently Repeat What Luis Says day.

"Walked into the station and demanded protection. Seems he suspects a hit is out on him."

"Gee, can't think why." I leaned over and picked up an empty coffee cup from the floor and busied my fingers picking it to pieces.

"He's in lockup," Luis said and then added, "for protection," with air quotes.

I tapped my index finger against the dash, something I was prone to do when puzzled. The gesture always helped me think. It annoyed Luis. I considered it payback for the premature death I was sure he was going to give me by way of secondhand smoke. "You know, yesterday, sitting there across from Alvarado and his five-hundred-dollar-an-hour mouthpiece, with this mountain of questions we needed to ask, all I wanted to do was ask him one question," I stuck the crook of my elbow out the window. "Why the fuck would he keep a dumbass like Gaines on his payroll?" Luis initiated a smile which never quite materialized as his features contorted. With a concentrated squint, he lifted the cigarette to his lips and twisted to settle his eyes on Alvarado and Peter. I followed his stare, matching my partner's frown. "Why Gaines?" I asked again.

Luis still appeared contemplative, but I wasn't done. "You're Alvarado. You have a lucrative business starting up. Bigger and more complicated with a lot more risk. Lots of cash rolling in. So naturally you pick a two-time loser like Gaines to help handle your entire network? A guy who's waiting on a third strike? A guy so dumb he gets caught with smack because he forgets to turn his headlights on and turns snitch?"

"Questions like that remind me how you made detective," Luis replied.

It took five seconds for me to comprehend the insult in that compliment. "Nice," I grumbled. "Why are we still sitting here?" We needed to be talking to Gaines about this and with him in lockup we no longer needed to follow Alvarado. And besides, I did not want to witness the makeup between Peter and Asshole, if there was going to be one.

Luis shrugged, stared at me too long, and way too intensely. Then he made me choke on my own spit when he casually dropped his cigarette out the window and said, "I thought, since we're here and all, maybe you wanted to ask Peter the whore for a date. And maybe you could get a few questions in about his boyfriend, too."

Oh, shit.

I Did Not Have Sexual Relations With That Man. Yet

Silence followed. A long one. Not long enough for me to come up with an appropriate denial, but longer than necessary to seal any doubts Luis might have had at his assumptions.

"Did you pay that boy for sex?"

"It would seem that way," I said with a lame attempt at humor which, unsurprisingly, fell flat when my voice came out tired and fatalistic.

"Meaning?"

"I didn't have sex with him, or intend to." I slanted my eyes, checking Luis's reaction. That was the truth as I saw it. "Of any kind," I added hastily at his unblinking stare. "But I did give him money for…contact." Time moved too slowly, emphasizing my speed-of-light heart rate. At any moment I was destined to either throw up or drown in my own sweat.

"I don't have time for any of your bullshit, Glass. Did you compromise yourself and this case?" Every minute, every second of him studying me was a second closer to the end of my life as I knew it. Bite the bullet and trust him, or lie and twist things to a better light? At this point I could have told Luis that I had suspicions about Peter. That I paid him for information. But I would never have done that to my partner.

Cop partnerships can be more intense than marriages. You ride along with this person, both of your guns weighing heavily on your belts, and you're completely responsible for this other human being for eight, ten, twelve hours a day, sometimes seven days a week. And not the kind of responsibility that means love and affection in compensation. With your partner, the compensation is protection. You leave the station house *knowing* that their life is in your hands, and that yours is in theirs. There's no honeymoon stage, no adjustment period. There's you and your partner, committing to an absolute trust. You can lie in a marriage and still make it work, but if you lie in a partnership, you put your partner's career, their *life* in jeopardy. And if they think you're willing to abandon that trust, how could they have faith in you?

Then there was the gay. The second part of the Austin Glass is Fucked equation. I wanted to tell Luis the truth, and while I trusted him implicitly, I was terrified. Lie or truth? To me, both options could mean the end of my career, and of our partnership. So I just sat there, suffocating from the combined heat and silence. I didn't know when or where, or even how, to begin. I wasn't someone who lied about important things. Cheat, yes. Lie, no. A fine line, but distinct in my mind. Instead of lies, I used off-color humor to make the truth sound ridiculous, so I didn't have to lie. But even after wracking my brain, I still couldn't come up with a way to do that here. Or even use humor to diffuse the situation. I was too nauseated to be funny.

"Did you compromise this case?"

Did I?

"Probably," I admitted. "Or, at least, my involvement in it." I could have made excuses about how I hadn't known he was a prostitute. Or that he was involved with Alvarado. How I hadn't slept with him. How I was having an identity crisis, and it had all begun as something very innocent. Really.

But Luis didn't care about those things. Luis wasn't worried about the fact that I had traded cash for the services of a whore. Luis probably didn't care that I might be gay. No, Luis was worried that there was a person close to Alvarado who we now wouldn't be able to pressure into answering questions because I had paid him money for sex. Luis cared about this investigation, and his career. And right now he was deciding if his partner's ass was worth covering or if he should feed me to the wolves.

"Tell me," he said.

And so I did. I told him, as succinctly as possible, about Peter, me, and everything that had happened between us. I didn't leave anything out.

And speaking of out, apparently I now was. Some people maintained it was very freeing to take that step. I didn't share their assessment. It did make me wonder, though. How did one go about being out when they weren't gay?

"He knows you're a cop?" Luis asked.

"Unless he's blind and stupid." I lifted my jacket to reveal the obvious badge and gun clipped to my belt.

"He solicited a cop?"

"He didn't know then, maybe. But even if he knew, he also had to have known that there was no chance I'd actually bring him in. Not if it meant confronting questions about why a hustler was in my car after hours, soliciting sex."

"Or maybe you're not the first cop on the down-low to approach him," Luis mused.

"I'm not on the down-low!"

Luis barreled on past my denial without acknowledging it. "So we go with that. A cop on the down-low to another gay. Maybe he'll be more receptive to questions."

"A gay? I don't think it's a noun." Not that I hadn't just used it in exactly the same context.

"You prefer homo?" His expression was so deadpan I couldn't tell if he was serious or not.

"I'm not—"

"Nah. You're not gay. Straight guys always chase around hustlers."

"An aberration. And you're taking that part very well."

He shrugged and looked out the window. "Querida is gay."

"Your daughter is gay? Where are all these gay people coming from? Gay friends. Gay daughters of friends. Gay sisters-in-law. Gay suspects. I ask one guy for a kiss and suddenly I'm living in Ancient Greece." I was going to hyperventilate. Panic will do that. "Maybe that's what happened. Maybe all these gays rubbed off on me or somethi— Ow!" I rubbed the back of my head.

Luis gripped the steering wheel so tight his knuckles blanched. "When my daughter comes to me at eighteen and says she wants to take a girl to prom, Denise tells me, 'God gives us difficulty to prove we're worthy of heaven.' Things will work out if we just love Querida more. Then Querida marries this girl, and now I have a beautiful grandson. Okay, I think, Denise was right. Then my son gets arrested for stealing cars, and she tells me it's God's way of saying I need to be paying more attention to my children. So I spend more time with Carlos, and now he's in college, his second year he made dean's list. Right again." When he became silent, I didn't chime in; he was going somewhere with this.

"When I complain to Denise that my partner makes our nine-year-old look mature," he continued, "she tells me 'God has a plan' and I need to figure it out. It turns out he's not so bad—this kid. He's a little dumb about some people, a little too soft about street kids, but after only six weeks as my partner, he makes himself a target so I can crawl to safety after being shot. He chases down suspects in two thousand dollar suits. Snitches trust him for some reason, and he asks a lot of questions no one else seems to ask. He's got good instincts. I start thinking that maybe God's plan is I make him more of a man and less of a boy. And then, one day, he can be an even better cop than me."

"How's that working out?" I hadn't taken my eyes off Luis, though he was watching the now-empty alley. Peter and Alvarado had gone inside, or maybe for a walk. I had been too riveted by Luis to notice.

He rubbed his fingers over the stubble on his chin and finally shook his head at me. "I think I was wrong. Some men will always be boys."

"Interesting," I replied, twisting to stare out the front window. Apparently I disappointed father figures as well as fathers. At least I was consistent.

"But sometimes my partner is already a better cop than I am."

I showed none of the elation or surprise I was feeling. Instead I fell back on what was natural for me when shown affection. Quiet.

My silence lasted about five minutes.

"I can't believe you're still whining about getting shot."

Luis nodded slowly and settled back, flipping the car on. "I was in the hospital."

"It was fourteen stitches and a tetanus shot. Your arm wasn't even in a sling. I'm the one who had to go to the department shrink for shooting the guy."

"You still got that shrink's number?"

Ignoring the insinuation that I needed to go back to therapy, I jerked my head to the restaurant. "What did you mean by 'go with' the gay, anyway?"

"It means, I'm going to drop you at your car and then go talk to Gaines and find out if he really was working for Alvarado. And you're going to go talk to the whore." He gave me a meaningful snort before adding, "And remember: he's a witness and possible person of interest."

Chapter Four

How to Interrogate A Prostitute. Or Not

Luis once told me I was an idiot for getting my degree in accounting when clearly I should have majored in psychology. He said this after a twenty minute interrogation led to a man's confession to selling his thirteen-year-old son in order to pay off a gambling debt. It had been the sixth time in four months that I had wrung a confession from a suspect after the other detectives' efforts had produced nada. My father called this ability "juvenile charm". Luis apparently agreed with that assessment. I called it the Bro Effect.

The trick was to know your audience. Read the jacket, find out the suspect's background, and lastly, from the second you enter an interrogation, you adopt the correct persona. Because of my easy smile, and casual attitude, I was nonthreatening. "The bro". The kind of guy who didn't think too hard or judge anyone too harshly. The kind of guy everyone can relate to.

Unless you were a red-haired hustler with mesmerizing freckles.

Peter had met the tripping-over-his-own-tongue, panic-stricken, flustered Austin. Entering the diner, I was acutely aware of that disadvantage, among others. Getting the upper hand was going to prove difficult. I had no idea how I was going to approach questioning him.

Peter had no arrest record to study. Given his profession, that was astonishing. Astonishing in the Joe-the-ex-cop-must-have-pulled-some-strings way. From Joe's ex-partner, Ron, I'd managed to glean some information about the guy. His name was Peter Martin Cotton. Peter Cotton. The bunny slippers finally made sense.

Joe had picked him, and two other kids, off the streets four years ago and illegally fostered them. According to Ron, the kid was dealing for Prisc Alvarado. Alvarado, it turned out, had been Joe's first failed attempt to rehabilitate a street kid. At the time of his death, and after eighteen years, Joe was apparently still trying with Alvarado. Which should have been an lesson to me about obsession. It wasn't.

To everyone's surprise, the diner had been left to Peter, not Alvarado, when Joe died, which explained Peter's constant presence there these days.

Ron had also informed me that Peter was devoted to the other two 'foster' kids Joe had taken in; Darryl and Nicolas, both around Peter's age, though Ron couldn't be sure about their ages or names. After retirement, Joe had severed most ties with his former partner.

Other than that information, I only had what I had gathered myself: He was a whore, he disliked me, he had six freckles over his upper lip that begged to be....

Okay, maybe I had enough to work with. Devoted to the other kids. That was a vulnerability I could exploit, if necessary.

How to Date a Prostitute

In a booth at the back of the restaurant, close to the kitchen doors, Peter's grey slipper dangled enticingly from the edge of his seat. From the way it hung suspended off his toe, I could tell his foot was crossed over his knee under the table. Though his back was to me, I imagined he was laughing with the youth across from him.

The black-haired boy, and, yes, this time I meant boy—he had to be sixteen, max—was blushing as they laughed and using an ink pen to scribble on a drawing pad. He raised his head as I came near, frowning only slightly, but his grey eyes were bright and warm and his smile remained in place. Was I about to intrude on a date?

Peter followed the other boy's stare, twisting in his seat. "What—" His smile was so breathtaking, in the split second I got to see it, that my hands briefly tightened into fists. Then the smile was gone. "Cai, get your things and go home." Peter's eyes never left me.

Cai blinked and flashed a confused squint to Peter. "But—"

"Now," Peter interrupted and began to scoot out of the booth; I stood at the end of his seat, caging him in.

Cai offered a shy, inquisitive peek under his black bangs while he grabbed a messenger bag, putting his drawing tablet inside. "Night, Rabbit." He directed a twitchy smile at me and hesitated before slipping out of the booth and disappearing behind the kitchen doors. I propped my chin in my palm as I took his place at the table.

"Have I been too subtly hostile?" Peter said, clasping his hands and leaning forward. "Was my I'd-only-have-sex-with-you-if-you-paid-me statement too vague? Exactly how do I get rid of you? A billboard? A letter in braille? Sign language? I could threaten to go to the cops, but I think we both can agree that would be pointless."

I couldn't place the reason for my nervousness. For my sweaty palms and racing heart. I wasn't intimidated by his words or his anger. I wasn't scared in the traditional sense. And let's face it, someone named Peter Cotton wasn't exactly ominous. It was just him and his furious eyes. He got to me. "Your freckles are adorable." Somehow I didn't think Luis would approve of that opening line. And, by his incredulous glare, I knew Peter didn't. That, or he was seeing spiders crawl out of my ears.

"You're not just short a few sandwiches," he said, lip curling up in disgust. "Your picnic is missing the basket and blanket. There's not even ants at your picnic."

I couldn't help the grin. "Tell me about Prisc Alvarado."

"What?" His eyes blinked wide, head jerking backwards. And then he quickly adopted an air of indifference.

"Is he my competition?" I asked.

"Everyone is your competition." Peter lifted his hand to his eyes and began lowering it incrementally. "It goes normal human beings, crazies, republicans, my hand, imaginary characters, corpses and then, in a moment of lustful psychosis, you." By the time he was done, his hand was below the table.

Ouch. "A little over the top, don't you think?"

"No." He tried to scoot out again. I laid my badge on the table and he hesitated, a brief pull of his brows as he stared at it.

"I really do need to know about Prisc," I said. "Officially."

He sat back down and crossed his arms over his chest. "I can't help you. And if this is some kind of ruse to get in my pants, it won't work."

"We've established how I can get into your pants. And I didn't bring any cash."

"That was a one-time offer."

"For me? Or does Prisc get a discount?"

At this rate, the sheer amount of time he spent glaring at me was making me immune to it. "Why the sudden interest in Iss? I didn't see your car stalking me today, but it can't be coincidence that he came see me on the same day you question me about him."

"Different car. And I wasn't stalking." Yes I was.

"Don't worry. Not like I could report you, is it?" He sneered.

"Are you genuinely asking? Because if so, yeah, you can report me." I reached into my inside coat pocket and retrieved my wallet, a pen and one of my business cards. I wrote two numbers on the back and slid the card in front of Peter. "That's my full name and rank on the front. The back is my badge number and the number to my direct superior. You can make the complaint to Captain Ashenafi Mangistu."

"You're making up that name," he challenged.

"No. He's Ethiopian, and he's very uptight, politically correct and there's not an ounce of corruption in his soul." Damn.

Peter eyed the card for a few seconds and then met my eyes as he reached over, palming it. "And what would he do?"

"Probably suspend me pending an investigation," I said honestly. "Internal Affairs would be called in. It's not like the movies, they don't all band together around me and create an impenetrable blue wall." My heart twisted in new ways that had nothing to do with my attraction for Peter.

"Especially not a faggot," he challenged, arms crossing in front of him.

Ouch again. I was going to need stitches if the jabs continued this sharply. "I don't know. Maybe one of them would try to convince you I'm a great guy."

"Superficial. You're a superficial guy." He focused on the window to his right. I studied him, checking for any sign of hope he wasn't going to report me.

"Everyone is superficial at first."

"You're vain."

"Confident."

"Arrogant."

"Self-assured."

"Aggressive and full of yourself."

"Cocky," I settled on. My smile returned.

"Where you come from that's a good thing?"

"I'm a little cute?"

He sighed and observed me, his eyes hard. "I thought you might be. I thought you were just shy, sitting out there in your car, watching the restaurant. Watching me. Then I thought you were just scared. And that's what made you be an asshole. Coming here and accusing me of making you gay."

"I was. Scared. Am. I am scared. All those freckles and your perfect face—"

"Stop fucking talking about my looks. Quit staring at me like that's all there is to me."

"It's not. That's not—"

"What do you know about me? All you see is this." He waved a hand in front of himself. "This weirdness of coming here all the time. You don't ask me my name or out on a date. I sat in your car for ten minutes and all you did was stare at me."

Oh. I laughed self-consciously. No one made me feel self-conscious, except my father. Leave it to Peter to have brought out that unattractive trait. I kept letting him be the catalyst of my worst behavior. "I was embarrassed." I ran a hand through my hair, felt the spikes pop out as it passed over the strands. "I didn't know— I don't know how to deal with this. That I'm physically attracted to a guy. I couldn't think of a way out. Or how to ask you out. I was going to say coffee. It sounded lame. Or to buy you loafers or sneakers or anything that kept me from thinking about those slippers. And then you started listing prices for other things that suddenly sounded a lot better than coffee."

There it was. The twitch of Peter's lips that told me he was hiding a smile. I waited it out, hoping I was thawing some of the ice. "Cai buys the slippers," he said tersely.

I tried to pinpoint what it was that had me so fascinated. I wasn't sure it could be defined.

"You're staring again, Detective Glass."

I didn't turn away from the accusation, but my fingers sought out my badge on the table, spinning it gently on the Formica. "I was curious about what a date would have been like with a guy. With you."

"Why don't you ask me and find out?" His answer surprised me, and maybe himself, if the way his lips pressed together and his eyes widened in shock was any indication.

"See, now there's a problem. You're a witness in a case." I ignored the stab of disappointment in my chest, even when it grew sharper as Peter's shoulders dropped in relief.

"Iss, you mean? You can't ask me on a date because I know Iss?"

"Iss?"

"Prisc. He doesn't go by that. Reminds him of when kids at school called him Prick. We call him Iss," he said, flipping my business card over on its edge. One hand still crossed his chest almost protectively. His t-shirt read 'FCUK'. Yeah. I'd agree with that exclamation. "Anyhow, I'm not in that life anymore. I haven't been in four years."

His use of 'anyhow' reminded me of his accent. "Where are you from, Peter Rabbit?" I asked softly.

It took a few seconds but then he smiled, the same one that took my breath earlier. And I was no less affected. "Mamma used to call me that."

Part of my intuition was knowing when not to talk. So far I'd proven unreliable in that arena when it came to Peter, but I knew that if I asked about his mother, his walls would shoot back up. So I sat there in silence, watching his long fingers tumble the card end over end, tap it a few times and then stop.

Instead of answering that question, he went for the original one. "We used to hook up. Nothing serious. He was the first guy that didn't pay me. I was sixteen, Iss was twenty-nine and Joe threatened him with jail time if we kept fucking. So we stopped. It wasn't a big deal for either of us. I mean he wasn't taking advantage of me. It just...was what it was." He pursed his lips and shrugged.

"And today?"

Another shrug as he met my eyes. "He was searching for a friend of ours. I didn't know where he was so I told him that."

"That made him kiss you?" That was not jealousy in my voice. It wasn't. I did need to release the death grip on my badge, though. Peter noticed and cocked his head, but didn't say anything about it.

"Iss," he began and twisted his lips a few times. "Iss still remembers the sixteen-year-old that told him everything. I'm not that boy anymore."

"Not that naïve, you mean?" I was hoping he'd grin and remember when he called me that. I was right about the first part.

"Been a long time since I was wet behind the ears, Detective. If I ever was." He smirked, but it appeared more sad than anything else. "Anyhow, no, I didn't mean it that way. *You're* naïve. Me? I was just taken with Iss. We talked about everything." He jerked his chin up at me. "What's he supposed to have done?"

That was my cue to throw a question back, because it was never a good idea to answer that question. Lawyers filed lawsuits for maligning a person's character. So naturally, I did it anyway. "He's been charged with human trafficking involving forty-seven Mexican nationals ranging in age from eight to thirty. The feds might add charges when they take over the case. Who was he after?"

"Iss? You've got the wrong guy, Detective," he replied. It was deliberate avoidance of my question.

"Sounds like someone still taken with him."

"No. I told you I'm that boy anymore. I'm just telling you that Iss isn't ambitious enough to do anything like that."

The indifference in his voice was what convinced me he wasn't a lover trying to defend his boyfriend. "What makes you say that?" The thing that had me intrigued was that there was almost a puzzle piece clicking into place with Peter's statement. Based on Alvarado's previous petty arrest history, he didn't seem capable of running such a complex scheme as human trafficking on his own.

"He didn't even deal anything stronger than weed or party favors when we were together. And Joe let him hang around after we stopped hooking up. No way he'd even let him in the door here if he was that shady. They were together just a few days before Joe died." I locked that tidbit of information away. Something about the way Peter looked out the window again almost made me doubt his veracity. Almost.

"What about Terrelle Gaines?" Peter began laughing. I thought that was my answer. I would have been blown away by the way he brightened, but I was too busy computing how our case was going to hell.

"Terrelle? Terrelle shakes down the older trannies because he has zero game. Even the younger boys have kicked his ass. Janine once beat him over the head with her shoe. Chased him down the street hobbling on one high heel and trying to hold her wig on with the other hand. No way would Iss deal with Terrelle other than to beat his ass."

The problem with this statement was that Terrelle had recently given us several strong leads. He'd developed a trust with Luis and me. And he had given us Alvarado. But I trusted Peter. Probably because I was so fucked in the head right now.

"Why was Joe meeting with Iss?"

"Iss was like me, way back when Joe started on Vice. Joe took him in, tried to set him on the right path." He tapped my card a few times, read it, and then flipped it again. I waited as he fell silent, trying not to push. Yet. "Joe doesn't give up. Didn't. Joe didn't give up. Even after eighteen years, he still tried with Iss."

"But you don't think Iss wouldn't be into anything big."

"Iss deals some E, sometimes the new stuff at the clubs, nothing hard. Not ever. Not even meth." He opened his mouth to add something, but then his lips disappeared behind his teeth.

"There's something else," I nudged.

He nearly broke my mind again when his fingers dragged through his hair. My physical response was so intense, my lips parted to expel a harsh breath. Christ, I wanted him. "I told him some of what I heard you say on the phone Saturday."

Oh, fucking shit hell. "About how Gaines had sold him out?"

"About how he should maybe go away, do nothing for a while. I didn't mention Terrelle. I just told him not to meet up with anyone."

I had to ask. "Why are you telling me all this?"

"Why wouldn't I? There's been a few assholes here trying to… But most of the cops have been decent. And I liked Joe. He wouldn't want Iss going down for something he didn't do. Okay? Now, that's as much as I know about Iss and anything he's done. I'm done with all of this, detective. Leave me alone."

"Give me a name. Someone that might clarify things. If it's not Iss, then I need someone who *is* ambitious."

He was already half out of the booth, but he considered my request as he stood there, flicking my card against his fingers. "I'll ask around." I slid out of the booth and caught his wrist as he pushed the doors to the kitchen open. He turned and regarded my hand, then schooled his expression into ice. "I said I'd—"

"Let me buy you coffee? Or loafers? Or goddamned sunscreen."

"I thought you couldn't—"

"Yeah, I'm also not supposed to pay for hookers or go home with guys. There's a lot I keep doing around you that I'm not supposed to."

"Am I going to finish a sentence on this date?"

"Depends on how often your lips are in range of mine." Where that came from, I didn't know. Didn't care either, because

Peter *smiled*. He rolled his eyes, but he did smile. Then he gave a slow, almost reluctant nod, and said the magic word. "Okay".

"Three o'clock, Saturday. I'll pick you up here." I checked his feet as I released his arm. "And wear the bunny slippers."

"Have they drug tested you recently?"

"I'll bring the results on our date," I winked. My grin stayed in place until I spun around. That was when I closed my eyes and took a deep, shaky breath as I headed to my car. Several minutes of deep breathing later, I was finally controlled enough to call Luis with what I knew.

After we set up an interview for the next day with Prisc and his lawyer, I drove home whistling. My case was unraveling before my eyes, but I had a date with Peter on Saturday. He might not even stab me in the face during it.

It amazed me what constituted a victory these days.

But my joviality was short-lived when I found Angelica making dinner when I arrived.

She Left With The Only Bottle of Soy Sauce

When Angelica and I took the plunge into dating, we each owned a home. I, the Victorian apartment building that I adored, and she, a two million dollar brick mansion three miles away in the most expensive neighborhood in Denver. When I proposed we had the only serious argument we'd ever had: about where we were going to live. Eight weeks before our wedding, the jury was still out.

I was probably going to give in. Move into her house and settle into our life together. I knew it, and she knew it. But it was a difficult loss for me because I'd invested so much time and energy into this little building. Angelica understood that, too. So she put up with our living apart. For now.

We almost exclusively slept at my place when we spent nights together, though it was getting harder to explain our lifestyle to our friends. We were monumentally independent. It took almost two years for her to allow me closet space and drawers at her place. But she was always able to make herself at home in mine. Go figure.

She worked as a junior partner in a law firm—my father's law firm to be exact. Her hours could best be described as horrendous. At worst they could be called excruciating. Most of the time, seventeen-hour days were the norm for her. Thus, she came over whenever her schedule allowed.

"Hello, lover," Angelica greeted me with a smile over the island that separated the kitchen from the living room.

"Are you cooking?" I sniffed the air. "There's no smoke. The fire alarm isn't sounding," I said with a heaping dose of suspicion.

"You scoff, but what are you going to do when I actually do cook something?"

"Check and see what aliens have invaded your body and exchanged your soul for theirs."

"You can peek under my skirt right now," she taunted, holding up a spatula and a steaming frying pan.

My smile faltered. I concentrated on the TV, snatching the remote off the end table and flipping it on. "You did not cook that," I accused.

Angelica's soft laugh filled the room. I avoided her gaze. I had been avoiding *her* actually, because I didn't want to argue. And I was going to venture a guess that my wanting to bone a guy would be a big point of contention. We were going to have to talk about it.

I sat on the sofa, remote in hand and flipped through the channels. Even if something was on, I wouldn't have noticed. The TV held no interest for me other than as an excuse to avoid her some more. She was on to me, however.

I wasn't acting any differently than normal. I never rushed over to her and kissed her or groped her after long periods apart. I needed distance first. Distance from what I saw and dealt with on the job. At least, that's what I told myself was the excuse. So I wasn't sure why she instantly figured out something was up. Woman's intuition?

"What's wrong?" Angelica asked, flipping open two beers and setting one in my hand. She gently removed the remote and placed it on the coffee table.

Curling up beside me, she rested an elbow on the back of the sofa. Her fingers played with the hem of her skirt, where her feet peeked out. I concentrated on these small things, hoping I'd find some measure of attraction that was even close to what I felt for Peter.

"How do you do that?" I asked with a rueful laugh and a pull on my drink while I stared at her tiny toes.

"Probably something to do with being in love with you. But mostly because I've known you since you were sixteen."

"That was an interesting day." Deflect. Deflect. Deflect. I couldn't have the conversation we needed to have.

Always able to read me, Angelica took the hint and went with the subject change. "It was. Your father had asked you to take that Testam girl to her junior prom. And when I got back from lunch, you were cowering in my office to avoid doing so."

"He *ordered* me to take her." I grinned, picking at the condensation-softened label. It peeled away in a stripe under my thumbnail.

"Lovely girl."

I chuckled at her sarcasm. "It was your fault I took her."

"I just mentioned it wasn't worth fighting over. It was one dance. I was getting a little tired of the arguments between you two."

"Arguments? I can count on my hands the number of words Desmond Glass has said to me since I was six—and most of them started with 'Son, I'm disappointed in you'."

"If you had spent half the energy on pleasing him as you did on the things that ticked him off, he'd start sentences off differently." Her hand rested on my shoulder. I shook it off.

"Old news, Angel. And I took the dimwitted pest to her prom, didn't I? See how well I can please?"

"And got caught in her bed that night."

"Her idea to do it in her bedroom three doors down from her parents. Not mine." I gave my best poker face. "How was I supposed to know she was a screamer?" I smiled and chuckled again. "Or her mother was too. Julia screaming in the bed, her mother screaming at the door to the bedroom. I blame you for my hearing loss from that night."

"Mmhm," Angelica said dubiously.

"Why do half my conversations with you end up about my father?" I sighed and set the bottle down on the coffee table, moving off the couch and into the kitchen. She didn't follow me.

"Maybe because half of what you do is about your father."

"Not anymore. I gave up trying to be a son when I realized he only wanted one in name." I peered into the frying pan. "Is this Chinese food?"

"Austin, is this something to do with that?" Or another woman was the unspoken question. Given my history it wasn't a huge leap. Angelica sounded more resigned than angry. There was an inaudible sigh somewhere in her breathing. "Is that why you've been incommunicado?"

The food was boiling so I switched the stove off and took a deep breath. "I think I'm gay. Did you reheat this? Because I'm not ready to try your cooking just yet."

"It's from Wang's, and, yes, it's reheated. I did make the rice." She finally followed me into the kitchen and lifted the lid to the rice cooker.

My hands dropped to the counter, and I leaned against it, pressing my eyes shut. "I think I'm gay."

"Microwaved eggrolls make me queasy. They're still lukewarm though. I think we can—"

"I think I'm gay, Angel."

"I heard you!" Something slammed against the counter. "Stop saying it."

"Sounds like a plan." I twisted around and pulled two plates down from the cabinet, eyeing her sideways. She was gripping a bottle of soy sauce tightly. "We'll talk about something else." Snatching a couple of serving spoons, I scooped rice onto the plates.

She released the bottle, placed her hand on my shoulder again and pressed her forehead into my arm. "Austin, this is just like the other times. You're panicking. Eight weeks before the wedding and you're *panicking.* This is what you do every time."

That had occurred to me, and it was my modus operandi when relationships got serious. Granted, it was usually a woman I ended up with. "We can talk about this. Or we can *not* talk about it. But don't just slip in comments." I tossed the serving spoons into their respective dishes, stabbing one into the rice.

"There's nothing to talk about. This is ridiculous. Gay, Austin? *Gay?*" Angelica's hand clamped onto her hip as she yanked the soy sauce off the counter. "Do you hear yourself?"

"There's a guy."

"What?" She whispered. I felt, rather than saw, her step back from me. "Did you...?"

"No. God, no. Nothing happened." *Nothing of consequence.* I crushed my hands into my hair, pulled at the skin of my face with my palms, wanting to rub myself out of existence. "Christ, Angel, I don't know how to *not* talk about this with you. I don't know how to *not* talk about *anything* with you. I've told you every single thing since we met. But Jesus, how do we talk about this?"

She clutched the soy sauce to her chest, twisting it in circles. "Okay. Okay. So there's a guy. Just one?" I nodded, keeping my vigil over the counter. "So, you've thought about one man?" She laughed then, expelled a relieved and frustrated breath and placed her small hand over mine. "It's normal, Austin. That's normal."

"It's not normal. It's all I've thought about for three days."

"It's one person. You're not gay for thinking intimately about one person, Austin. You're just panicking like you always do and searching for something. We'll wait it out and see."

"One person the last three days."

"So?"

"I focused all this energy on him I think because...I didn't want to think about the other ones," I said quietly. She was back to hugging the soy sauce.

"You're right. We can't talk about this. I'm going home." She snatched her purse up, still gripping the bottle. "Don't touch me." She jerked back when I reached a hand out. "What did you think was going to happen, Austin? Did you think I'd bring out the PFLAG buttons and march in the gay parade for you? Why can't you end a relationship like a normal person?"

"I don't—"

"It always has to be some dramatic ending. Something sure to drive her away. Sleep with her best friend, her mother, her sister. But you swore to me it wouldn't happen with me. You swore we'd talk about it!"

"That's what I'm doing, *goddammit*! That's what I'm fucking doing." I had never raised my voice to her. Not once in ten years. Not even when I was bitching about my father.

"Well, I can't talk about this! It's patently ridiculous. I can't talk about *this* eight weeks before—" She was halfway to exiting when she finally stopped her whirlwind departure. I thought she might add something but two seconds after the pause she was out the door, slamming it hard enough to shake the glass figures on the mantle.

And she took my only bottle of soy sauce.

It's Easy To Be Brave When No One But The Dead Can Hear

Leaving dinner to rot on the counters, I climbed upstairs. I sat on the bed, pulling off my tie while staring at the dark lines between each wooden slat on my floor. Maybe she was right? Maybe I wasn't gay, and this was just the anxiety of a groom-to-be. The stress *was* a familiar feeling. Not just the stress, but the doubts and the pressure. I could trace them all the way back to ninth grade.

So many students. The halls reek of bubble gum gloss, cheap hair products, and teenage sweat. Everyone, save me and a few random kids, are in jeans or casual wear. Skinny, newly acne ridden, awkward and short, I enter freshman year a mere shadow of my eighth grade self. Puberty has smacked me up and down the ugly tree and then dropped me on my face. I compound all of these problems by wearing the uniform required at my old school.

It isn't that I prefer to wear these clothes. I watch television. I know what kids dress like. But my father insists I dress "properly", even in public school. And what Desmond Glass Sr. wants, Desmond Glass Sr. gets. And what he gets is his son tossed in a locker before second period.

I press my head against the cool metal door, my fist pounding against it. "I'm Austin Glass! I kissed Mitzi Baylor for three and half minutes. Mitzi. Baylor. She was seventeen! I broadcasted pictures of my dick to the entire biology class. I've been kicked out of four prep schools. I'm the guy that spiked the headmaster's tea with X! I don't belong in a locker. Fuck!"

A pound on the other side of the door knocks the metal into my forehead, not hard enough to do more than take me by surprise. "What's your combo?" The voice on the other side is laughing.

I rattle off the numbers and then stumble out of the tight space. "Thanks."

"Mitzi? Is she even real?"

I cup two hands out of my chest and make a show of how 'real' she is. "Her tongue felt real."

"Dave," my savior says, holding out his hand.

"Austin."

"Well, Austin, do you have any cash?"

"You're going to shake me down now?" I tilt my chin up, mouth agape. He's taller than me. Same mousy brown hair as mine, same brown eyes.

Loads better looking, but not much heavier, considering he's about four inches taller. I'm debating whether I can take him.

"I'm going to take you to buy some clothes. Can't keep pulling you out of lockers all day. Got classes." His grin is infectious. For a second I think about using my multitude of credit cards.

"Thanks, but if I don't wear this, my father will spend an entire evening lecturing me on the perils of dressing like common riffraff."

"Sounds brutal. A whole lecture." Dave laughs. "I thought you were 'Austin Glass', kisser of Mitzis and spiker of headmaster drinks?"

"I was trying something new," I mutter. Now that I'm home, I'm attempting to get on my dad's good side. Not that it has gotten me far. My father still doesn't speak more than five words to me. Less 'I'm disappointed, Austin.' And more 'Well done, boy.' I'm not sure why I'm trying at all. "You know what? Fuck it. Let's go."

"I'll drive," Dave announces, dangling a set of keys with a Mustang key ring. "You can tell me about biology class on the way."

Dave takes me to Target for the first time in my life. We throw some clothes in the cart, and, later, I change in the front seat of his car. We talk about his dad, the cop, and my dad, the lawyer. His dad takes him to baseball games and let him sip his beer once. My dad, I tell him, has seen me six times in the last twelve years, four of those were to pick me up from schools when I got expelled. At least one of those times was for doing more than 'sipping' beer.

"That sucks, man."

"I guess. Thanks for the save, Dave." I laugh and tuck my other new purchases in the locker once we arrive at school. No one is tittering at my clothes this time.

"I gotta get to class, but we can meet after school. I'll introduce you to some people."

"Cool," I say and jerk a nod goodbye.

~*~

Jesse Chambroy makes my stomach lurch. I'm not sure if I want to throw up or smile back at him. He doesn't look at me often, just stares at Dave a lot. I'm glad because it means I can count his freckles, and also because I don't want to think about why he makes me feel that way when he smiles at me.

Jesse is a senior now, Dave a junior, and I'm just finishing my sophomore year. It's a weird friendship combination, but it works.

Somehow. Maybe because Jesse comes from money, too. So he and I understand things about each other, even though I'm not even sixteen yet and he's nearly eighteen.

I don't get what's going on with him and Dave though. Maybe it's just that they're both jocks? Dave on the baseball team, Jesse a football player. Or maybe it's that they've known each other since they were ten. For that matter, I don't really get the three of us—Jesse, me and Dave. The only thing we all have in common is that we like fart jokes and Kung Fu movies. But for all our differences, we've been inseparable for more than a year, talking about baseball, lighting farts and making Jesse watch Seven Samurai over and over until he gives in and says that it's the best movie ever made.

My father disapproves of Dave, but not of Jesse. Jesse's family is wealthy and socially connected. So Jesse comes over often, hangs out in my room and makes my stomach feel like I'm riding a roller coaster. I try not to sniff him as we sit on my bed, flipping through his book of sketches.

"That's a lot of blood," I point out, wincing at the picture of dark shapes nestled in pools of blood. The bodies are of men, muscled, with stretched lips screaming in pain. I wiggle uncomfortably on the mattress.

"It's my interpretation of Stonewall," says Jesse, examining my face closely.

"Okay. What's that?" I don't get why he's observing me with such force, but I feel weird. Hard, too.

"A riot that started the gay rights movement. So they didn't have to worry about getting hassled or arrested for being gay."

"I don't get it. Why didn't they just stop being gay?"

"Could you?"

"Me? I'm not a homo. You're a homo, asshole." I punch his arm and climb off the bed, flashing him an angry glare. I'm not angry, though. I know what angry feels like. This feels like fear. I'm afraid. I should be angry, but I'm afraid.

"Austin," Jesse goes back to his drawing pad, lifting a page up and smiling softly at it. "I am a homo."

Oh. What do I do with that? "Okay. I guess. I mean, you're not trying to make out with me or something, right?"

"No." He laughs, making my stomach do things it shouldn't. "Are we still friends?"

"Best friends, dude. Best friends." I force a smile. "You told Dave?"

He nods, laughing a little more. "Him I tried to make out with."

"No shit? Your nose isn't broken, dude."

"*I made him promise not to tell you. I wanted to be the one. He was cool though. Said you'd be fine. That— that maybe you were, too?*"

"*Me? What the fuck, man.*"

"*You haven't exactly been dating a lot.*"

"*Not any girls I like.*" I shrug, frowning. "*Definitely not any my dad would let me date. I'm not a homo, dude. Okay?*" *Am I?*

"*Okay. Just, you know, if you...*"

"*I thought we were going to the waterpark?*"

~*~

"*Austin?*"

"*Yeah? Huh, what?*" I blink at the dark room, struggling to my elbows.

"*I need a place to crash.*"

"*Jesse— What?*" My eyes slowly adjust until I can make out that Jesse is sitting on the end of my bed.

"*They found out, Aus. My folks found out.*"

It's midnight, I note, checking my bedside clock. I'm having trouble comprehending the conversation. "*Okay. Found out what?*" I blink a few times and rub my eyes, reaching over to click the lamp on. Jesse's cheeks and eyes are a black-and-blue, tear-stained mess. His blond hair sticks out with clumps of blood mangled in it. "*Jesus, fuck. What the fuck?*" I'm too concerned to ask how he got into my room.

"*My dad. Fuck, Aus. He kicked me out. After he'd kicked me around.*"

"*Okay. Okay.*" I sit up, pulling the covers off and grabbing my cell. "*We'll call Mr. Buchanan. You gotta turn him in. You gotta go to the hospital, man.*"

"*I've been already. It's just bruises and a few scrapes. They denied my credit card for the co-pay. He cut me off, Aus. He took everything and cut me off.*"

"*It'll be okay, Jess. Dave 'n me will look out for you. Wait here.*" I leave and grab some icepacks downstairs. When I get back, Jesse is staring out my window, shoulders slumped in defeat. "*Here.*" I hand him the packs. They sit unused in his lap.

"*Just let me crash here. I'm so tired. I'll call tomorrow. I just can't deal tonight, man.*"

"*'kay. First thing tomorrow, though,*" I yawn, slipping back into bed and waiting for Jess to join me. It's only the third time he's spent the night since he confessed being gay a month ago. Too groggy to sense the implications of everything, I close my eyes and begin to drift off.

"*I don't have anyone, Aus.*" *I'm not sure, but I think he's crying.*

"*Asshole, you got me and Dave. You got the whole Buchanan clan, dude.*" *His hand finds mine under the covers. I will myself not to shake it free. He's my friend, and it doesn't mean anything. He just needs his friend is all. And that feeling in my stomach? That's just fear for him.* "*We'll deal in the morning.*" *I yawn again.* "*Maybe we'll go kick your dad's ass.*"

His laugh is the last thing I hear before I fall asleep.

~*~

Jesse refuses to file charges against his father. I can't blame him, he still hopes for some reconciliation. He's eighteen, so his father doesn't legally have to house him anymore, even though he has four months of high school left. He moves in with Dave's family.

My father calls me to his study three nights after Jesse sleeps over. My grandfather sits in my father's desk chair, my father in the visitor's chair. I find the power play a little hilarious, though I do most of the laughing in my head.

"*You're friends with that Chambroy boy?*" *My grandfather settles an imposing glare on me. I've shot up five inches since freshman year and five-feet-six-inch Arthur Glass has to look up at me even while he's standing. Probably why he remains seated.*

"*Yeah. Best friends,*" *I say defiantly.*

"*A faggot? You had a faggot in your room and your bed? Are you a faggot, son?*" *My father doesn't say a word. His gaze is mild and expectant as he inspects me.*

"*No.*" *My heart is beating ridiculously fast. I wonder if Dave won't be getting a second boarder soon.*

"*See that you stay away from him. And that other hooligan. Don't think I can't change my will, young man. And your father can just as well put you out. We've had just about enough of your behavior. Your little stunts haven't been more than attention seeking up to this point. I understand that boys will be boys, but I won't have a faggot in my family.*"

"*No, sir.*" *I wipe my sweaty palms on my pants.*

"*Test me, boy, and I'll show you the meaning of the word poor.*"

"*Yes, sir.*"

"*Find some new friends.*"

"*Yes, sir.*" *Fuck you, sir.*

Five minutes later, I go over to Dave's.

~*~

Jesse is miserable. He stays out all night and disappears for days at a time. He's constantly high or drunk, and he's lost his third job. Dave and I watch helplessly as he slips away from us. It's weeks of dragging him home from back alleys when he calls, covered in his own vomit and sobbing, only to watch him sneak out again the next night.

We threaten to send Dave's dad out to get him next time, and that seems to work. We don't hear from him for a while.

Four days before he is supposed to begin college, he meets us at a diner, smiling and seeming content. Both Dave and I are relieved that we have our friend back. He seems ready to attend school, even if it is at a state college. The tuition is low, and the Buchanan's are letting him room there, if he gets his shit together.

"I love you guys, you know?" Jesse says, grasping each of our hands, then returning to his meal and chewing deliberately.

He appears happy, and I can't figure out why that feels wrong somehow. Maybe because I've watched his smile for nearly two years, and I have every part of it memorized. It just looks...wrong. "Okay, Jess, we love you too." Dave laughs.

"Yeah, man, glad to have you back," I say. "You need any money for books or whatever?"

"Nope. I got everything covered. I figured it all out. I'm going to make my dad pay."

"What? How?" Dave and I ask in unison. I can't speak for Dave, but I'm worried that Jesse's about to kick his dad's ass. Or worse, kill him.

"Seriously, don't stress about it." He laughs. "I just wanted to tell you that you don't have to worry anymore. I got it covered." He drops a twenty on the table. His hand has a new tattoo. The skin is red around the blue lettering. I squint at the $20 and silently question where the money came from. Maybe he's blackmailing his dad? "Lunch is on me. I gotta go." Before either of us can voice the thousands of questions, Jesse's out the door.

"What the fuck?" I ask, and pull the money over. "Think he's dealin?"

"Dunno, maybe. Maybe it's time I got dad involved? I think we have to quit covering for him." Dave scratches his head and pushes his plate away.

~*~

—Come over. Now—

I read the text from Dave and dart a glance at my father across the dinner table. He's looking over some stock portfolio or case file or anything except talking to me. Shocker.

—Can't. Dinner—

—Now! Important. Now! 911—

It's got to be about Jesse. It's always 911 about Jesse. I sigh and type back.

—Will try—

Scooting my chair out, I attempt to make as little noise as possible. No one lifts their head. And by no one, I mean my father. My mother hasn't returned from her European vacation. Not for two years. My clean getaway to the garage isn't so surprising.

My father bought me the BMW for my sixteenth birthday. He wasn't around when I got the keys, just left them by the door with a note that read 'drive safely'. Not even a happy birthday. The asshole. Every time I use it to visit Jesse and Dave I get an extra thrill. It's because of this car that I can so easily defy both him and my grandfather.

—On my way— *I type gleefully, expecting to have an adventurous night of Search For Jesse.*

~*~

The only emergency is Dave. When I get to his house, I have to let myself in. It isn't hard to find him, I just follow the rage. He is seething unintelligible words, skin so red he appears sunburned. He has transformed Jesse's side of the room into a disaster of epic proportions. The drawers are pulled out of the dresser, clothes strewn, feathers still drifting down from ravaged pillows. Even the mattresses are pulled off the twin bed.

"He's dead," Dave screams, "Fucker. Asshole. Hung himself on the tree in his father's front yard."

"What?" Where Dave is rage, I am devastation. I slide down the wall and grip both sides of my head.

~*~

After the funeral, Dave never talked about Jesse again. For six months after Jesse's death, Dave didn't talk to *me* at all. By that time I had become the model heterosexual and was well on my way to becoming the model son, too. In large part due to meeting Angelica.

My friendship with Dave tentatively picked up when I tried out and made the baseball team. When it was clear neither of us were going to bring up our dead friend, the mood shifted and we became more comfortable. There were always pieces missing, though. A movie we'd watch in which one of us would pause, expecting Jesse to mutter about dubbing. The odd refusal to go to the homecoming dance, where Jesse had been crowned in previous years. We skipped football games and pep rallies. Once Dave dropped a cd down the side of my car seat and pulled up a sketching pencil that Jesse had left there. Before Dave could throw it out the window, I grabbed it and stuck it in the console. We didn't talk about that either.

My grandfather died in my senior year. Dave was already on the police force by then. He was waiting outside the house while we held the open casket wake. I relished grandfather's death-hardened countenance, forever grim and cold. "I'm going to be a cop," I had said. "Fuck you and fuck Princeton. Fuck being a lawyer. Fuck your edicts about my friends. And most of all, fuck your son and his frigid wife. I'll be there for kids like me." For kids like Jesse.

It was easy to be brave when no one but the dead could hear.

How To Lock Yourself in A Closet without Realizing It

So there it was, everything I had avoided thinking about for the past thirteen years. First the feelings stirred by Jesse, then his seemingly instant descent into drugs and alcohol until his final 'fuck you' death. I started repressing my feelings way back then because of our friendship, then continued doing so because of my grandfather and his threats and watching what coming out did to Jesse. Lastly came my own 'fuck you' to my grandfather, followed by cementing my repressed status when I joined a profession where 'gay' was just another word for 'pussy'. Now that was irony.

In three short days Life had managed to sucker punch me in the gut and kick me in the balls a few times, then it kissed my forehead and sauntered off to wreak havoc on the rest of my existence.

I took two over-the-counter sleeping pills, downed some bottled blue cold medicine, and chased it all with a glass of Bourbon. Woozy, I lay down on the bed, fully dressed, and fell asleep with the alarm clock blinking 19:27.

Chapter Five

Endorphins, Escapism, Enough!

I woke up at five a.m. lethargic from the pills and disheartened from my fight with Angelica. I had two people in the world I could talk to, her and Dave. Neither of them wanted to join me in dealing with (or even discussing) this problem. Angelica for obvious reasons, and Dave because we just didn't talk about Jesse. Ever. It seemed I was going to have to work out this issue on my own.

Padding down to the kitchen, I thought about things while I made coffee and cleaned up from last night.

I didn't realize I had become appealing to women until after Jesse's death. Before that, I was struggling with my staring-at-Jesse problem, and I wasn't paying attention to girls or flirting. When Jesse died, and Dave drew away from me, the way girls reacted became a little more noticeable. The pressure to prove I wasn't gay was on. Time to get really into dating. Not that I was a wet dream. As one of my ex-girlfriends said, "You're cute. Like, dorky-cute."

The first girl I asked out was a sweet, but insecure, freshman with bubblegum breath and an eager smile. Because Mandy was younger, I thought there was a stronger chance she'd say yes to dating an older guy and she'd be happy to be with someone who didn't push for sex.

I didn't know anything about her, other than she was blonde, attractive and her family was "acceptable". All I cared about was bringing her home, showing her off and then ending the relationship as quickly as possible. That proved easy when her friend Natalie made out with me and then told Mandy about it. Mandy dumped me, Natalie became my girlfriend, and I learned how to come off as a stud without actually having to be one.

I jumped from girlfriend to girlfriend in high school, never having to actually have sex. The best part was when I started to bring home the 'wrong' girls. No question about me being a faggot anymore, with the added bonus of pissing off my dad and grandfather just enough to be satisfying, without actually risking anything.

With hindsight, I could see the reasons for my development. Some people might think it was the money that held me back, but that was only partially the problem. It was watching Jesse spiral. Watching what being gay did to him, cost him. And my grandfather reminded every day of what it would cost me.

Not that I was ready to acknowledge being gay. Not completely. Or maybe I was acknowledging it, just not eagerly. Funny thing was I'd expected when I admitted it to Angelica, something would click and things would make sense. But all I'd accomplished was hurting her and sinking myself into a depressive state.

"Enough," I yelled, throwing the last dish into the dishwasher. I wasn't going to figure things out by flooding my brain with memories and questions. It was time for some endorphins. I went upstairs, changed, and then it was back down to my basement where I vegetated on ESPN while getting in a few treadmill miles.

Hump Day!

Fact: Wednesday is commonly referred to as "hump day"— a.k.a Austin's favorite day.

"Today is hump day, Luis." I lolled my head to the side and blinked prettily at my partner.

"Don't make me lock you in a cell, Glass." I was never Austin with cops. I was Glass. It was a terrible nickname. I was not breakable; and being linked to my family name was distasteful. My dislike of that tether was probably why Luis was just "Luis" with me.

"What kind of gifts do people give their partner on hump day? Lube? Vibrators? Issues of Bazooms with a box of tissues?"

"The gift of silence," Luis replied. We stopped at a light, and he leaned over to grab his lighter, cupping his hand as he lit his cigarette. I sighed, my mind automatically imagining tongue rings, pink lips and pierced...things. All my orders to stop thinking about Peter accompanied Luis's smoke out the window. "Dios Mio, kids today." Luis rolled his eyes and shook his head in what appeared to be resignation.

Today's lovely motor-pool issued car had no working lighter, air conditioning or sirens. What it did have was the strong odors of meth, vomit, urine and bleach. At least I hoped it was bleach. I shuddered to consider what else it might be. And now, it smelled of smoke, too. I coughed and stuck my head out the window for a breath.

"Out of curiosity, when do I grow up and become a full-fledged man with a penis?"

"When words like 'hump day' don't make you giggle like a twelve-year-old," he retorted, blowing smoke my way.

"Wow, that long?"

We weaved through traffic at a pace considered slow by blue-haired grandmothers. It was another hot and sticky day, with both of us in suits. Luis, who, surprisingly, did not have a trust fund, wore the same mismatched blazer as yesterday, with a pair of nondescript green polyester slacks—which were wrinkled beyond repair. My new Brooks Brother's grey suit, specially made to remain crease free, fit me like a glove. He was comfortable, barely sweating. I could have squeezed my jacket out and created a neighborhood swimming pool.

We had just completed a four-hour long review of the evidence on the Alvarado case so we could be prepared for the afternoon's interviews. And we did it while boxed up in a tiny room, the air quality resembling that of a third world country. I had suggested lunch to clear our heads.

Half a block from the station, my cell rang. I clicked it on while waiting for my partner's reply. "Glass," I answered.

"I can't go out with you," Peter stated, sounding as if he was speaking between tightly clenched teeth.

I pointed at a McDonalds. Luis shook his head and went the other direction. I recognized the route to our favorite Mexican place. "Sure you can," I said into the phone, relaxing back into the seat without protesting Luis's decision. "You get in the car, I take you to coffee, we talk, you find out how charming and loveable I am, invite me in to your house, kiss me and take me to bed."

"You're frustrating," came Peter's reply. Luis glanced over with raised brows as he parked.

"I'm adorable."

"From a distance," Peter admitted—grudgingly. I calculated just how tight his lips were clamped by the way he had said it. Grudging or not, he thought I was adorable. Mental victory dance time.

"Up close, I'm sexy as hell."

"You're rich, spoiled and used to getting your way," he said stubbornly.

"Not true. If I had my way you would have kissed me and ridden me like cowboy while screaming 'yeehaw'."

I heard a choking sound over the phone. Or was it from Luis? "What makes you think *you* won't ride *me*?"

My turn to choke. And blush. I never blushed. Before now I would have thought the only way I would blush was from sunstroke. Luckily, only Luis could see it. And his brows disappeared into his receding hairline. A difficult thing to accomplish, considering it resided somewhere on the crown of his head.

"Yeah. I think that's how it's going to go," added Peter as the silence stretched. My brain broke again. Images flashed in my head that were really more graphic than I was ready for. "I think you're going to spread those—"

"Anyway," I sing-songed and cleared my throat, "about Saturday. I'll see you at three." I hung up quickly, checking Luis from the corner of my eye. I'd worry about Peter's buyer's remorse later. Right now I was too concerned with finishing that sentence. Spread those what? Cheeks? Legs? Lies? Rumors? Okay, I was just kidding myself with those last two.

"Soooo. That was not Angelica," Luis said.

"No, that was not Angelica," I evaded.

"Glass, tell me that wasn't the Cotton boy."

Well, if he insisted. "That wasn't the Cotton boy." I nodded gravely. "I think I'll have the Menudo today." I climbed out of the car while Luis went on a Spanish cursing rampage.

He caught up to me after I was already seated at a table, munching on chips and salsa. "I ordered iced tea for us both." Sitting across from me, he glared long enough that I grew fidgety and began picking my bottom tooth with a finger while staring at the ceiling.

"This is not at all funny."

"Which is why I'm not laughing," I answered, showing him how very serious I was by returning his glare.

"He's a *witness*. How many ways can I spell 'fucked up' for you?"

"I saw him first!" The sheer ridiculousness of that statement made me sit back. I didn't try to clarify what I meant, however.

"You can't work a case if you're involved with a fucking witness. You can't look at him objectively," Luis reasoned.

"Maybe not. Or maybe I can. Either way, no one will know this case better. That makes me the best choice to continue."

Penny, our usual waitress, plopped two iced teas at the table, disrupting the flow of the argument. "Hey, guys. The usual?"

Luis was still glaring, so I answered her. "Yeah, and a bowl of Menudo for me. New haircut?"

She twisted a brown strand of pixie short hair in her fingers and nodded. "Yup. Kinda drastic but this summer's so hot, and the hair was getting heavy."

"Looks great," I winked and added, "Brave, too."

"I still sometimes feel it at my waist. Ghost hair," she sighed, and we both laughed. "Back in a jiff with your food." Before tucking her pad into her brown apron and walking off, she gave Luis a questioning glance.

"What *is* it with this kid?" Luis picked up his interrogation, as if Penny had never been there.

"That's what I'm trying to figure out."

"That suicide last month. It really got to you. Wasn't your first db (dead body), wasn't even your first suicide I'd bet. You've been weird ever since then, though. Haven't been by the house. Haven't seen Angelica as much. Today's the first hump-day shit since. What gives?"

"Seemed like such a waste," I hedged, gulping the tea like it'd soothe the ache in my chest or cool the watering heat in my eyes.

"Junkie that hangs himself ain't surprising. It's a fucking public service usually." Luis was prodding gently, poking around like there was a button he just hadn't found yet. He'd already found it, I just was having a slow reaction to it being pushed—shortness of breath, rapid heartbeat, glaze of sweat on my upper lip. Where was Penny with our food? I checked over my shoulder, hoping to see her carrying a tray over. "He someone you know?" Luis tried guessing.

"No." The wide eyes I gave Luis should have been heard by him as "Drop it!", but he was still searching for that button, like a blind guy reading the Braille in a hotel elevator.

"Can't just be that he was a junkie, we see those every goddamn day."

"Drop it. Jesus Christ, this is lunch, not therapy." Thank fuck the food arrived. I ignored Luis's contemplative gaze and dug into my tacos. The bowl of Menudo sat off to my left, daring me. "I don't know what it is with the kid. He's—?" Christ, how was I going to put this without sounding like a fucking woman. "…appealing. Attractive. I don't know. He's something. Shut up." I held up a hand. "I don't give a shit if your daughter is gay or your whole fucking lineage is taking it up the ass. They're not me. Unless you have some unique perspective on why I'm suddenly checking out guys' asses, then I'm just going to go with the redhead that takes it up the ass and hope he has a shitfucking answer." Or a goddamn roadmap of how to deal with a sudden attraction to penises might be helpful, too. "I won't fuck up this case. That's all you need to know."

A sigh, then Luis picked up his taco and bit in. "Penny," he called over his shoulder. "Where's the hot sauce?"

I breathed out a sigh of relief as Luis switched to babbling about his youngest daughter, Mariposa, who apparently found a box of Oreos the night before and ate the whole thing, claiming her innocence through chocolate-cookie-coated lips.

My Father, The Anti-Hero

Questioning suspects while attorneys are present is like a game of chess where one side makes all the moves behind their back, and you have to trust they'll tell you which move they made. Of course, they always lie. So when Luis and I entered the room, we were as prepared as possible for any lie Alvarado might tell. But the asshole already had our king in danger.

"Did it even take convincing to represent him, Dad, or did he just have to mention I was on the case?" I sat down across from Desmond Glass, propping up an elbow and dropping a cheek onto my fist.

"My client mentioned you were working the case. It had no bearing on the agreement to handle it. And you will address me as Mr. Glass in these proceedings."

"Did my father neglect to tell you that he hasn't seen me in four years and barely spoke to me before that?" I asked Alvarado. "That $1500 an hour for Desmond Glass and there was no advantage for you, was there? He doesn't know me at all, Prick. Oh, I meant Prisc." No, I didn't.

"You may direct your questions to me," Desmond Glass said, crossing his legs and resting his hands on his knee.

"Good. I wanted to tell you something really important, anyway. I was going to call, but it's so much better in person. Your son, Mr. Glass, is a big homo." My father's back straightened. His eyes narrowed, and his mouth pinched closed so tightly I thought maybe he'd eaten his lips.

Now that was freeing, while also being useful. My father was speechless.

Luis took a seat next to me, flopping down some evidence files, and began rubbing the center of his forehead with his fingers. "Dios, mio," he sighed.

While my father tried to control his hyperventilating, I tried to get a read on Alvarado. He was sitting back in his chair, tapping the ends of the arms while focusing flat brown eyes on me.

I didn't see it. He and Peter. Peter must be right about my being superficial, because no matter how many ways I twisted it or how many angles I approached it from, Peter and Alvarado just wouldn't come together in my head.

"This meeting is a courtesy, detectives, between the district attorney and my client. We have nothing further to discuss with you." Good old Desmond—who now refused to acknowledge my existence in the room—directed his comment to Luis. That was okay. Something was whirring around in my brain, and I needed to continue my analysis of Alvarado to figure it out.

Alvarado wasn't unattractive, I decided. Older than me by quite a few years. Was that Peter's type? Big, tattooed Latin guys with cruel eyes and a tiny mouth? The exact opposite of me? Or maybe he had various types? Or he lied about finding me attractive? So which was it: Had he been lying about this guy, or lying about me?

Observing Alvarado, I noticed similarities between him and Peter. Wife beater t-shirt, baggy jeans, lots of ink, wide gauges in his ears. But Alvarado had a good thirty-to-thirty-five pounds of muscle on me. I'd guess steroids, since I couldn't imagine he'd take the time to actually work out that much. He was a shortcut kinda guy. Which also didn't mesh with how I viewed Peter.

Peter seemed careful—considerate in his actions. If Peter was with Alvarado, it wasn't for any romantic reasons. All that guff about being sixteen and enamored? It was crap. Something else was up. Peter was trying to lead us off Alvarado. But why?

Alvarado slowly brought out a piece of gum and folded it in his mouth. I watched him chew, growing more unsure with every second. "You and Peter were never together," I bluffed. His chewing halted briefly. I didn't even need the flicker of fear in his eyes. I already knew. Peter had lied. Alvarado was exactly who we thought he was: a scumbag human trafficker with a penchant for young boys. I stood up and gathered the files. "No deals. Our informant wasn't lying," I said to Luis. Time to bluff some more, because I still didn't think Terrelle Gaines had anything to do with Alvarado. If that was the case, then we needed to know where our informant had gotten his information.

My partner, familiar with my interviewing techniques, followed me to the door.

"Man, Terrelle don't know shit. You think I would trust that pendejo to be all up in my business?"

"Quiet," my father said, laying a hand on his client's arm.

"Gee, Luis, that pendejo who didn't know shit? He sure led us to a lot of evidence."

"Items we found in your home." Luis opened a file and began laying pictures on the table. "Passports, receipts for warehouses under the name Sambucho, Inc, a company registered under your conveniently missing wife Leila, where fourteen people who matched those passports were working as illegal day laborers. Papers that led us to Inez Castillo, Abelinda Villanueva and Guadalupe Portilla, picked up last night and this morning. Each identifies your client as the person who sold them as domestics to three wealthy couples."

Desmond Glass didn't even blink at the charges. He simply stared at the mirrored partition as if he knew the DA was behind it. Which he was. "Mr. Alvarado performed a misguided goodwill gesture by helping some of his fellow countrymen retain work in the US without green cards. Those three women are seeking asylum by accusing my client, and in the case of Miss Villanueva, we are prepared to offer proof that prior to coming to the US, she worked in a brothel in her hometown of Tanque. Further, he maintains his innocence with regard to how they crossed the border, but he is willing to give more information on the person responsible, as well as the locations of the children of some of those families. In return, my client requests immunity and witness protection under the purview of the FBI." My father checked his watch. "Should the DA care to make an appearance, we could move toward that goal."

The FBI? He wanted to get involved federally? Something was wrong. Really wrong. Luis had figured it out, I could tell just by his bland expression. I wished the epiphany would migrate my way.

"It's a cop," Luis explained, eyes directed at Alvarado. "Whoever he's turning over. A cop or bigger. But he won't give us the name, or he'd have made the deal already. The whole point of this meeting was for us to reach that conclusion. Then we'd instigate an investigation, and the FBI would swoop in and take over."

"Peter knows who it is?" I asked Alvarado. He rested penetrating brown eyes on me and said, "Man, who you think set me up with the guy?"

Fuck. I'm a complete and total moron.

Chapter Six

Once I Got Over Him Being a Scumsucking Criminal

We pulled into the diner's lot a half hour later, and Luis turned off the car. I grabbed his arm as he opened the door. "There's just no chance of you letting me do this on my own?" I pleaded.

His answer wasn't so much a laugh as it was a guffaw. He shook off my hand and continued laughing the entire walk into the restaurant. I hung my head for a minute, then followed.

The hostess—and I use the term loosely because she didn't greet us so much as give us a once over and raise her brows—met us at the entrance. We held up our badges. She curled her lips and stuck out her chin. "What?" I wondered if hostility was a job requirement at the diner.

"We're here for Peter," I said and checked behind her for him.

"Peter? Who the fuck is Peter?"

Luis cocked a brow at me. "Yeah, who the fuck is Peter?" His amusement was not catching.

"Bunny slippers, bad attitude, boyfriend named Cai," I snapped.

I checked hostess-girl's nametag. Matilda. Really? Matilda? "Rabbit. You mean Rabbit." She giggled, causing her chin to wobble hypnotically. Resting a hand on her ample hip, she smirked at us both. I attempted a smile in return.

Just as she shifted toward the kitchen doors and screamed, "RABBIT! COPS'RE HERE FOR YOU!", Peter walked out of the kitchen. For two seconds he stared at me. He blinked in surprise and started a half smile. His gaze bounced to Luis. He squinted and his eyes blew wide. Taking a backward step, he swiveled and tore off into the back. I stared, dismayed, at the doors swinging back and forth. Then I twirled on my heel and booked it out the door to follow.

"Goddammit, stop, Pete— Rabbit!" I shouted as he hopped over the retaining wall behind the restaurant and sped across the main street. "Motherf— I just bought this suit!" *And it's too fucking hot to chase your ass in it.* Fuck. There was no way that little shit could outrun me. I had been training for the FBI for ten years. And I was taller. Yeah, taller. I just decided that.

But that fucker wasn't just fast. He managed an even pace ahead of me and then did an imitation of my slide across the hood of a car—only the car he chose was moving. I looped around it and followed him across the street, already breathing hard.

Once on open ground, I closed in on him, but then he sprang over a pair of guardrails, jammed his feet into the side of a parking garage and somehow monkey-climbed the freaking wall! He then twisted his body, grabbed the edge of a windowless opening and pulled his legs up. He disappeared somewhere on the first level.

I stood there out of breath, four blocks from the restaurant and gaping up at the concrete hole he vanished into. That was how the asshole got those abs. Fucker trained in Parkour. Holy shit. I wanted him so badly.

Once I got over his being a scum-sucking criminal, that is.

"Yo, your boyfriend just whipped your ass." Luis's laughter carried through the car window as flung open the passenger door.

"What the fuck're you laughing about? We just lost him, and what the fuck was he running for?" I flopped into the seat and slammed the door as the car screeched out. Luis handed me a piece of paper.

"...Detroit Street..." I read the address, frowned, and then my lips did a slow curve upwards. "2A."

Unf Unf Unf

We made it there before Rabbit—er, Peter, *asshole*, liar. I waited patiently at his door while Luis watched the back gate.

His home was packed into the middle unit of a set of rundown brick townhomes smack in the heart of the most urban neighborhoods of Denver. I knocked and rang the bell. No answer. I had little choice but to wait outside in the muggy summer sun. I stank of sweat, but at least there was a small garden next door to offset the rank. I inhaled and played with the cuffs hooked to my belt.

We now had grounds for arrest, since he had fled, and I relished throwing cuffs on him. I almost hoped he ran again so I could see him do that shit all over. Then jump him and hold his wrists down and ram my tongue—

He ran. The moment he sprinted around the corner and saw me, he blinked wide, skidded and pivoted, hauling ass the opposite way. "Are you *kidding* me?" I shouted, giving chase. I was closer this time from the get-go, not to mention being newly familiar with his tactics. He made it exactly two blocks before my football tackle skills made themselves useful.

Perhaps not appropriate to mention to him that I played 'tight end' (but I did). And I was sure there were all sorts of 'wide receiver' jokes that could have been pertinent, but I was too busy struggling with—fuck he was strong—Peter to think of them. Maybe later.

"Hold—" I growled.

"—off me, pig!"

"—still," I grabbed his wrists. He twisted and bucked under me. I was sure he could feel my erection because he finally stilled and tried crawling away, instead of rubbing against my crotch by twisting some more.

Sadly, I couldn't enjoy this position for long because I had to get him cuffed. Though, there were much better ways I could come up with to cuff him besides behind his back. *Later*, I told myself again. With somewhat of a lesser struggle, I managed to get his hands cuffed and then throw myself off him and sit on the grass.

Peter lay on his stomach, breathing as heavily as I, and then he kicked me twice in the hip before I moved out of range. I found myself staring at his jeans-clad ass and his sparsely-freckled back where the shirt had ridden up during our fight. It was so wrong to be this aroused by him.

"Alright, we'll talk later about where I'm picking you up Saturday." Peter rolled over and stared at me with comically large eyes. "Right now I have some other questions."

"What is *wrong* with you?" He glared at me.

"I'm somewhat sure I'm suddenly gay," I shrugged, "My father and mother are hypocritical abandoning homophobic assholes. The former defending my chief suspect in the biggest case of my life—something I'm sure you had a hand in. I'm obsessed with your freckles, your bunny slippers and your lips—which I should be getting points for not kissing while you're incapacitated, by the way. I'm dating a whore while working on the vice squad—points to me again for not arresting your ass for that—and I'm ridiculously horny. Oh, and my fiancée won't talk to me."

He narrowed his eyes at me and bit his lip deliciously before pulling it through his teeth again and again. "I'm not a whore," he said. "Not anymore."

"Just a poet, and you don't even know it?" I held up the handcuff keys, attempting to dazzle him with my smile. "If I take those off, are you going to run away? You know what, *Rabbit*, never mind. You *lied* to me."

"Peter," he said quietly. "My name is Peter." I opened my mouth to respond but he interrupted. "I did what I had to do."

I leaned over and uncuffed him—because I was insane. My fingers stayed a little too long on his wrists. He pulled them in front of his chest and rubbed the chafed skin.

"We're not going to arrest you for lying. I mean we could, but we'd have to prove you were lying. Which is a stretch. Jesus, is that why you ran?"

Peter turned his head away from me and pushed off the ground. "Sure," he lied. Again. I recognized the lie now that my rosy glasses weren't so shiny. I was not seeing him as this ethereal, innocent boy any longer. I saw him for what I dealt with all the time. A hustler. Attractive street trash, but street trash nonetheless.

And you know what? It didn't lessen my attraction to him one iota.

"So what do you want?" He tucked his hands in his pockets. I sensed he was faking vulnerability.

"I came for that kiss." I flashed all my teeth in a grin as I stood up. He stared at me with that withering glare. "You know why I'm here."

He pulled his brows in and surveyed the park just west of us. "Your nose is bleeding."

"Fuck," I said, leaning my head back and pinching the bridge. "If I knew dating a whore would be this difficult, I'd have slept with you the first night."

"Call me a whore one more time," he warned.

"You're sensitive about *that*? Do I need to define the word whore for you?" I couldn't believe I was having this ridiculous conversation.

"I thought you'd refuse or leave me alone," he spat. Literally he spat, at my feet. "You know, being a fucking cop and all." He shook his head and huffed a laugh, biting his lip in that delicious way again.

Dear God, he'd broken my nose, charged me for sex, kicked me, made me look like an idiot, and all I wanted to do is bang the sense out of him with my dick. "I have no idea what to do with you, Peter." I sighed, pushed my hand through my hair, and began searching my pockets for a handkerchief or tissue for my nose.

Peter's fingers pressed under my chin, lifting it up. Using a bandana he pulled from nowhere, he dabbed away the blood under my nose. My heart beat like we were still on the run. "I don't like you," he muttered. "You're a closet case, and you're only interested in my ass." He rubbed my bruised nose. I whimpered. I was fairly sure he pressed harder than necessary.

"Sadist," I groaned. I was so hard right now, I could probably come if he accidentally rubbed my knees. Not the best time, since I saw Luis pull the car up across the street.

"You're too pretty," he murmured. I'd have grinned if my nose wouldn't protest.

"You want me," I joked.

"Against my better judgment," he admitted.

My fingers brushed against his stomach as I rested them on the ridge of his waistband. The shiver that I elicited thrilled me. "Hi," I said with a stupid grin and a wince of pain.

"So eager," he said, wetting the bandana with his tongue and wiping at my nose again. I cringed, immediately regretting the gesture as pain shot into my forehead.

"I like you," I said honestly. "Even though you're probably a criminal and are going to get me thrown off the force. And you kicked me. Broke my nose. Made me gay and refused to kiss me."

"You don't even know me," Peter reiterated, stuffing the bandana in my pocket, and contemplating me for a few seconds. He stepped back and released my chin. "You need a name, I guess?" He popped a brow at me.

"Yeah," I said, because that was the only coherent thought I had besides *unf unf unf.*

"I wish I could give you one. Even if I had it. Which I don't. I just get calls for favors." He shoved his hands into his pockets again, whipping the flop of hair out of his eyes. "Iss knows things. I can't risk it." The thought of him risking anything broke my heart a little. But it also made me more alert to my behavior. I was definitely more suspicious of his mannerisms at least. "But I might know someone who has more to give on Iss."

"I need something from you. Something that justifies my not arresting you."

He nodded once. "I'll talk to my friend again. That's the best I can do."

"Okay. And, Peter? Don't leave town," I said. "Next time it won't be me cuffing you. Joe's not around to keep your record clean." I was normally ruthless at my job. For a while Peter had clouded that instinct. Perhaps I'd see a bit more clearly now. "Besides, for our date Saturday? I was thinking less cell block and more movie house." I said brightly.

His lips twitched, but he didn't say no. I took that as 'Oh, you sexy devil, Austin, I want to do you right here, but I'm super-duper excited about our date so I'll wait'.

I was paraphrasing, of course.

Dave

Luis chewed me out the entire ride back to the station and continued his tirade for an extra fifteen minutes in the car after we arrived. I convinced him that Peter was going to come through with a name for us. That, combined with reminders that my law enforcement career, at least up to this point, had been impeccable and my standing in the way of him taking another bullet, finally shut him up.

I grew up Catholic. I was not above guilt trips.

He dropped me off at my Jag in sullen silence and left without a word. I turned on my car, and with nowhere to go, no one special to see, I drove aimlessly through the city.

For the hundredth time since Saturday, I wondered what the fuck I was doing. Apparently what I was doing was getting off on being lectured because I called Dave.

Knowing that he had spoken with Angelica. Knowing that he would not talk about Jesse—maybe even had purposefully forgotten him, like me—I still called.

"Buchnanan home, I'm Asa," a bright soft voice greeted me.

Asa was almost five and insisted on doing things like answering the house phone and helping her mom with dinner.

"It's uncle Oz, Asa. How's my girl."

"Mom says she's mad, and it's not nice for you to call her fat."

I cringed again, making a splinter of pain rocket into my skull. "You're right, Asa. That wasn't nice. And Uncle Oz thinks you have the most beautiful mommy in the world."

"Mom. Mom. Uncla Oz says you're the most beautiful mom in the world."

"Give mummy the phone, sötnos. Oz, the booties were perfect, but you didn't have to."

"Am I forgiven?"

"Always, Oz. I just teach you a little way to hold your tongue, yes?" Only the Buchanans used the nickname. I never told them how much I hated it. It didn't matter, when they said it, it was different.

I laughed. "I think you taught me well, beautiful. But admit you forgave me because I sent the can of fermented herring."

"Yes, this was very kind. But I think Dave will not talk to you after I open it."

"For your love, I'd do anything, Marta." I heard a mild scuffle over the phone, and the sound of lips smacking in a kiss.

"Are you quoting Oliver Twist to my wife?"

"I think that was just Oliver," I smiled.

"You know she won't let me ban you from the house for sending her that foul smelling crap. But I insist you be there for its opening."

"Oh, wow. I'd love to, but I'm busy."

"I haven't told you when yet, man."

"I'm monumentally busy. Weddings to break up, boys to chase, cases to solve. Busy, busy."

"I heard." The tone got serious faster than I was ready for. I pulled off the road into a parking lot and leaned my head back on the seat.

"Angel called Marta?"

"Marta first, then me. Wanted to know if I knew what instigated it." I checked out the park across the street. Watched a couple of toddlers bounce on the rides. Would I ever have kids? "Do I?" He added.

"Last month, Luis and I are part of the sweep of the meth house on 19th Street, near the old hospital. You know it?"

"I heard something about it. Dead kid in the back room."

"Not in the back room. In the backyard. Used his belt to hang himself in the tree. Seventeen years old." Silence. "You there?"

"Yeah."

"How'd we go eight years not talking about this? Not thinking about him at all?"

My father was always a lost cause. Telling him today wasn't even that satisfying. Especially since I felt like I had lost Angelica at this point, and now I was risking the loss of Dave, too. I had even fucked up with Luis. Slowly peeling my life apart helped me realize how lonely and afraid Jesse must have been.

"This isn't something we should talk about over the phone, Oz."

"Did you hate him because of that kiss?"

"Shit no! We were cool after that. He made a pass, I said no, it was over. I loved him. You know that. Christ, we'd been friends since we were ten. Just. Goddamn that asshole. We laughed about the fucking kiss."

"And then you told him I was gay," I accused.

"Oz, sometimes it'd take a snap of my fingers at your fucking nose to stop you from staring at him."

My laugh broke on a wrecked sob. I quickly stifled it all. When I had control again I answered. "I counted every freckle on his nose that first summer."

Another beat of silence, and then we both breathed out in frustration and relief. "You want Jake's and Terry's new number?" Dave asked.

"Okay," I sighed. A few seconds later I heard a beep announcing a text on my phone.

"I wasn't mad about the gay shit, Oz. I was pissed at what he did, not who he was."

Too much angst. I needed a break. "Angelica said she wouldn't march in the gay parade for me."

"Are you asking me to be your fella for the gay prom?"

"That's like the worst impression of a woman in the history of mankind."

"Do me a favor, Oz?"

"Sure?"

"Don't ask them about ass-sex when they answer the phone. Marta feels guilty when you have no friends to visit."

"No on the ass-sex. Check."

"Next week, Jays vs Sox?"

"My place, bring beer. Laters." Huh. No lecture?

I checked my phone and debated calling Jake and Terry. But I didn't know them that well, and I had no idea how to be gay around gay people. Was I supposed to develop an interest in shopping and Cher? Right now all I wanted to do was go home and watch some sports and do my second pastime: first person shooter video games. So that's what I did.

Chapter Seven

Thirteen Years Too Long

Why has it never been said in the history of the world that Thursdays suck? Thursdays are that awful place between halfway done and can't quite see the finish line yet. Thursday morning, stuck in the evidence room, *again*, with Luis—who had decided he was done bitching at me and would just heretofore grunt all responses. I was in a rotten mood. I was pissed at myself for making a date on Saturday. Seriously. Saturday? What was I fucking thinking? Like the anticipation between now and then was a good thing?

"There's nothing new in these boxes." I kicked one and sent it skittering by Luis's foot. He fielded it with his shoe and then shoved it back.

"Right now you'll sit there and look through these boxes while I try to figure out if I'm going to the captain to request your removal from this case. The less time we're searching through evidence, the more I'm inclined to head to his office. It's your call."

"I haven't fucked up the case," I insisted.

"A miracle because you've done just about everything possible to fuck it up."

"Bullshit!"

He pounded the desk and stood, leaning over, nose-to-nose with me. "Just let it go. Wait until the case is solved." Our volumes began escalating.

"I can't," I said—which being interpreted was, I wouldn't.

"A few weeks?"

"Weeks? Or months? You don't know. And I can't wait."

"Why the fuck not? Is this kid—"

"Because I've waited thirteen years too long!"

"Ai, Dios mio! You! Ya estoy harto de tanta hostia. Estúpido cabrón!"

"I'm Googling that." I sat down and began typing in my phone. "And if you just told me to suck your cock, I'm calling Denise." While I waited for the tension to ease, I watched the latest viral pet video.

"I said I'd had enough of this shit, you stupid stubborn ass."

"I love you, too. Which is why I say this with respect: If you keep rubbing your face like that, I'm going to have to lift up skin to look you in the eyes."

"This kid is involved, Glass."

"I know he is, but he was just used to throw us off Alvarado."

"That's little Austin speaking."

"A, he's not little. B, not even funny to go *there*. C, he'll get us a name."

"Says you and your—"

"Says me and eight years of being a cop."

"Eight years is still primary school. I wouldn't brag about that. He has until Monday to come up with someone. Or you bring us something we can squeeze him with."

"Deal." I exhaled, hoping I'd bought enough time that Peter could come through.

Luis grabbed his coat from the back of his chair and slipped it over his shoulders. "Let's get out of here and find out where those kids are before the DA agrees to that plea. Because it ain't here."

"Where to then?"

"Let's go beat down some SORs (Sex Offenders Registrants)."

"I thought uniform was on that?"

"They are," Luis said. "And so are we. Let's go."

Peter

By Friday Luis and I had visited forty-two registered kiddy offenders in Denver and its suburbs. By late evening we had four left on our list. The DA had already cut the deal with Alvarado hours earlier. Nineteen minors were rescued from various places, but those were only the most recent of Alvarado's victims. They were the ones Alvarado gave up. Luis and I were hearing reports of more from the dregs we'd been interviewing.

My cell rang a few minutes from the end of our sweep. Luis and I were parked outside a halfway house, where we had interviewed yet another sex offender. My partner lit up a cigarette while I picked up the phone. "Glass," I answered with a cough.

"The Manhole," Peter said. "Talk to Darryl Boerner. He'll be there until three a.m. He knows you're coming." He hung up before I could say a word.

"Peter came through. The Manhole?" I refused to peek at Luis as my lips pressed together and my chest and shoulders shook.

Luis groaned, "Shit." He dragged the gears into drive and hung a U-turn taking us into the depths of downtown.

My Job Sucked Sometimes

The Manhole was one of Denver's oldest gay bars. It was notorious for leather, biker types. Rumors were that a stairwell and basement existed where men had sex and, during the summer, 'watersports' were played on the patio. The heat of the day reminded me what time of year it was.

"This you can handle on your own," Luis announced as he parked out front.

The bar wasn't dark and dingy like I had expected it to be. Sunlight filtered in through a doorway which led out to the patio, and hanging fluorescent lights kept most of the area well-lit. The only dark spot was four steps from the entrance, where the infamous stairwell coughed up moans from two leather clad men humping against the wall. My partner steadfastly ignored them. I craned my neck to investigate and grimaced. I was definitely *not* gay enough for that, I decided. Luis wore the most put upon grimace in the history of man. "I'll wait here," he said, leaning near the door.

For early evening it was almost empty, only a smattering of men nursing their beers, hovering at tables or playing pool and darts. A few of the patrons walked by. They wore chaps. Just that—chaps, with nothing else. Their hairy asses waved around in the breeze. I grinned, checking my partner. Luis passed a hand over his eyes and curdled to cracker white.

Walking over to the bar, I leaned across the scuffed wood and flashed my badge, smiling with what I hoped was my charming smile. "Here to see Darryl," I said to the biggest, hairiest man I'd ever laid eyes upon. I dubbed him Grizzly Adams.

"Darryl! Visitor," Griz called out over his shoulder and poured cherries from a large jar into a little container. A skinny boy about Peter's age danced around the corner, lowering a set of headphones and looping them around his neck.

Darryl Boerner was on the feminine side of cute, with bright green eyes and wispy thin blond hair. He wore leather chaps, the hot pink variety, with matching pink short-shorts underneath. His arms and chest were bared around a vest that appeared to be a matching set with the pants. Old scars from track marks littered his inner elbows and arms.

"Why, hello there." He leaned right across the bar so, should either of us move an inch, our noses would touch. His lip gloss smelled fruity. "You rang, handsome?"

I flashed my badge again. He glanced at it with distaste and then back up to me, smiling in a manner I assumed was supposed to be seductive. There wasn't enough gay in the world to make me hit that. "Peter said you'd have something for me," I said placidly.

"So you're the gorgeous little detective," he mused. Tilting his head and twirling a bleached strand of shoulder length hair, he eyed me like I was a glazed donut. "Peter always did like 'em manly and pretty." He propped up his elbows on the wood and placed his chin delicately on the back of his hands. "I have something for you. Now what are you giving me, hmm?"

I slid a hundred bucks across the bar. He dropped a hand to cover it, and then tucked it somewhere. I refused to check, or even imagine, where. "Well?" I asked, doing my best to be devastatingly handsome.

"My, my, so impatient. For a hundred more you can to join me downstairs for about an hour."

"I'm spoken for," I lied, trying not to grit my teeth. "Just the info."

"Lovely, isn't he? Our little Peter Rabbit." He reached out to trace the top of my hand. "And so sweet. Had a face like an altar boy when he was just twelve. They *loooved* him to pieces. That delightful red hair, blue eyes so innocent, those darling little freckles. Made him call them daddy. He used to tell me they liked him to cry. *Don't, daddy. Please don't, daddy*," Darryl parodied in a soft high voice. The way Darryl said 'loved' made me want to get descriptions and kick off a pedophile-murdering rampage. "Does he call you daddy?"

"The info," I reminded him, this time there was a distinct bark in my voice. Nausea had welled up in my throat. Acid reflux of the emotional kind.

You know what was sick? What my selfish fucking brain was thinking? If Peter had been checked for HIV. That was my first thought when I heard he'd been raped at the age of twelve. I disgusted myself.

"Don't get your panties in a twist, sexy," Darryl said airily and picked up a napkin. He wrote an address down and slid it over to me. "Iss's stepbrother's house. Took me there once. Told me I was his special little boy." He batted his lashes, and I resolved to never do that again to Luis. "My phone number's down at the bottom. If you ever want me to call you Daddy." I didn't even want to think about that. "Detective...?"

'Yeah?" I looked up from the napkin.

"You hurt my Rabbit, and they'll write horror films on what I'll do to you." The way he said it was so casual, I could almost feel my skin crawling away.

"And what if he hurts me?"

"Chance you take with boys like us, ain't it?" He waved a few fingers at me, "Buh bye now," before putting his headphones on and dancing his way back from where he came.

I headed for the entrance. Luis hadn't moved. His gaze was fixed on the disco ball above his head until I approached. "Get it?" he asked.

"Got an address." I held up the napkin and had to restrain myself from running out the door to vomit. I needed those terrible images of Peter with sick old men out of my head.

Three hours later, the crime scene techs had cleared out of the stepbrother's house. We had two more victims, both adult women, safely being handled by victim services. But best of all was the brand new evidence on Alvarado, his step-brother, birth father and two cousins. And I had the added bonus of knowing Peter had been partially vindicated before I actually dated him.

I went home and showered until my skin felt relatively clean. It took a lot of scrubbing—until my skin was as pink as Peter's.

In a rare physical manifestation of human compassion, I ended up vomiting into the toilet until every wretch ended up dry.

My job sucked sometimes.

You

I dreamed of Peter in bursts. Things that made me wake up in a sweat and, at least once, near tears. I didn't cry. Ever. Not because I found it particularly unmanly or weak, but because, despite my naiveté with Peter, I was jaded as hell. With a little introspection I could have figured out that what I felt for Peter was compassion, but that would have required delving into the emotional shithole that was my black soul.

After the third heart-pounding awakening, I gave up the quest for sleep at about 2:00 a.m. Padding downstairs in my boxers, I heated milk in the kitchen and added bourbon to it, then plopped on the sofa. The television illuminated the room in weird hues as I flipped through channels. I wasn't even watching the thing. I kept picturing those animals touching Peter, hurting him, transforming those bright blue eyes into the lifeless expression that glazed over them every so often.

Across the room my cell phone lay at ease on the table. I eyed it for about two minutes before I went over, picked it up and tapped it against my thigh. I returned to the couch, shivering at least partly from the air conditioner. Lack of sleep had the same effect. Plus, I was terrified of this sudden need to protect this probably beyond-broken boy. Man. At twenty he was definitely a man.

And something else eye opening, I didn't *want* a boy. To deny being gay, at this point, was pointless. That battle was done. At least for now. What that meant, I didn't know. But I knew what I wanted; and what I didn't. I didn't want to be one of those men who touched him and thought about taking his innocence away. I wanted fully grown-up Peter; and he was no boy. Thank God.

I dialed and lifted the phone to my ear, stretching out on the sofa and throwing an arm over my eyes, blocking out the TV light.

Six rings later, Peter answered. "Do you know what time it is?" His voice was sexily sleepy.

I closed my eyes and breathed, just taking in his voice for a minute. "Tell me something good, Peter."

Silence, and then I heard a sigh, coupled with a yawn. I imagined him curled up in bed, hair poking out all over, eyes closed with those long copper lashes resting against his cheeks. "Cai finished painting our living room yesterday with a mural depicting Darryl as president." That was a disquieting and frightening image even without including Cai.

I didn't mean tell me about your boyfriend. Lifting the phone from my ear, I glared at it silently. "Tell me something *not* about your boyfriend," I growled, phone at my cheek again.

Peter laughed, a throaty sound that had all the dregs of sleep in it. I could hear, from the noises he made, that he was stretching while he yawned again. My imagination did wicked things with that information. "Cai's my brother, Detective." The way he said 'detective' made my boxers tent.

Mentally I was doing the prize fighter just-won dance. Until I realized he hadn't said anything about Darryl not being his boyfriend. "Darryl was interesting. I could take him in a fight."

"Huh uh."

"He weighs like fifty pounds less than I do."

"Darryl's scrappy and goes straight for the balls, Detective."

I smiled. "I like that much better than Alex or idiot."

"I need to get back to sleep. I have to be at the diner early."

"You work there too much."

"It's just till it sells."

"Then what?"

"Detective, can we not have this conversation at three a.m.?"

"One last question?" I took the silence as acquiescence. "Why vouch for Prisc?"

"Whatever you think you know about him, you don't know everything. To you, he's just a criminal. But to me he's the guy that drove me and Cai to school every morning and picked me up every afternoon. He found Joe the diner, helped him balance the books, took shifts when people were sick, got me my first intern—"

"I get it," I sighed.

"He got Cai a home. Everything else was just a bonus. But I'll owe him forever for that."

Jesus. "Tell me something good about your life," I whispered, needing to hear that he wasn't as broken as I thought him to be.

Peter breathed into the handset for about two minutes. I began wondering if he was about to hang up, or had fallen asleep, when he answered. "You." It was so quiet I almost didn't hear it. He hung up before I could ask him to repeat himself.

I fell asleep, grinning, with the phone still clutched in my hand and my milk souring on the coffee table.

I Am Now Fully Embracing The Gay

You

Jesus God when he said that word I swear my whole world pinholed to one person. I considered canceling the date. Because I was a cowardly asshole who couldn't handle the emotional turmoil. But my dick was way ahead of my brain—thank you, Jesus. It kept a stern navigation toward the right place.

You

An hour and half on the treadmill, thirty minutes on the rowing machine, another hour with free weights—and I still was anxious. One word repeating over and over in my head, creating a second layer of anxiety.

It wasn't just that it was my first date with a guy. It was the fact that I knew nothing about being gay. How did a homosexual go twenty-six years without knowing about gay sex, or gay kissing. (Did gays kiss? Oh wait, yeah, I'd seen pictures of gay men kissing.) Or dating guys?

The Internet was somewhat helpful—in that it gave me a hard on and made my eyes bulge at the same time. Rimming, felching, anal, frotting. *Frotting*? What? Oh.

Backroom sex, glory holes, oral. Enemas, HIV, BDSM, bottom, top, pitcher, catcher—I was getting a headache from information overload. And it appeared that most gay men fucked on the first date. Or before their first date.

You

That one word. Maybe nothing else mattered but that. Maybe all that mattered was that I wanted to hear his snarky comments about my tie and make him laugh in spite of his best attempt not to.

Maybe all that mattered was I was mostly accepting the gay.

You.

I narrowly missed crashing the car several times on the way over to Peter's home. And, like I'd imagined, I was nervous as hell. My fingers drummed on the steering wheel. I kept accidentally pushing 'seek' on the stereo instead of 'play'. My stomach decided I was fourteen or was riding a rollercoaster. And I had to turn the air conditioning on full blast so I didn't sweat through my chinos and plaster my plaid shirt to my body. Yes, that was what I wore. I also wore a tie. Not because ties were particularly comfortable. But because I fantasized Peter pulling me into a kiss by my tie, and that had my dick so hard, even cotton chinos were too heavy. I parked at the end of his block, hands like cling wrap on the steering wheel.

You.

My worst fear was that I'd end up like Jesse, alone and miserable, hanging from a tree. Coming out wasn't what was going to make me suddenly suicidal. I didn't have to worry about that. I wasn't a teenager, afraid of the loss of my parents or friends and no way to take care of myself. That loss was scary, sure, but I'd get past it. I had options. What I knew, beyond a doubt, was that if I continued to deny who I was, I'd end up with my service revolver in my mouth.

"Better cock than steel," I said wryly, checking my reflection one last time before I exited the car.

Chapter Eight

Holy Fucking Christ, Dear Sweet Mother of God

"Holy fucking Christ," I moaned. "Are you trying to kill me?" Peter had a new piercing, in his lip; or it was an old one he'd decided to actually wear. Either way it was there, in his perfect, kissable bottom lip. Well, if I thought I'd need something to keep me focused during the night, that was now covered.

"What's that?" He nodded toward the package I had tucked under my arm. It was just something to make him laugh—or, you know, question my sanity.

"A corsage," I replied, and handed it to him with my kiss-me-now grin. He said nothing and tossed it over his shoulder where it landed somewhere in the depths of his living room. I used the opportunity of following its path in order to peek inside. My jaw dropped. Almost every wall was covered in incredible murals.

The farthest wall was so realistic, at first glance I thought it actually *was* a patio door leading out onto grass and a wooden deck. Beyond the deck, and this was the only reason I quickly figured out it was a painting, was the summer rain. The real world was rain-free.

What I could see of the other walls were different and unrelated scenes: an aquarium with sharks, and starfish sucking against the glass. A baseball game with a field that reminded me of the one from my old high school. Darryl in a pink suit surrounded by Secret Service. I couldn't stop gaping at it all.

Peter was watching me, seemingly judging my response. "Wow. When you said Cai finished painting the living room, I had a whole different idea in my head." He quirked up a careful smile.

I cleared my throat, waiting for Peter to invite me in, but Cai emerged from the depths of the house to do it for him.

"Hi," Cai greeted me brightly. He had a rainbow of paint in his hair, on his jaw, nose, cheeks and neck, and sprinkled along his jean overalls; as well as what was once a pure white t-shirt. He carried a jar with a paintbrush swirling in a clear liquid. Another brush was tucked behind his ear, dripping yellow paint on his shoulder. I thought he may have been cleaning the wrong brush.

Cai was the kind of boy who made you automatically grin from his sheer guilelessness. The kind who attracted people through personality rather than appearance. Where Peter was ethereal in beauty, Cai was just plain goddamn capital C "Cute". His nose was a bit long and a little crooked— but a good fit for his face. Like Peter, his strongest asset was his eyes—not grey, not blue, but a mixture of both. But where Peter was ice, Cai was the sun. I thought his optimism might piss me off, but if I was in high school, I would have had a crazy crush on him.

It wasn't until I looked deeper that I noticed the network of scars running from his wrists to his neck, like an ice skater had practiced figure eights on his skin. There had been a futile attempt at hiding them under Celtic vine tattoos, but the damage was so extensive, it was impossible to hide.

"Hey, yourself," I replied, tipping my chin in greeting and resting a shoulder against the door frame.

He extended a surprisingly paint-free hand. I shook it, noticing the other hand was layered in paint. Though he was taller than I, by at least an inch, there was something almost delicate about him. "I'm Cai. Which you probably already knew, but still, I'm Cai. Some people call me Nikki because my name is Nicholas, but most people call me Cai. I don't really like Nikki, but I haven't told that to many people. I think Rabbit likes you though, so maybe you'll be around a lot, and I don't want to be stuck with Nikki when you could be calling me Cai. So…it's just Cai."

While he spoke, he jerked my hand up and down, going on about "did I want to see the bedroom?", because he had started a new mural that, "…looks like someone blasted a hole into the aftermath of the Battle of the Granicus River", and, "Really, it's interesting since some people say it went one way and some another". I stopped listening too closely after "Rabbit likes you". And I didn't pick up his voice again until, "Do you want to come in? I—"

"No," Peter announced at the same time I said, "Yes." And as if neither of us had spoken, Cai continued to babble as he moved aside so I could enter the apartment.

"—'ve just finished the living room, and now I'm working on the bedroom. Well, my bedroom, since I finished Peter's ages ago. And Darryl's painted his own room."

I wasn't sure what else Cai babbled on about as he led me by the wrist towards a hall just to the right of the stairs. I gathered he was saying something about paints and what types he used, but I got sidetracked by the walls.

Where most people might have had framed photographs, Peter, Cai, Darryl and Joe were depicted in various paintings with frames glued to the wall around them. There seemed to be a gradual change in all of the pictures as they boys aged. No smiles to almost smiles to outright laughter in two of the frames. Cai released my arm while I stared at the wall, enchanted. "You're talented, kid." And Peter *could* laugh without reserve. When would I get to see that guy? The unconstrained Peter.

"Thanks!"

"We're leaving," Peter announced and leaned over, pulling Cai's head down to plant a kiss on the top of his forehead. I wanted to be that forehead. Cai shut up suddenly and took a breath—something he hadn't done since I arrived—and exited back into his bedroom with a bright wave. I caught a glimpse of an unfinished mural on his bedroom wall.

"He's really talented," I said.

"He's a prodigy." There was a note of both challenge and pride in his voice. And I hadn't realized he had dropped his guard. Until now.

"Does he go out and do things or just stay here and paint?" I went back appraising the paintings, and waited for Peter to answer.

I thought I might be getting assessed again. "He doesn't sleep. It's part of the mania. He's going through puberty, so it's difficult to get his meds just right." Another challenge or maybe a test.

I frowned and tried to reconcile that fact. "He's bipolar?" I knew some about the condition from being on the job, but not a whole helluva lot. I'd seen what the depressive end of the bipolar spectrum could wreak, however.

"Yes," Peter answered. Once again I sensed a provocation in his words. I smiled and went back to studying the paintings. "He talks a lot in the manic stages." There was nothing but warmth in his voice now. Apparently I had passed the test. "It used to be worse, but still he— he says stuff he shouldn't." Peter, I noted in astonishment, was blushing a little.

"It's okay, Peter, I like you, too," I grinned and slipped my hand into his. He stiffened momentarily and then sighed, liberating his hand, but gently—not yanking it away. I did my mental victory dance again while I checked him out.

He wore black studded suspenders over another wife beater tee and a light blue cotton shirt, unbuttoned and hanging loose around his sides. Despite the suspenders, his jeans hung low on his hips, and as he moved I caught glimpses of pale skin and the elastic of his boxers. There were no bunny slippers, though—just nondescript sneakers. I sighed in disappointment.

"It's just because I asked for them, isn't it?"

I was imagining the twinkle in his eye, wasn't I? "Pretty much," he said, holding the front door open and trying to usher me out with his glare. So contrary, my Peter was.

The area where he lived was a tiny street where the cars lined each side and left space enough only to allow cars to pass each other by the narrowest of margins. I feared for my Jag, glancing at it as often as I did Peter while we walked in an amiable silence. It was almost as if a truce were in place.

"How long have you looked after him?" I asked.

"None of your business," he growled. Ceasefire apparently *over*.

I took a deep breath and pushed him against my car when we got there, caging him with my arms. Leaning forward, I dragged my nose, inhaling deeply, along his neck. "For some reason I can't get enough of you," I murmured in his ear. "I think you tease me with these rare glimpses of perfection. And then slap me with a dose of hostility. But mostly, I think you like me. And for some reason that pisses you off."

When I lifted my head to catch his eyes, I was surprised to find him smiling. "I don't like you," he repeated, settling his hands on my hips. "Much." Then he tortured me again by licking his lips, the gold ring glistening in the sun.

"But I have handcuffs and a nightstick." I waggled my brows.

He pulled his smile into his teeth and released it. "You don't piss me off as much, I guess."

"Meaning you want to be naked and covered in chocolate later?"

"I'm allergic to chocolate," was all he said to that. His fingers curled into my pants, pulling my hips close. But he turned his head when I leaned in to kiss him. "Where are we going?"

"Movie first." I tried not to sound disappointed, but it trickled through. If he kept everything so distant with me, we had no chance of working out.

Was he worth all this effort? Watching him with Cai told me enough to say, yes. Most definitely, yes.

He grimaced. "We should go. Unless you want to stand out here all day."

"I'm okay with that." Hips touching, the scent of him, the warmth of the sun, no hostility. Yeah, I was okay with staying right here.

I sensed, rather than felt, his fingertips at my belt. Then he jerked it, and freed it from the buckle. It was broad daylight. While not busy, there were people around. Not that I stopped him. Even as my button was undone and the sound of my zipper going down sped up my pulse, I just closed my eyes and tried to breathe evenly. I wasn't sure why I made the effort—I hadn't had a steady heart rate since his first smile.

I knew he was emotionally distancing me with this behavior. Of that I was certain. But I was somewhat helpless against him. What made Peter more compelling than the sun's gravity?

Something else I suspected as he leaned in, his breath quick against my cheek. If I let him turn this into only sex, that was all it would ever be. So even when his fingers slid dangerously low, I found the willpower to move away and zip up. "Later," I choked out as he lifted his glistening finger, opened his mouth ever-so-slightly and sucked the tip.

Dear, sweet, mother of God.

I was now *fully* embracing the gay.

He Was Nothing Like What I Thought

Somehow I convinced myself to move away and get into the car. I clicked the automatic door locks, and Peter slid in beside me, pulling on his safety belt. I liked that he did that. I didn't like that he put his feet on my dash, however. Arturo was delicate.

"You've had a shitty life," I said as I pulled out.

"No I haven't. I've had Cai and Darryl and Joe. There have just been bad bumps. Even the road to Disneyland has potholes."

He was rifling through my car, checking out the registration, pulling out bits from the console, flipping on the radio until classical music was playing low. "I've had a few potholes. They're mostly repaired now." When I turned my head, he was tapping a drawing pencil against his knee. Jesse's.

"Cai's why you spend so much time keeping the restaurant afloat?"

"Money is why I do that. Cai is why I breathe."

"What happens when he goes to college? That has to be soon, right?"

"Soon," he agreed. "He's sixteen, but he's ridiculously smart. He could be enrolled now. He loves high school too much, though." I loved this relaxed part of him. His hostility had all but disappeared. I decided to talk about Cai for a long while.

"Here or out of state?"

"Here. University of Denver, I think."

"My alma mater."

He grunted in response, finding my detective notepad. He couldn't read it; my notes were written in codes only I could comprehend. As he tucked it back into the console, I began to question if he wasn't nervous. The thought made me grin. That was an absurd notion.

"So Cai goes to college. What does Peter do?"

"Bus tables until the diner sells." He shrugged.

"That's all you want for yourself? No ambitions?"

Something painful flashed over his features, drawing his eyes into a squint. "That's all there is for me right now."

"You don't seem stupid," I said.

"You think busing tables is stupid?" he challenged, eyes dark with anger. Anger, apathy, hostility and sexual tension, those were the revolving elements of our relationship thus far.

"I think wasting your life busing tables when you're smart, is stupid."

"You think I'm stupid, but then I'm too smart to bus tables." He laughed softly, genuinely smiling. Oh God, that grin. My groin tightened.

"I think you're smart. At least a smartass."

"Pots and Kettles, Detective. Pots and kettles."

My eyes were on the road now, but I dropped my hand to the divider, just to see if he might ditch the bravado and take it. We went about six blocks before he did, gazing out the window as if he didn't care or notice. He had another case of buyer's remorse two seconds later and abandoned my hand, tucking his in his lap.

"Anyway, when Cai graduates college or the restaurant sells, I'll try a translating career." With the way he squinted, I wasn't certain he meant to tell me that.

My eyes widened, and I turn to him briefly, then back to the road. "You speak another language?"

"I speak six languages." He was trying to impress me. My mental-victory-dancing self was getting worn out.

I nearly ran us into a telephone pole while fixating on his smirk. "Six?" Sadly, what I was thinking was: 'Can he say 'fuck me' in all of them?'

"Yeah, before—" He stopped. "When I was younger, I was into foreign films. My mother was fascinated with Dr. Zhivago, so I started learning Russian when I was like seven. And then we moved in with Joe, and Cai got into graphic novels and that led to Manga and so forth, so that led to Japanese and Korean. And you can't live in Colorado without knowing Spanish. When Joe died I was working on my B.A. in Chinese Languages."

"What the fuck are you doing busing tables?" I said furiously. All that wasted talent just pissed me off.

He studied me for a long while, as if judging what to say. I had to pull over because, frankly, Arturo feared for his life at this point.

"We needed the restaurant income. I won't die if I don't graduate, Detective."

My turn to stare. "I get it. That's why you agreed to see me. Date the rich cop." Why should I have been surprised he was using me? He wouldn't kiss me, he didn't even particularly like me. I sat back and breathed, angrier than I'd ever been in my whole life—at myself.

"Now who's stupid? And insecure?" He flicked my ear. "Who didn't want to go out with who?"

It was disconcerting getting chastised by someone six years your junior. I was not insecure. I was a perfectly normal combination of arrogant and narcissistic. "Flicking me is not your way of saying you're into S & M, is it?" The eye roll in response was well worth another flick.

He gave me a suspicious glance, probably because I was grinning like an idiot. "What?"

"You like me."

I received a combination eye roll, lip twitch. "I like your *ass.*"

"Uh huh." I grinned my stupid grin the rest of the drive to the theater.

Falling

The movie theater was situated downtown. Of course, I got lost and frustrated. The more I cursed and roamed around, the more Peter hid a smile in his teeth.

"Stop laughing," I grumbled, wanting to kiss him breathless.

"Don't cops have to take some sort of test about the streets?" I heard his damn grin while I focused on the road.

"I know the fucking streets," I said testily. "It's just the shitty ass street designers built them sideways, probably to confuse the whores and junkies when they ran into a building instead of another street to walk." Ah, shit. Peter's eyes lost all trace of warmth. "I didn't mean…"

"What are you doing with me, Austin?"

Falling for you, I said silently. "I like you," I sighed taking his hand. He jerked it away. "Dammit, Peter, you're not a whore."

"*I* know that." He scowled at me. I took his hand again, stubbornly holding on as he tried to pull away. "You trying to make a point to your rich daddy?"

"No." I gave up on trying to work this maze of streets and pulled into the first lot where I saw a free spot; though it was fairly far from the theater. "Did you look me up?"

"Didn't have to look far. Apparently you're dad's a local celebrity. I saw enough."

"Which is why you tried to cancel our date," I surmised.

"Desmond Glass's boy fucking a male whore."

I attempted to smile at him. "Are we fucking?" He just scrutinized me with dull eyes. I was trying to read him, but he had this magical, well-rehearsed way of locking out every emotion. "Okay, here it is. My dad's an asshole. I spent most of my life pissing him off or pleasing him in one way or another. That stopped a long time ago. I also have ambition which makes walking around with a male whore something of a contradiction.

I'm doing it anyway. Because I can't seem to stay away from you. I've fucking tried. And I don't *want* to want you. That's just not how things work I guess." The quiet that followed had me swallowing a lump the size of a coconut.

"I'm hungry." Was that his way of forgiving me? Did I even need forgiveness for anything?

"For my cock?"

"Unless you're prepared to have it fried and dipped in marinara before I chew it, I'd think of something else."

"That sounds painful."

"Then I guess you'd better feed me real food, Detective."

"I'll hazard a guess that you want Italian."

Lips. That is all.

Peter ate enthusiastically but with a delicacy that surprised me. Every bite he placed carefully in his gorgeous mouth, licking off any remaining sauce from his lips. I barely ate my food because I fixated on the ritual before me. My mouth watered, but not for food.

"When are you going to let me kiss you?" I finally asked.

He sucked at his fork and then set it down. That was on purpose, right? That fucking had to be on purpose. "When you beg for my dick in your ass," he said a little too loudly.

Plates clinked and a few gasps resounded in the distance, and I *blushed.* "*That* was on purpose," I accused and smiled apologetically at the old couple gaping at us from a nearby table. Change of subject was in order. "Anyway, how'd you know I was a closet case?"

Wiping his lips with his napkin, he set it beside his cleaned plate. Both his brows and lips were lifted in amusement. "Have you ever done anything with a guy?" I shook my head and sat back.

"Guys don't need to woo or date," he said. "Most, anyway. We fuck. We suck. We sometimes become boyfriends afterwards. There's no courtship. Not always true, but for the most part." He shrugged.

"You don't think that you have a jaded opinion because you were— of what you…did?"

"Because I was a whore you mean? It's not that much of a stigma in the gay community, Austin." I longed to be the glass of water he lifted to his mouth.

"You seemed offended when I called you one," I pointed out.

"Because," he stared through the couple at the next table, then back to me. "Because of the way you said it."

"Maybe I just don't like thinking of you with other men."

"Or maybe you classify hustlers as worthless," he threw back.

"Maybe I did," I agreed, emphasizing the past tense.

He smiled and took another sip of water, standing up as he did so. "I have to go take a piss," he announced. The web of his hand blurrily displayed through the glass as he set it down. I locked on to the blue stain—that strange tattoo. Same place, almost the same design.

The first one I had seen was a little less defined, and reminded me of amateur tattoos done with a Bic pen and mom's sewing needle. Peter's tat was more refined than Jesse's, but they were identical in lettering: "ISS". With the s's overlapping.

A continuous mental image looped in my mind: Jesse sliding his money onto the table the last time I saw him. I didn't pay much attention to the tattoo back then, just thought it was weird. I did remember pondering where he got twenty bucks to toss down, so the moment stood out. Dave and I had made a pact. After months of seeing the money we gave him funneled up his nose or down his throat, we decided: no cash. We'd pay his rent, food, anything else, but nothing he could use to buy drugs or booze. Now I knew what we had done—what we had forced Jesse into. He had been whoring himself out. Ten years later, I finally understood a little of what our friend had been reduced to, and maybe, why he gave up.

As Peter walked away, I could almost feel the hiss in my chest releasing thirteen years of oppression. A dawning of understanding washed over me. Peter was the Jesse that could have been. And some piece of me believed the universe gave me a do-over.

Not only was I an asshole for reasoning like that, but it was dangerous. Peter was dangerous.

I didn't care. This was it. My heart pounding in my chest, I debated on whether to follow him or sit—or run. I drummed my fingers on the tabletop. Then I got up, leaving a fifty on the table.

Austin's Epic Intuition Fail

I felt like James Bond or Maxwell Smart— Inspector Clouseau?— furtively glancing left and right before following Peter into the bathroom.

"What are you doing?" he asked, briefly glancing at the hand I used to pull him into a stall. I raised my brows and tugged his belt loose once we were inside, door closed. "I thought it was obvious?"

"You want to have sex in a men's bathroom?"

"Huh? You said…Wasn't it a signal? Your coming in here? I read online that gay men did that."

"Yah, in the 1960's, Austin. Or at a Republican National Convention. Not on the first date in the bathroom of a restaurant. In *this* century."

Oh. Oh, well, while I still had the nerve. I sank to my knees and took a steadying breath and grinned up at him. "As long as we're here."

"You want your *first* sexual experience with a guy to be in the men's bathroom, trying to give your *first* blow job?" He was more amused than astonished, but both emotions were warring for his eyebrows which dipped forward and then lifted.

'You said you didn't kiss. I don't know. You make me ridiculous. I turn into an impulsive teenager whenever I'm around you."

He burst out laughing, combing a hand through my hair. "Just relax. It can't be more nerve-wracking than the first time with a girl, right?"

"I was never nervous with women," I answered, watching him unbuckle the belt that I'd abandoned. I chewed my lip nervously, pulling pieces of skin off and reaching up to grab hold of his hips. That seemed…I just wanted it over with. Band-Aid ripped off. Gay virginity out the window. Sexual tension eased. "I just didn't care what they thought. They were a means to— whoa, hello. That's a penis."

"That's a really shitty attitude toward women," he said quietly, thumb trailing down my cheek.

I knew what he was doing, trying to distract me from my nervous blathering, but all it managed to do was perturb me. "Are you really going to lecture me with your dick waving in front of my mouth?"

Outside the stall, a throat cleared. I stood up quickly as footsteps clicked on the tile and the stall door next to us closed. Peter was holding back laughter so hard his chest shook. "You have no shame," I told him, and that was when he grabbed my tie and pulled me into a kiss. A kaleidoscope of colors danced behind my lids.

FUCK!

I didn't register the lip ring at first, or his bared cock pressed against me, there were too many neurons firing in my brain, too many emotions and reactions zipping through my body.

If the guy in the stall next to us made another sound, I didn't hear it through the blood pounding in my ears. After minutes of his lips pulling and sucking on mine, until my mouth was raw, things slowly came into focus, like eyes adjusting to a dark room; only it was my senses that were becoming attuned.

I marveled that his hair was coarse, not soft as I had imagined it to be. My fingers twisted in the thick strands, locking in place as I held him close. Warmth emanated from his chest as it bumped against mine. He exhaled through his nose and his breath butterflied across my cheek.

Cinnamon and the scent of tobacco invaded my nostrils. He tasted mildly of garlic. That shouldn't taste good, I thought. But it did. And then I stopped thinking as his teeth grazed my bottom lip.

I parted my lips to sigh, and he used the opportunity to push me against the wall and invade my mouth with his tongue, cupping my jaw between his palms. I had kissed before, but this wasn't kissing—this was *being* kissed. No control on my part and only half aware of the whimper I made as he pulled away.

"Your phone's ringing."

"Oh," I said dumbly. The heat of his fingers soaked through my shirt as they moved up my sides. I fumbled for the phone in my pocket, mesmerized by his mouth—until he dipped forward. Closing my eyes, I offered my neck to his lips and teeth. "Glass," I answered huskily.

"Oh, Christ. I don't want to know," Luis said. The phone beeped when I dropped it. I scrabbled to catch it, fingers pressing on the buttons before I brought it to my ear again.

"I—Uh. What?" I had to stifle a moan as Peter bit the slope of my neck that led to my shoulder and then stepped back and began tucking in and zipping up.

"I'm standing over Alvarado's corpse."

Instantly, I sobered. "Shit. When?"

"Coroner is checking into it. Shot in the back of the head. No murder weapon found. No weapons here of any kind. Unless the killer took it with him, this won't be a self-defense case."

"Hang on," I said, watching Peter adjust his clothes. "Peter, does Iss have a gun?"

"Iss didn't like guns," Peter replied. *Didn't?* Iss *didn't* like guns?

Realizing his mistake the moment the words are out, slowly he raised his eyes to meet mine. "It's not what you think."

Fuck!

Chapter Nine

Austin Glass-Fuckup of the Year

"It's not what you think," Peter said, but my heart had seemed to stop. My fist was tight enough that I worried the phone would crack and my breathing was so labored, it was half a minute before I could speak.

"Did you get that?" I asked Luis, impressed by how calm I sounded.

"Yeah, I got it. It's not enough to bring him in."

Peter began reaching into his pocket. I stopped his hands with a gentle touch. "I need you to keep your hands where I can see them."

Luis said something, but I was too focused on Peter, whose fingers hovered at the waistband of his jeans. My heart was pounding, had been the whole time, but I was now aware of the skips in its beat.

"I just need to call Cai, okay? That's all."

I kept the phone connected, so Luis could hear in case something happened, but I placed it on the toilet paper dispenser. Shaking with fear and anger, I raised both hands in what I intended as a calming gesture, keeping my face placid. "Peter, I'm going to take you down if you reach for your pocket."

"Am I under arrest?" His jaw clenched and vibrated, genuine dread shining in his eyes.

"Not yet." Using the past tense when speaking about someone wasn't probable cause. And it wasn't even him saying 'didn't' instead of doesn't. It was the slow way his eyes came up to mine. That was when I realized his mistake wasn't just an accident of phrasing. Thus far, nothing connected Peter directly. It was only that one word that could be explained away by even the most incompetent of lawyers. I didn't have reasonable suspicion. Suspicion, yes, but not the type that would convince a judge.

Watching his lips part to expel a jagged breath, I recalled how good they felt when he pressed them against my skin. My throat constricted, a ball of humiliation pushing upwards from my stomach. My mouth still stung from his kiss. The attraction still hovering between us made me sick. All his lies, his manipulations, the hostility, the teasing, and I still wanted him.

"Then, I'm free to go?" He glanced at my cell.

I rapidly searched my memory for any reason to arrest him that didn't involve me outing myself as his potential lover, or worse still—as someone who bought his services. Something minor would work. However, my only thought was that twenty minutes ago I finally figured out why I was so obsessed with this man; was finally able to view my attraction to him objectively.

Two Epiphanies in Less Than An Hour. I'm On A Roll.

Staring at Peter's defiant gaze, I still felt the impulse to protect him, but my new found clarity was enough to stifle those urges.

I snatched up my phone off the dispenser. "Tell me there's a witness." Who didn't see Peter or anyone like him.

"Unconfirmed. We're still canvasing," Luis answered. "But there's a tentative time of death. Neighbor thought he heard the gunshot between eleven and eleven thirty last night. M.E. says that's consistent with his findings. Body's in rigor, but the heat is playing with body temp. He can't confirm better than 'between eight and thirty-six hours'."

"Naturally, the neighbors called 911," I said sardonically.

"One," Luis replied with a combination cough/laugh. One person had called. That narrowed time of death only if the neighbor could definitively identify the sound as a gunshot. I could ask Peter for an alibi for the last thirty-six hours, and he could mention to me that I was part of his answer. Or, and this was more likely, he'd lawyer up. In all honesty, I wasn't sure if I could account for my own whereabouts for the last thirty-six hours. No question I asked him would make things better right now.

"Let him walk. We can bring him in later if we get something more from forensics," Luis said. I murmured my agreement and hung up.

"You're free to go," I told Peter reluctantly.

Nearly a week had gone by since I witnessed Peter's current expression, that sad little smile while he stared at the floor. I now saw it as an aim to draw my sympathy. He pulled the door to the stall open, brushing his hand against mine in the process. It was enough to send my blood rocketing through my body again, but I gave nothing of my reaction away, not even acknowledgment of the touch.

"It's a little ironic that today I gave up fighting what's between us," he said quietly.

I met his eyes, my face a careful mask, while his seemed twisted in melancholy. "That I chose today to start, you mean?" The smallest of nods was my answer, and then he turned to leave.

"That's not irony. That's fate." When he exited the stall, I pressed the back of my head against the wall, following his movement with my eyes. "Did you do it, Peter?"

He stopped, hand on the door, didn't turn around when he answered, "Who's asking? My date? Or the cop?"

To me they were the same. Though, not lately, I had to admit. Lately, my title of 'cop' left a lot to be desired. "One and the same, Peter. The truth shouldn't change based on the questioner."

"I suppose if I trusted you'd believe me, I'd tell you that, no, I didn't, Austin." He turned slightly and met my eyes. "But, if you ask me again? I'll say I want a lawyer."

"Why are you so cryptic?"

"Why are you so difficult, pushy and conflicted? One minute you trust me, the next you have nothing but accusation in your eyes. I'm a whore, then I'm practically your boyfriend. You want to get to know me, but you follow me into the bathroom in order to hookup."

"My whole life has been upside down since I met you! A little confliction is—."

"Not my fault. Your confliction is not my fault or my problem."

The laugh that pushed out of me had more air than humor. "You're right. I'm not your problem. Not your type. Not your anything. I've ignored all your hostile rejections, the insults and the lies. You wanted me to leave you alone. I'm finally listening, Peter." Moving past him to the exit, this time I halted at the door, eye-to-eye with him. "Next time I come after you, it'll be to bring you in."

He didn't follow me out.

Temper, Temper

Detective Frank Marco looked and sounded like a pig: a squashed nose rammed between red, pockmarked cheeks, draping jowls, and a constant wheeze whenever he exhaled. He was also a remarkably soft-spoken guy with a gentle demeanor. Go figure.

By contrast, his partner, Max Delmonico, *was* a pig, though he could steal the spotlight from the prettiest of starlets. Delmonico had a hard voice and an even harder set of green eyes. Next to them, Luis was the poster boy for average.

By the time I arrived at the station, Alvarado's body was on its way to the medical examiner's office, and Frank Marco and Max Delmonico were gathered near our desks and locked in deep conversation with Luis, who was handing them files.

As I approached them, all three sets of eyes turned from their semi-circle of discussion to me. Was I imagining an apology in Luis's frown? I wondered how much Luis had told them. Probably everything. And considering who the detectives were, I would know in less than five seconds just how intimate and detailed Luis had been.

"Glass," Marco nodded.

"Well, if it isn't Richie Rich," Delmonico sneered. I exhaled with relief. Obviously Luis had said nothing about my relationship with Peter, or Delmonico's jibe would have included some form of 'fag', 'queer' or 'fudgepacker'.

"That's it? That's your big insult? A reference to a defunct comic book character? You need new material, Del." It wouldn't help. The only way to improve Del's wit would be to exchange his brain with that of a coma patient.

"What's up with your suspect?" Marco said to me. It took me a second to realize he meant Peter.

Luis had told them about him, apparently. Hopefully it was just that Peter and Prisc were lovers and had a recent disagreement Luis and I witnessed. "Said we should direct questions to his lawyer," I answered.

"What was your take?" Luis asked. The glance that passed between us was almost telepathic. 'Sorry,' mine said. 'You fucked up. Now you know. Get on with it,' Luis's shrug conveyed. He knew I wasn't going to make the same mistake, not with Peter, or ever. Unfortunately, I was about to make a bigger one in the next few minutes.

"He's hiding something, but I couldn't read if he's our perp." A partial lie. My read was Peter didn't do it, but I no longer trusted myself where he was concerned. "Any witness statements yet?"

Delmonico spoke up. "Regular train of boys running through that house. Prick certainly had a taste for the teenagers from what the nosy biddy across the street says. Some uniforms talked to her." Del flipped a few pages in his black notepad and started reading, "Here it is. 'Mrs. Millicent Waters was at a late mass yesterday. She saw three figures between the time she got home at ten and went to bed at 11:40-11:45. Which covers the time when Mr. Eduardo Ynez," he flipped a page up and over, "next door, says he heard the gunshot."

"How good a look did she get?"

Del flipped another page, shot me the bird and continued his recitation. "As I was saying, one with dark brown or black hair, thin, tall; definitely male." Del made air quotation marks, "Gangly," then went back to reading from the pad. "Not long after him, another one left, she can't say boy or girl—just long blond hair and, emaciated. Her word again."

Another flip of his notepad. "Last one she swears was a girl, but every neighbor says they haven't seen anything without balls enter the vic's house in the four years he's lived there. We'll assume they include his ball-busting wife. Just young boys other than that."

"The girl?" I prompted. Del's snickers and sneers were about to get on my nerves. Especially since the idea of young boys being anywhere near Alvarado made me think of Peter—whose hair, at ten at night, would have appeared dark brown. Though gangly he wasn't. I said as much to the group.

The only reason Luis and I were at the scene was to coordinate notes and descriptions that had come up in our own investigation. With deep regret, I had to share my next thought.

"My suspect has a brother. Gangly, dark hair, six one or two. Nicholas Cotton. Age sixteen." I jotted down the address.

Betraying Peter was easier than I would've thought.

"Lots of gangly boys with dark hair," Marco pointed out with a frown. His way of asking why I zeroed in on the brother.

"Brother was involved with Alvarado. Intimately." I hesitated. "And just spoke about him in the past tense."

"The girl," Del continued, scratching his nose with his middle finger while smirking at me, "Millicent says had a skirt clear up to her backside and a bra. Oh yeah, a golf hat."

I didn't rise to Del's baiting finger. For whatever reason, he didn't like me. By his "Richie Rich" comment, I had a feeling my wealth was his particular bone-picking. "Is that a look now? Golf hats?" I asked with a lift of my lip in distaste.

"You tell us. We heard you turned faggot," Del said. The blood drained from my face. My head whipped to Luis. "That in fashion, Glass?"

"Next time I bang your sister, I'll ask," I ground out, stepping up to Del and peering down. Even my three inch height advantage didn't intimidate him.

"You need me to turn around, fairy?"

"Del, knock it off," Marco said with a quiet sigh, staring off in the opposite direction of me.

"Fairy?" I said to Luis, jerking my thumb at Del. "Is he for real? Richie Rich and fairy?" I glanced at my watch again and shook it. "How do I get back to the 21st century?"

"Click your heels three times, Dorothy," Del said. I wasn't expecting him to get better at insulting me, so I was rendered speechless for a moment.

The heat of humiliation warmed my cheeks as my friend and partner said nothing in my defense. "You want to be my first gay experience, asshole? Turn around, because I'll click my heels right up your ass until you scream 'there's no place like home', bitch." I advanced on Del, fists clenched, fully intent on knocking him out. Before either of us could come to blows, Luis had the collar of my shirt, pulling me backwards, and Marco's arm shot out to block Del.

"Just keep your faggot ass away from me," Del screamed, bashing his chest up against Marco's hand.

Walking backwards—or more yanked backwards by Luis—I shouted back, "First it's your ass I have to watch. Now it's mine? You sure *I'm* the faggot?"

"Enough!" Luis yelled, pulling me to face him. How someone in his shape managed to toss me around like a rag doll, I'd never know.

"What the fuck, Luis? You're supposed to have my back. Fuck you!"

"This ain't grade school, Glass. I ain't your boyfriend standing up for your honor. You bring that shit to work, you handle the fallout."

"How the fuck did I bring it here?" I screamed, spraying spit in an unblinking Luis's face.

Calmly, Luis stared me down, "Five seconds to figure it out."

I needed ten. "Shitfuck. The interview." Of course—they had watched the recorded interview with Alvarado and my dad. "Goddammit."

"Shitstorm just started, kid. Del's got a loud mouth, and he don't like you."

"Fuck that. I'm more pissed that asshole stole our case!"

"No one stole shit. We're still working the trafficking angle."

"Our fucking suspect is dead."

"Which just means we don't have to subpoena financials," Luis poked a finger in my forehead. "And we can trace the others involved."

Oh. "Well, okay then!" I glared across the station at Del. "Why are we here?"

"Why are you still yelling?"

Because I was fucked. I was royally totally incomprehensibly *fucked*. "Because I fucked up," I replied, voice lowering. Even Marco was giving me a pitying look, and he had to partner with Del, the skeeze of the whole department.

"Yup," was all Luis said.

Nice. No sympathy there. I had to grin, desperate though it was. "Kiss it and make it all better, daddy?"

"Tell me again why I put up with you?"

"I always let you drive?"

"That's so you can stare at my cock."

"I hear gay men are allergic to polyester and bad fashion. Your cock will always be safe."

By the time we were at our cars, our banter had significantly reduced my panic. Folding his arms over top of the opened car door, Luis pointed his key at me. "Go see Angelica. You'll feel better."

"She's not taking my calls, or emails, or texts."

"That's why you go see her." He climbed into his car and drove off, leaving me to mull over that piece of advice. Or was it an order?

Revelations and Bruised Egos

How did it work to be gay and still be moved by how beautiful Angelica was? Even in her old college sweatpants and a ratty t-shirt she retained her elegance. Only the dark circles under her eyes gave me any indication she was suffering. It felt longer than four days since I'd seen her. A whole lifetime of revelations lived in the span of this week.

From behind the open door, a frame of music mournfully surrounded her. I barely refrained from wincing at the lyrics. "Can I come in?" I asked, hoping I sounded as contrite as I felt.

To my surprise, Angelica tried for a smile. Her lip trembled upwards and then twisted into a grimace. "I wish you wouldn't."

"Please?"

She stared past me, out onto her front lawn, eyes glazing and then tearing. The fact that I'd never seen her cry made me reach out. I wrapped my arms around her waist and kissed the top of her head, pulling her into my embrace. "We weren't even that good together," she laughed, hugging me back. "Can't think why I'm this upset."

"I'm sorry. It was selfish of me to come here."

She muffled another genuine laugh into my shoulder. "Austin Glass selfish? What else is new?" Her hands snuck under my jacket and flattened against my back. They were so small and warm.

"Ouch," I smiled through the melancholy. "Want my gun? I'll go get it for you."

"Ask me again in ten minutes," she said, taking a deep breath and pulling away. I dropped my arms, feeling the urge to fidget with my tie. A sudden recollection of Sister Francis's ruler slapping my fingers had me jamming both hands in my pockets as I stepped inside.

The main entry hall with its marble floors and vaulted ceilings was meant to be intimidating. Angelica often brought opponents here, leaving them standing there while she pretended to be engaged in a phone conversation. Fortunately, I was already too anxious to let it affect me as I followed her into the house.

She took me to the bar, which was diagonal to the sunken living room, and stepped behind it. "Bourbon, neat?"

"A double if I'm going to be here ten minutes. I want to be numb if you decide to shoot me."

"I do want to shoot you some days," she admitted tiredly, setting the glasses out and pouring slowly. "It's just so...you. Most days I want to shoot myself, for thinking I could change you from the asshole that leaves women at the altar."

"Honestly, Angel, I'm not panicking about the wedding. I know you still think that, but that's just not it."

She took a dainty sip, licked her lips and leaned across the bar, avoiding eye contact. "I went online to these websites that Jessica said might help. Would you believe there's a small cult of women in my situation?"

"Women with douchebag fiancés?" I drew circles along the rim of the glass, waiting for when, or if, she'd face me.

"Women left by gay men," she clarified. "Most of them kept blaming themselves. Saying things like, 'I should have known, he would only have sex a certain way' or 'He kept hiring the same contractor who didn't know how to build anything'. All I could think was, 'Not my Austin. No one would guess'."

"Least of all, him," I said quietly with a smile. That's when she turned to me, frowning.

"How do you not know something like that, Austin?"

"You bury it so deep that you forget it's there," I sighed. "And when it tries to surface, you grab someone, or something, and use it to help keep it buried."

"Melissa," she said. I nodded at the mention of my other ex-fiancée. "And Justine." She grabbed the bottle, stepped down into the living room and curled onto the couch.

I followed, sitting down beside her, resting my head on the back of the sofa, its leather caressing my neck. "And night school rather than college, double shifts, overtime to have an excuse not to date or spend time with whoever I was dating, no single friends, *no* male friends except for Dave, always women who wanted commitment," I added. "I never had to think of it again with them. Just plow ahead into family, kids, eventually work my long hours at the FBI."

"Until what? What changed? Did I do something?"

"You and a slew of events," I said honestly, hoping it didn't sound like an accusation. I was hoping for a lot of things tonight. "I just stopped giving a fuck what Desmond Glass thought after he ended his affair with you. You were so broken for a while after that."

"You *knew*? Before we started dating?" I nodded my response. "And you didn't say anything?" At the rate we were tossing Bourbon down our throats, we'd have to be spatula'd off her cream carpet soon.

"Because I didn't care that you were using me to get back at my father. Next to Dave you were the closest thing to family I had, and being with you was the only time being with a woman felt natural, pressure-free."

"Did you just compare me to being your sister," she scoffed, pulling her feet up on the sofa and using my lap as a headrest. "Because I knew you were demented, but…"

"A distant cousin, twice removed," I assured her, twisting the end of her ponytail in the ensuing silence.

"Austin…?"

"Yeah, Angel?"

"I think I did know."

"How's that?"

"Sometimes the sex was just awful."

My ego made a muffled cry from under that blow.

Stumbling home around three the next afternoon, I checked my voicemail as I let myself in the house. Luis had left a message, reminding me to be in early on Monday to pick through forensics' findings.

Spending the night talking had been cathartic, but the lack of sleep was pushing me into a coma. With the upcoming morning promising to be a smorgasbord of stress, I decided to forgo the gala and rest in preparation for Monday's hell. I flopped face-first on the bed and fell asleep in my clothes for the second time that week.

You're Invited to the Wedding

No amount of jogging or working out could ease the worry over today. Not only did I have Del's knowledge of my identity crisis to stress over, I had the fact that I was dating a prostitute who was both a person of interest in Alvarado's murder and his former lover. What I didn't need (but what the universe saw fit to jab my balls with in its quest to see how far I could fall in a week) was a phone call from my father on the way to meet Destiny—or Fate, whichever bitch was playing with my life.

"Glass," I answered, flipping my visor down against the sun.

"Austin," my father's gruff voice grated in my ear, familiar but distant at the same time. "Who is this *person* I'm hearing about; making you break things off with Angelica?"

I grinned maliciously. "That would be my ho-mo-seckshuul boyfriend. He's moving in this weekend."

Silence.

Then, "Don't be a fool. Think about your future and quit vying for attention. Do you think the FBI will take you knowing you're…"

"A faggot?" I finished gleefully. Huh. Way more fun than I'd thought it would be. Maybe I'd give him a coronary. "Fudge packer? Homo? Queer? Butt Pirate? Turd Driller? Cum drin—"

"You're not amusing. You're just destroying your life to get back at me. Go back to Angelica. She loves you. You love her."

Why Dad, I thought, you sound almost as if you care. And of course this had nothing to do with the fact that I might make news, right? *Austin Glass Homo-extraordinaire Strikes Again.* I was sincerely digging 'Butt Pirate', but the Homo-extraordinaire sounded like a superhero. How awesome would that be?

"I'm thoroughly embracing the gay right now, Dad. Guess what. I won't even be the one that gives. I'll take it, *Dad*. Right up the ass. And you know what? I'll like it." The thought even made me squirm. "I'm probably going to marry him I'll like it so much. Buy him a boat or an island or just some really kinky butt plugs. Oh look, a homo sex shop. I can sense those now that I'm gay. It's like a beacon, calling me home. A butt plug beacon. I think I need to stock up on merchandise." I didn't even know what a butt plug was. Mostly I was just trying to piss off my father.

"Now you're just being droll. Do you know he's a male prostitute?"

Daddy investigated Peter? Shock. Who knew he cared. "Was. Was a male prostitute. I noticed you emphasized the prostitute part, but not the male part. You'd feel better if I picked a less prostitooty boy?" Prostitooty? I might have gone a little hysterical as I neared work. The sex shop gave me an idea of how to handle the rest of my day, though. I pulled into its parking lot.

"I'd prefer you didn't do these things to piss me off." Uh oh, Daddy's cussing. Things must be bad.

I sighed, because regardless of what he thought of me, at one point I did love my father. It hurt like shit to love someone that just shut you out, but I was done with all of that. "I have to go now, Dad. Sign on the window says there's a special on cock cages." What the fuck was a cock cage? I wasn't ready for gay sex shops, obviously.

Silence.

Right about now my father was venturing how hard I was trying to get back at him by moving in with a guy whose last name I don't know. Of course he didn't know Peter and I had nothing to do with each other anymore.

"Don't worry, Dad, even though I can't legally marry Peter in Colorado, we'll be sure to invite you to the one in—" I grinned wider as the phone signaled Desmond Glass had hung up.

Givin' It Before Gettin' It—Always Beat Them To the Punch

Just seeing my partner cheered me up immediately. As he lifted his eyes over the computer monitor, I placed a giant butt plug on his desk. It reminded me of a mini beige traffic cone. "It's an early hump day gift!"

"Jesus, save me from idiots," Luis said, eyeing the plastic encased sex toy with an expression that could only be described as beaten.

"And, because I love you so much." I tossed an issue of Butt magazine next to the other present. No kidding, there was such a syndication.

"There's no being around you."

"No lube, though. Wasn't on sale," I whispered loudly.

"Just get to your desk, cabrón." Luis typed as I sat down. I presumed he was sending me the new evidence collected by the crime scene unit. Studying my inbox, I was proven correct. My eyes scanned the pages of financials as I removed my jacket.

"Alvarado's bank accounts *and* my partner has a new term of endearment for me. Things are looking up." I checked out my crotch. "Soon anyway."

It was no secret around the station; that was apparent from the collection of goodies in my drawers and atop my desk. I gingerly removed a framed picture of a man's anus and tossed it in an envelope addressed to Delmonico, placing it in my outbox. A muffled sound had me opening my center drawer. A vibrator switched to 'on' rolled noisily toward the edge. A few tubes of lube came tumbling after. "Hey, Luis. I was wrong. I *do* have lube. You like the cherry flavored kind?" I thanked the entire station and pocketed the lube and about six of the hundreds of condoms overstuffed in my second drawer. The banana was a quandary. I wasn't sure if it was meant as an innuendo or a snack from an admirer. I ate it, and left an issue of *Bears* magazine prominently displayed on my desk. Because I was thoughtful like that.

I was sure worse was to come, but I could take it. I'd keep telling myself that, hoping eventually it would be true.

Luis shook his head and tossed the butt plug and magazine in the trash. "You are several kinds of fucked up, cabrón."

"Uh huh," I mumbled around the banana. While I scrolled through the account, I seriously considered pouring some cherry flavored lube over the fruit like it was syrup, just because some of the guys were watching for my reaction to my 'gifts'. They got bored when I gave none.

Three hours later I was deep into trying to make sense of a spreadsheet while my partner was trying to run down the last of the passport owners by checking with snitches, hospitals and local illegal immigrant safe havens. "Luis," I double clicked on a few entries in the software program Alvarado used to keep track of money. Most of it was to legitimate businesses, or so it seemed. In reality, a lot of it was probably laundered through one of the enterprises or all of them. The trick was to find out which ones and trace the money backward. "Something seems off."

"I love it when you say that," Luis said, moving around behind me to see my screen.

"Has the accountant looked through this yet?"

Luis shook his head. "He's on it now. Why?"

"How much cash did we find at Alvarado's?"

He reached over and pulled a file off his desk and flipped through it. "Two hundred twenty-five thousand and some change."

"Well, assuming that money came from—"

"Glass! My office. Now." Captain Ashanafi Mangistu's dark face glared at me from his office doorway. Max Delmonico smirked just behind him.

I grabbed my jacket, standing up and pointing at the screen. "If that two hundred grand in cash was from the recent smuggling, then what's that exact amount doing in Alvarado's books, funneled through—"

"Now would be best." The captain's accent rolled across the station house, depositing its load of sarcasm in my ear.

Suspension Without Pay

An hour and a half after jerking my arm out of Luis's grasp without a word, I drove home. I sat on my sofa, pounding Johnny Walker Black like it was my new bride and this was our honeymoon. Well into my fourth glass, listening and thinking of nothing but the sheets of rain outside, my doorbell rang. It took four buzzes and continual hammering against the wood to finally register: someone was at my door.

I launched to standing, fell back into a wave of dizziness and laughed. Crawling seemed to be the best option here, and it got me safely to the door—but not before my shoulder was detoured by an end table. Using the knob I pulled myself up and opened to greet my visitor.

"Oh, good. I was wondering when you'd come to finish me off," I told Peter.

"Are you drunk?"

"Are you my mother?" I laughed. "Never mind, she can't raise her brows through the Botox. You can't be her." How he got his hands into his jean pockets while they were wet was something only sober me could ask. Drunk me just stood there and stared at his hard nipples poking through his wet cotton shirt.

"I need your help."

I laughed harder. Nearly doubling over. "You need my help? Naïve, clueless li'l ol' moi?"

"Please." I could barely hear him through the rain.

"Go away, little boy," I sneered and went to shut the door.

"Please." He pushed his hand against the wood. "Please. I'm begging you. They arrested Cai."

"I'm suspended. Can't help you." I huffed a laugh completely lacking in amusement. "Surprised you didn't try and take the blame."

"I did. But I was with Darryl at The Manhole. About thirty people saw us. He didn't do it, Austin. He didn't kill Iss."

"Not couldn't?" I asked with a lucidity I didn't realize I had. "Didn't? Not *couldn't*?" I cursed my curiosity.

Peter bit his lip, making my groin stir before he turned away. Down boy. "I need him out before they...Before they find out who he is."

"And who is he?" I asked, fully expecting to be lied to, ignored, the question bypassed.

"Nikolaj Strakosha."

Slow as my mind worked, synapses swimming lazily through whiskey, I pinpointed the name while Peter drowned on my doorstep. "The eight-year-old who took out Nikki the Nail?"

Chapter Ten

Who's Using Whom?

Although I was crazy curious about Cai, there was this perverse enjoyment of Peter standing there, getting soaked, looking as lost as I felt. My little bit of revenge backfired, however, when I noticed how his t-shirt stuck to his chest, and how his abs outlined out against the cotton. Instant sobering fantasies.

Peter's indecisive expression returned, manifesting in the pull of his bottom lip between his teeth and the squinting downcast eyes. I could almost hear his brain churning out the question, 'Use sex or not?' The fact that he turned me on didn't embarrass me nearly as much as his knowing how much he affected me. That, and understanding how naturally it came to Peter to use the information to his advantage. We were at odds, a still-frame: I—trying to breathe while ignoring my urge to push him over the sofa and lick the rain off his stomach, and he—considering how best to use my attraction.

"You could have me." He stepped forward. Instead of meeting my eyes, Peter appeared to be staring at the center of my nose. "Just *help* me."

"Oh, for fuck's sake." I sighed. "Just get inside and try not to whore yourself for five minutes." I yanked him inside the door.

"S-stop st-staring at me like that then," he chattered as my A/C unit delivered a frigid welcome.

Since I didn't want to turn off the central air, I sent him upstairs while I went to make something hot to drink. "Go take a shower and put on some dry clothes."

Midway to the kitchen, weaving a Johnny Walker induced walk, a resounding splat near the stairway grabbed my attention. I turned to see Peter's shirt on the bottom step. The green lump of cotton dripped rivers of rain on my floor, calling my attention to him. He paused halfway up the stairs, bending to see me through the railing, pale muscled chest inviting me through the bars. "Are you going to join?"

Yes. Fuck, yes. Yes on four different levels—one of them pleading. "No," I replied.

With my mouth drier than a Saharan summer day, I marched/wobbled into the kitchen, slamming the metal teapot down on the stove. The shower upstairs turned on. My eyes rolled upward to the ceiling as I stood, *literally* waiting for a watched pot to boil.

What would his naked skin feel like next to mine? How many freckles would I count on the inside of his thigh? What sounds would he make if I used my tongue along his stomach?

The next second I blinked and stood inside my bedroom, staring at my bathroom door. That was when the diseased portion of my brain began developing a personality and a voice.

I could have him. I deserve it even. Isn't it his fault I'm suspended? That my wedding is called off? Any way I want it. He's a whore. You do him a favor, he does you one.

And what would that make you, Austin? If you used him like that?

"A lot less fucking cranky, that's for sure," I muttered to my empty bedroom. And maybe my boner finally could stop wearing holes through my pants.

More than mildly disgusted with myself, I turned abruptly and swallowed bile before forcing myself to walk—not run—out the door.

"Austin?" Peter asked quietly.

Downstairs the teapot screamed.

Getting to Know Your Local Sociopath

"Tea's ready," I said, pretending that was the reason for my flight. I didn't wait for his reply, or turn to see if he was dressed. If I saw him there, in a towel, dripping wet, I wouldn't be able to control myself. My fingers already itched in memory of the last time I touched him.

I jumped over the last few steps in my haste to get downstairs. In the kitchen, I set up two cups of tea and stared at mine while it steeped. Why the fuck was I drinking tea? Across the room, on the coffee table Johnny Walker attempted seduction.

Peter stepped into the kitchen replacing my whiskey fantasy with one involving my teeth and the borrowed pair of blue and gold college sweats and t-shirt he wore. He grabbed the other cup of tea, eyes shifting along the countertop until he found the sugar.

"Would you like some tea with that?" I asked, watching him spoon four heaping mounds into his cup.

"I'd like a Coke or Pepsi," he retorted, opening my fridge.

"Beggars and choosers, Austin."

I wished he'd quit using my name. It was like an incantation, stealing bits of my soul for himself every time he said it. "Soda's bad for you."

"You're a little young for me to call you daddy, but when you say things like that…," he deadpanned, pouring milk into his cup and closing the fridge.

"Nikolaj," I prompted, pressing back against the counter and hoping either my jeans or polo were baggy enough to hide my erection.

Peter exhaled an indecipherable sigh and set his tea down. Was that frustration? Resignation? Fucking aggravating man—always so goddamn impossible to read. Pulling himself onto the counter, Peter gripped the edge and stared at his feet. "Did you ever love someone so much, you lost yourself in them?"

"Not sure I could tell you what love is anymore," I answered.

He frowned but nodded, as if he understood. "I was four when Cai's mom—"

"Your mom, you mean?"

He shook his head, and I followed a bead of water as it dropped from the tip of an auburn tendril, snuck past his temple and slid down his cheek. My tongue curled involuntarily against the roof of my mouth. "Do you know much about Nikki the Nail?" This time I mouthed a 'No'. I knew the story of Nikolaj Strakosha, The Boy Who Killed the Mafioso, because it had been a news sensation at the time, but I knew little of the crime family.

"In the 90's," Peter began, "Little Moscow—what we called our neighborhood in Sunny Isles, Miami—was run by the Briansky Boys. The boys being the boss Aleksandr Briansky, his number one Nikolai Dyachenko and his number two, Kaja Strakosha."

"Wait. Nikolai is your dad. But Cai is named Nikolaj?" I said, brows furrowing as that little wiggle of question tickled my brain. Nikolaj *Strakosha*. "He was Kaja's kid?" The same last names seemed obvious, but the first name was what threw me.

"Yes. But my dad and Cai's were like family—in the mafia sense as well as the brotherly way. Cai was named after my dad. Rofasa, Cai's mom, and Zhavra, my mom, were best friends, practically sisters. And their children couldn't be more like brothers if they shared DNA." He waited while I digested that, biting his lip and regarding me through his brows.

I was struggling with how attached he was to this kid. "Cai's not your real brother," I said.

"Cai *is* my brother. It doesn't matter that he's not related by blood," he huffed. "Same with Darryl. Actually no," he added. "Cai's both brother and son, I guess? If you had to label us at all."

I had a lot more important things to ask. Tons of questions that needed answering. So naturally I picked the one that would abso-fucking-lutely complicate everything. "So you and Darryl…?"

"Sometimes." Peter nodded. "When we're lone—"

"I don't need the details." My stomach was already moving like a group of otters were playing keep away with it. "Just move on."

"You asked," he said hotly.

"And now I'm un-asking."

"Whatever. Fucking frustrating," he muttered. *Ditto*, I thought. "It was weird with Darryl and me at first." He reached for an apple on the breakfast table, and then somehow expected me to concentrate on his words when he bit into it, causing its juice to glisten on his lips like cheap gloss. Come to think of it, that fucking lip ring was goddamn distracting, too. And he smelled like rain.

"Jesus Fucking Christ. Can you just tell the story?" I lashed out testily and tossed my tea in the sink, replacing it with a beer.

Peter stopped eating, his mouth hanging open in an invitation I didn't take. He began to chew again, slowly, eyeing me warily. "Okay…"

"You and Darryl and Cai…" I rolled my beer in a 'move on' gesture that caused bits of liquid to pop out of the bottle—which only reminded me of how long it had been since I'd gotten laid.

"Look, this isn't even important, is it? I mean you don't need to know what happened then, you need to know what happened with Iss."

"You asked for help and then laid a bombshell on me. I want to know more." I took a long sip of my beer and watched Peter over the rim of the bottle. Setting my Guinness down, I crossed my arms over my chest. "You're still assuming I'm going to help. I don't know that I can, but if I could, why would I? You're a complete baffling fucking mystery, and you've spent every day of our brief history lying to me. Even your name is a lie."

"I'm Pyotr Nikolaevich Dyachenko, if that's even the slightest bit important. They call me Petya where I come from. I have Tourette's. It used to come out as me twitching my nose when I was nervous. I don't do it so much now. Cai thought it was funny and started calling me bunny—which I changed to Rabbit—for obvious reasons. It was Joe who gave me the last name Cotton to play off of Peter Rabbit and Peter Cottontail. Not really lies. Just…bending things a little. Okay? My name isn't a lie."

Pyotr. Peter. Something else caught my attention. "Bending things a little? Telling me that Alvarado didn't deal more than club party favors?"

"I told you. I did what I had to do. I told him you were interested in me. He threatened Cai if I didn't lead you off the trail."

"Threatened him how?"

"The day you came in to question me about him, he said I was to tell you, or do, whatever I had to so you'd back off. Except for the part about him not being ambitious and only dealing weed," he shrugged, "the rest was true."

"And he and Joe?"

"Joe wanted to save Iss. Iss didn't want to be saved. He used Joe and Joe let him. Only time he ever stood up to Iss was when he said to stop hooking up with me."

I had been right about Alvarado after all. In order to not think about how closely Peter and I resembled Joe and Alvarado, I focused on the other thing that caught my attention. "You're the son of Nikki the Nail." I wasn't clarifying who was who at that point. I was trying to wrap my head around who Peter was asking me to help. I had to have that wrong.

"Yes."

"The Russian mobster that Cai shot in the head."

"Yes."

"Your father?"

"Yes."

"And you want me to help Cai."

"Yes," he breathed with such conviction that my eyes closed, and my breath became a distant memory. "I'm trying to explain it."

"I'm listening." Enraptured was a better way to describe what I was—a child at story time, hearing a reading of The Godfather.

"My mom and Cai's mom were inseparable, even though Rosafa is Muslim and my mom is Catholic. Darryl's mom was a crack head, and his dad beat the shit out of him. So everyone was always at my house." He grabbed the beer from my hand and took a pull before I could stop him. I yanked it back, but he appeared unaffected. "The Family started meeting at our house too. There was a lot of talk about a snitch early on before Briansky got arrested."

"You know a lot about this. What were you back then, like seven or eight?"

"Ten, when my dad started grooming me. Eleven, when the organization went to shit." He gazed at my beer. "Can I have one of those?"

"Did you turn twenty-one in the last week?" For spite, I took a long drink. Peter rolled his eyes.

"Darryl—"

"Real name?"

"Daniel," Peter answered. "Daniel Corozzo. Son of Tony Corozzo." He twitched a smile. "Tony the Pipe. Lowest of the low in The Family. And probably the only one not in jail or dead by now."

I rubbed my temple trying to process the information. "Interesting combination: Nikki the Nail's son, Kaja Strakosha's and Tony the Pipe's?"

"Catholic and Muslim. Albanian and Russian. Very weird. But we were more than friends. We were all family." Peter nodded. "Darryl—Danny, I mean—was like a pariah. He wore pink shirts and painted his eyes with glitter. Sometimes he curled his hair in ringlets. You can imagine how that went over with the Family." I didn't stop him when he retrieved a beer. It seemed to me that Nikki the Nail's son earned at least the right to one beer. "He was older but so fragile. One day I let him paint my toe nails pink, and that was it for him. We were bonded for life." He laughed. "And Cai by proxy."

"Why did Cai kill Nikki?"

"To get that, you have to know how things went to shit and how we three kids were involved," he explained. "My dad and Kaja mostly did enforcement. Things that had me puking when I got home. Darryl and Cai just sat with me while I...well, I didn't even have to tell them. They just knew. And Cai, he's four years younger than me, nearly six years younger than Darryl, but he's smarter than us and the combined IQ of the whole household, ya know? So when things started to fall apart in the organization, the three of us knew the score."

I jerked a nod for him to continue when he squinted at me. My detachment was all pretense. I didn't relate or understand. How could I grasp a ten-year-old being primed as an assassin or "enforcer".

"Anyhow, my dad was a good guy outside of all that. Which sounds weird, but he was. To all of us. Even Darryl. Which is why we never suspected he'd hurt Kaja or Cai."

He took a sip of his beer and set his jaw tight. I wanted to reach out to him but there was this canyon of distrust between us. While he continued to dwell on past memories, I waited, picking the label off my beer with a thumbnail and watching the shadows of his past relived in his face: a frown, a tremble of his jaw, a hard swallow.

"Months after my grooming started, Briansky gets arrested, along with most of the high-level men. Fingers get pointed, and everyone blames Kaja—the Muslim Albanian. He's not Russian—not one of us. There's a split between my dad and Cai's, everyone sure that Cai's dad snitched on Briansky. My dad gets put in charge. And Cai gets a permanent place in our home. As a 'guest'."

"Why wasn't Kaja in protective custody?"

"Isn't it obvious?"

"He wasn't the informant," I said.

"Nope. But my dad had me shoot him anyway."

Jesus. "So, you killed Cai's father, and he killed yours."

He chewed his lip so hard, I half expected blood to dribble out. He bowed his head and settled his eyes somewhere off in the corner. "My hands shook too badly. I shot Kaja—*Uncle Kaja*," Peter emphasized with a chatter of teeth that wasn't, I knew, a result of the rain and my A/C. "I hit him in the knee. Which was funny to everyone in the room. Big joke. Ha, ha. 'Your son needs practice, Nikki', and, 'He needs a smaller gun'. They ruffled my fucking hair, like it was so cute I missed. While Uncle Kaja is screaming and crying through a gag."

The shuddering breath Peter took at this point tugged my heart hard enough to pull me to him, wrapping my arms around his waist. Turned out he wasn't as affectionate as I. He pushed me away.

"You want to hear this or not?" Peter glared. I stepped back, hands raised. "I had to tell Cai this story, and it was a lot fucking harder to do that. I'll manage, okay?"

"Okay," I acquiesced, estimating how brutal he really was. Impenetrable? Or was there something inherently good about him? How did someone come back from that with any kind of empathy for the world?

He set his beer down. "Three nights later I find Cai sitting on the sofa, gun in his lap and my father in his favorite lounger, a bullet through his brain. I remember the playoffs on the TV so clearly. My dad's team—the Dolphins vs. the Ravens. Dolphins were losing. Why isn't dad yelling? Oh, might be that missing part of his head and face..."

Peter—Age Twelve

Peter's faking laughter with Darryl as he opens the door, but the smell of blood and feces is enough of a blow to knock the smile off his face. It takes him a minute, maybe two, to comprehend what he sees.

The Dolphins game is loud in the background, cheering crowds celebrating through clouds of blood and brains. Cai sitting on the sofa, calmly, legs crossed, with a gun three times bigger than his hand resting in his lap.

"Police will be here soon I think, Rabbit," Cai says, staring at Nikolai Dyachenko's slack form.

"Motherfuck! What did he do?" Darryl's sandals clack across the living room as sirens grow closer. "Oh, shit. He's dead. Shit! Shit! What'd you do, Cai?"

Peter's still trying to assimilate the scene before him when Darryl grabs the gun and Cai, jerking both off the couch. It's not Peter's first dead body, but that's his father. His papa who just a few hours ago made him eat spinach. He's maybe not thinking as quickly as he usually does. "Papa?" Peter says, staring at the corpse like it'll stand up and grin, despite the cavern in its head.

"We gotta go," Darryl screams, grabbing Peter by the hair and jerking him toward the kitchen. The sirens are practically on their doorstep by the time they all stumble out the back door, Darryl shoving Cai and yanking Peter the entire length of the lawn.

"I turned myself in," Cai says, still calm. It's such a rational voice that it reaches in and flips Peter's switch to on.

"We'll talk later," Peter responds shakily, taking the gun as both he and Darryl physically shove Cai through the gate at the far end of the yard.

"They'll see," Cai insists. *"They'll see he needed to die. Let me go back. They'll see."*

Fucking Cai and his logic. Peter can't focus, can't think about anything but getting away. He ignores the splatter of blood on his brother's face, the chunks of something grey dangling in Cai's black hair as they tear down the alley. *"Cai, so help me,"* he pants, *"if you take one step to return, I'll knock you out and carry you. Then we'll all be fucked."*

They run in silence after that, slowing down only so Darryl can find a car old enough to hotwire. It ends up being a relic from the 70's or 80's, a Camaro. Cai has to clamber over the center console to get in. Darryl's already pulling a screwdriver out and working on starting it when Peter sits down.

There's a collective holding of breath while they drive past two police cars. The smell of onions and garlic fog the air as Peter and Darryl breathe out the pizza from just half an hour ago. Had it only been 30 minutes since his life was normal?

"I drugged his drink, Rabbit. So it didn't hurt."

"Not now, Cai."

"He killed my dad, Rabbit."

"I know," Peter says. Darryl casts a sideways glance at Peter, gaze flickering on the gun.

"Are you mad, Petya?" Cai asks, in that bizarrely innocent voice.

"No, Cai. Never mad at you. Okay? Just don't talk for a while— don't say anything." Darryl takes the gun and slides it under his own seat as he drives. Then he reaches over and grabs hold of Peter's hand, squeezing it, before lacing their fingers together.

Peter stares out the window as Little Moscow turns into swamps, then rivers, then forests. *"I've got forty bucks,"* Darryl says after a few hours. *"We'll need gas soon. How're we going to get money after that?"*

They discuss robbing some place with the gun, but decide against that kind of attention. By day three on the road, they have a system of stealing wallets from guys whose pants are around their ankles in rest stop and gas *station restrooms. Driving nights is all they can manage, since Darryl isn't legal to drive and they can't afford to be pulled over. The journey is long.*

It's not until the fourth week that Peter gives his first blow job to a trucker outside a roadside diner. No risk, no fuss, no screaming asshole scrambling after them with his pants down. Though that did happen once when Peter used his teeth because the guy shoved his head down and made him choke.

Easy sailing after that. Between Darryl and him they can pull a hundred bucks a night if they stop at busier spots.

Jealousy, Thy Name is Austin

"The original plan was to go to California," Peter told me, either ignoring my dismay or too busy visualizing his past to pay attention to me. "We were passing through Denver when Darryl said he was done driving for a while. So we settled here. Was only supposed to be for a month or two. We just never left."

"I don't get it," I said, my voice hovering between horror-struck and disbelief. "You were okay with him killing your father because your father killed his?"

"No. Cai...Cai is super smart, Austin, but he's not *street* smart. He didn't kill my father for revenge. He did it because he thought it was right. He was eight. And angry and scared. Intellectually he was off the charts smart, but emotionally he was just eight years old."

I thought back to the show I'd watched about this killing. Some news magazine show aired it about a year after I was graduated from the Police Academy. Cai's voice on the 911 call was so small, but eerily cool.

"Hello? I just killed my Uncle Nikki."

This whole story didn't mesh with the Cai I had met. "They'll have his fingerprints in the system. They'll get a match eventually," I said, still in a state of shock.

"How long will that take?"

"A week, probably less. They'll run it in AFIS, but then someone will have to visually identify the prints. It'll depend on how many partial matches AFIS spits out and the quality of the old crime scene prints. And all they'll have are the prints at the scene, not a name to match. Unless he's been arrested before?"

"No, never arrested."

"They'll have his prints from back then. That's all."

"They find out who he is, and all they'll see is the boy who drugged and killed Nikki the Nail. They won't understand. And they won't believe he didn't kill Iss."

"*I* don't believe he didn't kill Iss. A neighbor saw him leaving the premises. And with what you've shared tonight, his being capable is no longer a question for me."

"I'm telling you he didn't do it!" Peter jumped off the counter, fists clenched at his side.

"How do you know? You obviously think he's capable of it, too. You keep saying 'didn't'. 'He didn't'. Not he *couldn't*," I said, repeating myself.

"Cai doesn't lie to me, Austin. He'd never lie to me." I made a scoffing sound. "You don't even understand. He had a break down after what he did to my father." Peter folded his hands in front of his face as if in prayer and took a deep breath. "For a year afterward he'd start crying hysterically just out of the blue. Then he'd go silent for days on end. We had to drag this rocking chair through ten states because he wouldn't sleep without me or Darryl rocking him."

"He's bipolar," I argued.

"The cycles don't last that long in kids. Trust me, I know all about his condition, Austin. It's asking a lot, but just trust me. Please. He didn't do it."

"Because you know who did?"

"No. I'd fucking turn them in if I did."

"Even if it was Darryl?" I asked quietly, remembering the 'emaciated' blond that Millicent had described.

"Darryl was with me," he reminded me.

"The whole night?"

Peter had the grace to blush, though I didn't read it as embarrassment as much as shame. "We...did a show."

Oh, Christ. I downed the rest of my beer and went in search of something stronger.

Johnny Walker and Austin Glass: A Love Story

"I don't want to know," I said, pointing my bottle of whiskey at him from the coffee table.

"I needed a mortgage payment." He followed me, trying to take the bottle.

I moved it out of reach and countered with, "What you need is a fucking leash and some goddamn morals!"

"Morals are for rich trust fund babies whose worst problem is their daddy doesn't love them," he spat.

Whiskey, glass, pour, toss back, glare. Repeat. "Cop out," I slurred in retaliation, pointing the empty glass at Peter.

"Don't get drunk. Fuck. I need you sober," he yelled, snatching the glass out of my hand.

"There's the problem right there. You need me sober. You need my help. You need something from me." I laughed, tossing the bottle on the sofa, ignoring the glug glug glug as it emptied over my cushions. "And I just need you."

"Need me to what?" He asked with a huff, tipping the bottle right-side up.

"Nothing. I just need you," I whispered and flopped into a nearby recliner.

I heard his swallow over the drumbeat of blood in my ears. "You don't even know me."

"Which makes it really weird to be falling for you, don't you think?" A pleasant numbness spread throughout my body. I didn't care about what I just said to Peter. Didn't notice the awkward silence or care that I was giggling and suspended from my job and being used by a whore to help a sociopath. I just closed my eyes to it all and let Johnny Walker lead me back to our honeymoon suite.

Chapter Eleven

I Will Never Drink Again. I Need a Drink.

Sometime during the night I began dreaming about Feudal Japan. It was a specific interest of mine, developed accidentally due to a combined lack of elective choices during my second year of college and an open class in Asian History. The dream, in hindsight, was surely my mind's way of desperately searching for common ground with Peter. It found a miniscule thread of commonality in the fact that Peter spoke Japanese, and I had a fascination with samurai warriors. A less-than-slim thread. A fucking gossamer strand of spit. But my brain latched on, and thus began my nightly fantasies of swords colliding. Which, in turn, birthed my hangover.

Mid-battlefield my samurai dream-warriors began stabbing into the grass while a team of gong ringers marched behind them. "Sweet Jesus, make it stop," I whispered, grabbing my head as I woke. A supernova of light hit my eyes before I fell off the bed, shutting my lids tight. The gongs continued in the form of my doorbell, as the teeny samurai began work on the sides of my skull.

"I'm coming," I moaned, stumbling to my feet and nearly falling into the hallway. I staggered downstairs, head held tightly between two curled fists. Peter's shirt tangled around my feet on the last step. While I tried to lose its hold on me, my shoulder hit the wall, my leg the sofa. And after stubbing my toe on the umbrella stand, I answered the door hopping on one foot, green cotton still dangling off my ankle.

Between my cries of "Ow, fuck, shit, ow", I wasn't sure whether to soothe my broken toe or block the sunlight lasering into my pupils. I did manage to kick off the shirt, soccer-style, past my partner and onto my front stoop.

"Morning, Sunshine," Luis said, shoving a Styrofoam cup of coffee in my hand. At least I thought it was coffee. There was a vague aroma of espresso, but the cup surely held the contents of Satan's stomach.

I mumbled a gruff, "Hey", and raised my eyes from the cup to thank him when my gaze caught something as the door clicked shut. I blinked twice and canted my head to see around Luis, hoping I was only imagining one of my steak knives buried through a piece of paper and driven into my four-*thousand*-dollar, custom-made door.

Fucker.

"Nice outfit," Luis motioned at my boxers and then frowned, turning to follow my line of sight. He pulled the note off the door, reading it aloud—with way too much volume, in my opinion. "I borrowed the Jag. I didn't steal anything. Unless you count your...anal virginity," Luis choked out the last words pretending to cough into the fist holding a laptop bag.

"Changing," I growled, wincing at my headache and snatching the note from Luis's fingers. I was fucking blushing as I stalked upstairs to change. I wanted to stomp up them, but I had a thimbleful of dignity left. I wasn't wasting it on a tantrum.

Upstairs, standing under the shower spray, I actually checked my ass—like I wouldn't have already known if someone had been up in there. Jesus. I needed my head examined. My hangover chose that moment to remind me of the samurai battalion still digging their way out of my skull. Mother of God, I needed a drink.

No need for a suit today. I felt a pang of loss in my gut. Dressed in chinos and a light cotton shirt, I returned downstairs, headed past Luis who sat poring over files on my table, and grabbed good old Johnny off the corner table for another round of oral pleasure.

"I need a drink."

Luis checked his watch and gave me a bemused frown. "It's ten in the morning."

"I'm aspiring to maximum cop cliché." He just gawped at me. I pulled a glass out and started to pour, then paused mid-stream as Peter came in. He took one glance at me, grabbed the bottle from my hand and just kept walking past Luis and into the kitchen. My hand was left clutching...air.

Only about four drops had made it to my glass. Luis had the same number of wrinkles in his brow as he tried to understand what he just saw. And Peter had ten times that volume of recrimination in his glare.

"I was drinking that," I said mildly.

"And now you're un-drinking it," he mimicked.

"I have a hangover."

"I don't care," he replied, tilting the bottle high over the sink and challenging me via maintained eye contact while he dumped the liquid down the drain. I hoped it was the drain, at least, and not my floor.

When did my life become a series of lectures and scoldings from a twenty-year-old whore?

I childishly wanted to grab the bottle of Jaeger in the liquor cabinet. And then drag Peter upstairs and rip off those suspenders he was wearing, tie him up with them and—

"You took my car," I accused.

"I wanted to go see Cai at the jail. And change."

Luis cleared his throat, and we both turned to glower at his intrusion into our exchange. I rubbed the bridge of my nose and stalked into the kitchen. Much as I wanted to slam cabinets, the sharp thud of swords in my brain reminded me to close them softly. After pouring a glass of water and taking a few aspirin—or was it ten?—I joined Luis in the living room, trying to forget that when I had walked by Peter I could smell cinnamon.

I was going to be mature about this. And ignore him.

"Shouldn't you be at work?" I said to Luis.

"You didn't finish telling me about the accounts yesterday," Luis replied, turning a laptop screen to me. I leaned over to glance at it.

Immediately the idea of working buoyed me, then I remembered Peter could hear us. With a scowl, I looked up at him standing a few paces behind us. The way Peter was staring at the screen nagged me. "You recognize some of this?"

Peter eyed me sideways and nodded. "I recognize the vendor names from when I took over the accounts after Joe died."

"Glass."

"Which?" I asked, ignoring Luis's abbreviated warning about sharing case information with Peter. What the hell. I was suspended and off the case anyway.

"Cai," was all Peter said.

I rubbed a hand over my face and sighed. "I said I can't do anything. One, I'm suspended. Two, he's probably guilty, and three—"

"I don't need you involved. I need you to pay your father's *fees*."

There wasn't a juror on earth who would convict me of murder right now. "You're going to barter information about Iss's death for money?" Why the fuck was Luis smiling?

"I'll do whatever I have to."

"Christ." I huffed. "My father?"

"Is the best defense attorney in the state."

"Ay, Dios mio." Luis exhaled noisily. "This can only end well."

"I'm not on the case." I pointed out to Luis. "I don't have to follow the rules." Shit. Was I really going to do this? How much information did Peter have? More importantly, how much could I trust him? If at all?

"I have records," Peter said, as if reading my mind.

"Not my father," I insisted. "I'm not paying my father."

"He's the best criminal attorney in town. I know. I looked it up."

"No, he's not," I sighed. "Angelica is." To Peter's non-vocalized query, I responded, "My ex-fiancée."

Peter nodded at me. "You get her there today. I want him out before the fucking P.D. gets Cai held without bail. I'll give you more information than you can handle."

Devious, conniving, scheming, deceitful, manipulative… I ran out of synonyms on my way upstairs.

I *AM* My Own Worst Enemy

Angelica and I had parted on amicable terms, though she had asked me to give her time. I was breaking the promise to stay away by calling her, and not for completely altruistic purposes. Part of it was that Peter was going to supply information. The other part, the largest part, was Peter's voice echoing in my head, *"Please."* That entreaty was so earnest and plaintive, I couldn't help but be moved. Peter had me so twisted up in him that I wanted to believe the faith in his brother was justified. For both those reasons, I phoned Angelica from the privacy of my bedroom.

"Are you really moving in with a male prostitute?" she asked when Pauline, her secretary, patched me through. There was anger and hurt lurking in her question, but amusement puddled around there as well. Ten years of friendship seemed only warped, not irrevocably broken, by our breakup.

"I would, if I thought it might give my dad an aneurism. Did he seem close to one when he told you?" I asked hopefully.

Her breath was loud in my ear. "Three days is not giving me time, Austin." All amusement evaporated from her voice.

"I know. But I have a case for you."

"The last time you gave me a case, it ended up costing the firm twenty thousand dollars."

"Pro bono cases are good for the image." I threw in, "Besides, I'm paying for this one," before she could argue.

"Austin, abuse cases belong with family court attorneys. You can't keep sending me these types of—"

"It's Baby Capone," I interrupted with the press's nickname for Cai. The receiver was silent, then there was a flutter of papers, and what sounded like the TV in her office. She was probably checking for a frenzy of reporters surrounding the courthouse and flashing pictures of Cai.

Almost everyone knew the Baby Capone case—if they were alive at the time and in any way involved in law enforcement. An eight-year-old boy taking out a mob boss was headline news. His age made it interesting; his disappearance made it legend. Rumors were that Nikki's son—Peter, a kid himself—killed the boy and then also vanished.

Anticipating Angelica's disbelief I added, "They don't know they have him. Fingerprints will take time, then they'll have to put two and two together." Considering it was Del and Marco on the case, two and two might take longer than the fingerprints.

"Then how do you know?" she asked astutely.

"I may or may not be involved with Nikki's son."

"The male prostitute?"

Déjà vu. "That would be Peter."

I imagined Angelica was salivating at the thought of representing this kid. Yet she would still be upset about doing so would be a favor for the man who screwed up our relationship. Namely, me. Regardless, the importance of the case wouldn't be her chief reason for helping. My asking would be, despite all that went on between us. "What else do I need to know?" she asked me. "...Pauline," she called excitedly to her secretary.

"Bond is decided at three p.m. today," I answered. "Kid's processed under the alias Nicholas Cotton. According to the brother, he's got an IQ out of the stratosphere and is bipolar. There might be some argument about your being hired by a non-legal guardian, since Peter's not actually his brother."

"And?" Before I could answer with my brilliance, she began talking to someone else. "...wipe my schedule for today, and get me guardian ad litem papers. Also I need..."

I waited until she was done instructing Pauline, and then asked, "And what?"

Her huff made me grin. "What's he being charged with, Austin?"

"Oh." My brilliance could be measured in milligrams. "Murder."

"Whose?"

"Prisc Alvarado. Brother's ex-lover, human trafficker on a case Luis and I were working."

"He do it?" Angelica, when down to business, was short and to the point.

"I thought the kid was half angel when I met him. Story the brother told makes me think he's got black wings. Still, Peter's convinced he didn't do it."

"Detectives on the case?" More paper shuffling around her muffled voice. She switched me to speaker phone.

"Delmonico and Marco," I informed her.

"Can you hustle me through to Nicholas?"

"He goes by Cai. And, no. I'm suspended."

"Because of the prostitute?" I heard disappointment in her sigh.

"Because I threatened to shove my foot up a fellow detective's ass in front of half the station."

"You are your own worst enemy, Austin. What about Luis? Can he get me in?"

"He's working another angle of the case. They'd have his badge if he started consorting with the defense attorney."

"Okay. Then I have to go if I want to have any time to talk to Cai before the bond hearing."

"Angel?"

"You're welcome."

I smiled into the phone after she hung up.

Awkward. Life is Awkward.

Monty Python could have made a full-length movie on the amount of awkward that was Luis and Peter in my living room. When I reached the landing at the bottom of the stairs, they both turned to me in hopeful relief; Peter from the wall dividing the kitchen from the main room, and Luis six feet from him on the sofa.

"I see you two have made progress since I've been gone." I went with sarcasm to break the quiet. Grabbing the bottle of Jaeger I'd rejected earlier, I took a seat next to Luis. "Angelica is on her way to Cai. Your part of the bargain is waiting." I nodded Peter toward the laptop on the coffee table in front of Luis.

"A boca de borracho, oídos de cantinero," Luis replied.

"English. I speak *English*, Luis."

Peter failed to hide a small smile. "It's a Mexican proverb. It means don't listen to the drunk guy, all you'll hear is the bar."

Before I could do my Bogart-Casablanca impression, Peter seized my Jaeger. I was going to get really tired of his parenting. As soon as he didn't smell like cinnamon, and his thigh didn't press quite so closely to mine. Why did he have to sit directly next to me? Wait, I knew that answer—Manipulation 101.

Fucker.

"That one," Peter leaned over my lap, finger almost reaching the computer screen, "is one of our food suppliers. And that one, laundry services. Payroll company. Garbage pickup." Luis scrolled down, and Peter quickly pointed again to another row in the spreadsheet. "That one is the company that leases the diner."

Peter's arm nestling against my stomach *could* be explained by the way he had to lean across me in order to point. I *maybe* could reason the hand on my thigh was bracing him. I *possibly* could rationalize that the gentle squeeze of his fingers was supposed to be reassuring. But when his hand moved up the inside of my thigh, then quickly back to my knee, I ran out of excuses. "That's his auto body shop and this one here, that's Leila's sister's hair salon."

"What are you doing, Peter?" I asked agitatedly. Or thought I had asked. When no one responded to my question, I realized the lack of air in my lungs made speech impossible.

I found my voice when Peter removed his hand and sat back against the opposite arm of the sofa. Pointing to the spreadsheet, I cleared my throat and asked, "How are you recognizing these abbreviations?" Did I sound as hoarse to Luis as I did to my own ears? His furrowed brows could be interpreted as deep thought, or a result of the hitch in my breathing.

"Cai worked at the auto body last summer and Darryl gets his hair done at the hair salon. As for the others, I tried to take over the accounting when Joe died because I didn't want Iss around. I couldn't make the figures work, so I had to call him anyway."

Looking over the list of abbreviated names, I thought of something else. That was a lot of businesses for someone like Alvarado. "Did Iss own all those businesses or have a piece in them?"

Peter shook his head and shrugged. "No way he owned anything of Leila's. But she owned some of his. Once Leila got her Green card, it was just business between them. And most of the vendors on that list are owned by cops."

Luis's jerked his head up from studying the laptop and turned to Peter. "Cops? How do you know that?"

"Joe told me. I don't know which cops, but he always said he kept the business in the blue. 'Cops is always better than regular peeps, Pete'. Think I heard that about a hundred times."

My eyes met Luis's and both of us understood the implications of that. We knew there was a cop involved, but cops? Plural? Were they all laundering money? It seemed likely since there was no way a simple cleaning service charged a small diner five grand a month. But according to the books, the cleaning service which contracted with the diner got paid that much the previous month. And I'd seen Colorado's Finest Diner, what the fuck could they have been cleaning? Certainly not tablecloths.

"That explains the cash at Alvarado's house. Dench died and Alvarado didn't have access to the diner to launder it," I said and immediately shook my head. He should not have had that much cash in his house. There was no way I could make that work in my head. Alvarado was a piece of shit, but he wasn't stupid. He wouldn't keep evidence around. "But if he was taking care of the diner accounts again, why didn't he funnel that money in? And those passports? Why did he keep all of that shit at his house?"

"He didn't." We both turned to Peter as he continued, "I…put those in his house."

That statement effectively slapped me back to my senses. "You set him up?" The guy didn't even seem guilt-ridden as he shrugged nonchalantly.

"I thought they were Iss's. I found them in a safety deposit box that Joe got for me. I think I signed for it about three years ago. Joe had fixed up an identity for me. He was doing the same for Cai and Darryl. I figured that was what was going to be in the box. Instead, I found that stuff."

"Could be bullshit. Alvarado said this kid intro'd him to a cop on the take," Luis interjected.

"He lied," Peter said, standing up. "I've been out of that life since Joe took us in. Iss was just pissed because he figured out I put that shit in his house."

"Quiet. Both of you. I need to think." A bevy of thoughts chugged through my head. All that money, all the passports, left in a box only Peter had access to. "Ron said Dench would do anything for his boys." I examined the computer, then turned to Peter. "I need Joe's records for the diner."

"What are you thinking?" Luis asked.

"I think the passports and I.D.s were evidence to start an investigation. But an investigation wouldn't be able to do much with cash. The money could only be for one thing: Peter and the boys. I think Dench was hiding those passports and that money because he was about to turn himself or Alvarado in. Did you put everything from that box in Iss's house?" Peter nodded slowly, a frown of denial pulling at his brows. "And you're sure Joe put them in the box."

Another nod. "No one else had access."

Luis caught on. "Dench was going to turn on everyone? Or he could have been planning to run, leaving the kid here with the evidence to turn in. What will the diner records tell you?"

"Dench, Alvarado and who? If I can separate the legitimate businesses from the ones here on Alvarado's spreadsheet, I can track the other partners." I shook my head again. "No, I'm wrong somewhere. Missing something or someone. This much money? Monthly? How many people would he have had to smuggle?"

Peter shook his head vehemently. "Joe was not involved like that! Iss did all of Joe's accounting. All of it. It was Iss's idea to buy the diner in the first place. Joe couldn't say no to him really. But Joe would never—"

"Never say never, kid." Luis alt-tabbed on the computer and pulled up a list. "These are the disappearances or people who 'moved away' which match with Alvarado's travel. I included unsolveds."

Luis's most valuable skills were his ability to find people, to acquire snitches and to recognize patterns in suspects. He could look at a case and figure out which scumbag was our most likely doer. I thought he had some geographical sixth sense—or instinct. Sort of how serial killer programs could pinpoint the radius of where a suspect lived. For this case, it helped that he was from Mexico City, too.

"There are two hundred and thirty names here," I breathed.

"Two hundred and thirty-nine." Luis added, "You're right. Not enough to account for all that money."

"How long ago did you go back?"

"Not how long. How far."

"Huh?"

"This only covers the towns and cities I could cross check with Alvarado's recent travel. Some of these towns have little-to-no telephone access and the local police weren't helpful in a lot of cases. I couldn't delve any further. There was a full-scale war between two cartels near where Alvarado was last seen. Some missing niece or daughter of the Jiménez cartel lord. I don't see us getting more information from down there. But that's not the important information. What is important is that even if there were five hundred, it still wouldn't match up with the amount of cash rolling through Alvarado's accounts every month."

I scanned the amounts on the list again and concentrated on the sums less than two grand. "These small amounts here, here and here. Who do they belong to? There has to be two different sources for the cash. Five and nearly ten grand to these businesses," I pointed, "Only one and two to the others." I looked at Luis. "How long till forensics is done with the accounting from each business?"

"A week?" Luis answered. "Probably two."

"They're probably spending most of their time on the big money. Which is probably drug money. I think the smaller amounts are the trafficking funds. I can work on that end. Meanwhile, we need Peter to study the inventory of evidence from Alvarado's arrest to see if anything is missing. With cops involved, we can't be sure we have everything." Peter was texting when I turned to him. "I need the balance sheets from the diner."

"Already ahead of you, Detective. Darryl's emailing them," he said, holding up his phone to show the text. "Will all this help Cai?"

"Depends. If Cai didn't kill him, then the partners probably did. Let me ask you something. How did you know Iss was dead?"

Peter's darted a glance to Luis and shook his head at me.

"I've got to get back to the station." Luis stood after reading Peter's silent message: *Not while he's here.* "Bring him by tomorrow," he nodded in Peter's direction, "We'll see if he notices anything missing. I'll leave the laptop here."

I walked Luis to the door. My partner stopped with the door half open, his voice low. "You should have contacted your union rep to fight the suspension."

I shrugged. "It's a week. I deserved it. And besides, by the time they reinstated me, I'd be back on the job."

"It's on your permanent record," Luis pointed out. "The FBI will take it into consideration."

"I'll introduce them to Del. They'll be more impressed I didn't shove my foot up his ass."

He chuckled, then got serious. "Don't trust him."

"Too late," I replied with a weak smile of my own.

"My neck is on the line with this. He helped today, but the setup of Alvarado is enough to arrest him."

"I know."

"He lies one more time…"

I nodded at the unspoken threat and shut the door behind him. The knife was no longer stuck in it. Crossing my arms over my chest, I leaned against the wood just inches from where Peter'd stabbed the blade through the mahogany. My brows raised expectantly.

"I went over there to kill him," Peter said with an amount of stoicism that would make Zeno proud.

Maybe I'm *Dating* the Sociopath?

"Pardon?" My eyes blinked so many times it could have been considered a tick.

"Darryl and I got back from our gig, to find Cai hysterical in the bedroom. He's crying like I've only heard him do when the depressive cycle hits. One time when he got like that—I went out to make macaroni and cheese. It took like ten minutes. Fucking microwave," he set his jaw. "Ten minutes because he has to have the cheese sticking and burnt to the macaroni. I came back in the room, and he'd used a bottle of turpentine and had my lighter—Cai tried to set himself on fire."

My brows shot past my hairline and probably landed somewhere in the back of my neck. But I didn't say anything, so Peter continued. "So okay, Friday we get home late. Darryl and I hear this sobbing, and we're frantic." Peter rubbed the tattoo on his hand. "Cai was holding his hands in his lap, rocking back and forth." He begged me to understand with his glance into my eyes. "Iss had branded him. Tried to rape him, then fucking branded him as a message to me."

Jesus, this case was complicated. This whole fucking boy's life was complicated. I rubbed my temples. "But Cai wasn't raped?"

Peter shook his head. "He wasn't even upset about that," he laughed tiredly, rubbing the meaty part of his palm between his eyes. "His fucking hand. He's hysterical because Iss destroyed his canvas."

"Huh?" That was becoming a recurring response of mine.

"Cai's skin. When he was younger, he got into a manic phase and carved it up—we covered the damage with tattoos, and since then he's had this thing about his skin being a canvas for artwork."

"And you think Cai didn't kill him?" And Peter thought *I* was the naïve one.

"I know he didn't, because two other people were there when Iss tattooed him. Cai's best friend Rachel, and some kid that held him down. Cai said Rachel got him out of there."

"How do you know he didn't go back and kill him? You were willing to do it," I pointed out.

"Because he didn't try and stop me. We all wanted him dead for it. And they both were creating alibis to cover for me."

As a cop that admission was a twist to the gut, but as a human being? Maybe part of me wanted the man dead, too.

"They told the cops this?"

He nodded. "I think Cai did, not about me going there—but about Rachel taking him home. Rachel is MIA, though. She disappears for long periods. Usually after she scores."

Oh, good. An addict for an alibi.

I flopped down on the couch. The middle cushion was the only thing separating me from Peter while I attempted to pull all this information in. It was too tiring. My eyes were trying to close. "You should have told me all of this from the beginning."

"I didn't know you. You didn't know me. I just wanted Iss out of our lives. I'd have even given up the restaurant, but the day I was supposed to meet you...that Saturday you came to the diner and saw me that first time—"

"You were the no-show informant I waited two hours for?"

"Yeah. I planned on giving you everything. The passports, the money, the accounts. Then Cai's tuition came up, and just like that we were broke. The mortgage was next and the restaurant was the only income we had."

"Not the only income," I pointed out without mentioning the money from his and Darryl's "gig".

"So I called Darryl, and we used this snitch everyone knows to pass you the info about Iss. Then I went to his house, hid the stash, and that was supposed to be that. Iss in jail, restaurant safe and those people being looked for. But then you were always hanging around, pushing your way into my life. No matter what I did to send you away." He bit his lip around a half-smile and fisted one of my pillows to his chest. I let my eyes fall shut.

"You still should have told me," I scolded, before settling my head onto the armrest, bare feet propping my knees up in the middle of the sofa. "Have you been baking?"

"Cai's other favorite, cinnamon rolls," he whispered. My eyes flew open. He hovered over me, bracing himself on either side of my head.

"What are you doing?" My voice cracked on an unsteady breath.

"You're hard."

"Yeah well, I keep trying to explain to my dick that you're a lying, manipulative whore, but it has selective hearing and chooses to focus on that last part." I immediately regretted saying it. Hurt flashed in his eyes. But Peter never gave me any emotion for long.

His hips pressed against mine. He was hard, too. My brain fogged and my hands moved of their own accord to his hips, pulling him closer.

"Try to think of me as a person, Austin. I know that's a novel idea for you, but I'm not just a whore."

I wasn't sure why he felt it necessary to say that while rocking his hips into mine. "Peter...?"

"Hm?"

"Shut up." My fingers closed around the back of his neck and I pulled him into a kiss.

Frotting Should Replace Baseball as the National Pastime

Our lips clashed together, teeth clacking, making me wince and him grin. I'd had better delivered kisses, but the Fourth of July had fewer fireworks than this one. Just one more incongruous Peter-phenomenon in a list long enough to satisfy Santa's naughty roll.

The slight rock of his hips opened my lips for an intake of breath. His tongue swept in to steal it away. I delved fingers in his hair, gripping it in a fist and pulling him tighter to me. He responded by nipping my bottom lip and rubbing his cock harder into mine.

"Wrap your legs around me," Peter ordered bending his elbows to cradle around my head. He scooted us both down the couch.

"I'm older. I should be on top," I said stupidly.

He laughed gently, skimming a hand down my side, his lips trailing heat across my jaw. He paused, his breath damp and hot along the curve of my ear as he whispered my name. Then he pushed hard with his hips, my zipper and his pressing together almost painfully. My brain skittered to a halt.

"Yeah. I know. I'm shutting up." Okay. I could handle being a homo. Clothes on and rubbing against each other like teenagers was the best pre-sex experience I'd ever had. Sadly.

"I'm going to make you come without even touching your cock," he promised.

"Oh, God. You're a control freak," I groaned, pulling harder at his hair. He nipped at the skin on my neck. Every touch of his lips was like kindling. I slipped my hand from his hips and down the back of his pants, more heat from his skin to my palm.

"You're seriously…making…me consider…a gag." He rolled his hips, making my back arch with the zing of heat that shot from my groin up my spine. He thrust again, and my other hand clenched into a fist.

"Now who's talking…Oh, Jesus…" I forgot what I was going to say as he trailed a tongue from collar to earlobe. Done talking. Couldn't through the moans anyway. And somehow in the middle of all that, I wrapped my legs around his waist and began rocking into him.

Control was never my issue. Not in bed, not in life. Overthinking was my problem, which was what I was doing as Peter made me realize what I had missed by repressing who I was.

Do I move my hand up or in? Am I supposed to stick my fingers in his ass? He's on top. Does that make me the woman? What do women do in this situation? They never stuck their finger in my ass, that was for sure.

"Stop thinking," Peter whispered. How he knew was anyone's guess. Experience? Or my twitching hand in his pants was more likely.

"I can't reach," I laughed. Delightfully, he laughed too. Though both of us shut up as he covered my lips and sought my tongue with his. The smell of cinnamon enveloped my senses, but it couldn't overpower the tang of sweat. My hand moved up his back, slipping under his shirt then back down again seeking to map out every inch of his damp, warm skin. His breath quickened as did the pace of his hips. He curled his tongue around mine, sucked at it, drove me to slamming my hips against him until our lips were wet from breaking apart with the force of our rubbing.

My fingers twisted and tangled tighter into his hair, then started to cramp, but the pace of his hips wouldn't allow me to unclench them. I used that hand, instead, for leverage to hold his mouth close. My legs locked him tight to my hips, the friction between was insane, an inferno ready to explode. Until it was overshadowed by the sensations in my groin. Toes curled, hips stuttering, breath held, I came quietly, with a clipped moan and a deep shudder.

It took Peter another few minutes, which time I used to explore his jaw with my mouth and teeth. My hands concentrating on his skin, the pockets of muscles tensing and shifting along my palms. Soft skin, wet from perspiration, rough with stubble—and he even tasted of cinnamon.

When I heard his soft pant against my ear, felt his hips still and his body tense, another shudder ripped through me.

Gay sex, one. Straight sex, zero.

Chapter Twelve

Gay Sex 101 With Professor Peter

Lying under Peter was awkward, but not completely so. My legs cramped, necessitating the return of my feet to the cushion. Other than that, the weight of him against me was comforting, so I stayed relatively motionless. I started another skin-adventure on his back, the pads of my fingers trailing down the shallow channel in the center.

I was still guarded, half expecting the curve of Peter's lips to bolt after his other fleeting smiles, leaving him with a scowl—or worse. I scanned his face, searching for hints that now he'd scored, Hostility and Apathy would be back up to bat. His mouth held only a serene smile—a vision I would pocket away forever. Just in case.

I continued to study him, committing every freckle to memory. He wasn't as untouchably beautiful as I once thought. He had an ethereal quality in the pinkness of his skin and the deep blue of his eyes, but still, his nose was a little too pointy, with a tiny ball at the end. His cheeks had a few acne scars; and his top lip, though shaped exquisitely with a dip in the middle, was too thin.

"You're staring again," he chided softly, dusting his mouth across mine. I marveled that even that small bit of contact made my heart stop, sputter and speed ahead.

My fingers continuing their journey along his sides, under his shirt, cruising along the curve of his ass. Every inch of him was hard and soft, rough and smooth. I could hardly breathe with the force of want he elicited in me. "I was just thinking you're not as perfect as I imagined," I replied.

Instead of being affronted, Peter laughed. That sound also hit me deeply with a burst of warmth. I could see the appeal of drugs. If this stomach-sinking, dizzy, falling-through-space feeling was anything like taking heroin? Sign me up.

"And here I was thinking you were more perfect."

"That's the orgasm talking." I smirked.

"So orgasms give me beer goggles, but they make you start seeing flaws?" His eyebrow moved slowly up.

"Saturday."

"Today is Tuesday. Does coming also make you muddled?" His smirk was going straight to my groin, not a completely unpleasant feeling—except for the sticky mess soaking through my pants.

"*You* make me muddled. Saturday was when I started having clearer vision when it came to you."

"Ah. Because you thought I killed Iss," he said, starting to get up. I sighed at the loss of his smile and pulled him back down.

"Partly," I nodded, "Yes. But also because of this." I reached for his hand braced against the sofa near my ear and blind-felt for the 'Iss' tattoo-marred skin.

The center of Peter's brow creased as he looked at me and cocked his head. "Because Iss tattooed me?"

"I've seen the tattoo before," I said, brushing back the fall of auburn tickling my forehead as he leaned over me. I had to smile when it fell back in place—having yet another reason to touch him tenderly. I didn't see Peter as accepting gentle gestures, so I was glad for the excuse.

Peter pushed up to his knees and lifted my feet to rest on his lap as he sat down. I was as surprised by the abrupt move as I was by the affectionate contact. He frowned, rubbing the blue ink and resting his wrist against my ankle. "The tattoo," Peter said, "…Jess?"

"You knew him?" I propped on my elbows, doing the math in my head. Peter would have been ten?

He responded with a shake of his head "I knew of him. It was like last year when Joe told me about Jess and Iss. How did you know Jess?"

"Back up to Iss giving you that tattoo," I said instead of giving him an answer. Talking about Jess was too painful. I sat up, grimacing as my air conditioning reminded me that my pants had a spreading stain in the crotch.

"Shower first," Peter said, and I had to grab his wrist to keep him from going.

"No, shower later. Tattoo first."

He shook my hand free and bit his lip. I wasn't yet immune to that particular enticement, but I kept my breath quiet as it tripped in my throat.

"Iss and I are counting cash one night. Pretty big night for sales. I took in around twenty grand in three hours dealing at a newly opened club. Those kind of numbers get you noticed. Not that I understood that's why Iss did it at the time. I was too busy being angry over being made his possession."

He blew out a breath and unbuttoned his jeans, dropping them to the floor. He was more easy in his nudity than in conversation. I, on the other hand, just went from sated-to-*boing* between his letting go of his pants and their hitting the floor. This wasn't the way I wanted to see Peter undress for me—shrugging off his clothes in a puddle next to my sofa. However, I wasn't going to complain. There was no bad way to see Peter naked.

"Are you paying attention, Detective?" Peter asked, smirking while grabbing my ankles. I had to look up from his crotch to answer—which made responding irrelevant.

"That's rhetorical," I said, yanking my shirt over my head while he dragged my pants past my hips. My back smacked against the sofa cushion.

"So, I'm on the bed at his house," Peter continued, while my brain held up protest signs that read 'Iss Schmiss'. "Iss comes out of the bathroom with a homemade tattoo gun and says if I don't give him my hand he'll knock me out, break my fingers and do the tattoo anyway." Iss Schmiss, the protester chanted as Peter knelt before me completely naked, lifting my ankles in the air and knee-walking between them.

"You planning on repeating this story in about five minutes?"

"Five minutes? We'll have to work on your stamina."

Either I was crazy, or stupid, because I stopped him before he could touch me. If his hands even brushed my skin, my brain would stage a sit-in until I bent over.

When had I started thinking about bending over?

Peter finished hurriedly, "It is—was— it *was* Iss's way of protecting those he thought belonged to him. I just had to show it if I got busted and ask for Detective Joe Dench. That's how I met Joe."

Before the last words were out of my mouth, he brushed aside my hand and climbed between my legs, folding my knees to my chest. "Story's over now. We have to go to the court soon."

Court? Oh. Cai's bond was being decided at three. My brain had officially declared itself on strike while my other head took over the thinking.

"Breathe, Austin." I immediately obeyed the gentle command.

"I don't need an entire lesson on gay sex in one hour." I swallowed.

"I'm going to take a lot longer than an hour," he promised. We had two and some change before he had to be at the courthouse. That was my last recollection before Peter's cock touched mine and rendered all thought moot.

When the doorbell rang, my head tilted back at the same time as his mouth lifted from my lips. Peter moved to the inside of the sofa while I scooted from under him. As I grabbed my pants, the chime sounded again. "Coming." I threw Peter's jeans at him with a look that dared him to say a word.

He chuckled, sliding up one pant leg. We were moving methodically, not hastily, which proved a mistake.

Before either of our pants was waist high, the front door flew open, and in walked my best friend.

Dear God, I'll Take That Lobotomy Now. Thanks, —Austin

"Ready for the ga—" Dave's grin fell as his jaw unhinged and then clacked back together, "—me." In rapid succession he dropped the six pack of beers from his hand, causing me to yell a frantic, "Oh, shit," while he croaked, "Fuck, I didn't—" and dropped the pizza box upside-down, both of us turning our backs to each other. "Fuck. Oh, fuck. I'm really sorry, Oz." Then he started laughing.

"Jesus Christ. Can I just come out to someone in a normal fucking fashion?" I jerked my pants closed while Peter and Dave continued to laugh. It was only luck that I didn't catch my balls or pubes in my zipper. Knew I shouldn't have given him a key.

"Sorry," Dave sputtered, now laughing uproariously while picking up a beer at arms-length. It spewed yellow liquid across my hardwood floors as he headed to the trash. Midway he stopped and blinked. "Pete?"

"Detective Buchanan," Peter smiled tentatively, buttoning the top of his jeans.

"You know each other? Never mind. Answer in a minute. I'm going to go take a shower. I can't have a fucking discussion like this." When Peter started to follow me, I shook my head and nodded to the guest bathroom. I wasn't going to have Dave thinking about Peter and me showering together.

"Stain on your crotch says you already had a fucking discussion." Dave chuckled. I froze halfway up the stairs, praying for a natural disaster, before finishing the climb to my bedroom.

My shower would have made lightning look lethargic, as would the speed with which I pulled on jeans and a t-shirt. Foregoing shoes, I jogged back downstairs to find Dave rinsing a towel off in the kitchen sink.

"Thanks for cleaning up the beer," I said, not even bothering to explain what he witnessed. Dave and I had jacked off together plenty of times. Our friendship didn't lend itself to embarrassment. Hence his laughing at catching me with another man on my sofa and my being perturbed rather than humiliated.

"Isn't he like twelve?" Dave nodded to the hallway where the guest bedroom lay.

"Twenty," I shot back. "How do you know him?"

"Busted his boyfriend a few times."

"Prick?"

"Prisc."

"That's what I meant."

"No, you didn't."

"No, I didn't," I agreed.

Dave nodded, stepping over the back of my sofa and sliding down into the comfy seats. I hoped that Peter and I didn't leave any mess on there. As surreptitiously as possible, I examined the leather.

"I cleaned it off," Dave said. "A bed too much work for you two?"

He was taking this astonishingly well. "No," I said carefully. "It was unexpe— Why are we discussing my sex life like it isn't stunning news?"

"Stunning, is it? At your first 'fabulous', I'm outta here."

"Comes to that, I'll shoot myself. Don't worry." We sat in silence for a few seconds before I added, "Luis told you about the suspension?"

"Nah. Didn't have to. Word got around."

"A party just for me? I don't know what to say, Dave. I'm touched."

"Del's an ass. You should have kicked it."

"To be fair I didn't threaten to kick his ass so much as to shove my foot deep up in there."

"Surprised he didn't report that as sexual harassment."

I grinned. "Beer?"

"One of yours. The cans I brought will explode." He crossed his ankles on my coffee table.

From the kitchen I brought two opened bottles of Guinness, handed one to Dave and retook my seat next to him while he flipped channels, settling on a repeat of last night's baseball game. Far too many of my pay channels were sports related—I even had international sports. Maybe I was overcompensating?

I was trying to stop thinking about Peter's naked body when Dave stole a spot in my thoughts. "Lemme ask you something, Oz. You tryin' to destroy your career?"

"Only if I can do so in a blaze of naked gay glory," I replied sardonically. I wasn't the least bit defensive. Dave was only looking out for me.

"Fucking a witness, threatening Del in the middle of the station, Oz? If anyone but Luis told me this shit, I'd fucking say they were lying. No way would Austin Glass do anything to risk his chances with the FBI."

"The FBI is overrated," I lied.

"Oz, what's up, man?" We still hadn't managed even a glance at each other since I sat down. My head fell back, eyes closed while my fingernails stripped the label off my bottle. I didn't have an answer for him. Thankfully, Peter made his appearance, watching me as he sank into the recliner.

Maybe Peter was the answer. The problem *and* the answer. The answer without being a solution. Another tick in the inconsistent life of Austin Glass.

He was wearing my sweats and college t-shirt again. The welling of emotion that came from seeing him in my clothes was impossible to explain. Everything I felt for Peter was impossible to explain.

And he had a beer.

"There are two cops here," I warned, an eyebrow going up at Peter.

"I can fuck you, but not drink your beer?"

Lord, give me strength, and a steady hand for when I shoot him in the face. I stood up and snatched the beer from his hand, setting it down on the coffee table and breathing out as I sat down again. "I did not say you could fuck me and—"

One side of Peter's lips ticked up. "Way you were bent on that sofa a few min—"

"Say it," I warned, 'and I'll shove my foot up *your* ass!"

"Kinky," Peter murmured, not hiding his grin.

Dave took a swig of his drink, still staring at the screen. He hadn't spared us a glance during that whole argument. "Have you got some sort of foot-in-ass fetish? Del's ass and now Peter's."

"I think it's just feet. He's obsessed with me in slippers," Peter said quietly, tapping something into his phone.

"Christ. I'd choose a lobotomy over being with either one of you right now." I scrubbed a hand over my face.

"Can I log into my email account on that?" Peter asked, nodding at the laptop. "Darryl sent the accounting records."

Uh—Help

Having downloaded both sets of records—one set from the computer Luis brought, and one set from Peter's mail—I began perusing them while Peter and Dave chatted. And by 'chatted' I mean that "uh" littered conversation when one person had seen the other naked and was probably doing his utmost to not think about where the other guy's dick had just been—namely in the his best friend's ass. I could have corrected that assumption, but I was too busy doing the this-isn't-happening avoidance thing by staring at the computer screen and endeavoring to work.

At least three other detectives were probably slogging through the evidence on this case. Marco and Del were following the trail to their killer, while Luis and I were following it to our missing passport owners. It seemed the week and a half we'd been working on it, this case had tripled in value.

"I heard about your brother, Pete," Dave said. "How's he holding up?"

Peter shrugged. I read his intense concentration on the TV as he didn't want to talk about it. I winced at his flat-eyed stare, identifying it as his prelude to sarcasm. "Great. They locked him up with a guy who lit his parents on fire and watched them scream while they tried to get out of the garage. It's a great learning experience for Cai, who last month cried for two hours when a bird hit his window and died."

Dave stared for a beat, took a long gulp of his Guinness and turned to me, "So," he coughed, "you're gay."

Three fingers rubbing against my temple didn't ease the pain that shot through my skull. I jabbed the 'print' button and went to retrieve the sheets from my office, not caring if Peter and Dave sat in awkward silence, or killed each other.

When I returned a half hour later with the print outs, Darryl was sitting in my spot, his skinny jeans-clad thigh pressing against Peter's. What infuriated me most was not that Peter had invited someone to my house, or even that Darryl was sitting in my place. Nor was it that Peter was sitting on the sofa next to Darryl. What enraged me was my reaction to Darryl's hand casually resting on Peter's knee: Fury.

The heat of my own anger unbalanced me. It buzzed through my veins like a swarm of hungry red ants. My skin crawled with it. I had no right, no reason, to feel jealousy. I'd known him what, a week? We weren't boyfriends. We hadn't even fucked.

"Christ," I muttered, shoving those feelings deep, deep, *deep* down into the pockets of my soul. I determined to bury them further down than the memories of Jesse had been.

"Darryl," I greeted, taking Peter's old seat on the recliner. I tossed papers on the coffee table and shoved them across to Dave.

"Hello, pretty little detective." Darryl smiled devilishly, green eyes managing innocence and sin as he stroked Peter's thigh and stared at me. Peter, leaning over to take some of the paperwork, was either oblivious or indifferent to the touch. My eyes were fastened to Darryl's fingers.

Before I could remember my gun was in Captain Ashanafi's desk, Dave grabbed a few of the pages and, like Peter, began looking through them. "What are we looking for here?" he asked.

Grateful for the pull away from Darryl and Peter, I leaned forward and flipped my laptop so I could see it side by side with Luis's. "Clues to who owns these businesses. Forensics is still—" Darryl's fingers twitched up Peter's thigh. My eye ticked. "Why are you here?" I was too riveted by his hand touching Peter to give Darryl the glare he deserved. A dim voice in the back of my head said, 'touching what's mine'. I tried to smother, stuff and toss the voice away.

"He brought me clothes for court," Peter answered for him, brows drawn inward with confusion. He followed my gaze down, eyes bouncing back up. I'd never seen him grin so quickly.

I tried to reason why that would require Darryl being here. In my house. When no explanation was delivered, I asked, "Why didn't you go to him?"

"Isn't it easier if we all drive there?"

"All? All of who?" I asked, not wanting to hear the obvious answer.

"Us." Peter swept a hand among Darryl, me and himself.

"Why would the three of us be going to listen to Cai's bond hearing? I did my part."

"Moral support?" Dave threw in with a blink of interest. I'd respond to that if I didn't think he was being completely facetious.

Bastard.

"I can't pay his bond," Peter said quietly.

Darryl, throughout this back-and-forth exchange, stroked Peter's thigh and glared at me. I smothered a possessive growl. "That's not my prob— Is there a reason you need to molest him?"

"It's called being compassionate, prettyboy. Did you want me to just call him a whore and ignore that he's hurting? Or maybe you'd like me to leave you alone with him so you can take advantage—"

"Stop it, Dare," Peter said, not harshly enough to please me. "His lawyer says bond is going be like a million dollars or more. If he gets it at all. I can't put up the restaurant as collateral because it's going to be under investigation now. Our house isn't worth more than a hundred thousand, if that."

"Are you asking me, or is this another tit for tat?"

I could see his wheels whirring, trying to come up with the answer that would play me best. Would he beg? Offer himself? Try and seduce me again? Was anything he said real? Never mind. Those were all irrelevant. What was relevant was that Peter Dyachenko had me at a smile.

"I'll pay you back," he pledged with a face so steeped in earnestness, I almost believed him.

"How? Don't answer that." Whoring himself out if I had to guess. If I was jealous of Darryl's hand, the idea of Peter being with anyone else was a physical weight on my chest, crushing the air from my lungs.

But I had no right. Zero right. Nada. Nil. Neither the justification, nor a reason to be possessive. Of all the feelings I had for Peter—lust, warmth, protectiveness, anger, frustration—jealousy was the most confounding. And it had to go.

"You're a dickhead with a badge, prettyboy," Darryl snarled. "He—" Peter's hand cut him off with a gentle squeeze.

"It doesn't matter how. I'll sign whatever papers you need."

The sickest part of me—the one that had worried about Peter's HIV status, the one that said I had a right to his body because of what he put me through; the rotten, evil section of my soul that said Peter was mine—that was the portion of my mind that slithered up to my ear and hissed the venomously seductive, 'Imagine the ways he could pay it back'. "Okay," I said, ignoring the devil inside, "For starters, how about you stop lying to me."

Dave continued his quiet watchfulness, but the shake of his head was reproach enough. He thought I was an idiot. He wasn't wrong.

"Hear that, Rabbit? He wants the whole truth. How's this for truth, prettyboy. Peter doesn't even like boys."

"This is like the Desperate Houseboys of Denver," my best friend quipped, looking from my stunned face to Peter's guilty head drop, to Darryl's satisfied smirk. Dave got up and went into the kitchen. I vowed that if I heard corn popping, I was going to bludgeon him with my fireplace poker.

"He has a pair of come-stained pants in the bedroom that argue for the prosecution," I said flippantly. I wasn't buying Darryl's taunts, but Peter wasn't offering any rebuttal. If he wasn't at least bisexual, then I felt completely used.

"Darryl, would you stop, please?" I knew that pleading look in Peter's eye. He needed for Darryl not to alienate his golden goose.

"Why? So he can treat you like a whore? He calls you one often enough. Can't you see how he'll want to get paid?" He gripped Peter's arm, pulling him to the front door. I got up to stop them—or shut the door behind them. "Come on. We'll get the money some other way. Cai wouldn't want you to take it from him."

I couldn't argue with Darryl's logic. Or fault it. He was doing what someone who truly cared about Peter would do: stop letting him sacrifice everything for Cai. I sighed and considered committing myself to a sanitarium. "You don't have to pay me back. Get your clothes on, and we'll go."

Peter's lips hinted at a smile. Darryl dropped his hand, releasing Peter who stood by the entryway. Darryl was still dubious, and his thin shoulders held the stiffness of self-righteousness, but he appeared less angry.

With relief, I propped my ass on the back of the sofa as Peter headed to the guest room. Instead of passing, he stopped in front of me and cupped my jaw. My lips parted before he leaned in for the kiss. I fisted the edges of his shirt, yanking him closer, until his hips were warm under my hands, until the twinge of pain from my tilted position faded under the softness of his mouth, until I forgot all my objections and reasoning.

He pressed into me with an arch of his hips, supporting my neck with both hands as he controlled my mouth with his. Peter liked control, and who was I to complain when it felt like this? I had no breath, each exhale stolen by his teeth or tongue. Whether it was that lack of oxygen, or just the dizzying feel and smell of him, my heart sped up. He eased back just enough to suck in my bottom lip briefly before pulling away. My mouth chased after him.

With a quiet, "Thank you," Peter left me there, stupefied, shivering, and desperate.

And that asshole Dave looked on while sharing a bag of popcorn with Darryl.

My Ass is A No Fly Zone

After both Peter and I changed into more appropriate 'court clothes'—which for him meant less holey jeans and a tucked in button-down shirt—the three of us piled into Arturo, leaving Dave to man the house. Or, as he said upon our leaving, "Gonna watch ESPN without a wife and four kids drowning out the game and changing the channel to Nickelodeon."

We were driving in silence until I couldn't stand it anymore. "What did he mean you don't even like boys?" Darryl was smirking in the back seat. Peter sat in front, wearing his impenetrable gaze, which I was beginning to understand meant that he was upset or sad.

"It means he likes T with his A. He prefers ladypenis over the real thing. Gay for pay. Norman Normal. He's a breeder. Het-er-oh-sexy," he mimed sign language.

"Darryl," Peter sighed long-sufferingly. "Would you please shut up?"

Gay for pay? How did that explain Alvarado. For that matter, how did it explain Darryl. "Is he on medication?"

"Don't encourage him with the option of legal drugs."

"You're not contradicting him."

Peter licked his lips, and my heart sank in my body before rebounding with a much less vibrant thump. "He's...right."

"And you're...straight?"

"I'm okay with men. Maybe I'm partially gay? I don't know. I don't label it. I like both. But, gun to my head, I prefer women."

"Then—"

"I prefer you overall." Peter grinned. My heart rate exceeded the speed of sound.

In the back, Darryl scoffed loudly then, maturely, made a gagging sound. "He couldn't find his prostate with his head firmly up his ass. Seriously, Rabbit, what the fuck?"

"I would just like to throw out there that we can all stop talking about putting things up my ass. No fly zone. Do not enter. No parking."

Peter's smile made me squirm in my seat and resume silence for the rest of the trip to the courthouse.

What's That You Say?

Angelica met us on the front steps of the building after I texted her. As we entered the courthouse, I expected Peter's piercings to set off the metal detector, but surprisingly it remained mute. I just then noticed he wasn't wearing his lip or eyebrow ring, and obviously he'd taken out his other piercings for this. Such random maturity from him mystified me.

On our way through security, Angelica briefed us. "The Feds are here," she said, throwing her soft leather briefcase onto the scanning belt.

I tossed my wallet and keys into a tub, digging in my pockets for change. "They know."

"They know," she agreed with a firm nod, not losing pace as she grabbed her case and clacked down the marble hall. Neither of us looked back at Darryl and Peter, but the patter of jogging feet told me they were behind us.

"What's that mean for bond?"

"Depends on if the D.A. decides to hold back today and let the feds handle their case first. I doubt it. Big case, lots of publicity. They'll both be vying for his blood. I think Will (Will Schoemaker—the District Attorney) has the upper hand. He has a stronger and more relevant case."

"Just a witness that saw him hours earlier," Peter argued vehemently.

"Time of death has moved. Coroner put it between ten and midnight. The neighbor that heard the shots is retracting his statement. He says it could have been later. Biggest problem now is that they know who they have. Will is trying him as an adult."

She finally stopped moving in front of a large set of polished wooden doors which opened into a courtroom. "Peter, right now you have to worry about two things. Cai might be denied bond, and you are probably going to be at least questioned, if not detained, by the Federal Prosecutor."

"Why would they deny bond?" I asked. At sixteen Cai was hardly a hardened criminal, but I knew the answer even as I asked. "They skipped town."

"He knows how to disappear," she affirmed. "And they'll use the fact that the feds want him in order to prove he has a history of violence."

"He's not going to get bond," Peter said, all emotion drained from his face. My earlier thoughts bore out; when Peter was most emotional, he shut down.

"I didn't say that. He hasn't been charged with a crime by the federal prosecutor yet. That's in our favor. And there's no murder weapon or witness who saw the actual shooting."

I failed to catch Angelica's careful wording. "Then why did they jump to prosecute?" I was confused. Most prosecutors wouldn't even file with that kind of case.

"Cai's girlfriend is making a deal. She says Prisc raped Cai, and Cai went back there, got a gun from the living room, and then she heard a shot."

"That bitch! She's a lying smack addict," Darryl screeched, his voice echoing in the enormous halls. Half the courthouse turned around.

"She's lying," Peter echoed. "Prisc didn't rape him. And he didn't go back there."

"She was pressured," Angelica said, "Cai says she's terrified of jail. But, Peter, they have evidence he went to the hospital and requested Cambivric."

"What's that?" He and Darryl asked nearly at the same time.

"It's a drug they give rape victims to reduce the risk of exposure to HIV," I said, leaning against the wall. Dammit.

"Oh God," Peter whispered pressing his hands against his forehead. "Fucking stupid. How did I not know?"

"Let's get through this, and then we can help him. His mother is here now," Angelica soothed with a hesitant pat to his arm. "This works in our favor. But you're no longer his legal guardian, you're a suspect in your father's murder at worst. And at best, you're complicit in Cai's flight. There's only one person the courts would even consider releasing Cai to…"

Her pause made my brows rise while my brain went through every person that could have a single—

"Austin?" Angelica smiled.

"Say what now?" I said, doing my best Wile-E-Coyote-plan-backfired blink.

Chapter Thirteen

Three Against One—And Not in the Fun Way

I grasped for the nearest metaphorical branch to avoid being pulled over the edge. "I'm not approved for foster care. They're not just going to release him to me."

"You don't need to be," Angelica informed me. "His mother was flown in. You just need to have her staying with you."

My thoughts flat-lined. Peter stared at the floor with his fucking typical unreadable expression. Darryl glared under perfectly arched and plucked brows, as if anticipating my negative response. And Angelica's attack was double-barreled: her damn kitten eyes *and* her placid smile.

Fuck!

"Austin, he's a good kid. I'd take them myself but with his case and my others, the work hours for the next few months are going to be ridiculous."

"There's an entire fucking world out there and you pick me?"

"You have a stable home—"

"I'm a single man very recently outed. He's a sixteen-year-old boy!"

"You're a decorated police officer—"

"Working on the guy he killed's case!"

"Allegedly."

"No, I'm pretty sure I'm working on the case. No alleged about it." Only, I wasn't. When I got back to work, I'd be off this case.

"Why do you have to be a smartass about everything?"

"Because everyone else thinks I'm a fucking dumbass. I have to do something to prove them wrong." No one was making an argument about this arrangement but me. If Luis were here he'd suggest they just shoot me and get it over with. *This* was just a slow, cruel, torturous death of my meticulously planned future. "What you're asking me to do is literally toss my career away. Much as I despise Delmonico and think Marco is an idiot, I can't take their chief suspect into my house. What kind of message would that send?"

"That you think he's innocent, and they should start hunting for the real suspect. They're not even looking anymore, Austin. They're sitting on their complacent—"

"I wouldn't look either!" I yelled, catching the attention of various whispering passersby as my voice echoed in the halls. "There's a fucking witness, he was at the scene, he's done it before. Who the fuck could possibly believe he's innocent besides these two dipshits," I hiked a thumb at Darryl and Peter, "who apparently think he's the next coming of Christ. But not me. I am not joining the Cult of Cai."

"I believe he's innocent," Angelica said.

"Did he tell you that?"

"You know I can't reveal anything he said. But I think I've made myself clear."

Damn her gentle smile. Damn her calm, rational voice. And damn her reproachful, guilt-laden eyes. And damn Peter, too, while I was at it. And his fucking bunny slippers that made me interested enough to pay attention to him in the first place. I was burning those fuzzy fuckers the moment I saw them again. Which reminded me, he was suspiciously silent.

He didn't make his usual plea with his eyes, or use his body and my feelings for him, he didn't even raise his gaze from the marble tile. Despite all of Angelica's cajoling, what finally had me considering agreeing to do this was Peter's lack of comment.

Maybe he understood the gravity of my situation. I needed to believe that. I needed to believe he comprehended the fact that, should I go back to work, taking Cai in would make me a pariah amongst other cops who would already have enough trouble dealing with my being gay. Even Luis would probably distance himself from me.

But, if I didn't say yes, Cai would likely spend months awaiting trial in a jail cell. Could that kid survive? Even with Angelica up to bat for him, I was only mildly convinced of his innocence. It seemed everyone who spent time with this kid developed some sort of blind affection for him.

I wasn't kidding about the Cai Cult. And I had reached my fill of Peter's complete and total lack of self. There's sacrifice and then there's martyrdom. Peter teetered too close to the latter relative to his 'brother'. Besides Peter being a whore, besides his shaky morals; and his, at times, anti-social personality, the largest hurdle between Peter and me was going to be his absolute and total devotion to Cai. That kind of reverence was abnormal.

Wasn't it?

Ultimately, I had to admit that the question wasn't about Cai at all. It was about Peter. It was about how much was I willing to give up for someone who was a complete stranger little more than a week ago. He lifted his face from studying the floor. The entreaty in Peter's eyes alone might have compelled me to do it; the slow rise of deep blue, shining with such hope, slammed into me like a boxer's fist.

"It'd be the end of my being a cop," I said to him. "Not just the FBI. I'd be frozen out of every agency." He nodded succinctly, remaining stoic. "What is it with this kid?"

"I owe him," Peter stated solemnly.

"Owe him what?"

"Everything. I owe Cai everything." He didn't explain that statement. I wasn't expecting him to, not with Angelica watching us with an intensity that bordered on rude. The devil inside me questioned if she wasn't suggesting this whole scenario in order to ruin my career in retaliation for my sins. "And he's my brother," Peter added to my stare.

"Your firm'd better give me a job after this," I muttered to Angelica.

"The firm would have given you a job long ago had you not shown your buttocks to one of the senior partners," a modulated voice behind me said.

My back instantly straightened, and I rotated slowly on stiff legs to face my father. "Maybe the senior partner shouldn't have told a fifteen year old boy that he was an ass?"

"I don't see the correlation," Desmond Glass said, giving Peter and Darryl a look so full of distaste, the tip of his nose nearly became one with the space between his eyes.

"Really? Calling me an ass...me showing my ass? You got nothing?"

"Your dad's a silver fox, prettyboy," Darryl informed me while giving my father the once, twice, and three times over. "If I was into old men, and he didn't already have something long and hard stuck up his ass..."

Maybe I could like Darryl.

"Why are you here?" I asked my father.

"Angelica has requested I represent your...friend. Which of them is it?"

"Both," Angelica said at the same time Peter and Darryl muttered, "Neither," while I contributed my ever-intelligent, "Huh?"

Everybody Hurts

Angelica took the crossed-arms-hip-jut stance and made it formidable. And she did it at only a little over five-feet four inches tall and wearing a pencil skirt tight enough to show every mole. "Any minute now I'll have the press outside, a boy fighting for his life in there," she jerked her head to the door behind her, "these two boys questioned by federal agents and prosecutors, and a sixty-year-old man and his thirty-year-old son cannot manage a professional conversation?"

"Are you thirty?" Peter asked with a jaw drop.

"I'm twenty-six," I said indignantly. "Twenty! Six!"

"I apologize," my father said diplomatically—to her. To me he nodded swiftly and then swiveled his gaze to Peter and Darryl. "I'll need to be briefed before we meet with the prosecutors." He pointed his leather attaché case down the hall and motioned for Peter and Darryl to move ahead.

"Austin?"

"Just go with him, Peter. And for God's sake don't lie to him. You can see Cai if he makes bond." *And if you're not arrested.* I was already suspicious about why he hadn't been arrested yet. Even if they knew he wasn't responsible for Nikki the Nail's death, they had to assume he had some culpability. Maybe his age at the time was factoring in?

Down the hall a stream of suits filed into a side room. From the way they held themselves and the dark suits they wore, I read FBI all over them.

"Men in suits," Darryl sighed, catching the line of men and pointing a slim finger. "Eeny meeny miney homo..."

I almost felt sorry for the them. Them being the FBI agents.

Catching Peter's brief flicker of fear, I reached out and brushed my fingers against his just before he walked away. He fisted his hand, which was the only acknowledgement I got for the gesture. The last I saw of him was Darryl leaning over and whispering something in his ear.

"With everything happening all at once, the pressing question in the front of my mind is: Do you love him?"

"I met him a week and a half ago, Angel. Of course I don't love him." I laughed harshly.

The marathon-long talk with Angelica over the weekend had been cathartic, yes, but between us both, the level of melancholy that settled in over those sixteen hours was draining. Now it was as if that feeling was a physical being possessing me; and instantly the sadness and guilt enveloped me.

"Yet you'll risk your job, me, your father, your friends for him?"

I shook my head, "No. I took a few risks because of him, but not for him." How did I explain this weight to her? As succinctly as possible considering she had to go defend Cai soon. "Since I was sixteen there's been this heaviness in my chest. The second I'd meet a woman who wanted to settle down, the pressure eased. As it got closer to the point of actually getting married or moving in together, the pressure would start bearing down again. So I'd fuck it up and find another one and another."

I peeked into the courtroom to make sure we still had time—and maybe to gather myself. When I turned around she was leaning back against the wall, both hands wrapped around the handle of her carrying case resting against her thighs. "I didn't have that with you, Angel. The pressure, I mean. Not in any unbearable way. Probably because you and I were something more than lovers. But last month it started to change. Right after that kid I told you about hung himself." I took a place next to her, crossing my legs at the ankles while the wall supported me. "At first Peter was like that moment when the pressure eased, but it never quite lifted until I acknowledged I was gay."

Saturday, during our long discussion, we had talked about her affair with my father. We talked about Jesse and Dave. I held her while she cried. But she didn't ask about Peter. And we didn't discuss my new found sexuality.

"Just like that?" She asked.

"As terrifying and painful as our breakup was, the pressure evaporated," I snapped my fingers. "I wasn't obsessed with, or in love with, or even enamored with Peter. It was that feeling of relief that I was chasing." I wasn't going to explain to her that it was more than that now. Things were too strained.

Neither of us would be over this soon. That much was clear by the awkwardness of our stances. While we were dating, and even before that, we would hold hands or I would wrap my arms around her shoulders, and she would lay her head against my arm. Now we stood shoulder-to-shoulder, both hurting and missing what we had, neither of us reaching out to comfort one another.

"This is a good case," she said quietly.

"It is," I agreed.

"After this I need time, Austin. It hurts to see you."

It wounded to hear that. "Okay. I'm here. Always. Whenever you want."

She took a deep breath and brushed her shoulder purposefully against mine, before pushing off the wall and stepping through the courtroom doors.

The Lying Onion

"He's with me," Angelica told the bailiff at the doors when he stopped my entrance behind her. I followed her in, acutely aware that I had just tried to open my jacket and flash my non-existent badge. I couldn't remember the last time I had worn a suit and not had it, and my gun, weighing along my belt.

Inside, the courtroom was empty save the necessary people: myself, three at the defense table, two at the prosecutor's, two bailiffs and a court reporter. The only person out of place sat primly on the bench behind the defense table.

Rosafa Strakosha, for that was who the woman behind the hijab had to be, sat with her hands folded neatly in her lap. Only part of her hair was covered, the black tresses matching neatly with the hijab's silk material and appearing almost part of it. Like Cai, her nose was wide and long, her lips full and broad. I set her age at late thirties, early forties—and only because I did the math using her son's age as a guideline. She could pass for thirty, easy. She turned red-rimmed eyes to me and then lowered them. Her reaction made me curious as to how we would mesh living together. A gay man and an Islamic woman. Something else to worry about, along with the plethora of other things.

I slid into the bench across from her. Not because she made me uncomfortable, or that I wanted to appear in favor of the prosecution, but so that I could read Cai's face throughout the bond hearings. He wouldn't be able to speak much, that was

Angelica's job, but I wanted every opportunity to judge him. In fact, the whole thing wouldn't take longer than maybe ten to fifteen minutes—not enough time to get a superb read on the boy. Which reminded me—I twisted in my seat to check out the gallery. Why was the courtroom so empty?

I should have known then that something was different about this whole case.

When the deputies brought Cai in, I studied him closely, seeking signs this kid had put bullets in the back of two men's heads. His skin looked taut and his eyes hollow. Stress was not playing kindly with him. Orange did him no favors, either. The vibrant color against his olive skin made it almost seem jaundiced. There was an air of innocence about him—maybe in the way his shoulders were hunched or the constant blinking? I couldn't place what it was. He dragged his bottom lip through his teeth multiple times; his lips were red and raw from the gesture. He never raised his eyes, even when the judge entered.

I understood why Angelica was so adamant about my standing up for this boy. He was way out of his element.

"All rise. Superior Court of the State of Colorado, County of Denver, the Honorable Judge Morris D. Whitaker presiding, is now in session. Please be seated and come to order."

Judge Morris Whitaker was a tall, heavyset black man in his early sixties. I'd been in his courtroom many times, and he'd been to dinner at my parents' house, with my father, on different occasions. He was a genuine believer in the justice system, but he was fair—and liberal, something I never believed my father could handle in a friendship. And something that would benefit the defense.

"Attorneys of record?"

"Angelica Jackson for the defense, Your Honor."

"Good afternoon, your honor, Will Schoemacher for the prosecution."

Judge Whitaker read through paperwork. I listened quietly as the bailiff read the case number.

I was just getting comfortable in my seat when the charges were stated. My jaw dropped as I heard the words "Felony Murder with deliberation". First degree murder. They were charging Cai with premeditation? I was absolutely sure that was only because of Cai's history. I could see second degree murder, but not first. The boy had been raped.

"Mr. Schoemacher, what is the state recommending for bond?"

"Your honor, the defendant is charged with first degree murder with deliberation. He left the home of the victim, retrieved a gun, came back to the victim's house and shot him execution style in the back of the head. In addition, Mr. Strakosha is a suspect in another premeditated murder and has a history of fleeing from previous crimes. He has a network of friends and family more than willing to hide his whereabouts from authorities. His mother has close relatives in Albania tied with organized crime, and the two men he has lived with for the last eight years have a history of criminal activities. We are asking for remand, Judge."

"Remand you say? Shocking." Judge Morris smiled. The court let out a nervous laugh. "Ms. Jackson?"

During bond hearings each side is heard only once. The point of the hearing is to decide bail amounts or remand/release. Remand in a felony murder case was sometimes granted, if the defendant posed no flight risk.

"Judge Whitaker, Nikolaj, who just recently turned sixteen, trusted Mr. Alvarado, a close family friend, enough to get into a car with him, as he had done many times in the past. Nikolaj was driven to Mr. Alvarado's home at two in the afternoon and assaulted for seven hours. His girlfriend was finally able to help him escape when Mr. Alvarado fell asleep from excessive narcotics use. Mr. Alvarado learned of Nikolaj's escape," Angelica continued, placing a hand on Cai's shoulder, "and then dragged Nikolaj back, threatening to kill both my client and his caregivers. Nikolaj feared for his life."

"Is this your motion for an affirmative defense, Ms. Jackson?" Judge Morris grabbed a file from his desk and perused it, then shot Angelica a glance over his bifocals.

"It is, your honor. Additionally, I would like to add that Nikolaj's mother is here. Mrs. Strakosha has been in federal witness protection since becoming a witness against her husband and his partner. Her willingness to leave the program in order to be here speaks volumes as to family ties. She will also be residing at the home of a local decorated police officer, along with FBI and US Marshal protection." She pointed in my direction. "Detective Austin Glass is ready to post bond for Nikolaj. I believe it speaks to Nikolaj's intention to fight these charges that a decorated Denver police officer is willing to take the boy into his home and post his bond."

Oh yippee. A woman hiding from the mob. In my house. With a murderer. Joy. And speaking of Cai…

An affirmative defense. So Cai did kill him. Not that I blamed the boy one bit. Hell, I'd go dance on Alvarado's grave, if anyone bothered to claim his body, let alone bury him yet. I seemed to have made the right decision notwithstanding my previous objections.

"What about your client's friends, Ms. Jackson. Is he willing to adhere to a no-contact order?"

"Judge Whitaker, the two young men in question have taken care of Nikolaj since he was eight years old. Furthermore, the prosecution's characterization of two federal witnesses seems unduly harsh, seeing as how they have no criminal records after the age of twelve, and both Pyotr Dyachenko and Daniel Corozzo were set to testify against Nikolai Dyachencko before his demise."

Oh, Christ. Peter was like an onion of lying layers.

"His demise?" Will sent a wide-eyed glare of incredulity at Angelica. "What Ms. Jackson fails to mention, Judge Whitaker, is that her client is the person responsible for Nikolai Dyachenko's *demise*—which was accomplished with a gunshot to the *head*."

"Nikolaj is not charged in that case, your honor," Angelica said with a serene smile. "Mr. Schoemacher is well aware of that fact."

"This is a bond hearing, not a preliminary trial, counselors, save your arguments. I've heard enough. FBI agents, US Marshals and a detective vouching for the boy and taking him into his home is enough to convince me that he isn't a flight risk. Wait," Judge Whitaker chuckled when the prosecutor took a breath as if ready to speak, "The defendant will surrender his passport if he owns one, and he will wear a monitoring bracelet that confines him to Detective Glass's home. Bond is set at one million dollars. That should be enough to ensure everyone gets Nikolaj to court."

A million dollars. Shit. The bang of Judge Whitaker's gavel was like pressing a button on the toilet, with my money resting in the bowl.

I left the courtroom before finding out the preliminary hearing date, and called to arrange a money withdrawal from my private banker. Due to the hefty balance in my account, getting the money wired wasn't going to be an issue—even after hours.

Revenge is Best Served Using an Albanian Woman and the Sociopath She Calls Son

"Neat trick having the courtroom cleared," I said to Angelica. "How'd you get Will to agree to that?" The fact that we weren't surrounded by reporters was no longer shocking.

"I threatened to petition a gag order, and he knew Judge Morris would issue it."

"Bought time to avoid the press."

"That was the idea."

We were standing outside the courthouse awaiting the completion of Cai's paperwork so we could take his mother to my home. Rosafa had insisted on staying as close to Cai as possible, but after an hour inside, Angelica and I ventured outdoors into the evening sun until all were ready.

"No coincidence that my father and the feds were questioning Peter and Darryl while that hearing was in progress?"

"No, it wasn't a coincidence," she agreed. "Desmond and I made the appointment specifically. Cai asked me to keep Peter out. This seemed the best method."

"Clever," I said. "You know the feds aren't going to go after an eight-year-old case where an eight-year-old was the shooter."

"It's doubtful," she concurred.

"Then why pursue an affirmative defense? He can't be innocent, Angel, at the same time as declaring he did it in self-defense."

"I can't talk to you about the case. And don't badger Cai about it, either, while I'm not there. His Miranda rights are in effect."

I gave her a two fingered salute and shot off a frustrated puff of air. "What's the mother like?"

She truly grinned then, and my immediate thought was, '*Something wicked this way comes.*' "Oh, Austin," she laughed delicately, "I quite possibly have revenge without even intending it."

Whatever my response was, something akin to a parachute fail mid-fall, it made her laugh harder. "What does that mean? Because from where I'm standing, hounding me into allowing a killer in my house was fair enough revenge."

"I did not hound," she hedged.

"Angel?" My voice sounded desperate to my own ears, but she took no pity on me. Before she could answer, Rosafa exited the building with a contingent of black-suited men close behind.

Cai's mother held no judgment in her appraisal of me, but she turned to Angelica immediately after the once over. "Thank you, Miss Jackson."

"You're quite welcome," Angelica replied with an outstretched hand which the older woman took. Angelica laid a hand atop their clasped palms and inclined her head my way. "This is detective Glass."

"Austin," I said, holding out my hand.

Rosafa's grip was as firm as her nod. "You paid the bond, Detective Glass?"

"Austin," I repeated, "And yes. It shouldn't be long now before we hear my private banker weeping." Either she was tired or she didn't get my joke. That was okay, it was a lousy joke.

"They said they will take Nikë in patrol car. The officers would not allow me to ride with them."

"You can ride with me," I said, picturing Cai with the abject misery of someone who'd been arrested, jailed, and was facing life in prison, carted off once again in a patrol car.

"Actually, Austin, the Marshal service needs to drive us. We also need to pick up her bags from the hotel and talk about a few things."

More than grateful to have less time around a woman who was examining me like I was belly-button lint, I offered a brief smile. "Peter and Darryl still in there?"

"No. Your father drove them home."

"I'll see you at the house." To this day I maintain that I did not run to my car.

Since I had to give my information to the county clerk, and was recorded as Cai's place of residence, the police department called to confirm when I would be home in order to set up the home monitoring system. Without Peter and Angelica to rain down sheets of guilt, I began to process the fact that this boy was going to be in my home, ruining my career. I spoke tersely to the officer making the appointment and hung up, continuing my drive.

"Jesus Christ, what have I just done?"

I answered myself silently, *You're tethering Peter to you, using Cai as the chain.*

Home Alone VI — Avoiding Mother and Son

Peter was waiting on my front stoop, resting his waist against the wrought iron railing next to Darryl, who sat on the top step. When they saw me, Darryl stood and Peter tilted to see beyond me.

"They're bringing him in an hour and half," I said.

"Rosa?" Darryl asked.

"When Angelica and she are done discussing things." I slipped past them and unlocked the front door, holding it open so they could go inside.

"Did he look okay?" They asked in unison, though Darryl's was a variation of the question. It was then I noticed the grocery and duffle bags they carried in.

"He looked tired," I said tactfully. I couldn't ask the questions I wanted to about Rosafa, not without giving away that she was a federal witness. I had a feeling both boys knew, however. And I really didn't want to ask questions. I wanted to take Peter upstairs and finish that kiss we started earlier. "What's in the bags?"

"Cai's paints and clothes. Groceries. Rosa will want to cook, and Cai has sugar...issues." Peter smiled fondly.

"Issues?" I showed them to the kitchen and watched them unpack. They unloaded Pixie Stix, Pop Rocks and Skittles by the bagsful onto my counter. "That's not sugar issues. That's a candy factory."

Darryl grinned over his shoulder while stuffing my cabinets and fridge with various items. The only things I recognized without reading labels were eggplant and rice. Or maybe I saw lettuce or cabbage? "Cai will be having major sugar withdrawals," Darryl said.

"He uses it sometimes to combat the sadness." Peter shrugged.

"Cai's got sugar and Peter's got—"

"Darryl," Peter warned.

Peter's got what? Intravenous drug needs? A whip collection? He masturbates using those slippers? What?

I really needed to get over those slippers. I kept fixating on them because it was so out of place with his personality. But the more I learned about Peter, the less I was beginning to think he was as hard-edged as he liked people to believe. The way he kissed, the way he touched me, and his patience with me—those didn't fit with who I perceived he was. It was time to stop basing everything I thought about Peter on the fact that he was a prostitute.

"Do you two want to stay here?" Both of them turned slowly to me. Peter's mouth was parted, his eyes wide. Darryl tilted his head.

"As in move in?" Peter asked, clenching and releasing fists against his thighs.

"As in, stay here for a few nights a week until the preliminary hearing. Bond may be revoked then." Move in? I remembered when even the thought of that sent me from the person I was dating into another woman's bed. This, though? This made my heart skip beats in a whole new way.

"Sure, a few days I meant." Peter exhaled loudly. "Thanks. I can sleep on the sofa."

You can damn well sleep in my fucking bed. "It's a pull out, you two can share." *Over my dead, rotted-to-dust corpse!*

After Cai murdered me, of course.

"Be right back," Peter said to Darryl and took my hand, pulling me upstairs two at a time.

"Remember to use protection," Darryl sing-songed.

"I don't have my gun," I answered idiotically.

I followed Peter heedlessly, or more specifically, my penis followed blindly. How many blow jobs can we fit in before Rosa and/or Cai get here?

In the bedroom, Peter slammed the door with his foot and shoved me against the wall, pushing my blazer over my shoulders.

"We need to talk." *Oh, shut-the-fuck up, self!* We didn't need to talk. We needed to suck, or fuck, or do things that I had been waiting a week and half to do. Things I had been waiting my whole post-pubescent life to do! Things that had to do with stuff coming in my mouth, not words coming out of it.

"Say, 'Suck my dick, Peter'. That counts as talking," he said, devouring the thoughts from my head with every press of his tongue and lips against my neck.

We needed to talk. I had no idea what to expect from Rosafa, or how to take care of Cai. I wanted to know what Darryl had meant about Peter having something like a sugar obsession. I wanted to know about—Oh, fuck. Peter's tongue teased between my now-opened shirt panels, leaving a hot trail down my chest and stomach.

My hands delved into his hair, releasing the herbal scent of his shampoo and cinnamon—a scent I was sure he sprinkled on. I inhaled it deeply, using the wall to push my hips to his mouth. "Suck my dick, Peter," I echoed.

He scraped his teeth along my side. "Now say, 'Please', Austin." His fingers pried at my belt.

"Please, Austin," I grinned, pushing him further down, until he was on his knees.

My Ex-Girlfriend Was Right—Men Do Suck

His lips closed over my cock. My grin quickly disappeared under a gulping breath. I automatically closed fists around his hair, guiding his head, my gut twisting with the same heat of his mouth.

"Fuck," I breathed, quickly sucking in another swig of air. In a state of rhapsody, I looked down, watching his fucking porn-star mouth work over my cock. My thumb grazed over his cheek where long copper lashes rested. He blinked them away, a sea of blue open to my gaze. My head fell back, eyes closing with that image while I exhaled in bursts.

I tried to remember anytime I had felt even the smallest fraction of this pleasure. Nothing came to mind. It wasn't just the sex, it was Peter. It was the image of Peter with his perfect red lips gliding up and down my cock, and his deep blue eyes, gazing up at me with a fascination I could read clearly.

"Peter," I moaned, stroking his hair, bleeding it through my fingers. He yanked my hips hard, burying my cock in his throat and twisted his head in such a way that my legs threatened to give way. My hands flew to the wall for support. He shoved my ass hard against the wall, licked around the head, drove me crazy with his tongue, and then swallowed me again. I saw stars.

Thrusting forward with every slide of his tongue, my breath stuttered, held, stuttered again before I was just panting every exhale. His tongue ring clipped over the ridge of my cock. "Fucking...fuck." I jerked in his grasp. My knees trembled, and pleasure expanded from my groin like tipped bottle of heated oil. The intense wave of heat tore through my body. I tensed, grabbing Peter's hands, crushing them as I shot into his throat. He didn't stop sucking—making my body jerk with his tongue ring bumping up against my sensitive head. I laughed breathily, pushing him away and sliding down the wall to sit with my knees near my chest.

"Christ...I can't...That was..."

The doorbell rang before I could finish. Or maybe I couldn't have finished anyway. I was spent—in every way.

"Good?" Peter laughed, placing his hands on the floor at either side of my hips and leaning forward to my ear. "Hope you took notes. There will be an oral quiz later."

"Notes? Fuck. I don't think I could repeat that if I had a video and step-by-step instructions."

Video...mm.

Chapter Fourteen

Understanding Everything—Unfortunately

I was smiling while quickly throwing on clean khakis and a shirt. I felt like I finally had a handle on decoding Peter's actions. Little things were coming to me, each with a depth of understanding.

So far, I knew he shut off when he felt frightened, angry or confused. I imagined that had to do with his having been a hustler and lived in a household run by a mafia enforcer; or a combination of those two. In each circumstance, having the ability to turn off sentiment was essential. All the moments of warmth he showed me were a little more momentous because I knew this tidbit about him.

Today I got another piece in the Peter puzzle. He used sex to express gratitude and elation—or his version of them. Maybe also to avoid painful or uncomfortable subjects?

When I had agreed to help him with Cai, he responded by initiating sex. No, not just sex, intimacy. Peter had been intimate with me. He'd shown me patience and warmth.

The same thing just happened downstairs when I asked him if he wanted to stay here. Immediately I was dragged up to my room and attacked.

Most people showed gratitude or happiness in a smile or a bouquet of flowers—Peter sucked cock.

Not a whole lot of debate on which of those choices was my favorite.

Not a big surprise, either, that as I jogged down the steps a few minutes after him, I considered all the ways to make Peter grateful—frequently. But at the resounding slap I heard, my feet skipped the last three steps in one bound, my smile crumbling simultaneously with my landing 'thud'.

Peter stood in front of Cai's mother, his cheek slowly reddening even as the rest of his skin paled. His jaw clenched, his nose gave a slight tick; and then his face became blank with a single blink of his eyes.

"You take my boy from me, Petya! Whore yourself? This is what you do with my child and your life?"

"Hey," I intervened, standing between them, my back to Peter. "You hit him again, and I'll arrest you."

"Stay out of this, prettyboy," Darryl said, somewhere behind me. I didn't bother to check, but I knew he was next to Peter.

"You are not family!" Rosa glared at me.

"It doesn't take family to understand that blaming a boy who was twelve years old, is on the wrong side of insane." I wasn't going to ask which kind of 'family' she meant.

"We did what we had to do," Peter said, a repeat of his earlier assertion to me.

"You did what you had to do? You sell your body when your mothers cry our hearts onto your empty beds?"

Peter said nothing in defense of himself or Darryl.

"Mama Rosa," Darryl began in a stern voice, "We couldn't stay. Not after what happened. Would you rather Cai go to juvie?"

"Nikë is better now? Raped by drug dealer? Taking test for AIDS? Going to jail for murder? What have you two done?"

"That's hardly his fault," I said, but Peter seemed to disagree.

"It's my fault, Rosa. I—"

"You. You are a stupid boy! I should slap the backend not the face." She stepped around me and pulled both Darryl and Peter into a hug. She was taller than Darryl by an inch, and Peter was a few inches taller than she, but Rosa seemed to dwarf both of them. "Stupid boys." Each "boy" had his chin in her hands as she looked them over. I summoned all my detective skills to handle the scene I was witnessing. Nothing. For all my experience, I threw up my hands in defeat. There was no understanding these people. "You go call your mother," she told Peter.

"Does she know?" Peter asked, lip white under the force of his teeth.

"I tell her some. You tell her everything. She is flying here soon. Go now." She turned to Darryl as Peter slipped off with his cell phone tucked against his stomach. "You, help me cook."

I was left standing there as Darryl trailed after her into my small kitchen. "What the hell just happened?" I asked the empty room.

Darryl called from the kitchen, "You just met an Albanian mother."

From my point in the living room, I watched Darryl and Rosa pull things from the cabinet and fridge, until Rosa looked up and raised her brows at me. "Vendosur tabela." Rosafa flitted her hands in my direction. Having not had interaction with a mother—other than Dave's, who was a soft spoken and soft-all-over woman—I didn't know what Rosa expected. I checked behind me in case someone *there* was the something I was supposed to do. "You fix table," she ordered.

"I don't have table," I replied, still reeling from the questions battering around in my head from these encounters.

"What kind of person has no table for eating?" She tsked.

"The kind that lives alone and eats drive-thru food?" I retorted.

"Maybe you live alone because you eat garbage. You think of that?" She appeared to be massaging someone on my counter. I leaned over the half-wall which served as a breakfast table to see her rolling dough, not noticing Peter until he leaned against me, sending a thrill of heat down my neck.

"I live alone because I'm an asshole. Since my fiancée just found out I like *cock*, I'll continue to live alone" The word emphasized around a mild sentence sounded even more harsh. I didn't care. I was hoping the shock of my words would shut her up.

"Elton John does not live alone. Doogie Howser does not live alone."

She had me there. Peter and Darryl were hiding smiles, one burying his against my shoulder and the other grinning at the eggplant he was chopping.

I didn't have to come up with a response, thankfully, as the doorbell rang, signaling the end of this round.

Cai was here.

How to Win Friends and Alienate Albanian Table-lovers

Shoulders drooped, his hands rubbing along the wrists, eyes downcast, Cai looked broken and defeated. That was my first thought. My second was that Kelly Fitzpatrick, the patrol officer who last week praised my self-described death-defying capture of Prisc Alvarado, could eviscerate me with his glare.

Officer Kelly "Mick" Fitzpatrick carried a satchel which he opened immediately upon entering, and from which he pulled a black box. "I'll need a flat surface," Mick said.

I flourished a hand at the living room, giving the officer free reign and ignoring the way he harshly bumped my shoulder as he walked past.

Peter wrapped a hand around the back of Cai's head, enfolding the boy into his arms. Darryl ruffled Cai's hair as they both murmured things that I couldn't decipher. I was busy watching that scene instead of Mick, until he was finished setting up and cleared his throat.

He had completed installing the home-monitoring system and called everyone's attention to the black box sitting on my mantle; then began a list of do's and don'ts with regard to the judge's orders.

"You cannot leave the house without prior authorization. You cannot drink alcohol, partake in illegal substances or associate with known criminals. Do you understand, Mr. Strakosha?"

Cai nodded, eyes wet and wide, pushing a soft, "Yessir," from his lips.

Mick continued the explanation, tossing a not-unexpected sneer my way. If this is how a patrol officer treated me, my fellow detectives would be a nightmare to deal with. With that done, Mick took his leave. Not before throwing a last caustic glower at me. I, of course, smiled brightly and gave him two thumbs up, dropping the act as soon as the door shut behind him. I shifted my gaze to the small group of embracing houseguests, which now included Rosa.

My whole adult life had been about being a cop, and my entire future was wrapped around the FBI. I should've been angry at Angelica for lying about Cai's innocence. And at both her and Peter for beguiling me into ruining my career with a misrepresentation of the facts. At the same time, I had difficulty imagining this boy killing anyone. One look at Cai's face, his innocent eyes and his childlike smile, and I couldn't find the will to be angry at any of them, or even to fault him for killing Alvarado.

Not that I agreed with vigilantism, but there was a small part of me that sided with Cai. When the kid lifted his eyes, the gratitude set in their grey depths whispered the shameful fact that I actually approved of what he did.

Besides, I agreed to all of this. My choice. I had to stop blaming everyone else.

"Your paints and sketchbook and some clothes are in the guest room," Peter said, pointing to my hallway.

"Enough. We will eat now. I cooked Bourek," Rosa announced, pushing everyone towards the living room with waving hands. I looked at my watch and saw it was nearly ten in the evening. I couldn't remember the last time I had eaten.

"What's Bourek?"

"Heaven in puff pastry," Darryl answered me. And no exaggeration here—he pranced to the kitchen to retrieve a pan from the oven.

Once everything was laid out on my coffee table—Bourek, pita bread, feta cheese salad—we sat down to a morose meal. The only one who enthusiastically devoured his food was Cai. His attention was single-mindedly focused on the Bourek, which resembled egg rolls made of puff pastry and were stuffed with, I hoped, beef or lamb. But hey, I braved menudo, right?

Though the Bourek tasted, as described, like heaven, dinner was a subdued affair. Everyone focused on Cai, watching for signs of a breakdown. Between Rosa's disapproving tsks every time someone had to lean over to put something from my coffee table onto their plate, and the continued silence, I grew uneasy half an hour into the meal. At the most recent 'tsk', I considered asking Rosa where she might find space for a dinner table, but the thought of her answer made my ass clench.

"You all decide your sleeping arrangements, I'm going to bed. Dinner was fantastic. Thank you." I stood up at the same time Rosa and Darryl did. Peter grabbed the leftovers and carried them in the kitchen. I was not going down the possessive road of 'get your ass upstairs'.

Waiting until he made a return trip to the living room, I told him, "You're welcome to join," in lieu of begging.

"I'm going to stay up with Cai for a while," he replied.

There it was again. Cai above all else. Silly to expect more after the short period we knew each other. From now on, I'd keep reminding myself just how short that period was.

Darryl and Rosa were busy loading my dishwasher despite already knowing I had a maid who came in to do just that. I didn't miss their not-so-casual glances our way.

I said my goodnights and avoided two-stepping the climb upstairs by the smallest of restraint.

In my silent, lonely room, I stripped to boxer briefs and crawled into the cold sheets, trying not to conjure up images of Peter climbing into Darryl's arms.

Whore-Colored Glasses

I woke up to Peter spooning me from behind, his teeth chattering in my ear, "Cold," he whispered while he insinuated his legs between and over mine.

"Try clothes," I said, feeling his body mold against me.

"You're warm."

"If you're here about the oral exam, I'm playing hooky," I said groggily.

He yawned in response, nuzzling the back of my neck. "Too tired to get off," he murmured and settled into the embrace, hips pressed against my ass. His nudging hardon started a chorus of beats in my pulse. I stiffened—in more ways than one.

I wasn't used to this Peter. The one who affectionately cuddled with me while he shuddered from my air conditioning. "Good," I lied. A brief flicker to my bedside clock read 3:22 a.m.

When his hand slipped down my chest, resting against my stomach, my brain twitched on as the slew of questions chugged through it. "I thought you were sleeping with Darryl?"

"Are you telling me to go sleep with Darryl?"

"I'm trying to figure out why you're here."

"Because I like you and you invited me?" He rolled off me, and I twisted to watch him push a hand through his hair. In the diminished light, the strands resembled the shade of oxygenated blood. A sense of foreboding started a shiver at the base of my spine.

"You like me, Darryl, and who else?"

"Are you asking me if you and me are exclusive?"

"Definitely not. We barely know each other."

"I haven't decided if I like your jealousy," Peter mused.

"I'm not jealous over a guy I met a week ago." Yes, I was. Fucking ridiculously jealous over a guy I met a fucking, lousy-ass, goddamn week ago.

"My father married my mother three days after they met."

"Your father also killed and maimed people for a living. How about we just place him in the Not-To-Emulate pile?"

"And obviously you can't marry me," he continued as if I hadn't spoken.

"Obviously."

"It's not legal in Colorado."

"Which is of course the only reason I wouldn't marry a whore I met a week ago, who plays me like the Philharmonic's conductor, and alternates between hostile, affectionate, murderous, manipulative and horny. We'd have to put Sybil on the fucking license."

"Who's Sybil?"

"A woman with multiple person— you know what? That's not the point." I twisted full around to sigh at him.

"I thought we were discussing a question, not a point."

"Then answer the fucking question."

"I did. You just had your whore-colored glasses on and didn't believe me."

"You like me."

"Yes."

"Or you feel obligated to me?"

The beat of silence was my answer.

"Okay. So what if I do?" He shrugged, pulling his knees up and leaning back on his hands. The sheet fell below his waist. So did my attention.

Christ. "Because it's just another way of whoring yourself!" I forced myself to search his face for a response. He lifted a shoulder.

"Again. So what? I'm attracted to you. You like me. You want me. That's why you're doing all of this, right?"

What was I going to answer? That I wanted to save him from himself? That I didn't want what happened to Jesse, to happen to Peter? That Rhonda Pendergrass had given me a taste of what was to come, and that I was wrapping a chain around Peter if I had to, in order to keep him from becoming that.

"I'm just supposed to accept your obligatory fucks and call us even?"

"Maybe I'd be up here for a different reason if every word out of your mouth wasn't 'whore'?" He said it so calmly, just resting back on his hands, staring at the ceiling, breathing slowly, that it was hard to tell if he was angry. It took a little work on my part, studying the way his mouth trembled an in the dark, to consider maybe he was *hurt*.

"Yeah, well, I'm an asshole," I said.

I could barely make out his flash of teeth. "Do you think you could quit analyzing things long enough that we can get some sleep?"

Curling over on my side, back to him, I waited to see if he'd take up his previous position. The bed dipped and moved as he shuffled down into it, but the only touch he offered was a hand slipping briefly over my hair. "How's Cai doing?" I asked, swallowing a lump of emotion.

"I...wanted to warn you," he hesitated.

"Warn me?" I twisted again to check over my shoulder. Were they disposing of a third body downstairs?

"He's painting your living room as a thank you."

"Huh." I frowned and thought about the work I'd seen in their house. "My decorator might screech, but I'm okay with that."

"Your decorator? *Seriously?* How did you *not* know you were gay?"

"Never mind, it's not me that's the asshole, it's you." I responded, punching my pillow and getting back to my sleeping position.

Peter snorted.

"Go to sleep, Detective." I was already halfway there when he murmured those words.

Blow Job or Coffee?

The next time I awoke, the clock read 4:07 a.m. Peter's nose was once again nuzzled into my neck, his hand casually strung over my hip. And he was snoring. Loudly. Or maybe it only seemed loud due to the proximity of his mouth to my ear. It was, I guessed, what caused my way-too-early wakeup call.

I felt guilty about doing so little yesterday with regards to the case—besides attempting to tank Del and Marco's part of it. I needed to get some energy and get cracking. Luis would expect I had made some progress—suspended or not.

Mornings were never my thing. Coffee, a workout and random places to rest my face were required before I could fathom work. Sliding out of Peter's embrace, I stumbled to the shower and started pushing myself to alertness.

Once I was scrubbed clean, teeth brushed and eyes half-way to opening, I threw on clean underwear and sweats, then sat on the bed to pull on my socks and sneakers.

"Coffee?" Peter mumbled and sprawled across the bed.

"No blow job?" I leaned over to tie my shoes.

"Sure," he stretched, catching my sideways glance when he pushed the sheet off his waist and exposed his bare cock, an appendage which I'd spent the better part of the shower trying *not* to think about. Now there it was, curving up against his lean stomach and—

"I was joking," I lied.

"No you weren't," he yawned and flexed his hands until the muscles in his arms and chest tightened. My stomach flopped lazily.

"No, I wasn't," I agreed. "Maybe when you're not comatose." I rotated back to grin at him, but he was asleep. I wanted nothing more than to lick him from chin to groin. Congratulating myself on my restraint, I instead covered him with the sheet and went downstairs.

Cai Redefines Dork

The entire living room: floors, cabinets, sofas—everything—was tarped using my two-hundred dollar, Egyptian cotton sheets. Skittles wrappers and empty Pixie Stix straws littered the area and sugar-dust glittered all over. The phrase 'while bits of sugar-dust danced in the sheets' popped in my head.

Cai was sitting on the back of my sofa, wearing jean overalls that were twice as big as he was and thin with wear. They were the same pair, I dared to guess, that I saw him in the second time we met; and they had enough paint to satisfy a Skittles commercial. Oddly, his white t-shirt was pristine.

He stared across at the mantle, or wall, which I noted was no longer cream-colored, but midnight blue. The contrast with my red, brick fireplace was stark.

"Are you trying to will the monitoring box to stop working?" I grinned, walking into the kitchen to start the coffee.

"Um...no?" He frowned and continued zoning out. The wall being the centerpiece of his world.

I watched him while I got the machine ready—this boy who had Peter so enthralled. The bean grinder switched on, and he tilted his head like a bird catching a hunter's footsteps.

"I give up then. What are you doing?"

"Um...watching paint dry?"

"Do you always answer in the form of a question?" Throwing a leg over the sofa, I planted both feet on the cushion next to his and sat beside him.

"No?" he said, flaming cheeks framing his dimpled smile. Okay, he was charming in his own way.

"So what are you doing?"

"Oh...but..." His blinked at me. If his brows weren't pulled together in such befuddlement, I'd have thought he was fucking with me.

"Watching paint dry? Literally?"

"Can't, um...start until it's done. The primer's done. I can't start until the primer's done. Painting. I can't start painting until the primer's done."

I could only stare back at him. It was like he thought faster than he talked, but didn't wait until he had a full sentence. Was that his meds? "I have an Xbox," I pointed out and then went to point at my laptop as well, only to see a sheet covering my coffee table. "And somewhere under that mess is a laptop. I even have porn."

"Oh...um..." More blushing and a small shuffle away from me. "I, um...porn..."

"Gay?"

"I—" He studied his knees. "Reckon I'm not sure, sir."

I remembered why he was in his predicament suddenly and cursed my own stupidity. "Sorry, that was insensitive. I also have tons of regular movies."

Smile flashing, he said, "Yessir. It's okay," in a strained voice.

"Sir? Sir's my father. Actually never mind. My father is 'Dick'. I'm Austin." His skin practically glowed with shades of red most artists would kill for. "It's okay if you are, you know?"

He laughed boyishly and granted me another shy, approving smile. I had a feeling all his smiles today were just the smallest bit forced. He was trying, I speculated, to keep us all from worrying about him. "Hoped maybe I was like Peter," he said. "Don't think I am."

"Why would you hope that? Do you think something's wrong with being gay, Cai?" The temptation to ruffle his hair was extreme enough that I gripped the edges of the sofa on either side of me and scrutinized the wet spots of paint spattered on my sheets.

"Oh...no." He laughed again. "Just...well, better chances, right?"

"Chances at what?"

"Love?"

He blushed brighter and laughed harder at my look, wiping the back of his hand along his forehead and leaving a cheerful, blue stain of paint behind. "Cai, I might just join your cult."

"My...cult, s—Austin?" He bit one side of his lip. Was that something he's learned from Peter? Or Peter from him? Cai's gesture was unique in the way his nose wrinkled up. It was adorkable. I definitely wanted my kids to be like this one.

Minus the whole cold-blooded killer part.

Unless they were girls and just starting to date. Then I might arm my kids with grenades.

"So what are you going to do with my wall?"

He followed my gaze, head tilting in deliberation. "Something like Starry Night with a more modern gothic feel?"

My head canted the opposite of his as I, too, examined the blue space. "Not that tree, though. It's too creepy."

"The dark, deformed church?" He murmured. "Kinda makes a beautiful sense, don't it?"

I closed my eyes and pictured Van Gogh's masterpiece. The small peaceful town, the brilliant blues of the tumultuous sky, and the golden moon and stars. Among all those bright, hopeful hues, the tall dark tree-like structure could be a distorted version of the church below.

"You think churches are evil?"

Instead of answering he said, "I didn't kill him, sir…Austin." He had the softest voice, his accent buried beneath breath. I strained to hear him.

"You're pleading guilty."

"Yessir. Ms. Jackson didn't approve, either, but then I told her I did it. And how it'd be easier to prove than innocence. Don't think she believed me."

"*You* gave her the strategy?"

He started another blush, piling it on the others. Soon, I was going to have to turn up the air conditioning, before he overheated the house. "Yessir. But I don't want you to think I killed him. I would have. But I didn't. But Miss Jackson can't let me lie in court, you know?"

Which was more shocking? The 'I would have', the 'I didn't', or the strategy?

Or was the most extraordinary thing that I believed him?

"I can understand those feelings."

"Think so?"

"No," I said.

We stared at the wall. The coffee maker huffed and puffed in the background before exhaling in completion. Then silence.

"I was saving myself," he murmured. "Antiquated and silly, but I was."

Before I could joke about antiquated being a big word for a sixteen year old, I told myself Cai could school me seven ways to Sunday with his IQ. While my brain scrambled for something clever to say, he schooled me in another way.

"Did you know that diagnosing bipolar disorder in children is nearly impossible?"

Interesting subject change. I wasn't sure how to go with it. "No, I didn't." I'd let him talk, that was how.

"I tried to kill myself once. Peter stopped…um…hustling, then. After that…he watched me so closely. Kept track of everything. My moods, my actions, the way I slept. Always right beside me and checking my temperature by kissing my forehead or sitting by me at night. Then he started going with Iss more. Dealing drugs. That's how he got caught." He picked a loose thread off his knees and chewed it. I stayed silent. "Iss— Peter told me. He told me to stay away from Iss. But Peter's love is like a vise, and it squeezed so hard."

I closed my eyes and took a deep breath. "It's not your fault, Cai."

"It is," he nodded vigorously. "He told me to stay away from him. I just was so tired of everything. Of being smothered. Told what to do. Don't stay out late, Cai. College applications, Cai. Don't go to Rachel's house, she's bad news. Take your meds. Stay away from Iss."

"It doesn't matter if you went in Iss's car to defy your brother, or even that you stayed in Iss's house. Iss was more than fifteen years older than you. He was a big guy. And, most importantly, you didn't want it."

Working on Vice, I knew the only way to get this through Cai's head was to repeat it over and over. For everyone around him to repeat it. It had to be ingrained. Thoroughly. Much as I wanted to hug him and stop that flow of tears, having a man touch him might trigger something. So I sat there and stared at the wall as his tears fell and hoped my words comforted him.

"Peter never cries.' He laughed, smudging his face again as he wiped it with the meaty part of his palm.

"I'm sure he does. Just not in front of anyone."

Cai shook his head, inhaling the paint fumes that were making me lightheaded.

"You really don't know him." Movement out of the corner of my eye had me checking his fingers, they drummed against his knee in a tidy rhythm, until he reached into the front pocket of his overalls and pulled out some more Pixie Stix.

Without glancing over, he offered some to me. I plucked one out of the fanned bundle and ripped the top open with my teeth. Both of us tipped our heads back and poured the sugary powder onto our tongues. My mouth watered, creating a paste that made my tongue shrink with its tartness.

"This is vile stuff," I slurred, swallowing ungraciously.

"It's awesome. You're just too old."

"Old? You little shit." I tossed the crumpled wrapper at him, bouncing it off his head. If not for the crusted tears on his face, the moment might have been funny.

Out of the blue he extended a key, lifting the palm of my hand to accept it. "What's this?"

"When you came by Saturday, Peter kept trying to get you out of the house."

"Yes?"

"You need to see why. And bring it back here." The smile he gave me was a mixture of naughty and shy.

I squinted at him and stared at my palm to consider the key. "It's not a porn collection or sex toys is it?"

"You really don't know Peter at all," he mused. "He'd never keep that stuff where I could find it. But that right there? That's the key to knowing Peter."

The brass teeth grinded against my skin as I fisted it. My ticking pulse could be measured with parade drums. I was so eager to drive to their house, calling Cai on his terrible play with words slipped my mind.

Chapter Fifteen

Did I Just Agree to More Pussy?

As I stood and readied to leave, Cai spoke up again. "I have an ulterior motive for having you go to the house."

"Of course you do," I said. "You wouldn't be Peter's brother without an ulterior motive for everything."

Cai's attention fastened to his knees. "That wasn't very kind."

"You're right." Properly chastised, I sat next to his feet. "I'm not a very kind person, Cai."

"Cruelty is an effortless answer to fear."

"Who said that?"

"Um…me?"

"You're too wise for your own good."

"You're too cynical for yours," he tossed back, blush and half-grin firmly in place.

"The motive?" I veered us back to the original topic.

"Begone?" Which brought a raised eyebrow from me, followed by a, "My cat," from him. My lips turned down in distaste. He winced and added, "She's litter box trained."

"I don't care if she can flush the toilet. I hate cats."

"Oh…um…okay." His smile dimmed to a point and disappeared. I checked my shoes for puppy fur, and Cai for my footprint.

"I guess it's independent?" I sighed.

"She. And yes. She sleeps a lot, too." His hopeful lip-bitten smile drew a resigned shoulder—slump from me.

"Keep her in the guest room?"

"Yessir."

He looked so happy. I wanted to roll my eyes. "She has a carrier?"

"Yessir, in Peter's room, under the computer desk."

"And stop calling me sir?"

"Yessi— Austin."

"Kid?"

"Yes?"

"You'd better fucking cure AIDS or something." I got up to leave.

"Austin, sir." He stopped me again. I gave up on getting him to stop calling me sir. And nearly abandoned the prospect of leaving.

"You have a dog, too?" I asked. "Maybe parakeets and a family of illegal aliens in the basement? Or genetically engineered humans that you've created to answer everything in the form of a question?"

He blinked and stared. I was either not funny, or he felt very guilty. "Don't snoop?" He said—or asked—even his commands were questions.

"The 'key to Peter' is just out there in the open ready to be seen?" I answered dubiously.

"Did you know Peter didn't finish school past seventh grade?"

Rubbing my face with both hands, I decided Cai was going to parcel out information in bundles of riddles. He would be a great teacher, though, if he went that route; he would always lead the students to discover the answer rather than being told it. "No, I didn't," I replied. The knowledge made an awful sense and brought back my protective feelings toward Peter.

"Even back before we left home, he had a lot of trouble with school. I think he was glad not to have to go to class. But Joe made him and Darryl both enroll in high school. He was sixteen, and they put him in remedial classes because he was so far behind and didn't read well. He just couldn't catch up. He never asked for help. After a few months, he dropped out. But Joe made him get his GED."

"Whatever you're trying to tell me is not computing. Are you saying Peter isn't smart, Cai?"

"No. I'm saying Peter hated school because he couldn't do most of the work. And he only let me help him with a few college courses when he was near failing. He won't ever ask for help for himself. But he's smart. A different kind of smart than you or I. He doesn't think like we do."

"Cai?"

"Yessir? Um…Austin, sir?" He winced again.

"*No one* thinks like you." That brought on another blush. I hesitated. "Anything else before I try to leave, *again*?"

He shook his head no, and became immersed in the blank wall. I grabbed the remote and flipped on the television.

Just for fun, I clicked until I saw a cartoon. Cai's attention slowly drifted to the screen. I left him watching Scooby's and Shaggy's fearful run from a zombie.

Demons

I decided to do my morning run by jogging to the house the boys shared. I estimated it to be about two miles, not even close to my usual workout. By the time I arrived, I'd barely broken a sweat. To prolong the run I did a few laps around the nearby park.

Cheesman Park had a haunted history involving unmoved graves and ghosts. That sordid tale was nothing compared to the rumors about the park now. This century it was known more for gay cruising.

Much like the bar where Darryl worked, rumors abounded of casual sexual encounters in parked cars or in the clusters of trees encircling the park. My first lap revealed they were more than rumors.

As I rounded a corner, a guy in his mid-to-late thirties zoomed toward me with his shirt off. My pace slowed as we made eye contact. I made the mistake of following the curve of his neck down his chest and over his sculpted stomach. It was the first time since meeting Peter that I'd allowed myself an open admiration of another man. The breath I held released when he passed, and I picked up my pace. Seconds later, he joined me at my side.

"Hey," I said, hiding my surprise behind a smile. Dark hair, hazel eyes, very muscular. Hot body. My cock seemed to agree. I was embarrassed by my attraction. Maybe I hadn't fully embraced the gay.

"Hey, yourself. I haven't seen you here before."

"First time."

"That so?" Other than his body, he wasn't gorgeous. Not ugly in any sense, just a regular guy, like me. "Well, First Time, I'm Interested."

Don't say it, Austin. Don't say it. "Where?"

A white set of teeth and small crinkles at the corners of his eyes said he approved of my answer. "My car's on the east end of the park." He pointed directly across from where we were. I kept running. Thinking. Running.

Fantasizing.

My heart beat more rapidly from envisioning his mouth wrapped around my cock than the physical exercise.

It was established that Peter and I weren't exclusive. He'd given me the same idea. We barely knew each other. But I wasn't ready for casual hook-ups if I was embarrassed by just admiring a guy. Instead of letting my cock lead the way, I mentally kicked myself and said, "I think I'm taken, man, sorry."

Mr. I'm-Interested just smiled and jogged on as I slowed.

Goddamn Peter for being the one I wanted.

My eyes never strayed from the path after that. I stretched my usual hour run into nearly two hours. Thirty minutes of which I sported a woody capable of impaling anyone who ran into me. It was not a comfortable feeling. At least my sweat cooled against the summer sunrise. When my legs began to protest, I turned out of the park and walked the remaining blocks to the townhome. Letting myself into Joe's house, I returned the key back into my sock and took a look around.

For three young men living together, the house was remarkably clean. Cai's paint cans were the only clutter in sight, and even they were semi-neatly stacked in the far corner. The TV was maybe a 32" screen, at least five-to-ten years old. The furniture was threadbare, and bits of paint dotted its pilled, green-plaid surfaces. On the battered coffee table, a fan of men's magazines was on display next to a stack of cork coasters. I hadn't noticed these things the first time, because I had been so blown away by Cai's artwork. Now that I could see the furnishings, I was puzzled.

With as much money as Joe had supposedly pulled in, his belongings would have been rejected by secondhand stores. Weird. If Joe was raking in money from his illegal activities, it wasn't spent anywhere in his home. I had to check out the diner's books. Which meant I needed to get out of there quickly.

I stopped in the kitchen briefly, picked up a box on the counter and tilted my head at the aroma of cinnamon. It was strong enough to seep through the foil covering the pan on the counter. When I lifted the aluminum out of the way, a tray of cinnamon rolls answered every question I had about Peter's scent. I grabbed one, polishing it off before reaching the bank of doors in the hallway.

I opened each one, trying to find Peter's room. It was in the far back, connected to the yard by a large picture window. The room was spartan—a desk with a computer, a simple double bed, a dresser and a bookshelf. All had seen better days. Standing at the threshold, I considered spying—because that's what cops do. It would have been creepy though. Looking for evidence was not the same as prying into Peter's personal life for my own edification—which I would have been doing. And which I deeply longed to do. I'd have to settle for what was out in the open.

The paintings on Peter's walls, which I could attribute to Cai, danced with a purity of colors. There were no scenes or discernable images. Just bright swirls of green, purple, red mixed with indigo and black. I likened the murals to the backgrounds of a children's book. Cai had painted joy on these walls.

Other than Cai's paintings, the room was bare of personality. No pictures. No vases. No memorabilia—unless one counted the unfinished liquid near Peter's computer. Some dark-twisted *evil* percolated in that coffee cup near the keyboard. I steered around it, while shaking the box of cat treats I'd found in the kitchen.

The moment I opened the box, something crawled out of the depths of the crumpled comforter. I immediately backed up and stared at the thing.

Demons should not be that small. Were demons small? Or gargoyles. Was it a gargoyle?

I was being facetious, but really, seriously, "What. The. Fuck?"

While I debated whether to leave it here, Begone stretched onto her back and fell off the side of the bed. She grappled wildly until one claw saved her from an ass-meets-floor encounter. The thing dangled there far too long for me to believe she could figure out how to extract her claws on her own. But I didn't want to touch it—her— *it*, to help.

For one thing, the...cat?—looked maimed, or burned. Her random tufts of fur were indiscriminately stuck between bits of pink skin. It was like a four-year-old had used dust bunnies from under the bed to create a collage of fur on a burlap canvas.

Begone also reeked. The thing was a walking biohazard of stale tuna seeped in sun-soured milk.

As if the smell, scarred flesh and bent tail weren't enough, the poor creature had an ear missing, and a marbled white and grey scar from the top of its head down to its black nose.

"I'm supposed to take you home," I told the thing. Begone continued to grasp at the comforter to keep Peter's thin carpet from devouring her. Then she started purring and batting at…nothing. There was nothing *there*.

"You couldn't just smell disgusting and look like an ad for animal cruelty? You had to have the crazies, too?"

Purr.

My brain launched an immediate argument about the beast.

You've already ruined your career, your marriage, possibly your partnership, definitely your reputation, and most likely your house. Are you really going to draw the line at taking a cat home?

It's not a cat.

It means something to Peter.

Everything that belongs to, is about, or has even a cross reference to Cai, means something to Peter.

While I carried on my internal discussion, the cat pushed its back claws into the side of the bed and back-flipped onto the mattress. It finally yanked free from the covers, sticking a furless ass in the air and flopping on its side—without incident this time. While it bedded down, I got to the real reason I was in Peter's bedroom.

Indebted to a Fucking Hairball With the Crazies

The cheap bookshelf reached from floor to ceiling, where it leaned in the direction of the eastern window, as if the wood was still trying to reach for the sun; or the books shoved into it were too much of a burden. They were piled, stacked, stuffed and crammed between college notebooks and packets of computer printouts. Most shelves contained textbooks on Japanese, Russian, Chinese, Italian and Spanish, accompanied by dictionaries in each language. I pulled a few out and flipped through them, discovering Peter had highlighted in each book and written marginal notes.

The notes were vast and detailed. Words circled and the definitions in ballpoint on both sides. I traced my thumb over his writing, feeling the dips in the paper.

The highest shelf contained a different selection of books. These were on parenting, teenage behavior and more than a few on Bipolar Disorder. My heart twisted as I summoned an image of a teenage Peter, suffering through these textbooks, learning how to take care of Cai. It was both heartbreaking and poignant. Reluctantly, I closed the book and checked the other shelves.

How fluent was he in all these languages? As I sat down to flip through the notebooks, the thing—I refused to say 'cat'— rubbed its head against my elbow.

"I've been at homicide scenes that smelled better than you," I told it.

Purr.

"Dogs are okay, but I don't like cats."

Blink.

"Do you know *why* I like dogs and not cats? Because when you're talking to dogs, they don't walk away in order to rim themselves."

Begone continued to orally pleasure itself, while I did my creepy, stalker impression and read through Peter's notebook. I told myself it was only one, and that wasn't too much nosy digging. Then guilt knocked on my conscience. With a sigh, I returned the notebook to the shelf and gave the masturbating cat a grimace.

"You're like a self-published pet porno." It ignored me. "I don't want to see this again," I warned it, flapping a hand at the self-gratification show.

Begone looked up at me from her pretzeled position and blinked.

"Christ," I muttered, dragging a hand through my hair. Why had I agreed to this?

On my way to fetch the cat carrier, I bumped into Peter's desk, jostling the mouse and knocking the screensaver out of function. Up popped a newspaper article with a small picture of Angelica and me, taken at a fundraiser a few months ago.

Detective Austin Glass, son of criminal defense attorney, Desmond Glass Sr. Esq...

I rolled my eyes at my father's title as much as the fact that he was mentioned, prominently, in an article about *my* medal.

...was awarded the Distinguished Service Cross today. Detective Glass entered a convenience store with his partner...

And that word 'partner' would take on a whole new meaning once the press got hold of the new gay Austin. I skipped reading the rest of the article. I knew the story. I now also knew that Peter was nosier than I.

My fingers tapped against my thigh during my not-so-brief time staring at the screen. They were as anxious to check Peter's computer history as I was. The physical effort it required to turn away from the screen was excruciating.

I took a hard look around the room and tried to decipher what it was that I knew about Peter. The fact of it was, I didn't know much. I knew about Cai. I even knew about Darryl. But I barely knew anything about Peter. Except that Peter had no self-identity beyond Cai. He obviously had ambition to do something, if the bookshelves held any clue. He was proud that he spoke other languages, as I remembered him almost bragging on our first date.

My fingers began to tap faster. That certain 'something' was tickling my brain, telling me I had the picture, I just needed to fill it in.

"Why? Why did you say you owed Cai?" I asked his bookshelf. "Why is everything in your life about Cai? You ask me to help Cai. You give up everything for him. You rescue him, protect him, parent him."

I had just started mentally going through my previous conversations with Peter, searching for clues, when a metal clank from the front room diverted my attention. I assumed two things incorrectly: first, that it was Peter or Darryl; and second, that I had nothing to worry about.

Surely either of the guys would have known I was here. Cai would have told them. No one called out to me. There was only silence and then what sounded like a loud bowl of Rice Crispies. I had closed the door earlier, to keep the cat corralled, so after confirming that it was still sleeping on the bed, I opened it just long enough to slide through.

What greeted me in the living room wasn't Darryl or Peter, but flames swarming over the sofa and across the front door like white water rapids. Moments later, a sea of smoke rose up and curtained the room.

Coughs leaked out of me, then became a constant rhythm. With the front door blocked, I peddled backwards until I felt the wall. Bending to where the smoke was thinner, letting the walls guide me, I started to make my way toward the bedroom. A paint can knocked into the toe of my sneaker and disappeared before my watering eyes. I sunk lower to the ground.

Not being familiar with Joe's home, I floundered into the hallway, getting twisted and turned around as smoke fogged the narrow corridor. Fire sizzled against wood and cloth, breathing out heat against my skin, making me grateful for the sweat from my run. On my belly now, I snaked across the floor, blindly searching for any door that wasn't open to a room filled with smoke. I needed Peter's room where I had closed off the cat.

And wouldn't it have to be the fucking cat that saved me?

Begone's howls rose above crackling plastic, while paint cans exploded like popped corn, their lids bursting off, then flying out to smack the walls. One teetered to a rest near my hand. More howls. I followed them while smoke coated my tongue with every cough.

Movies don't capture how quickly smoke follows fire or how swiftly it spreads. It was instantly overwhelming. The heat intensity was like a Miami summer turned up a thousand, smothering degrees. All I could think about was opening that door and trying to fill my lungs with something besides black, hot air. I struggled to get to Peter's room, solely focused on getting out the window.

My chest hurt, and I knew from training that heat inhalation was just as dangerous as smoke, so each inhale was a practice in Lamaze breathing. In, in, in. Out. Out. Out. My fingers walked up the door, dragging my torso and head into the smoke as I fumbled for the handle.

I tested the knob for heat, in case a fire raged on the other side. It was warm but manageable. And by the sound of that cat, there was an ample supply of good air in that room.

A river of smoke followed me as I collapsed inside, slamming the door shut while coughing and spitting out black phlegm onto Peter's carpet. Smoke continued to slither under the door. Displacing Begone, I seized the comforter and stopped the flow. I grabbed a t-shirt from the nearest drawer and wrapped it around my fist, smashing out the window. There was no stopping the coughing, even as fresh air flowed in.

The cat's howls were like claws on a chalkboard. *Jesus, shut up!* I instantly regretted my instinctual inhale. A fresh set of coughs twisted my lungs dry. The roar of fire grew closer.

In a graceful sweep, I scooped up the cat, coughing my own howl as it nail-gunned its claws into my chest. Planting a foot on the bed, I launched myself out the window and into the backyard.

Frankenstein Ass

My shoulder ached from the landing, and for some reason my ass did, too. However, nothing was as agonizing as the fucking cat claws that now ravaged my chest in Begone's attempt to scramble out of my arms. I fought the animal, along with the urge to scream, while my oxygen deprived lungs attempted to suck down air through their pain. *Slow breaths, Austin.*

From seeing the first whippet of flames until landing on my side on the grass, it had only been around two minutes. I allowed ten seconds to lounge on the ground, time enough for the fire to leak into Peter's bedroom and French kiss the shattered window. A flame licked out a few feet above my knees. I scurried away and leveraged myself to standing.

Grabbing Begone's scruff, I pried her claws out of my chest, making pained hissing noises as I swerved to the back gate. Cat hanging in one hand, I fumbled with my arm, pulling my cell phone off the Velcro holder. I punched in 911, just as I kicked the gate open.

The way the townhomes were situated caught my eye. A row of connected families, held together by kindling. At seven a.m. all three were most likely occupied.

"911, what's your emergency?"

"Detective Austin Glass," I rasped out.

"Are you injured, Detective?"

"Yes." This time I was louder, pushing as much sound into my voice as possible, which resulted in a choked coughing fit. The problem was I was trying to make my way from the alley all the way around to the front with a burning pair of lungs. I also had something wet sliding down my legs, a chest bloodied from scratches, a jerking flea-ball in one hand and my cell in the other. "Fire. Detroit Street. 1400 block."

I repeated the address, hanging up before the operator could ask questions. At townhouse-door-one, I began kicking with the shoe that wasn't slick with blood. I couldn't scream, but eventually someone came to the door.

"Get out. Fire." It was all I managed to say before the world swam out of focus. I stumbled forward, caught in a pair of chubby arms—or breasts, it was hard to tell.

I heard yelling from all sides and inside the house. Begone slipped from my fingers. Didn't see which way she went but I tried to get out words to the effect of "Hope you get run over by the fire truck. Fucking cat." What actually came out of my mouth was, "Ho tk fkcat."

"Oh, dude! You're bleeding," a heavily accented voice said. I blinked up into a blurry face with skin the color of toffee, only then realizing I had crumpled to the cement walkway. "We gotta move you, dude, 'kay? Just don't go all whacked."

Fingers attached to my wrist and the waistband of my pants and pulled. I wasn't moved so much as dragged/scooted over the grass. With a wedgie severe enough to permanently add two octaves to my vocal range, I waited, bled and moaned on the sidewalk with a slowly growing community of indistinct faces surrounding me.

The entire world was speaking in rapid Spanish, huddled in a circle around me as if preparing for a beat down. Someone pushed me to my side and jerked down my sweatpants. As Peter's neighbors discussed my ass in a language I didn't understand, someone put that goddamn cat against my stomach. It squirmed its way under my t-shirt to hide.

Why couldn't you hide under the fire truck tires?

I heard sirens and banging, most likely from the fire department. The sea of people opened to allow two paramedics in, then reclosed behind the kneeling attendants. I couldn't see where I was situated on the block, until firemen started to move people away. The skyline revealed itself. I looked past a grey haired EMT to see I was three houses from the inferno that engulfed Peter's home.

As a mask was being slipped over my face, and my sweatshirt was being cut open, the cat attached itself to me once again. I groaned, hissed and mentally promised the EMT my babies as he pulled the thing away.

"Can you tell me your name?" He asked calmly, as if he hadn't just removed a furry demon from my stomach like an *Aliens* re-enactment.

I breathed in a heavy dose of fresh oxygen. "Austin," I replied, resisting the urge to add Darth Austin at hearing the sound of my muffled voice.

"Austin, I'm Jase. Are you the officer who called in the fire?"

"Yes. Bleeding in back."

"Maureen's got you."

I processed another set of hands flitting down my back and over my ass. If this many people were going to be seeing that part of my anatomy, I was going to have to start using a Stairmaster.

Jase flashed a pen at my eyes and checked my pulse with two fingers. "Did you fall or hit your head?"

"No."

"Did you lose consciousness?"

"No."

"Any allergies?"

"No." He continued asking me questions pertinent to medical history. I answered for a minute or two, but as the cognizance of what happened finally pushed through, I began to panic.

My phone was still clutched in my hand. I batted away Jase's fingers in order to dial Peter's cell. It rang twelve times before a voice came on to tell me that user was not answering. I hung up, dialed again. As the phone continued to just ring, I grabbed the EMT's sleeve and twisted it in my fist. "Get a patrol car to my house. Now!" Big mistake yelling. Huge. It was nearly impossible to get the address out between the coughs that followed.

Jase's face twisted in confusion, wrinkles becoming more obvious as he frowned.

"Fire was deliberate." My voice was hoarse, but it wasn't as difficult to breathe. Talking hurt, but wasn't impossible. "The people staying at my house live in that tinderbox over there." The slow slacking of his features gave me hope he understood what I was saying. He picked up his handheld radio and called in to emergency dispatch.

"I need to get to my house." I tried to sit up and weaved as a wave of dizziness crashed into me.

The EMT flattened a hand against my shoulder, gently pushing me back down. "A patrol car will be there in a few minutes, officer. We need to get you to the hospital."

"Dizzy," I said.

Jase nodded. "Smoke inhalation. It's always worse than what people think."

I was too worried to contemplate going to the hospital. If the fire was meant for any of the boys, they were in danger. And my fears were being heightened by the fact that Peter wasn't answering his fucking phone.

Maureen began dressing my wounds, giving me an idea of just how extensive they were by the size of the bandage. I didn't stop them as they loaded me onto the gurney on my uninjured side. But they would have had to pry the phone from my cold dead hands.

My wounds weren't serious enough to warrant a siren, so when Peter finally answered the phone, I heard him clearly.

"Where the fuck have you been?" I barked. Jase cleaned the wounds on my chest with antiseptic. I tried not to make any noise as it bit into each scratch.

"I was in the shower. Why do you sound like you're in a tunnel?"

I was getting him a waterproof phone! "Are you at my house?"

"Course. Is something wrong?"

"Are you alone?"

"I'm not all that turned on by the Darth Vader voice."

I tightened my mouth and pulled the oxygen mask off my face. "I don't want to have phone sex, Peter." Jase choked a laugh, unsuccessfully trying to cover the sound with his fist. "Joe's house just burned down," I said delicately.

The swallow I heard was about as much emotion as I expected from him. "Are you hurt?"

Was I hurt? His first question. Now I couldn't breathe at all. If I wasn't careful, Peter was going to steal my soul. "No. I'm fine. Cai's pet is fine. I don't think anything else survived. Is Darryl still there?"

"Everyone's still here. Did you really save his cat?"

"Have actual tests proven that's a cat?" The ambulance doors opened, and Jase tried to take my phone. I held up a finger which Jase ignored as he pulled my mask back on.

"What's that noise?"

A flurry of hands and voices around me drowned him out a little. "Gotta go. Stay at home," I said falteringly as the gurney jostled me.

The doorbell rang just as he asked, "Are you in the hospital?" I hoped to God it was the police I'd sent and not....

"Don't let anyone but the cops in. I'll be home soon."

I hung up as the speaker system started to page someone.

Jase and Maureen rolled me into a half-sheeted cubicle in the emergency room. "Good luck, officer," Maureen said.

"Yeah. Thanks, guys." As they were leaving, I picked up my phone to call Luis and then remembered. "Hey, what about the cat?"

"FD will take it to the pound," Jase said, walking backwards. "You can pick it up there." He gave me a thumbs up and vanished out the automatic doors.

"Officer Glass, how are you feeling?" The nurse was a big woman. Amazonian-large with a thick middle and bright floral scrubs. I focused on her long fingers wrapping around the curtain and pulling it closed around us as she entered.

"Less woozy. Can I make a phone call in here?" I looked for the nearest exit.

"Let's wait until the doctor has a look at your wounds and I've taken your vitals. Looks like you're going to need some stitches." She smiled kindly as she looked at the chart. When she started pulling on rubber gloves, I prayed that Peter liked scars.

Because I had a feeling I was about to get Frankenstein ass.

Chapter Sixteen

Hospital Admissions

Nurse Jackson's posture could have been used to end an exclamatory sentence. Even as she gently drew away the bandaging from my backside wounds, her body was ramrod straight. Considering her size, the effect rendered me cowed.

I twisted to look at her over my shoulder. "How many stitches?"

Cleaning the excess dried blood off, she leaned closer to my ass, increasing my embarrassment level. "The doctor will say for sure, but between you and me, I'd say ten?"

That didn't sound so bad. "In the biggest laceration," she continued. "The other two will probably require less. Maybe none." Balls of blood-soaked cotton fell from her hand into a nearby silver trashcan. She had big hands. I couldn't stop thinking about it. Man hands.

After taking my blood pressure, getting a patient history, examining my chest and applying an ointment to the inflamed scratches, she pulled a sheet over my hips and slid my chart into a nearby plastic holder before vanishing through the curtains. I lay there, bored, glaring at my blank cell phone. The resident finally arrived just as my eyelids drooped.

"Officer Glass, I'm Doctor Wicks." A bright white smile beamed at me between beautifully shaped red lips and skin the color of polished mahogany. "Mind if I take a look?" He nodded to the sheet. I was alert now. Every part of me was alert now. This was not a good day to start openly admiring men.

"Unless you can faith heal from there?"

He laughed magnificently, rich and baritone with enough treble to raise the fine hairs along my ear. When he pulled the sheet off my ass, I focused on the pain, hoping to quash my erection. "When was your most recent tetanus shot?"

"A few months ago." There was no way I would turn to look at this guy while he examined my ass. When his fingers gently moved over my skin, I prayed he'd have no reason to look at the front of me right then.

Half-naked, lying on my side, with only a thin sheet covering the front, an erection would most definitely be noticed. I tried to imagine Nurse Jackson attempting a penile examination with a metal rod. Unfortunately, her size and manly hands had the opposite effect. If my growing cock was the icing on a shitty day's cake, Peter's arrival in the face of my unwelcome woody, was the cherry on a turd sundae.

"You're hurt," Peter said redundantly, by way of a greeting. Naturally, he had zero expression to clue me in to his thoughts on the matter.

"It's a few scratches."

"From the cat?"

"When I see tests to prove it's feline, I'll believe it. For now, it's just a demon-thing. Hey, didn't I tell you to stay at home?"

Wicks rolled his traveling stool to where I could see him, interrupting Peter's response. "I'm going to numb the area with an injection, officer," he informed me. "You'll feel a small pinch. Then we'll get these stitches in, and your friend can take you home."

"Stitches?" Peter went around me to look. Everyone was going to be staring at my ass today. I was ordering that Stairmaster the moment I left the emergency room. "The cat didn't do that," Peter stated.

"Thank you, Captain Obv— ow!," I growled, twisting to glare at the smiling doctor who was feeding a syringe into my butt cheek. My glare switched to Peter in the wake of the doctor's obliviousness. "Why are you here?"

He stood there, gripping my keys tightly in his palm, the keychain medallion dangling between his long fingers. It was his only sign of emotion. Anger? Fear? Or annoyance? "Darryl and I don't have a place to live."

I closed my lids for a second, then focused in front of me, my deep inhale trying to mask my hurt. Peter moved slowly around to my front, pausing at my knees. I couldn't look at him, couldn't breathe through my humiliation. To say that Peter's arriving with an agenda was painful was an understatement. "Stay at a fucking hotel for all I care."

"Okay," he answered, but made no move to leave.

"Get out of here, and leave my keys."

"You'll need a ride home."

"Hoping I'll change my mind about you staying with me on the ride home?" I sneered.

"No."

The tug of the needle moving through my skin was all I felt as the doctor began sewing. He cleared his throat gently. I didn't give a shit if Doctor Hotness was embarrassed by our conversation. I was angry.

"No?" I echoed. "That's it?" I thought Peter came because he was worried about me. Maybe cared about me a smidgeon? Instead, I found out he needed something else from me. I was livid, frustrated and dangerously close to wanting to punch his face in just to see something, anything besides apathy.

"Cai said thank you for saving the cat."

"Get out, Peter," I replied tiredly. He could shatter my soul right now, it was so fragile sitting there in his palm.

"You need a ride home," he repeated.

"Stop calling it 'home', like it's *your* home. It's my home. You were just visiting. Emphasis on were."

"Okay. You need a ride to your home."

"All done," the doctor said quietly. No smile in his voice now. Peter and I had sucked the joy out of the room. "I'll be back in a few minutes with some prescriptions and instructions on how to care for the wound."

Neither Peter nor I said a word as Wicks left. I stared at the metal trashcan, Peter stared at me.

"Do you even have money for a hotel?" I ground out.

"I can get money."

Another moment of pathetic tension enveloped the space between us. I wasn't sure how much more of this my heart could take. It was already on the verge of collapse. One more soul-crushing event short of deadened. The thought of Peter turning tricks again, or 'a gig' would be too much to bear. "Just stay at the fucking house."

"Home," he said.

"Whatever." I answered despairingly.

"I liked it when you called it home."

My stomach released a swarm of fluttering.

I squinted up at him, trying to understand how he could pack so much into words without a single emotion showing on his face. Then the flood of understanding showered over me. "You could have asked me when I got home."

A hint of a smile passed over his lips. He looked to the curtains, either in hope or worry that we'd be interrupted again. What was his smile indicative of? That he cared? Peter was robotic only when certain emotions threatened to overwhelm him.

"Come here," I ordered, the same soft tone I used way back when I realized he hadn't stolen my money. He didn't immediately step forward, waiting a few seconds before his hips were parked in front of me. His eyes turned down to watch my thumb brush against the breadth of skin visible between the cargo shorts and t-shirt. "Are these my shorts?"

"My clothes were dirty." There was no missing the quiver in his voice, even as he tried to muffle it by barely moving his lips.

"You're such a little shit sometimes," I said, tugging at his shirt until he crouched in front of me. I searched futilely for anything in his face to tell me what he was thinking. "How many hospitals did you call before finding me?"

A one shoulder shrug, then, "This one was closest to our house."

"Is it so hard to admit you care?"

I'd never seen such a direct, expectant gaze from him. "You tell me. Is it?"

"Touché," I replied, pushing still-damp hair off his brow. "You scare the hell out of me."

"You have all the power, Austin."

My laugh was rueful. "Is that what you believe? Do you think I have any power when it comes to you?"

Footsteps and a tentative, "Officer Glass?" from the other side of the curtain made Peter straighten and move back. The fist in which he clenched my keys was covering the spot my thumb had traced. I also noticed the ridge of defined flesh above the waistband of his boxers. My clothes, it seemed, were just a bit too large for him. I resolved to buy him a closetful in my size. And…were those my underwear?

"All clear, doctor," I called out.

With Peter in the room, I stopped taking an interest in how attractive Doctor Wicks was, or what he was saying.

"Let me just get you on your way with the prescriptions. A nurse will be by with some scrubs you can wear home."

My gaze was constantly floating to Peter's bare legs and stomach. I succeeded in retaining less than half of the instructions for caring for my wound because of the distraction. Wicks left with his jovial smile and a small chuckle as Peter took the prescriptions and instruction sheet from my hand.

"Are you hard?" Peter eyed my crotch.

"No," I lied.

"Because of the doctor?"

"I just said I wasn't hard."

"He's a lot older than I am."

I couldn't help but smile at Peter's insecurity. It was about time *he* had some for a change. "He also smiles a fuck-load more than you. But you're the one I'm taking home."

"We could try—"

Nurse Jackson interrupted Peter this time. "Here you are," she announced, handing me a pair of green scrubs, slippers stacked on top. The cost of both combined could be around $.50, but I had a feeling my bill would move the decimal two places to the right. Good thing cops had decent health insurance. Which only served to remind me, I was probably going to be out of work longer than the week's suspension.

"How long did he say for these stitches?"

"Seven-to-ten days," Peter and Nurse Jackson said simultaneously.

Shit.

"No showers for 48 hours, officer," the nurse added as I toed off my bloody sneakers. "Unless you can tape a plastic watertight seal over the stitches." The clunk of my sneakers hitting the ground was like a cue at the end of a joke.

A trail of darkened blood caked my ass from cheek to foot, and soot speckled like mold across the rest of my body. The only clean spaces were where the cat claws had ravaged it and the attendants had cleaned around each gash. I leveraged to get a better view. The doctor had warned me to be careful while I was numb, but I hadn't expected to only feel the slight tug of flesh as I sat up, gingerly leaning to one side. Looking down at my filthy legs and chest, I could only imagine the fun of sponge baths.

"We'll help him," Peter assured Nurse Jackson, smirking at me when I raised brows at him.

"He's lucky to have a brother like you," she said with a gentle hand on Peter's shoulder. I choked out a noise that sounded remotely like Jeffrey the Tailor.

"Yes, ma'am." Peter grinned.

Little shit.

"You're ready to go, officer. An orderly will be by in a few minutes to wheel you outside. Oh, and before I forget, there's another officer here to take your statement."

"Thanks," I said, thinking decidedly non-brotherly thoughts about Peter.

The nurse exited, leaving the curtains trembling in her wake.

"Who's 'we', Peter? Because that better be me and you, and not me, you and Darryl. Or me, you and Rosa. Or me, you and anyone. If I wanted that many people to see my ass, I'd become a wh— stripper."

At the correction of my language, Peter's smile became one of those moments that threatened to stop my heart.

"Turn around so I can get dressed," I said, twirling a finger at the ground.

"No."

"No?"

"You're going to need help."

He was right, but I was still suspicious. I was right to be. The scrubs took longer than necessary to put on, mostly because Peter kept breathing onto my skin when he had to lean forward to tug up my pants or when he assisted in lifting my hips. At one point I would have sworn to almighty God that he blew into my ear. I nearly fell off the table.

Fucker.

I had to meet the officer taking my statement with a raging boner. And wearing scrubs.

With no underwear.

When I was stopped by an officer Briggs, I succinctly told him the story from when I entered the building until the ambulance took me away. I made sure to mention the strong odor of turpentine, which I was certain had something to do with my dizziness. Peter waited for a few minutes, listening in stoic silence, then exited to retrieve the Jag. Neither of us told the officer that Peter was the homeowner. Maybe he just wanted to get home. Or maybe he didn't care about Joe's house. Or maybe neither of us trusted the police *not* to arrest him.

Briggs asked a few pertinent questions, fishing for information that I had anything to do with the fire. Satisfied with my responses, he left me his card and then left me longing for my badge and gun as he radioed in. I wheeled past him, feeling a little sorry for myself.

Hump Day Goes Down in Flames

Standing outside the hospital doors, waiting for Peter to pull my car around—the car no one but me was supposed to drive—I filled in the time by calling Luis. It was better than thinking about someone else handling my baby and one true love, Arturo.

"Happy Hump Day, Luis." I grinned. His slow sigh was music to my ears.

"The whore staying with you?"

"Peter," I corrected defensively. "His name is Peter."

"Is Peter staying with you?"

"Not even a, 'Happy Hump Day'?"

"Can it, Glass. This is important."

Luis's tone narrowed my eyes at the ambulance bay, my smile twitching downward. "Yeah, he's staying with me. What's up?"

"Was he there last night?"

"Yeah, all night until I left at five-thirty-ish this morning. Going to tell me what this is about?"

"There as in, you saw him, or there as in he was around?"

"First time you've questioned my honesty, Luis," I said quietly. My Jag pulled up, and I held a finger up for Peter to wait, turning my back on the car.

"Not questioning your truthfulness," Luis said after a few seconds. "Your judgment, but not your honesty, Glass. Now did you see him or not?"

"Give me a time frame."

"Three to three thirty."

"He came up to bed at twenty after three," I said, squinting in remembrance. "And he was still there when I woke up again at four, and after I took a shower. I'm guessing his brother and Darryl will vouch for him before that."

"A murder suspect and another whore?" Luis huffed. "What about the other one? Darryl."

"Ask the two cars of feds outside my house if either of them left. Black SUVs, no shame and no technique."

"You're under surveillance?"

"Their witness is under surveillance," I said. "Protection most likely. Now will you tell me what happened."

"The diner's toast. Five injured. Fire started in the kitchen. Alarms were disabled."

I silently tumbled this information around. "Ask me why I called you, Luis," I said, pondering how I was going to tell Peter this news.

"Your place in flames?"

"Joe's house," I corrected his guess, and then told him what happened.

"Fire alarms disabled there, too?" he asked.

"Until you mentioned it, I didn't even think about it, but, yeah."

"Same doer. He hits the diner first, house next."

"Couldn't get to my house past the feds," I speculated.

"Or didn't know they were all there."

"Or that," I agreed. "But the feds weren't trying to hide their presence. Maybe the fire starter wasn't after the kids. Maybe the doer was after someone else. Any of the injured names released to the press?"

"Not yet."

"Maybe our fire starter was after some*thing* else?"

Luis grunted. "Get that kid here to look over the evidence."

Looking down at the disaster that was me, I sighed. "Give us fifteen minutes."

Driving While Intoxicated

Sliding into the passenger seat was an adjustment in attitude. Immediately, I went for the steering wheel and bit back a curse when my hands came up empty.

"Buckle up," Peter ordered. He waited to pull out until I had complied.

"Head to the station downtown. The big building on 14th."

"Police plaza?" He frowned and swerved off the road, parking the car near a stop sign. "You need to take a shower and get into bed."

"You can get me into bed later. Right now, we need to look over that evidence box."

"You want Darryl there, too? He looked through most of the stuff."

"Is he at home?"

Peter's smile killed me. "Yes. He's home."

"Was he last night?"

"Sure." Peter answered. "I carried him to bed before coming up to you. Why?"

"He was drunk?"

"Asleep. He takes Ambien and Benadryl because of his weird shifts at the club. Doubled the dose last night because he hadn't slept since Cai got arrested." Peter tapped the steering wheel. It was so like what I did when my mind was buzzing, I had to check his face. A miniscule wrinkling of his lips as they pressed white was my only clue that he was puzzling things together. "Why? Did someone get murdered?"

"Why would you say that?"

"Don't do your fucking interrogation thing on me."

"I wasn't." Yes, I was. "The diner's gone."

"Another fire?" His fingers gripped the steering wheel so hard his knuckles blanched.

"I'm sorry."

"Was anyone hurt?"

"Yes. We need to drive. Now, Peter."

"Fine. To the restaurant."

"No. We get Darryl and then to the police station. You both need to interview with Luis and stay out of the way of the cops at the scene."

"My friends are there." It was the second time I'd heard a tremble in his voice.

"Peter, you can't help them. All you'll accomplish is getting in the way, or getting questioned under suspicion of arson for the insurance."

"I was with you."

"Darryl wasn't, and I didn't see you for part of the evening."

"He needs a lawyer." The white knuckle grip threatened to break his fingers, I put a hand over his, gently prying them away.

"Peter, *you* need a lawyer." The way I was positioned, angled off my stitches, prohibited leaning across, but I wanted to grab him and shake him senseless. "Get out so I can drive."

"You can't sit properly," he argued.

"Then get moving." He pulled onto the road and took my hand.

I picked up the phone, intoxicated by the way his hand stayed in mine, shifted gears and returned to lace our fingers together. As awkward as it was to speak into the cell and hold his hand, I refused to move it after I'd dialed.

My Father, The Philandering Asshole

I didn't miss the way Peter looked at me when I asked to speak to Desmond Glass.

"Whom shall I say is calling," Nina, my father's assistant with bigger boobs than brains, asked.

"*Who* shall I say is calling," I corrected spitefully.

"That's what I asked," she replied, wheezing her squeaky voice into my ear.

Oh, Lord.

"Nina, tell my fucking father I'm on the fucking phone or I'll fucking wring your fucking gold-digging neck." The fact that she had slept with me behind my father's back may have played a part in my assholeness.

Unsurprisingly, she hung up on me. "Cheating, conniving, dumb, stupid, *bitch*!"

I took a deep breath and redialed. "You need a lesson about how to treat women," Peter said.

"Nina, *please* put my father on the phone." I smiled at Peter with teeth clenched so tight, plaque could crumble off.

"I'll see if he's in."

I knew damn well he was in, I could hear his cigar humidifier. Which meant the cow was in his office. Most likely under his desk giving him a blow job. This bothered me why? I wouldn't have recognize my mother if she gave *me* a blow job. Why should I care if my father banged his dumb secretary?

"It's your son," Nina whispered loud enough to shatter glass.

"Austin?" My father said into the receiver. Not 'son'. Not 'boy' as his father referred to me. Just Austin, the client. I heard papers shuffling and a thump. What I imagined was dipshit Nina bumping her head as she tried to stand under the desk. I wished it had been her skull cracking against my father's nuts.

"You have more than one son?" The silence and measured breath wasn't something I thought about at the time. Later I'd put it together. But now, I was too focused on Peter's hand in mine, his thumb tracing circles over my skin. "Your clients are about to be interrogated downtown."

"Are they in custody?"

"No. They're coming in voluntarily, at my request."

"I'll need a few hours to wrap things up here."

"You mean unwrap Nina's mouth from your cock," I snapped.

"Don't be crass, boy." Ah, there it was. The earth was back in its orbit now. I bit back an automatic apology.

Even after all these years bile rose up at the mere thought of apologizing to my father. "Meet us at the downtown station in two hours."

"Very well. Have them call the office immediately." He hung up without so much as a goodbye.

"*Asshole*," I muttered and laid my cell on the dashboard.

It didn't take long to reach the house. Seconds after I hung up, Peter hit the brakes at the mouth of the alley. "I should warn you, there's reporters everywhere."

Fuck.

"They better not be in my fucking parking spot."

He drove on, flipping the visor down as various types of cameras and video equipment were shoved near the windows.

"Detective, is Nikolaj Stakosha innocent?"

"Detective Glass, has he told you how he murdered Nikki the Nail?"

The shouts were muffled through the glass. I ignored them and gently grabbed Peter's arm as he crawled the car past them. "Listen, don't respond to any of them. Not 'no comment'. Not 'yes', not 'no'. Don't even move your head in affirmation or denial."

He turned the car off and looked around, then calmly met my eyes. "Okay."

"Whatever they ask, you don't say a word. Whatever I say, you don't repeat, don't agree or disagree, just walk past them. Some of the more unscrupulous reporters will not hesitate to edit your nod or comment, attaching it to a different question."

"Okay."

"Keep your eyes on the ground."

"*Okay*," he sighed.

When we climbed out of the car, we were swarmed. I pushed Peter ahead of me as questions accompanied the jam of microphones and cameras at our mouths.

The last thing I needed was to alienate the press. With my job on shaky ground and my fellow officers cursing my face, I wanted allies, not enemies. So, although I wanted to scream at them to get off my lawn, waving a cane and smacking my lips; as coolly as possible, I closed the gate behind us.

At least with the press here, an arsonist wouldn't have a chance at my house.

Would It Be Okay If I Stomped My Foot Until Someone Let Me Fucking Shower?

My living room smelled of herbs and garlic. A lot of garlic. The aroma was overwhelming all other senses. It didn't help that it was nearly noon and I had only eaten that cinnamon roll hours earlier. The way my stomach rumbled in appreciation said it was more interested in food than the rest of me was. What I wanted was a shower and a change of clothes. Green scrubs were comfortable until you started smelling cinnamon and male sweat, and then they were just an embarrassing show of your manhood.

"Is it true?" Cai asked, chewing his lip and then his thumbnail.

Rosafa exited the kitchen, a kerchief tied to her hair, clothes covering all her skin. No wonder sweat beaded the exposed parts of her face. With so much going on, I forgot to ask her about Muslim propriety. Too late now. "It is all on fire?"

"We can talk more later. Right now we have to get downtown. Cai, I'm sorry but the cat will have to wait. It escaped and is probably at the pound."

"Are you okay?" He asked, wide grey eyes taking in my appearance.

"Yeah, kid." I grinned at him, watching the relief roll out of his shoulders with a breathy laugh.

"I go get the cat," Rosafa offered. "There is casserole here. You need to eat."

"I will, when I get back," I promised. "Really we'll talk and eat when we get back. Both of you need to stay inside. Don't talk to the press and don't let anyone but the police or fire department inside the house."

"Cai, I'll get Begone," Peter said, ruffling his brother's hair as I had wanted to do hours ago. "Do what he says."

"Where's Darryl?"

Peter turned from the kitchen and looked around, as if my question had just reminded him that our party was missing one person. "Probably still sleeping."

"No, he went to the hospital," Rosa informed us. "He said your friend is hurt."

"It's Tilda, Rabbit. Darryl saw her on the news," Cai pointed at my muted TV as all of our heads swiveled to the screen. The news had changed, obviously, but tickers paraded at the bottom announcing the injury count had risen from five to seven. Peter immediately picked up his phone to start texting.

"I need to shower. Badly. Tell Darryl to get here," I ordered and climbed the stairs, suddenly aware of the sharp pain in my ass, and not at all from what a few days ago I'd assumed would be its cause.

Peter's Trick

Because of the wounds, I had washed my hair in the sink and was now sponging off the dirt away from the shower's spray, turning off the water between rinses. Peter's conversation filled in the quiet spaces.

"Flowers... Tilda loves daffodils... No one else we know?...We can come get you... We don't have the money to—... He said we could stay here... I don't know how long. Days maybe? Enough time to get some cash together... Insurance is going to whoever got hurt, Dare. Just set up another gig."

Doubtful Peter knew that I could hear him speaking on the phone through the bathroom door. Or maybe he didn't care. But the conversation was battering my already bruised spirit, and I wished I weren't hearing it.

"Then set up a private one if Kevin thinks it's too soon. We need the cash!" His whispered hiss slid under the door and sucked the air from the room. My forehead pressed against the tile.

The sponge in my hand released a gush of water meant for a final rinse, but in the heated squeeze of my fist, it drained out unused. I drowned out the rest of the conversation by keeping the shower at full blast and standing out of the jets as I sponged myself clean.

Once finished, I toweled off and harkened back to my discussion with Peter at the hospital. I was trying to find the place where I had incorrectly concluded Peter and I had reached an understanding about us. How could I have been so wrong?

It also reminded me about what he was going to say. Maybe the clue to what had been going on in his head was in the statement the nurse had interrupted: *"We could try—"*

We could try what? A threesome? We had been talking about my attraction to the doctor. Was that his answer? Was it all about sex with Peter? Maybe I had been reading things into his behavior that I had wanted to see. Maybe I should just forget about it all.

Wrapping the damp towel around my waist, I tucked in the edges and opened the bathroom door. Peter was lying on my bed, arms stretched above him and shirt riding high on his abdomen, exposing the thin trail of hair from bellybutton to waistband. Maybe it was all about sex with me?

"Peter?" His eyes were closed, body still except for the deep rise and fall of his chest.

"Hm?" The sea of blue opened up, tugging at my breath until it surrendered in a heavy exhale.

"Is your friend okay?" *Don't do that 'gig'. What were you going to say at the hospital? Am I just a means to an end?* Today was like reliving the first time I brought him home. Coming out of the shower with him lying on my bed, me pulling clothes on under my towel, avoiding looking at him as if he were the sun and I'd go blind from staring.

"Not really, she had some smoke inhalation problems and burns. But we'll take care of her. Everyone else we know is okay. Lots of people got hurt from trying to get out too fast. And some cars hit each other in the parking lot."

The towel fell as I buttoned my khakis, I leaned to pick it up, powerless to stop my gaze from meeting his. "Good," I whispered, eyes following the curve of his neck. I cleared my throat and tried again, "Good."

"You like me stretched out on your bed." The come hither smile wasn't sexy, it was pure torture for me.

"We have to go," I replied, ready to throw everything I felt for Peter in the nearest trash and tie up the bag. Let it fester there with my already condemned sanity.

"Why are you pissed?"

"I'm not," I said, sounding defeated and more tired than I'd felt in years. I was worn out more from my confused status with Peter than because of the fire, my job, Cai and any number of other things combined.

Grabbing a shirt from my closet I whirled around when his palms whispered over my naked back. "Ask me!"

"What?" He laughed nervously.

"Ask me for money, Peter." I grabbed his wrists and pushed him against the wall.

He looked everywhere but at me, no attempt to free himself. He was definitely stronger than I, but right that second I didn't care if he was being patronizing. If it forced him to answer me, then patronizing I'd take.

"No," he murmured.

"Ask me for money, goddamn you." I punctuated it with a slam of his wrists, hard enough to jar, but not painful—I hoped. The next time my shirt wouldn't be there to cushion it. I was that pissed.

"I have!" He spat back, easily extricating his hands and pushing me away. I grabbed his arm, turning him around.

"For Cai. For sex. Not for you. You'd rather go fuck a bunch of strangers—"

"I don't fuck anyone but Darryl anymore," he denied. "It's just a show for a bunch of voyeurs. No one gets hurt."

"I get hurt!"

"I don't have any other way, Austin."

"You have me. Ask me," I said, hating the pleading sound in my voice.

"No."

"Jesus Christ, why the fuck not?"

"Because I don't want you to be a fucking *trick*!" The shout was so loud I felt the vibrations along my spine.

I had no time to process his admission. His lips crashed into mine, sending my back into the wall. Whether from the pain clawing up my spine from my injuries, or the pleasure from his heated lips, I moaned loudly, folding my hands into his hair.

Chapter Seventeen

My Ass!

This was what I'd been waiting for. Peter, stripped of emotional restraint, wildly tugging and biting, sucking at my mouth, fingers like claws in my back. I pulled him closer, my lips parting invitingly. He invaded my mouth with his tongue darting in time with his grinding hips. I hoped to God that his frantic hands weren't going to move lower; the last thing I wanted was to interrupt this because I was screaming in pain. Thankfully, his grip eased, hands caressing instead of groping, mouth gentling against mine.

"We don't have time for this," I mumbled, curling my tongue along his upper lip.

In response, he dragged my bottom lip leisurely through his teeth before releasing it, leaving it throbbing with pleasure. "Then…stop kissing…me."

"I don't think I can." I kissed his cheek, his jaw, his eyelids. His mouth. I leaned into him and lost myself in his taste.

My phone shrilled on the bureau next to us. I ignored it, focusing instead on the slide of stubble against my jaw, the rough hands trailing sun-like warmth over my ribs. I lifted my chin, directing his mouth to my neck, but he had something else in mind.

I was in too much of a hazy stupor to resist when he flipped me around. My hands flattened against the wall, heart racing as he resumed kissing my neck and skated his tongue down the center of my back. He cupped and squeezed my crotch, then unbuttoned my pants. They glided silently to my feet. I inhaled sharply as my boxers slid down just enough to expose my ass. I barely comprehended what position Peter was in, and what it could mean. My last functioning brain cell was consumed by my excitement.

The room was silent, save for my harsh, escalating breaths. Bracing against the wall, feeling his hands and lips at the base of my spine, I nervously complained, "My ass hurts."

"You've been sticking the wrong things in it." I sensed his lips twitch against my skin. "Use my cock next time," he said, reaching around and snapping the elastic front of my boxers. "Hurts less."

"Asshole," I muttered.

"Was that a directive?" He bit the uninjured side of my ass, sending a trill of heat from his mouth straight to my cock.

"No," I replied breathily. I heard the rustling of his clothes. My fists clenched as I looked over my shoulder. Something brushed lightly against my stitches. My hips bucked away. "Ow. Fuck!"

"Sorry. I'll kiss it better."

"About time you kissed my a—*ah, Jesus, God!*"

He flicked a tender spot near the stitches. "Don't be a jerk."

I ground out, "What are you doing?"

"Applying ointment because you were too stubborn or stupid to wait until I had put plastic over—" he flicked again, causing a string of expletives to explode out of me, "—your wound."

"All right, already. Fucking-hell-shit-damn! You bastard!" My cell interrupted my tirade, playing an old NYC cop show theme. Luis's persistence was a pain in my ass—a second pain in my ass. With gritted teeth, I stretched for the phone, punching the answer button while trying to ignore the fact that Peter was on his knees fondling my ass. "Glass— ah, mother-fucking-shit!" I muffled a groan when Peter began applying the cream, as unprepared for his touch this time as I was the first. Delicate or not, it fucking hurt.

"I don't want to know what you're doing, just get your ass here," Luis said. "You're late."

"Yeah." *My ass is occupied at the moment.* I garbled out an apology between pained, choppy exhales and did my best obscene-phone-call breathing into the receiver.

Luis, neither impressed nor aroused, hung up.

After slamming the phone down, I pressed my forehead against the wall, unleashing another stream of curses. "What the fuck is that you're spreading on there, acid?"

"It's Neosporin. Be good, or I'll poke you again," he warned.

"Asshole." I laughed breathily. "Also not an instruction. Especially in the context of poking."

"Nice. You kiss your mother with that mouth?"

"I don't know my mother."

His fingers stilled. "Why?"

I didn't want to talk about my mother. Not while my ass was bared and Peter was on his knees attending to it. There were other things I wanted to discuss—or enact. But the words tumbled out anyway. Because I could cockblock myself better than any fucking phone. "She left for Europe the day my dad brought me home, and she didn't come back."

"She's back now," he said softly, resuming his task.

"Good for her."

Given the positions we were in, I was unnerved by the silence—I didn't know what to expect next, but based on the immediate history, I was convinced it would be unpleasant. "She's dying," he said.

What to make of that? Was I supposed to feel something? I didn't. Maybe a little numb. "Well, I'm sorry for her. Are you done back there?"

He pulled up my boxers as an answer and snapped the elastic back into place at my hips. Grabbing my pants, I jerked them on and turned around. So much for Peter at my naked ass. I wasn't going to ask the very wrongly-timed question of how he liked it.

"That's it?" He looked up at me, brow pinched.

"What do you want me to say? I don't know the woman." I moved to the closet, turning my back on him to grab a shirt and tie.

I heard more rustling behind me, and then he was leaning against the closet door. "Then why are you angry all the sudden?"

"I'm not angry." I yanked a shirt off the hanger and shoved my arms into it, fingers shaking so badly I could barely button it. Peter gently brushed my hands aside to do it for me.

"Sero-something. Liver disease?" he hedged. Both of us watched the quick rise and fall of my chest; another dead giveaway that I was upset.

"Cirrhosis," I amended. "And fuck her. I don't give a shit." The muscles in my mouth were beginning to hurt from being pinched.

He nodded, remaining silent while his fingers ascended the button ladder. "You didn't ask me how I knew about it."

"My asshole father and his passive-aggressive way of getting me to help. He told you, assuming you'd relay it. I'm surprised he gives a shit. When she croaks, he'll be free and clear to continue schtupping that fucking gold-digging bitch of a secretary."

He smiled indifferently, flipping my collar up before reaching for the tie and winding it around my neck. Wisely, he changed the subject as my anger amplified. "Schtupping?"

"It means—"

"Do you think I'm stupid?" He pulled tight on the knot and glared at me.

"It was just an old-fashioned word. I thought— Never mind. And, no, I don't think you're stupid. Anyone who teaches himself seven languages without finishing seventh grade is not stupid."

"Sixth grade." He smoothed out my tie and looked up at me. I frowned, checking the knot. "I didn't finish sixth grade. I wasn't good at school."

"Even more impressive," I said softly, thumbing his lips. "Thanks for the help."

He nodded again, pulling away to sit on the bed, propping up on his hands. "I'm not fluent in them, either."

I grabbed my suit jacket from the closet as a distraction, trying to think what he was driving at. "It's not like you to belittle yourself."

"That's not what I'm doing." He blew a puff of air, sending his hair flying wildly off his brow.

"Then why diminish your accomplishments?"

"Why use words like 'schtupping' and 'diminish your accomplishments'?"

"Because they're words I know?" Jesus, I was becoming Cai, answering questions with questions.

"Exactly."

If I had a list of my most used phrases with Peter, this would be zenith among them: "Huh?"

"You and your big words and fancy education. Your two-thousand dollar suits and your ridiculous million-dollar haircut that barely needs to be combed after a shower. You're either pushing me away by calling me a whore or trying to fit me into your world by making me more than what I am. I'm just Peter. A guy who didn't finish sixth grade and had to have his younger brother help him with college work."

I was stunned by this progression of conversation and required restraint not to lash out at him. Or check my hair. "Why are *you* so angry now?"

"Why are you trying to make me some gifted student who magically learns things and has a great future?"

"Why wouldn't you have a future?"

"I have a future, just not one that fits into what you expect!"

"And just what do I expect?" Our voices progressively grew louder.

"Some fancy linguist or interpreter or something like that. It's not going to happen."

"Because you won't ask for help? Is it money?"

"Oh, it's always about money with you, Austin, isn't it?" He stood up, our noses barely inches apart. My eyes flickered to his lips, tongue darting out to wet my own.

"You're lucky my ass hurts or I'd throw you on the bed and show you exactly how much it isn't about money with you!" I twisted on my heel, snatching the cell off the bureau and slipping it into my pocket as I shrugged my jacket on.

"And if your ass didn't hurt I'd fuck you so hard into the mattress you'd forget every word except 'more' and 'please'!"

I froze in the doorway, heart marching like an army platoon, and came face-to-face with a wide-eyed, red-faced Cai.

"Oh, um…yes…well…there it is," he mumbled, eyes darting frantically around as he pointed down the hall. "I—there's—they—" His face was so red I half expected the glow to light my way downstairs as he zoomed away mid-sentence.

When had I become so self-involved? Answer: always

"Shit," Peter muttered, ready to chase after him. I stopped him before he could get out the door, slamming it shut and closing him in.

Cai had dialed my anger down to simmer, allowing my tone to come out calm. "This conversation isn't over," I said.

"We're not fucking, so if that's what's—"

"Peter, goddammit, you're the one with a mood disorder!" He glared at me. I sighed, running a hand through my hair. "How did we go from helping me with my tie to your screaming at me?"

After too long a wait, he answered, "I don't get you. Your mother is *dying* and that doesn't even merit a thought. You've haven't known us two weeks, but you do all these insane things for Cai and me, and Darryl even. What matters to you? What do you want from me? It's not just sex, and I don't have *anything* else."

I had been so focused on my own problems that I had completely disregarded Peter's. He'd lost his home, his books, his livelihood—and was about to lose his brother. He was now completely reliant on me. He was even wearing my clothes. Not even minutes had passed since he'd had to help me with my expensive suit, and before that I'd told him to ask me for *more* money. If he was keeping some kind of tally, he was destined for a terrifying number at this point.

I prodded, thinking I'd show him that not everyone expected quid pro quo. "I don't expect— Peter, Joe didn't want anything from you, did he?"

"To be near Iss."

"What?"

"Iss wanted me. Joe wanted Iss. By keeping me, Joe had a hold on Iss." I was understandably confused. It must have shown on my face, because Peter looked away and added, "Iss was obsessed with me—or that I reminded him of that guy you both knew; Jess. He'd call me that sometimes when we f—" I watched as his eyes widened slowly and turned to meet mine. "Oh, *now* I get you," he said quietly.

I blinked slowly at his accusing look, almost taking a defensive step backward. Not that he was giving me more than the faintest clue of his anger and hurt. I read it in the tiny lines formed between his brows and the slack parting of his mouth. "Jesse's hair was blond and his skin less fair, but you could be his brother," I admitted.

He sighed, shoulders almost imperceptibly deflating. "So I'm supposed to be him for you, too?"

"No." I stepped closer to Peter, fists clenching at my sides to avoid shaking him. "However much you look like him, you're not him. It's like comparing honey and sugar. Jesse was uniform, no complexities. And he was weak. When things got difficult for Jesse, he stood on the hood of his father's car, hooked a belt over a tree limb and around his neck, then kneeled down. There's not even a miniscule part of you that's either passive like that or would give up."

"Then I don't know what you want from me. I have no hope of paying you back, and you know it. Not only that, you don't want me to earn money the only way I know how. I don't know if I'll even get back to school. You tell me to stay, and then tell me to go. You push everyone out of your life: your mother, father, that woman you were with. I don't have any footing here. I don't know where to step. If I go the wrong way, do I get shut out? Does Cai?"

"Whatever else happens, Peter, I won't turn my back on you. You have a place to stay until you get on your feet. I'm not finished," I remarked when he opened his mouth to interrupt. "No strings attached." Which meant he was free to make money however he saw fit. Not a situation I was happy with. "Unless you want strings."

"You don't see how insane that is?" His eyes were so wide and glassy I could see my reflection cast in their blue depths.

Our dynamic was shifting. For whatever reasons, Peter and I were done being coy. It was time I laid it all out there. "Goes hand in hand with being crazy about you, doesn't it?" I smiled ruefully and stood there letting the room try to breathe out our tension. My exhale was a tangle of shaking stutters, letting him know how difficult those words were to say.

"You're such an ass," he whispered. "Why didn't you just fucking say that in the first place?" My eyes had closed again as he approached, winding his arms around my neck and pressing our foreheads together. The scent of toothpaste and my shampoo hovered around us. Our labored breaths filled the silence.

"What kind of idiot thinks I do this for just anyone?" I gripped the sides of his t-shirt and pulled him in.

My eyes opened as he lifted my chin. "How did a privileged boy like you get to be such a fucked up man?"

"I think you were introduced to the reason yesterday."

"Your dad was…decent to me and Darryl." He scowled, then bit his lip. When he released it, I refrained, just barely, from pushing him backward onto the bed and doing obscene things to that lip.

"He should be. I'm paying him enough." Pulling away just in time for the phone to ring again, I answered it tersely and told Luis we were on our way. Again.

The tension in the room had all but disappeared. Only my irritation at a discussion about Desmond Glass remained. "Let's go." The subject about my father was hopefully dropped for good.

Speaking of parents, I hadn't yet asked Peter about his conversation with his mother. I wondered if he'd be receptive to questions about her. Now that we were on better footing, would he open up to me? I was listing the various ways to broach the conversation as we stepped into the living room and found yet more obstacles to our leaving.

Two of the FBI agents I'd seen surveilling the house that morning were in the living room. One was on the sofa and the other leaning against the mantle. They looked casually menacing in a way only men in semi-cheap suits could be.

People Should Be What They Look Like, Dammit!

From the kitchen, Rosa pounded something into oblivion while glaring at the living room. Cai, curled up in the arm chair, was doing some staring of his own, but with less of a glare than an interested gleam at the younger agent sitting on the sofa. I guessed younger, by the broad stretch of shoulders and the rich chestnut colored hair which stood in stark contrast to his aging counterpart across from him. They were the FBI version of Luis and me.

"Detective Glass," the older one nodded. "I'm agent—"

Peter brushed past me and headed for Cai, pulling him out of the seat and speaking in tongues—or probably just Russian. Same difference.

The younger agent turned around and stood up.

"I *haven't* said anything, Rabbit," Cai protested, playing keep away with his arm. "And I don't *want* to go to my room." The scene would have been humorous if I hadn't felt the sharp edges of an approaching headache.

"Agent one and Agent two. That's all I need to know right now. Whatever you're here for, it'll have to wait until I get back from the station. And I'm taking him." I jerked a thumb at Peter.

"They are here for me," Rosa said.

"Good. Then you can find a place for them to sleep, if they're staying. But hear this—I've given up my living room, guest room, job, career, heterosexuality and my stance on no pets in the house, but I'm not giving up my room. I'm drawing a line." Testosterone flowing, I grabbed Peter's wrist and yanked him out the door, aiming us both toward the back of the courtyard. He didn't make so much as a token resistance.

I released his hand to open the gate to my private parking spot and swore under my breath at the new scene before me. I had forgotten about the press.

Though there were only five or six talking heads, between the cameramen and giant cameras, it was overwhelming when they converged on us like rats on a fallen crumb. Questions and microphones flew at us as we waded through to the Jag. Neither Peter nor I answered, until one question halted Peter at the driver's side door. My irritation grew exponentially by the second.

"Changing teams, Austin?" Diane, a brunette with a pageant smile, had a hand propped on her hip and flecks of evil in her glossed lips.

I flashed her a look of surprise, then quickly masked it. "Helping the unfortunate," I clarified. "Your mother still dating your ex-husband?" I tossed the keys to Peter and leaned on the top of the car. "She always did like your leftovers." Her brown eyes narrowed in anger and I knew she'd forget to ask about Peter, which was exactly why I'd chosen that particular subject change.

She feigned casual laughter and shrugged. "Now both of us can talk about how much you suck in bed."

"*Sucking* in bed is probably why he's changing teams." Peter smiled benignly at her and flicked the door open.

My eyes rolled to the afternoon sky and then closed, head hanging as I choked out laughingly, "That wasn't the team she meant, Peter." I didn't have time to explain she meant associating with criminals, Peter was already behind the wheel with the door closed. "Give your mom my best." I faked a smile and gingerly climbed into the car, slamming the door shut behind me just as she responded with, "Why? You never did." Ouch.

"Sorry," Peter muttered, starting the car and slowly backing out. I wanted to push his foot down on the pedal and run over a few of the reporters. Diane first. It was weighing on me how many enemies I had created in less than two weeks.

"I should create a list of ways to be unexpectedly outed: Partners discovering my obsession for a hustler, friends finding me half-naked with one, boyfriend announcing I suck cock to reporters."

The car jolted to a stop. I grabbed the dashboard before my head thunked into the, windshield. "Boyfriend?" Peter asked, brows lifting.

"I'm not backtracking." I looked ahead, ignoring my jitterbugging heart, ignoring Peter and the reporters and the world; and my own inclination to, in fact, backtrack and say 'boy and friend'; or sputter out some other kind of insincere denial.

"Okay."

I eyed him sideways, searching for his reaction. Per usual, he showed me nothing but inscrutability. He shifted gears and pulled out of the alley.

He was a careful driver. Something I didn't expect from his hard living. Did that come from being caretaker to everyone around him? Peter was a forty-year-old parent living in a twenty-year-old's porn-star body. "At some point all of this is going to catch up with me," I said.

"What is?"

"Gay, boyfriend, job loss, career in the toilet, gay, criminals in my house, criminals in my bed."

"You said the gay thing twice."

"It deserves double billing."

"I like that best about you."

"I should hope so. Hard to be a boyfriend without the gay thing."

"Not the gay thing. The fact that you embrace every decision you make when you finally make one."

Oh. "I like your cock best."

"Liar." He smiled. "You like my mouth."

"I like everything about you." I watched him swallow hard and heard his breathing speed up. "Except that I come third, behind Cai and Darryl."

"You don't," he denied, pinching his brow.

"Everyone does. As your boy— Whatever-I-am—"

"I thought you said you were my boyfriend?"

"That sounds juvenile."

"If the mentality fits…"

"As your boyfriend," I continued with a growl, "I'd like to be bumped up on the list. At least to above Darryl."

"There's no list. There's just," he took a breath, "differences in interactions."

"I'd like a few interactions changed, then. Specifically those with your dick in, or near, Darryl." Or anyone else.

"Are you asking me for exclusivity?"

Was I? "Yes."

"Because not too long ago—"

"Things have changed since then."

"Since last night?"

"Yes."

"What changed?"

"You saw my naked ass."

"That was more significant than sucking your cock?"

Yes. "You didn't attempt to poke things up there," I pointed out.

"You're hurt. I'm not sadistic." He turned left, swinging the car along the curb as we arrived at The Manhole. "Next time I see your naked ass, don't count on my self-control," Peter said. A change of subject was in order.

"I thought he was at the hospital?"

"He was." At that moment I knew Darryl had gone to the club to set up the gig as Peter had requested. I wasn't going to think or talk about that. And neither was Peter, apparently.

Darryl leaned against the wall just outside the entrance, dragging a finger down the chest of a man whose neck was nearly the size of Darryl's waist. "He's not going to the station like that."

"Okay." The smile Peter gave me was tilting on the wrong side of malicious. "You're going to tell him that?"

"Yes," I said cautiously.

"Do you know what Darryl does here?" He honked the horn and pointed at The Manhole.

"Bartender? Dishwasher? Go-go dancer?" I couldn't remember what he'd said Darryl did. The latter seemed most likely. And though I'd been in few gay bars, I was sure somewhere I'd seen go-go dancers. Of course none of them were scrawny, if I recalled scenes from various Vice raids.

"Part-time bartender. Part-time *bouncer.*"

"He weighs less than my fist!" The subject of our discussion lifted a delicate finger off his prey's oiled chest and held it up to us in a 'one-minute' gesture.

"When you look like him, and your dad's in the mob, you learn to take care of yourself. Ever since he saw The Matrix, he's been obsessed with martial arts. Darryl's got a black belt in Jiu-Jitsu." My jaw unhinged like screws were yanked from under my ears.

I focused on Darryl's bright red jeans and the protruding hips jutting out of the waistband. Unconsciously I licked my lips, caught myself and deliberately turned to Peter who was eyeing me with interest. I was not checking Darryl out, goddammit.

"People aren't always who they seem, Detective. Am I anything like you thought?"

"No," I admitted. *You're a million times better than I could have imagined.* And that was the problem. Looking at Peter, I realized that I was never going to get over him. A distressing thought when I considered I might not ever *have* Peter.

"I like it when you look at me like that," he murmured, lifting his fingers to my brow and tugging gently on the strands of hair that had escaped my gel. His hand smelled faintly of soap and leather. I turned my face to his wrist and gently pressed my lips against his pulse, inhaling to find a trace of his usual scent. The moment was so remarkably tender, I forgot to exhale for a few seconds. My pulse raced, demanding a new breath. It was exhilarating, but terrifying, to be this vulnerable in front of him.

So, naturally, I had to ruin it.

"That reminds me. Did you quit smoking?"

His hand dropped, gripping the steering wheel once more. "Cai steals my cigarettes and flushes them." He scowled. "I gave up."

Excellent. "Remind me to buy him a boat. Or an island. Or something useful for sixteen-year-olds. Like lobotomy equipment for his human experimentation." Peter arched a brow and looked at me like I was green and from planet Zeezob; and then his gaze skirted to my left.

Darryl knocked on the window. I got out and pushed up the seat so he could slide in. He folded into the backseat with a gentle "Toodles" to the big guy. "Dennis wants to take me to Hawaii," he announced with a cross of his legs. I rolled my eyes and got back into my seat, carefully avoiding sitting in a way that might have me screeching like a ten-year-old girl.

Darryl apparently noticed my scowl. "What goat horned his ass? If you plowed him so hard he can't sit, Rabbit, he should be beaming with joy."

Peter's shoulders shook. He turned away from me, not only to check for oncoming traffic, of that I was sure. "I thought maybe he was jealous of you and me, but now I think he just wants you," Peter baited.

I was not joining in this discussion. Eventually the subject changed to the house, their injured friend and the fire and what they had lost. The pictures, Cai's paintings, books and little things, like Joe's pipe and Cai's last tooth. Things that I hadn't even thought about. It reminded me, once again, that Peter was taking punches left and right and not even staggering. His maturity and resolve astounded me.

There wasn't any salvation from Peter at this point. I was falling too hard.

"Another reason we're going to the station," I said. "You'll both have to speak to an officer about the fires." Just more shit to do for the Day That Never Ended.

Austin Glass Starring in: Screwed Without Orgasm

An hour later, Luis and I waited in a cramped room with the boxes of evidence from Alvarado's house. We had sorted out the small and large baggies containing papers, passports, IDs and money, leaving the rest—weaponry, drugs and paraphernalia—in the evidence lockup. Peter, Darryl and my father were meeting with the officers investigating the fires in a separate interrogation room.

It was just me and my partner, quietly going over evidence and giving wide berth to the elephant in the room. The elephant being the large number of rancid stares I had received as we entered, along with the large plastic rat that someone had planted on my desk. No one, not even Luis, who knew I was coming in, had hid that from my sight.

"On a scale of one-to-ten, how screwed am I?" I lifted a bag, pretending to stare at the contents. I couldn't concentrate on it. Couldn't care less whose passport I held.

"A hundred," Luis grunted.

I kept my smile, forced though it was, and lifted another baggy. "That'll be my first hundred since high school biology."

Luis slammed down a stack of papers. "What the fuck are you doing with your life?"

"Dating hookers, learning the gay, housing criminals, pissing off my fellow cops, and taking in what everyone says is a cat, but which I'm definitely sure is not a cat. I'm undecided on its actual species. I think it's a cross between a rat and some kind of alien life—"

"It's all a big joke to you?"

"No." I sighed. "It's all a big fucked up, confusing mess to me. What do you want me to do? Cry? Rant?"

"How is this for funny. Del and Marco are looking into your connection to Alvarado's murder."

"Now that is funny," I murmured, no smile on my face now. If they wanted to connect me, there wasn't much I could do. There wasn't any evidence of my guilt, but I also had no proof of innocence.

"You bring this on yourself with the shit you're pulling." Luis rubbed his forehead with his palm and dropped his hand hard onto the table.

"Yeah, well, now I'm in too deep, Luis. There's no way out. Even if I wanted one. Which I don't. I'll make peace with the end of my career. Some day. But I'm not on the wrong side here."

"You are so sure of this that you take me down with you? I trusted you, and you let your dick drag us both down into the sewer."

"This doesn't have anything to do with my dick," I shouted, knocking the chair back as I stood and barely feeling the resulting pain. I was finally filthy fucking pissed off. "It's about right and wrong and a sixteen-year-old kid who was raped for hours by a drug-dealing pimp. Even if Cai is guilty, I'm on his side."

"Sit down." Luis glowered and leaned back in his chair. I obeyed the order, but not without petulantly scraping the chair hard against the concrete floor. Luis pushed both hands through his hair. "It's always these kids with you. I should have expected it. But look, I get the money you give them, and the calls to DHS, and I even get you shelling out for this kid's lawyer. But all three of them living with you? Kids of men we work to put away? One of those kids is a killer; maybe they all are."

I crossed my arms over the table and leaned forward, my voice a loud, angry growl. "You're not listening to me. For once in my fucking life, I'm not looking for a criminal. I don't care if he did it. Get that? I don't give a fucking shit. And if I lose everything because of this, so be it. I'm doing what's ri—" I trailed off as I lost Luis's interest. He was looking to my right. Peter, Darryl and my father stood in the doorway.

Desmond Glass cast a disapproving curl of his lip at me. Darryl had the opposite kind of grin. And Peter? Peter's smile held the sadness and despair I felt, and something else, too. I didn't know what it meant, but it elicited a profound warmth in my chest.

Career Plague

The table spanned the majority of the room, and the evidence lay in piles covering almost every inch of it. Peter and Darryl were reaching left and right, exchanging items to be looked at and discarded.

We were tightly slotted into our cookie package, three on one side—if my father could be counted as being on a 'side'—and two on the other. Peter was to my left, Desmond in the corner to Peter's left, and Darryl and Luis across from us. Elbow room was nonexistent, which was unfortunate because Peter's kept brushing up against mine, drawing attention to his pale, freckled arm and making me lose track of why we were there. I kept wanting to trace through the soft copper hair dusting from elbow to wrist.

But my predicament wasn't half as uncomfortable as Luis's. When Darryl stretched for an item across Luis, he made sure to brush against him: a shoulder against a shoulder, his hand skimming Luis's, his face just close enough to be awkward. My partner's responses were like a spastic attack. He scooted sideways, yanked his hand away, jerked his head back. I spent so much time laughing at Luis's reactions that I was instantly aware when Darryl suddenly lost interest in pestering my partner. A frown passed over his elfin face. He leaned across the table and began to push baggies around, lifting them in quick succession.

"What are you looking for?" I asked.

Luis removed his palm from his brow, his eyes darting after Darryl's hands. "Something you don't see?"

"The beer place," Darryl responded absently.

Peter sat up and began helping. "Right. I remember that."

"Beer place doesn't help much." Neither of them looked at me.

"Not beer," Peter said, "Lager."

"Yeah, Lager. That was it. It's not here."

"Lager? Was that a name or an inventory item?" I started reading through the papers and tax forms they'd dropped.

"Neither," Darryl said, pulling a large pile in front of him and following my lead with slow reading. "I just remember Rabbit 'n' me having this laugh about how they probably did really well at Oktoberfest because we saw the address was on the mall, and it said 'barn lager'. Which probably didn't sell at any other time of the year." The mall must've meant the 16th Street Mall, where every year an Oktoberfest celebration was held. "Like who drinks beer from a barn?"

Luis and I both wrote down 'barn lager'. For some reason it seemed familiar to me, and I kept circling the word barn.

"I think there's more stuff missing here," Peter said and chewed his bottom lip. "I'm sorry. I can't remember what they were."

"This was everything you found in the safety deposit box?"

My father finally made a noise, in the way of clearing his throat. "Hypothetically."

My gaze found the ceiling and glared. "Hypothetically speaking, is this all that was in the safety deposit box?"

"Yeah. Except the money." Darryl said. Peter slumped back in his chair and nodded.

"And there was no indication of another box?"

"I didn't find one," Peter said.

"Mine was empty." Darryl shrugged.

"You both had one?" They looked at Luis as he leaned forward, and both of them nodded in answer. "And the other boy?"

I could see comprehension slip slowly over Peter. Moments later he picked up his phone. "Hey, kiddo… Yeah, we'll be home soon… Okay… Okay… I'll call Dr. Sherman later about—… Yes, I'll call her later about your prescription… We'll work it out… Listen, I—… Cai… Cai, stop talking for—… Cai!" Peter rubbed the spot between his eyes. "I need to know if Joe got you a safety deposit box?… Cai? Are you there?…" Peter looked up and nodded, slowly. "No, I'm not going to look into it... Yeah, I promise." He grabbed his pencil and wrote the name of the police credit union and pushed the paper to me. "Okay, no one is going to... We can talk about it when I get home... Me, too."

When Peter hung up, there was a collective inhale as Luis picked up the phone to obtain a search warrant for Cai's safety deposit box. However, it was late and there wasn't enough of an emergency to awaken a judge. Luis came up empty-handed, but with news that squeezed the breath from my lungs.

"They want probable cause to get into the box," he said.

Christ. Unless Cai gave permission to examine what was in the box—and thereby maybe incriminating himself further—Luis was going to have to tell the DA the truth about the evidence at Alvarado's house. We'd have to explain that Peter set Alvarado up and that we covered up that information.

I should've been forced to wear a full body condom, because I had now completely fucked my partner, Peter and myself.

Chapter Eighteen

Predictions and Predicaments

"I'll speak to my clients alone now," my father said. His inherent understanding the dilemma was a tribute to his skills as a criminal lawyer.

"What's going on?" Peter asked, looking to me for an answer.

"We need a warrant to get into that safety deposit box. In order to apply for a warrant, we need to have permission or show probable cause. If Cai won't give permission, the only way we can show probable cause is if we show there's a likelihood of more evidence being stashed in there. Evidence that either of you, or Joe or Cai hid there."

"Cai being arrested isn't enough to look through it?"

Luis shook his head. "Not unless they could show he used the box to conceal evidence."

"As in, he visited the box immediately after Iss's death. That'll take time, searches through security footage," I explained at their blank looks. "Warrants aren't all inclusive."

Peter worried his bottom lip hard enough that I saw the imprint of his teeth. "This is stupid. Cai can just—"

"Don't say anymore," Desmond ordered, rising from his metal throne. Peter closed his mouth with a snap.

After that, the room stifled us all in an uncomfortable silence. Peter scraped at the tattoo on his hand. Darryl flicked his thumbnail against the back of his teeth. My father took in deep breaths and released them from his nose. Luis and I went about packing up evidence. My monotonous voice read item after item while my partner pencil check-marked the paperwork.

I was too busy trying to solve Peter's problem to actually pay attention to what I was doing. Finding a solution was like trying to pinpoint the original design in a moving kaleidoscope.

Angelica and my father were going to encourage Cai to deny us access to the box. And Cai wasn't going to take much convincing. He didn't seem to want us in that box. Whatever was in there could link him to any number of crimes. It wouldn't be much of a dilemma for Peter. He'd go to jail to protect Cai. It would be moot. We'd get into the box anyway. It would just take longer. Or maybe we wouldn't. My father would side with Angelica in fighting a warrant on the box. She was a good lawyer. Either way, I couldn't stop Luis from arresting Peter at this point, even if I begged.

"Item 43: Mexican Passport number…"

"Have you found all the people?" Darryl asked. Since I was off the case, and not entirely in the loop, I looked to Luis to answer. The rest followed suit.

He took the bag from me and checked off the list before adding it to the box. "Most of this group," he nodded to the table. "Some of the others we tracked down were smuggled months and years ago. We haven't had a chance to interview all of them. They all have forged passports and green cards, unlike these people," he held up a passport.

Peter's eyes were riveted to the evidence on the table. "Is that what Joe was doing? Forging green cards?"

"Joe and Alvarado, among others, near's we can tell," Luis said.

"So he wasn't selling people?"

Luis was quiet, but all of us were staring at him expectantly. Except my father, who was taking notes on his legal pad. Fifteen-hundred dollars an hour, and he couldn't afford a fucking laptop? "People were offered forged green cards for a hefty price," Luis said. "They thought the money went to the cartels. If they couldn't pay upfront, they smuggled in drugs and cash to pay part and went to work doing whatever Alvarado ordered to pay the rest. Unpaid labor for most of the men. Prostitution for most of the younger women and children."

Darryl brought his knees to his chest and rested his chin on them, hugging his legs a little too tightly. "Why didn't they just go back to Mexico or wherever?" He had more of the callous attitude I expected from a whore. He was jaded and flippant, but he cared more than he let on.

"If they thought the cartels were running the operation, back home was more dangerous than staying here. Cartels don't give refunds for unsatisfied customers," I said drily. Darryl lifted his lip in a sneer and went back to pressing his mouth into his knees. "Traffickers don't explain the contracts, either. People don't understand what kind of work they're going to have to do to pay their way."

When everything was tucked away, my partner loaded it all on a dolly and took it to the evidence room. I waited outside the door while Peter and Darryl met with my father.

I was leaning against the wall, head back and eyes closed, when the brush of a sleeve indicated someone's presence next to me. I lifted a lid, spotted Dave and smiled. "Thought you'd hang the other day and watch a game with me later. Where'd you disappear to?"

"Called away," Dave explained. He rubbed the back of his neck and mimicked my position, eyes closing. "How's the case going?"

"Just caught a break. Looks like there's another safety deposit box." Before I could start tapping my nervous fingers and toes, I stuck my hands in my pants pockets and crossed my ankles. It didn't help, but at least the tapping was muted.

"Sounds like a good lead."

"Yeah." Dave stared at the opposite wall. His leg jittered. The nervous energy so mirrored my feelings that I considered he had bad news for me. "You heard something from Del and Marco on the Alvarado murder?" I fished.

"Captain already tore down the target sign on your forehead, Oz." I breathed a sigh of relief. "I gotta head out. It's late, and Marta wants KFC tonight."

"Hey, thanks for looking over those papers the other day," I called out as he walked away.

He turned, gave a tentative smile with a two fingered salute and walked backwards a few steps. "Sorry I couldn't find anything."

"Dave?" How did I thank him for standing by me? While the halls were filled with disdain at my presence, Dave hadn't hesitated to let people know on which side he stood.

Turned out I didn't have to thank him. "Whatever, Oz, our bromance transcends your fuckups. Rockies/Padres this Friday?" He asked loudly, by way of announcing to the entire station where I stood in his eyes.

"Can we drink the beer this time?"

I received yet another glare from a patrolman passing by. Dave noted it and tried to grin, but his smile wasn't reaching his eyes.

"You and me, a six pack, and your big screen."

"It's a date."

"Quiet," he yelled. "I don't want the whole station to know I'm queer for you!"

I pulled a chuckle from the swirling depths of my throat and went back to looking casual while I waited. If I could make it through the day without Peter getting arrested, I might have to actually *thank* my father. I barely resisted shuddering at the thought.

They arrested Peter an hour later.

Bedraggled and Empathizing with a Cat. Where's My Gun?

We had filled out paperwork for Peter's release. The officer in charge of the arson investigation had given me an interview and us paperwork. The City Pound had given us one carry box, one demon and paperwork. The fire department had given us a list of hostels and shelters, the insurance company's phone number and...paperwork. The entire day had added a headache, blurry vision and a cramp in my hand to the literal pain in my ass. I sat in the passenger seat, disoriented and anesthetized, my temple pressed against the car window.

It was dark and closer to morning than night by the time we journeyed home. Houses and streetlamps whizzed by in a blur of light and shadow. The past weeks of my life were an imitation of the transient scenery out my window. As was this entire day. Blink. Another scene. Blink. Another.

Darryl was driving. Peter was curled up in the back seat, sleeping off his arrest. He snuggled the box filled with the incessantly mewling cat. Darryl was the only one with energy. He tapped the steering wheel rhythmically while mouthing songs only he could hear. I was too tired to contemplate what that music was; and I was too drained to do what I wanted: to crawl back there with Peter and banish from memory that look of fear when had they cuffed him. His mask of indifference had fallen back into place moments later, but I would never forget the terror in his eyes before they shuttered and blanked.

Begone began to yowl. My ears made an attempt to crawl into my head, but I didn't give in to the urge to scream. Or shoot it.

I know just how you feel, cat.

Lectures Make Me Hard

The parking lot behind my home was empty. Reporters would be back in the morning, but it looked, for now, like we had one less shit-storm to deal with. As I reached for the door handle my shoulders relaxed.

"I don't know if you're what Rabbit needs," Darryl said, gripping my keys on his thigh and staring out the windshield.

"And you are?" I said, equally quiet so as not to disturb the subject of our conversation.

Darryl rolled his eyes and gave me a look of contempt. "You're such an asshole sometimes."

"I've been advised of that. It's good to be consistent."

Darryl smirked unexpectedly and dropped the keys into my palm. "I hope you're what he needs."

"Where do you fit into what he needs?"

He looked over his shoulder at Peter and smiled. "I used to be the one who took care of him." If he was implying that I was the reason things were different, I wasn't going to apologize. Darryl turned to me once more, focused. "Rabbit's the rock we cling to when we're drowning. He needs a mountain to hold him up, not another storm that'll wear away at him."

The poetry of those words shocked me. Not just because I had realized their truth long ago, but because they were in Darryl's voice. "You should be a writer," I said, uncomfortable with his scrutiny.

"You should be serious once in a while." He grabbed my ear and pulled me closer. I let him, because I was too damn bushed to fight off a black belt in Jiu Jitsu. "Hurt him, and I'll tie you up, spend days cutting your balls into deli-thin slices and feed them to that cat."

I yawned in his face. "Honestly, it's not a cat," I insisted when he released my ear.

"Dare, knock it off," Peter commented drowsily as he sat up and looked out the window.

The ceiling light ticked on as Darryl opened the door. Peter's face was half in shadow, but the illuminated side was imprinted with my seat design. I'd never had the opportunity to think of Peter as cute. Right then, he was ridiculously so.

"Why are you grinning?" Peter yawned, managing to look even more adorable as he tried to simultaneously give me a suspicious glare.

"Darryl told me to be your rock. People say I can't follow directions. I gotta disagree." I pointed to my crotch.

Peter laughed quietly.

"Loser," Darryl said and grabbed the cat. It yelped as he yanked the box. I opened the door and flipped the seat up so Peter could scoot out.

The driver's side door slammed, and the distant echo of Begone's howls told me that Darryl was almost inside the house by the time Peter gathered up all our paperwork and dislodged himself from the backseat. He lost his footing partway out and fell into my arms.

"Well, hello there," I said, nose-to-nose with him.

His eyebrow shot up. "You're really strange tonight. My arrest makes you horny and goofy?"

I palmed the hair away from his face and kept an arm circled around him. He smelled like sweat and cigarettes. I didn't care. He felt amazing. "You look cute."

"Fumbling and exhausted?"

"Vulnerable and unguarded." He took that as a cue to mask his near-smile and pull away from me. "Shit. Goddammit, Peter, I thought we were getting somewhere."

"We are. I just...things are happening so fast with you. I can't sort what's real from what's just these intense situations we're forced into."

"Join the club," I muttered.

I took a deep breath and shut the car door quietly, bending to pick up the papers he'd dropped when he stumbled.

He crouched down next to me, adding forms to the pile. "I like you. You like me. I keep saying that. Can't we decide what that means later, in your bedroom or someplace quiet? Not out in the parking lot where reporters were, and maybe still are, lurking, along with ex-girlfriends, and friends." He paused. "Ugh, Cai's inside. With Rosa and Darryl and the FBI. Privacy isn't an option, is it?" We both stood, Peter running a hand through his hair.

"Go back to the part about my bedroom." I clicked the car alarm, tucked my keys in my pocket and used that free hand to cup his neck, pulling him into a kiss.

Still warm and languid from sleep, his body sighed into mine. His lips parted, tongue leisurely delving into my mouth as if he'd been waiting all day for me to take this initiative.

He tasted of apple juice. He tasted of cigarettes. He tasted of salt and sweat and every one of my fantasies. I sucked his tongue, my pulse climbing unsteadily. He moaned, and I dropped the papers to the ground, ignoring their fluttered protest as I held Peter to me.

The hot heavy sounds of our breaths, the feel of his body against mine, the taste of him, all of it overwhelmed the outside world. The night closed in around us, sheltered us from nosy neighbors and other interruptions. There was just us, molded together, with his hands on my hips and mine cradling his face.

My stomach fluttered with warmth. "Peter," I breathed, tilting my mouth and capturing his lips again. He answered with a whisper of my name, fisting handfuls of my jacket.

His needy moans urged me to push him back against the car. I reached down, buckled his knees with my hands and lifted him atop the hood. His shorts rode up and my hands lingered at his thigh, rubbing up under the fabric, feeling the soft copper hair under my palms. He folded his legs around my waist, grabbed my collar and yanked me into him again.

I crashed into his mouth and met his tongue with a fierceness born out of weeks and years of denial. Seeing him spread out on my car, his stomach heaving with breaths, lips wet, eyes hooded and dazed; my cock ached with how badly I needed to fuck him, how desperately I wanted to watch his body jerk with the force of my thrusts. I shuddered with need, digging my nails into my hands. I took a deep breath and got myself under control.

This wasn't about me. It was about Peter. My stone angel, battered by the world and refusing to back down from it. Peter, who never asked for anything for himself.

I took advantage of his vulnerable state to be the aggressor. Gripping the sides of his shorts, I jerked them down below his waist, pulling him to the edge of the car at the same time. His t-shirt rode up, revealing pale skin with sharp shadows of muscle. With a gentleness I didn't feel, I traced each one with my tongue and dragged my mouth along the valley at the center of his stomach.

Looking up, I whispered reverently. "You're exquisite."

His muscles quivered against my lips; his feet dropping from my back as he curled his fingers into my hair. His throat moved in an unsuccessful attempt to swallow a moan; it was almost too loud when it escaped. Loud and plaintive. "So damn gorgeous," I continued, gliding my hands further up to bare his chest.

"Austin," he murmured, arching his back and pulling my mouth closer to his skin. The passive order drove the blood from my brain to my cock.

My tongue dipped into his belly button. He writhed in response. I kept him squirming plunging in and out, licking deep, until his moans became grunts and his hips undulated against my chest. Climbing higher, I tasted every freckle, every inch of skin on my path to the darker, larger brown discs on his chest.

He inhaled sharply as my teeth grazed his nipple, fastening his fingers into my scalp as I gently pulled the metal ring with my tongue. He panted each breath with every light pinch or pull of my teeth. My eyes flew up to judge his reaction.

The moonlight illuminated the ghost of lashes trembling against his cheek. His rabbit-quick heart beat against my lips, hammering in time with my own. His hips began to rock faster in invitation. I dropped my hands lower, tracing the carved edge of flesh that led into the waistband.

"Tell me what you want."

"Anything," Peter gasped evasively. He didn't push my head as I expected, though his fingers relaxed and tightened in my hair until the gelled strands softened in his grasp.

"Tell me," I repeated. I wasn't going to be satisfied unless he had asked me for something. I'd prefer begging.

"Austin?"

"Peter," I said, smiling evilly while plucking teasingly at the button of his shorts. He moved fluidly, propping up on his elbows. I almost lost it when his lip disappeared between his teeth. Then I recognized the crinkling of his eyes. In that second an intrinsic puzzle piece locked in place.

Peter wasn't shy. He wasn't being coy or seductive. In Peter's world, everyone wrested a price for an action. Peter was calculating what price I would extract and deciding if he could pay it. He never asked for anything for himself because he was already paying for everyone else.

It was on the tip of my tongue to reassure him that this was as much for me as it was for him, but it wasn't. I was nervous, inexperienced and knee-buckling scared. I hid it well because he was so damn fucking hot that my brain kept firing synapses to the area that controlled my cock.

Fear had a tight grip on my emotions. Standing in the middle of a parking lot wasn't helping matters. The feel of his skin against my palms; the subtle trembles he couldn't hide; the way his chest heaved from being overly aroused, all that did a lot to maintain my erection. Barely. My heart beat erratically, not only from arousal or the public display we were putting on; I was wholly terrified to take that last step. There wasn't a drop more of denial available after tonight.

"No strings, Peter." It hurt to say those words. I wanted strings. Strings and chains and possibly glue. Superglue. Triple-bonding, weapons-grade epoxy.

It wasn't the acceptance of a blow job stopping Peter. It was the asking for it. And, more specifically, it was me he had to ask.

I waited, patiently.

His eyes flickered. The blue disappeared in a spill of black, and the tip of his tongue curled up to lick his front teeth. "Suck my dick, Austin."

Gay Sex Three, Straight Sex Nil

When those words computed, I would have testified in court that my cock jumped in an attempt to escape my zipper.

Taking a deep breath, I glanced around us, checking to make sure there wasn't a group of videographers ready to upload our tryst into Internet infamy. I heard music a street over; it faded quickly, and the hush of the dark morning settled back around us. Sweat pooled in the small of my back and trickled down my neck. I took a deep breath of summer air and reached for his shorts.

My body refused to allow me a suave, steady hand for my first blow job. He was wearing *my* shorts. Shorts I was familiar with. And my fucking fingers were behaving like chopsticks. I shakily fumbled with the small plastic button, and I accidentally—on purpose—twisted it off in frustration and then went for the zipper.

To my ears, the zipper was audible in space. Peter's breath held, his stomach still and tense. Either he was anticipating what was coming, or his zipper was really loud. I met his eyes.

Anticipating. He was definitely anticipating.

His tongue poked between his teeth, daring me. I held his gaze while slowly pulling his boxers down. He lifted his hips, bringing the heat from his body closer to my face. I shuddered a breath and scooted the boxers down to his thighs. He lowered back to the car. My hands made a shaky trek over dips and curve of his hips, stopping when I felt the tip of his cock brush the edge of my thumb. I looked down.

As much as I wanted this—fantasized in vivid detail about the feel and the taste of him—it took serious resolve to wrap my hand around his cock.

The feel was familiar, and that took the edge off my anxiety. It also helped that I was aroused. Excruciatingly so. My tongue rolled along the top of my mouth, anticipating the slide of velvet skin and slick of precome. It wasn't the nine inches every gay ad peddled—for which I was grateful. The length was still a problem, though. More than six in—

"Did you forget the lyrics?"

"Huh?"

His mouth tilted in a smirk. "If you're going to break into song, we're going to get arrested."

I checked my position, realized I'd been standing there with my mouth half open, holding his dick like it was a microphone. "I'm deciding how this works."

"The word 'suck' should give you a clue."

My eyes never left his cock. "This relationship can only take one smartass if it's going to survive." Pornos and previous blow jobs were all I had to go by. They montaged in my head, trying to give me instructions. Lick the base. Slowly slide the tip of my tongue along his shaft on the way to rimming the head. Fondle the balls. Pump the shaft.

Too many instructions.

A single, clear drop glistened in the slit. My mouth watered. *Start there*, my brain told me. *Right fucking there.*

His smirk grew. "I—" My tongue dipped into the slit before my mouth closed around the head of his cock. Whatever he was going to say was lost in the hiss of breath pulled through his teeth.

I sucked hard, hollowing out my cheeks and drawing a long, "Fuck," from Peter. Swirling my tongue over the tip, I twisted my hand at the base, stroking up.

His head tipped back. "Fuck," he whispered again. "Oh, fuck."

My heart was nearly wrecked from the speed of its beat. His pulse was beating just as raggedly along the vein my tongue nestled against. It suddenly became less about slot A with tab B, and more about making Peter moan louder, jerk his hips like that, catch his breath, bite his lip.

In the heat of the moment, I spat on his cock, breath toying with the wet head, attempting a porn-quality blow job. I held his hips, swallowing more of his length, no hesitation, seeing how much I could take. When my gag reflex kicked in, the rhythm changed. It became a slow bob up and down, wetter and wetter, teasing, screwing with him, until, with every breath, he gasped out a curse.

"Fuck. Fuck. Fuck." He fell gently back onto the hood, knee tensing under my hand. "I'm gonna come." I ignored the warning, grabbed hold of the base again and pumped, lips sealed around his cock. I winced internally, preparing for the taste of come. This was for him, I reminded myself. His fingers clenched in my hair and yanked back hard. My mouth slid off with a wet pop just as his body tensed, air exploding from his lungs like gunfire. He held my face still against the tip, come spilling onto my mouth and chin. The strong scent soared through my nostrils. He shuddered the rest of his breaths, hand dropping from my hair.

His orgasm was the most erotic thing I'd ever seen.

Before I could say something witty, like "Nngh", he sat up, grabbing my hair again. I watched, mesmerized as he squeezed his cock dry, pressed a wet thumb into my lips and smeared the come on my mouth and cheek. My eyes widened as he moved in for a kiss.

His breath heated my lips. "Lick it off." It was a taste I'd have to get used to. It was definitely not ambrosia, but the way Peter stared at me intently while I licked my lips clean was. I wasn't sure what to feel, other than…claimed. I obviously liked it, my cock was hard enough to drill concrete.

I wiped the rest away with my sleeve and leaned in to his mouth. "Going to pee on me next?"

He licked the remaining come off the underside of my lip and fed it to me with his tongue. My cock called a timeout, begging for mercy. "Only if that's what you're into. Not my thing," he said, sucking at my chin while unbuttoning my pants. All functioning was centered below my waist, so it took a moment for my brain to catch up to his actions.

"No strings," I reminded him, a gentle hand on his wrist.

He bent forward whispering in my ear. "Unless I want them." My pants fell to my ankles.

A sauna couldn't stop my shiver. "Do you?"

He didn't answer. "Leave your jacket on." He pulled down my briefs to mid-thigh. "I have a price tonight."

"It wasn't coming on my face like we were shooting a scene from Peter Does Austin?"

He grinned, unbuttoning my shirt. I loved that he got my sense of humor—or attempted humor. "You look good in my spunk."

"Not swallowing it?" We apparently were going to go for round two. Outside. In the parking lot. Fucking nuts.

"Not as sexy."

"Not as dominating, you mean."

"That too."

"I'm not into the dom/sub thing."

He shrugged. "Me either. I just like…"

"Taking charge?" I arched a brow.

He grinned wider and pulled my shirt apart, dragging it and my jacket over my shoulders. Curling my tie around one fist, he gripped my cock with the other. "You like it."

I did. Public sex, too, it seemed. I looked around, cautiously. Empty alley. Dark windows in the distance. Crickets chirped, a horn honked from a few streets over. Other than that, the city was silent. Or, maybe I was so wrapped in Peter, I didn't notice much else.

"Brace yourself." He jerked the tie and pulled me into a kiss. In situations like this, one always had a choice. Mine was to obey or topple over. Obeying included his wet, warm lips against mine. Obeying included his tongue plunging into my mouth. Obeying included his hand stroking my cock. All in all, obeying was the first and best choice. Not just the only one.

He released me to cup my jaw and pulled back. "I want to watch you get off."

I opened my eyes and blinked the fog away. "Huh?"

"Jerk off. Masturbate. Stroke your cock 'til you come."

"I get it," I interrupted the string of euphemisms. "Christ, you're bossy."

"And you're blushing."

"I'm not blushing," I lied. "I'm aroused. I want to fuck you. And it's hot out here."

"You blushing is hot." He pulled his shirt over his head and flung it on the hood before dragging my hand to my cock. I gripped and started my practiced strokes. The fingers that fumbled at the newness of pleasuring him were now on their home turf. He leaned back on his hands, displaying his chest while he watched. I concentrated on that scenery to avoid his eyes. And so he couldn't see the embarrassment in mine.

It didn't take long for my orgasm to build. Not with the moonlight soaking into his pale skin, detailing each crease and outline in his muscled stomach. And not with him slowly stroking his cock back to life. When he stuck a finger into his mouth and sucked like it was a straw in a thick milkshake, I closed my eyes and tried to control my breathing.

I was so focused on my task I didn't realize he'd sat up again until I felt his hot breath along my ear. "Fucking hot." He kissed my jaw slowly and hovered over my lips. Our eyes met. Were my pupils that dilated? So black only a sliver of color remained at the edges? "Are you close?"

I nodded. "Do...I get...a prize?" I asked, feeling his hand brush against mine. I waited for him to take over the stroking.

"Uh-huh." Fucker was smiling as he slipped a finger into my ass.

He swam out of focus at the first knuckle. My hand stuttered. By the second knuckle I was dizzy with the need to come. My stroking intensified. When his finger crooked, I choked out a cry. "Shit."

"Please don't."

"Jok-ah-ing? Now?"

God. God. God. The words became a chant as he pushed in again, hard and fast.

"Beg for more."

"More," I panted out. He added a second finger and fucked into me over and over. His voice was low, whispering things against my lips. I felt his breaths, but his words were drowned out by the thump of my pulse.

My eyes slammed shut, a blurred myriad of dots dancing against the curtain of black. His pace accelerated in time with my approaching climax. I dug my nails into the car's paint as I tensed and came hard, gasping out an explosive breath.

I stood, legs quaking, gulping in air, rivulets of sweat racing down my cheek and over my nose. I shook and flexed my aching hand.

"Now that, Austin, was hot."

I opened my eyes to Peter's soft, satisfied smile. Closed them as he pulled out of me and prayed to God—who I'd probably just pissed off in my litany of blasphemy—that I wasn't blushing.

I rolled my eyes as they opened. "I aim to please," I said with more air than voice.

"Bend over and spread, in that case." He wrapped his arms around my neck and softly kissed the sweat from my lips. I mumbled something nonsensical and quickly lost the English language as his tongue stole it away.

We were breathing heavily by the time we broke apart and looked down. His shorts were stained with my come, and his hips and thighs glistened with the same DNA. My pants were lying flaccid around my ankles. Both of us smelled like a locker room, and neither of us made a move to get dressed.

"We should go inside," I said.

"We should rent a room," he countered.

The thought had merit, but, "Cai's release depends on my staying here."

He sighed, lifting his hips and pulling his shorts up. I heard the zipper as I bent to retrieve my pants. "Where's the button?"

"It was poorly sewn on," I muttered, jerking both underwear and pants up. My waistband hit the edge of my ass, reminding me of the stitches. The lack of pain was a surprise. "I think your come cured my pain."

"Magic come. I should sell it."

I glared at him and merely cavemanned a response. He tilted his head in consideration, lips flicking between his teeth. "What," I asked at his scrutiny.

"No one's been jealous with me like you."

"Iss wasn't jealous?" I asked incredulously.

He hopped off the car. "No, I mean no one is jealous in the way that you are jealous."

I was buttoning my shirt while we talked, but stopped at that. "I'm not—" There wasn't any way to deny it. Why bother? He took over the buttoning in an odd parody of the day before. I watched him with a smile. "You know I'm taking this off in about five minutes, right?"

"You know the FBI is probably inside on your couch, right? Anyhow, I like that you're not…possessive."

"Like hell I'm not," I said.

"Okay."

I exhaled in exasperation. Everything was 'okay' with him.

"Do you think you're in love with me, Austin?"

"Yes," I answered automatically, then reversed it after several seconds of stunned silence. "No!" I rubbed my aching chest and began to snatch papers off the ground. He was stone for all the movement he made. Fuck. Fucking. Fuck. What the fuck did I just say? "I'm not in love with you." I couldn't get out of there fast enough. Flinging the back gate open, I strode quickly to the front door, only to struggle with the handle. His footsteps echoed behind me moments later.

"Austin—"

"Shut the fuck up, Peter." I whirled around to face him, teeth raw from being clenched. "Just shut up. You don't love me. I don't love you. No one loves anyone."

His eyes were filled with pity. "You're so fucked up," he said.

"What the fuck do you know? You're a wh—" *Goddammit!*

The door opened. I pushed past a startled Darryl, slamming the papers on the end table and booked it upstairs.

The Truth Sucks. And It Is Awesome.

I didn't even have time to pace more than four steps before he came in and shut the door, leaning against it.

"Are you in love with me?" I asked, grinding my nails into my palms.

"Yes," he said simply. "But not yet."

I gaped at him. "Oh, fuck you and your inscrutability, Peter." I jerked off my jacket and yanked at my tie.

"I wasn't trying to be— Fuckit. What do you want me to say? That after a week and half I can't live without you? Be reasonable."

"Reasonable? I can't even *spell* that fucking word since I met you."

"Here are the facts, Austin. You've been engaged four times. You've cheated on every single one of them." Fuck the fucking newspapers and their biased articles about me. "You're cruel sometimes and superficial and spoiled and really fucked up emotionally. You talk about my being inscrutable, but you treat nothing as if it matters to you. Something terrible happens? You make a joke and shrug it off. You feel too much? You get angry and lash out at me. So no, I'm not in love with you. I'm fighting it every fucking step! I just wish I could stop it."

Chapter Nineteen

He Loves Me. He Loves Me N— Fuck This.

"If it helps, Austin, I don't believe you're in love with me." I said nothing. "I told you what I liked best about you was the way you jumped into whatever decisions you make. But it's also your worst fault."

"You've decided you're gay," he continued, "and now you're determined to live that way. I'm the easy fallback so you don't have to question that decision. Just like you don't question any other decision once it's made. When things start to fall apart, you don't retreat, you barrel on. There's only two scenarios for the people in your way. We get knocked aside, or we watch you splinter apart."

"I can see how it'd be difficult to fight loving the guy you're describing," I said. "What's not to love about an emotionally stunted, single-minded, reckless, unthinking guy like me?" Tearing the tie from my neck, I whipped it to the floor alongside my jacket and exited to the bathroom with a hard slam of the door.

Love? Why did I go there? Why did I think Peter would be right beside me when I chose that route? By all rights love, to me, was a fairy tale. Who had I ever truly loved besides Jesse? Dave, and to some extent, Angelica, maybe?

Had I loved Jessed? Or was I just remembering the emotion of a confused teenager? Maybe I wasn't gay. Maybe this was stress.

Maybe he looked so much like Jesse that I....

Had to be. Because I didn't love anyone. Not romantic love. Comfortable love. I knew what that was. I could handle that. Friendship, companionship—

Jealousy. Obsession. Awe. Heartache in the best way possible. His kiss. His touch. His smile. His strength. His fucking hot body.

Those were not symptoms of stress. Or comfortable love. Those were what I felt for Jesse.

Peter knocked gently. "Can I come in?"

"I'm busy. Washing jizz off my face." I turned on the faucet for effect and peeled off my sweat-slicked shirt.

Peter looked like Jesse.

But Peter was nothing like Jesse.

The stark glare of my sterile bathroom surrounded me. "Are you in love with him?" I whispered to my haggard reflection.

No. I wasn't in love with him. Another puzzle piece clicked in place. "*Yes*," Peter had said. "*But not yet.*" I didn't love him, and he didn't love me, but that was where this was headed. I had to get out of this circle of denial. If I had felt this for a woman, I wouldn't have questioned it at all. Run, yes, questioned, no.

If I did love him, what then? Did men love each other? Was that even real? What if I loved him and he never loved me back? What if his kind of love was different?

Gay love. It wasn't the same, right?

I looked at my reflection. "You're gay. You're gay. You're gay." It didn't change anything. He didn't—couldn't—love me.

Being gay was irrelevant. *You can make it about anything you want, but that won't change the truth.*

He said he was falling for me. Deep down I didn't believe him. Fundamentally I believed that I was unlovable. And hadn't that borne out with my mother and father?

Lying to yourself has failed you every time. Losing Peter would be the worst of your failures.

"You are fucked up," I told the reflection. *So get over being fucked up.* "He's going to break you." *Yeah, but isn't it worth it?*

"I have cake for your pity party," Peter said.

How could I not love you, Peter.

"And pony rides," he added.

"Christ. Is this how you treat Cai? No wonder he's rebelling."

"Cai doesn't throw tantrums or sulk in the bathroom."

I washed and dried my face quickly and threw open the door. "I'm not sulk—" *Hello.* Peter still hadn't pulled his shirt back on.

He displayed himself, hands bracing on either side of the doorway. The shorts hung low on his hips. The missing button left a gap, revealing the edges of the clipped hair. Sculpted ridges along his hips formed an arrow pointing right to his groin. My mouth went dry and my doubts faded in a cloud of want.

"I just wanted...Look, you're also sweet and funny and charming. And there's a...goodness," he fumbled with the word, "—you're a good person. And not self-righteous about it."

"And?" I said brusquely to cover that his words were making me lightheaded.

"And I can't always see past those to the bad things," he admitted. "And I have to, because you're too dangerous to love."

"I'm falling in love with you. Is that better?"

He dropped his hands from the door and backed away, brows furrowed, eyes wide. My hardwood floor stuck to his now bared feet. "There you go again. You made a decision, and it won't even matter about the truth!"

"What's the truth?" I stalked him across the bedroom.

"People don't fall in love in two weeks!"

"A week and half," I corrected. "You're just scared. And you want me right there with you."

"With good reason. What you're feeling isn't real. You're wanting someone else, and you're projecting him on me!"

"Don't tell me what I feel. Maybe I don't love you. Maybe I've just convinced myself I do. But despite all your faults, this is the closest thing to love I've felt. So maybe I'm in love with you, *but not yet!*"

He took another step backward and then another. "That's the problem. You don't think I have faults. I'm just Jess to you. The perfect—" He buckled backward onto the bed. I landed gently atop him. "—memory."

I pinned his wrists. "You're obsessive about Cai. Snarky. Treat people like you're a parent. Bossy. Controlling. Sleep with men for money." My knee split his legs apart, and I pushed between them. "Sleep with *me* for money! Use sex to deflect conversations. Manipulative. Act forty instead of twenty. Contradict yourself. Tell people what you think they want to hear."

"That's the same as manipulative." He bit his lip.

"Bite your fucking lip too much," I growled.

He lifted his chin and deliberately ran his tongue over the edges of his teeth. "You like it."

The Solution To All Problems is a Blow Job

"Blow jobs are not going to solve our problems," he whispered in my ear an hour later.

"I'm really tired. My ass and dick are sore. We can test that theory when we wake up."

The air-conditioning ticked on, blowing against my sweat-dotted skin. I shivered and pulled his hand closer to me. He kissed and sucked at the slope of my shoulder, instantly sending needed warmth into my blood. "I have to take Cai to the doctor for his prescription in a few hours."

I soaked in the details of a perfect moment. He held me close, my naked back to his bare chest. The metal ring from his nipple imprinting on my skin. His cock, soft and wet, lay against my ass. It all should have felt strange. It should have felt uncomfortable. But when I looked down at our laced hands resting against my stomach—men's hands with long fingers and sprinkled with sparse hair—all I felt was the world finally tilting in place. Peter had righted the ground under my feet. I was normal for the first time in my life.

"He has a mother, Peter. She's supposed to do those things for him." He rolled away from me. Another shiver passed over my skin, coldness seeping into my bones.

"I take care of Cai."

Fuck, were we ever going to get this dance right? Three steps forward, ten steps back. I flipped around to face him. "You're indebted to Cai you mean."

"Just go to sleep, Austin. It's not your concern."

"Tell me what he has over you?" I was ninety-nine percent sure of the reason, but I wanted to hear him admit it. I believed he needed to tell someone.

"He's my brother. Even you can understand family." He offered me his back, tugging the sheet up.

Ouch. Even me. The guy who had no family. I could snap back at him, but I didn't want to fight again. I wanted to rewind the last three minutes to that feeling of rightness. Deciding to drop the subject, I folded myself around him. Time to lead some forward steps. "I'm done fighting with you." I pressed my forehead against the back of his head, resting my fingers on his arm. He relaxed into my embrace and brought my hand to his lips, kissing the palm.

"Me too," he said. "Done fighting any of it."

"Tilt," I whispered.

"Huh?"

"Exactly," I said. Drifting off into sleep, I felt hope blanket around us.

Dreams Interrupting Fantasies

I awoke on my stomach with the bad taste of a disturbing dream lingering on my tongue and Peter's fingernail promising interesting things as it scraped down my spine. "Lower," I mumbled sleepily into a puddle of drool. The dream was quickly becoming a distant memory.

"Your butt cheek looks ravaged."

"It had a brutal workout yesterday. It's earned a little leniency in the attractiveness department."

He sat back on my thighs and spread my cheeks. I thanked the pillow for not tearing between my teeth. "How's it feel?" he asked.

My ass? Or what you're doing to it? My mouth was not cooperating with what I wanted to say. "Please."

"Can't. I have to go soon," he said huskily. "I'm going to put some more stuff on your cuts and cover the stitches so you can shower. This is going to hurt."

"I need to run before I shower. We can tape it up after." Feeling like we were on shaky ground from last night, I wanted us to do something routine. "Want to run with me?" I asked.

I looked over my shoulder when he climbed off and watched him gather a box of plastic wrap, a tube and medical tape off the bed. It warmed me that taking care of me was the first thing on his mind. Or maybe the second, I thought, recalling the way his finger had dragged along the crease of my ass before he had slid off me.

Peter tilted his head, chewing his inner lip as he glanced at my bedside clock. "Cai's appointment is at eleven. It's nearly nine-thirty. When I get back? Should you be running with stitches?"

"Maybe not," I admitted. But the thought of running with Peter, maybe even on a daily basis was appealing. More than appealing. I checked the clock, too. We'd had about three hours of sleep. Not even that could erase my smile. Rubbing my eyes, I untangled my legs from the sheet and swung them off the bed. "Did you go downstairs like that?" I asked, staring unabashedly at his naked body.

"Borrowed your jeans. Took them off again when I saw your bare ass."

"I had a sheet on. How did you see my bare ass?"

He smirked, then offered me the backside view as he walked into the bathroom. My cock sent a waving hand to my brain. "Don't even think about it," he called over his shoulder. "It took twenty minutes to wake you up, and now we don't have time." The door clicked shut, and my smile fell.

Without Peter as a distraction, the dream from this morning was suddenly a heavy weight on my spirit. I had dreamt it just moments before I had fully awakened, when my subconscious drew me towards a memory rather than a fantasy.

Six months ago Marta and I were sat at her breakfast table. We had been surrounded by soft sunlight from the wide kitchen window. Asa had just turned three and was squirming in her mother's arms. In the dream-memory everything was the same, except both of them were blurry, and only part of the conversation was clear.

Marta kissed Asa's freckled cheek. "Håll dig lugn, mitt lilla barn."

"Hole day lung, meet Lila Barn?" I asked.

Marta laughed. "This is good, Oz. You learn yourself Swedish."

I smiled and stirred the coffee which magically appeared at my elbow. "What's it mean?"

"Hold yourself still, my little child."

Barn. Child. Barn lager. I'd never taken the time to find the name, but Marta had opened a store not too long ago. Dave's nervousness came back to me from yesterday.

But barn could have meant anything—in any language. Swedish, Danish, Norwegian, Dutch. Come to think of it, I recalled seeing bairn as a Scottish word in a book once. So the word alone wasn't causing the gears in my brain to shift into overdrive. It was a preponderance of the clues gathered into one nightmarish thought.

Alvarado, at the very least, smuggled illegal aliens into the country. The cash Luis and I were tracking was probably money being laundered through enterprises owned by, according to Peter, cops. Back when Peter saw the list of businesses on the computer, he'd only recognized a few. Was one of the businesses Marta's?

There were too many coincidences to actually be coincidence. A foreboding itch started in the back of my head.

Dave had arrested Alvarado.

Dave's strange visit the other day.

Dave's nervous tapping last night.

Dave's Swedish wife who ran a Swedish children's clothing store.

Barn, the Swedish word for child.

What did lager mean?

Throwing on some jeans and a t-shirt, I hurried down to the living room to grab my laptop, only to freeze on the landing as I stared at the far wall.

Everyone's a Critic

"Jesus," I whispered.

Cai turned around, a rainbow of speckles dotting his face, arms and hands. A large streak of blue fit into the crease of his smile and there was a yellow blotch next to one dimple. "Um. Not finished. It's not finished. The mural. The mural is not finished."

"Jesus," I said again, words failing me. Not finished, but no less spectacular. Or at least the third of it he had completed was. From across the room, the gothic style church looked as if each individual brick was painted in detail, including the grooves and cracks. They weren't the traditional red or grey bricks, but a mixture of blues, reds and yellows which, like the rest of the painting, were surreal colors creating a realistic image.

"Stunning work," Agent One said, leaning against the wall just outside the kitchen. His gun was holstered neatly against his ribcage, and he was sipping what smelled deliciously like coffee.

"Stunning," I agreed. Since words were failing me, I wasn't above borrowing. I smiled at Cai's pleased bounce onto his toes. "Have you slept at all?"

"Um. Yessir?" His face turned an unusual shade of crimson.

"You're a terrible liar, Cai," I chided. The agent smiled into his cup. "That coffee?" I asked.

"I took the liberty." The man nodded at my coffee maker. "I hope you don't mind."

"If you left some for me, I might kiss you." The agent's brow rose.

"Riley is gay," Cai announced. Riley coughed, spilling his coffee down his chin.

"Interesting," I said and narrowed my eyes at the man who disappeared into the kitchen to clean off his shirt. "Riley is also my age. Did you notice that, too?" In a moment so reminiscent of Peter that my heart ached, Cai bit his lip and turned his blushing face back to the wall. "Peter's going to be down soon to take you to your appointment." I nodded to the overalls where the blue material peeked through streaks and splatters of paint.

"Oh," he looked down, "Lost the time." He quickly cleaned his brushes and started to jog out of the room, stopping at the open partition to the kitchen. "Um. See you tonight?" His fingers toyed with a beaded necklace around his neck. Had that been there before?

"I'll be here at ten," Riley nodded.

"Great!" Cai grinned and tossed a wave before vanishing down the hall.

"He's a sweet kid," Riley said once the door to the back bedroom shut. The emphasis on 'kid' was a relief.

"Sometimes easy to forget he's a kid." I poured a cup of coffee and hesitated in the kitchen, eyeing the makeshift tarp over my coffee table. The laptop was still there from Tuesday.

"If you say so." He held out his hand, his smile creasing the corners of his eyes. The lines spoke more to the frequency of his laughter than his age. "Agent Riley Cordova."

I shook the outstretched hand. "Austin Glass." It stung to have to drop the detective prefix. Had I already decided not to return to duty? No. "I'd love to shoot the shit, but I have some neglected work to look into." After holding the coffee cup up in a gesture of thanks, I retrieved the laptop from under the tarp and sat on the sofa, feet propped up on the coffee table.

Cordova sat next to me, ankle crossed over his knee and an electronic reader in his lap. I spoke without looking at him. "The FBI afraid of the big bad homo molesting their straight agents?" The words were light but my fingers tapped my password with unnecessary force.

"It would be unprofessional and inappropriate to call you defensive and reactionary, Detective Glass."

"So you'll just imply it?" A rueful grin wiped the hostility from my face. I could get to like Riley Cordova.

"I'm implying," he paused considering his words, "that you're taking the defensive against perceived offense, not an actual one."

"No coincidence you're gay and assigned to this case?" I asked with an accusing tone, waiting for the laptop to boot up.

"No coincidence," he agreed. "Mrs. Strakosha made some demands about the men on her personal security detail."

Oh.

I was an idiot. Not that I was going to apologize. The sting of rejection from my colleagues was still sharp. The memory of dildos and lube rattling to the front of my desk drawer was a vivid reminder of where they stood. "Well, welcome to homo-land."

He laughed and went back to reading. "Welcome yourself, Detective."

I chuckled, opened my web browser and forgot about agent Cordova. After navigating to the search engine, I typed in 'barn lager'.

Schizophrenic News

My first impression of the search results was that 'barn lager' was not proper Swedish, or Danish or any other language. The first entries were a mishmash of sites with one word or the other. Nothing sensible combined both words except a china pattern from Pottery Barn. My search led nowhere.

I navigated to an online translator service. The Danish translation of "child store" made sense. In Swedish and Norwegian it meant "child bearing". None of it got me any closer to an answer. Maybe I was wrong about the whole thing. A small laugh escaped as I breathed out.

"Good news?" Agent Cordova asked.

"Very. I'm the king of wild accusations it seems." I tapped the plastic trying to think of where to search from there. Maybe there was a beer place locally. I typed 'barn lager Denver', hit enter, and began to read down the page.

The ninth entry demolished my smile.

I almost missed it as I scrolled through the same results from the last search. The second-to-last link was in Swedish, and I was offered a button to translate the text. I clicked it.

Barnlager.com—We carry baby clothes, children's clothes and toys made in Sweden—16th Street and Wynkoop, Denver

16th and Wynkoop. Smack dab in the middle of the 16th Street Mall. I opened up the site's front page and skimmed over the pictures of toddlers in play clothes before delving deeper in. It took ten minutes, but I found what I was looking for on a list of importers. Asa's Playground was midway down the page.

It didn't take much of a leap to figure the name of Marta's shop.

Half-Wit's End

"Fuck." I dragged a hand through my hair and went on a hunt for the spreadsheet files from Luis and the restaurant. Was Asa's Playground among the companies listed? Wouldn't I have noticed that before? But that day I'd been distracted. Darryl and his wandering fucking hand.

"Bad news so soon? Things change on a dime around here."

"You're telling me," I muttered. "Two weeks ago I was straight." And at the height of my career. I put the spreadsheets side by side and began comparing the data.

"Is that when you decorated the house?"

My head rose and then turned to the agent. He was smiling but pretending to read. "It would be unprofessional and inappropriate to say 'fuck you'," I deadpanned.

"Not to mention sexually harassing."

Since he didn't look up, my stare went unnoticed. "Everyone's a fucking wit lately." I turned my attention back to the files.

Nothing on Asa's Playground mentioned. Was I reaching? I scrolled down the list again, slower this time.

"You're missing some numbers there," Cordova said, peering over at my screen.

"What?"

"Scroll up a few lines. Stop." He pointed at my screen.

I hadn't been checking the spreadsheet line numbers, just the names. I worked backward, up the list stopping at line one thirty-nine. The next number up was one twenty-seven. "Shit." Were those missing when I first saw the file? I gave myself a mental pat on the back for printing out the original files. Setting the laptop aside, I lifted the tarp and began searching for the papers. They weren't there.

Maybe Cai had moved them? Or Rosa. I scoured the living room for them. Checked my office. Nothing.

Maybe Dave had taken them home to review.

And not told you about it yesterday when you mentioned them?

Oh, Yay. Peter Pissed at Someone Else For a Change

I grabbed my coffee cup and went to think in the kitchen. What was I going to do? What could I do? What should I do?

Confront him? Give him time to hide the evidence? *This is Dave, you're talking about.*

What did I *know*, anyway? Nothing for certain. Barn lager wasn't even a common saying in Swedish. Otherwise there would have been references of the phrase all over the web. Marta would not use incorrect Swedish for her company. Would she?

Anyone could have moved the papers.

So what if Dave knew Alvarado. I knew him, too. And I wasn't involved with his laundering.

And yesterday? He had just been nervous. Dave had been nervous about standing next to the homo who slept with a witness and whose career was only missing the final knock of the gavel before it ended.

Normally I wouldn't question my instincts. I was good at what I did: piecing information together and seeing the error in an equation.

You're just wrong this time.

The address was downtown—the 16th street mall, just where Peter and Darryl remembered.

Barnlager.com.

The missing pages. Dave had them in his hands. *You left him here alone.*

Dave has your laptop password from the fantasy football league.

Fuck. Fuck. Fuck!

No fucking way was I turning him in. It was a selfish thought, but I couldn't get past the fact that Dave was my last ally. My only remaining friend. The one person I could call family.

I was pacing a stripe into the kitchen floor when Darryl walked in.

"Oh, God. Please tell me you two aren't still fighting," he moaned. His eyes were half-masted and crusty with sleep. That didn't stop his mocking voice. "I love you. No you don't. I don't love you. Yes you do. Wah wah wah. Some of us wanted to sleep!"

I wasn't rising to the bait. Instead, I changed the subject. "You slept with Rosafa in tighty-whities and a tank top?"

"I think her virtue is safe with me." He lifted his pink blindfold off his neck and used it as a headband. "Thank fuck there's coffee. Who's the stud on the sofa? I vaguely recall him as I stumbled to bed last night."

"FBI. Rosa's personal guard," I said distractedly. Why hadn't I picked up the phone already?

If Dave admitted to laundering? Trafficking? Murder? What then?

"What are you worked up about?" I followed Darryl's sneer to my fingers drumming on the countertop.

"Nothing."

"Why does Rosa have a security detail?" Darryl asked. I watched as he poured the last of the brown liquid into his cup. My own mug sat half-empty and mourning. "I thought she wasn't in witness protection anymore."

It was a valid question, but other things were on my mind. "How the fuck should I know? Ask her."

"All right, dickwad. I will."

The doorbell rang. Agent Cordova stood and peeked in through the archway to the kitchen. "That's probably my partner Agent McCleary. Would you mind if I answered your door?"

"Go for it." I wasn't paying attention. I didn't care who came and went in the house.

Darryl runway-walked back to the bedroom without spilling a drop of his coffee, all while somehow managing to ogle Cordova's butt. Waterboarding wouldn't have made me admit I was watching Darryl's ass as he left.

It wasn't even that great of an ass.

"Detective Glass, this is Special Agent Dan McCleary. He'll be on day shift in the house." Rather than come to me, Dan McCleary held out his hand and kept it there until I had to exit the kitchen to shake it. Speaking of great asses, Dan McCleary clearly was one.

Let the dick contests begin.

McCleary was an unpolished, semi-attractive man in his late thirties or early forties. His hair was grey. His suit was cheap. His cologne was cheaper, and his attitude was a hundred percent asshole.

He gave me an instant boner.

One day I was going to have to analyze why whores and assmunchers gave me wood, while nice guys like Riley left me feeling blasé.

Maybe I just wasn't responding because I knew Cai had a crush on him.

Yeah that was it.

Before I could lie to myself some more, Darryl's voice bellowed from the bedroom. "Over my dead perfectly-posed body!"

The guest room door banged open. Darryl strode past me in a blur of blond hair, his skinny legs disappearing upstairs.

"I take it he just found out what Rosa being in WitSec means?" I proffered, raising my eyes to the ceiling. Upstairs the pounding on my bedroom door gave way to muffled yelling.

Rapid Shift in Parenting

In the search for distraction from thoughts of my best friend's possible criminal activity, my mind began meandering after Darryl's question: *"Why does Rosa have a security detail?"*

Answer: Because her life is in danger.

Question: *Why is her life in danger?* To answer that question, I had to think laterally.

Whom does the FBI guard?

Answer: Important people.

Who are the important people to the FBI?

Answer: Celebrities, statesmen, politicians and witnesses. Rosafa Strakosha is not a politician, statesmen or celebrity. Therefore, she is a witness.

Why does Rosa, a plain old witness, get to pick her security detail?

Answer: She's important enough that they bow to her requests.

The subject of my thoughts emerged from the bedroom, wrapping a leopard print hijab over her head. "You have to wear that?" I asked.

"You think I wear this in summer because it is so comfortable?" She brushed a hand over her ankle length black skirt.

"I think if God wanted you to wear that, He wouldn't have invented heatstroke."

What kind of info would Rosa have for the FBI? Albanian syndicate crime was a growing issue, I knew that much. I also knew that there were a recent slew of arrests across the nation. All of them were part of an Albanian organized crime family. What had the DA said in court? Something about Rosafa having relatives tied to the Albanian mafia.

There wasn't time for more thought on the subject. Peter came charging down the stairs, hair still damp and unbuttoned shirt billowing behind him. "The fuck you are, Rosa. The fuck you're taking Cai."

"He is my son," she said calmly.

"Settle down, boy." Agent McCleary stepped in front of Rosa, hand reaching inside his jacket. Cordova moved closer to Peter. So did I.

Cai came dashing out of the hall, clothes stuck to his body and hair dripping wet. "Um. We can go now. My anklet blinked. That means we can go." He pulled at Peter's arm desperately. His giant feet sloshed in a pair of checkered Keds. He looked like he'd pulled his clothes on *while* he showered.

"He's not going with you. You don't even know him. He doesn't need more shit in his life."

"He is my son, Petya."

Darryl's eyes brimmed with angry tears. "He's ours now."

"Peter," I tried to reason. "This isn't the time. Things can be discussed when we—"

"You see? Peter. Not Petya. Not Pyotr. I'm not Petya, he's not Danny and that's not Nikë. I'm Peter, that's Darryl and he's Cai. That's who he is now. He's not your Nikë. You don't even know how to take care of him."

"Rabbit, please," Cai begged. "Let's go."

"I will learn."

"Oh, you'll learn? You'll learn in the few weeks before he has the stress of starting college? Did you even know he was going to college? No? Do you recognize when he's sick, Rosa? Not once since you arrived have you noticed he's hypomanic. Do you even know what hypomanic means? Didn't you ask why he's not more upset after being raped? Didn't it occur to you that his behavior wasn't normal for someone about to be tried for murder? But you're going to learn? Right."

Cai crushed his hand against his eye.

Cordova stepped between Rosa and Peter. "I think you should leave, Mr. Dyachenko."

"Knock it off, Peter," I said. "This can wait."

Rosa looked unsure, her eyes darting down. "He wants come with me."

"Bullshit!" But Cai's fingers dropped from Peter, and he blushed guiltily, tears wiped away before they fell. Peter looked at his arm where Cai's hand had rested and then turned in slow motion to face his brother. "Cai?"

"We have to go," the boy whispered and looked at me with despair.

I didn't know which of them sounded more in pain. But I knew Cai was the one going to jail if he missed his psychiatrist appointment.

"Let me get my shirt on and some shoes, and I'll take you. Come upstairs and wait." I smiled in what I hoped was reassurance and followed him up. Peter and his chewed lip would have to wait. Darryl and his tears would have to wait. Rosa and her bodyguards, my breakfast, my career, the case—all of it would have to wait.

Chapter Twenty

How to Adopt a Teenager Without Your Consent

Cai sat on the bed while I finished getting dressed. When I turned around, he was tearing off the end of his fingernail, a line of red surfacing where the nail had been decimated. He stared at the blood for a second, then went to work on the next finger.

I knew he needed to talk, but we needed to go. If he was late, or didn't show up, he would violate the terms of his home monitoring. Time was ticking away while I stood across from him, sneakers and socks dangling at my thigh. I struggled with how to handle him.

The problem was that I didn't know where to start. Why was he crying? Was it his disorder? Was he having a depressive episode? That could only be solved with medication. Which just made me antsier to get him to the doctor's office.

Or was he embarrassed about downstairs? Was he upset about Peter? The trial? The rape?

Christ. When I listed it like that, I was surprised the kid wasn't a basket case. What was I supposed to say here anyway? It'll be okay?

What a crock of shit. Nothing for this kid was going to be okay.

Suck it up?

I think Peter might actually shoot you if you say that to his brother.

A nervous laugh erupted from me and brought Cai's eyes to mine. He fought a flow of tears, blinking and squeezing his lids tight. Only a few escaped and slid down his cheeks.

Shit. If this kid stuck around long enough, I was going to teach him how to be a real man. You know, by bottling up his feelings and letting them fester until an ulcer formed. A man wasn't a man until the denial of feelings made him physically sick.

"What's the address of the doctor?" Changing the subject. Genius!

"Dunno." He sniffed and brutally wiped his eyes with the back of his hand. There were still droplets of water cascading from his wet hair over his cheeks. But fewer tears.

"Do you know the way there?" My genius tactic was working; the tears had almost stopped.

He shook his head and began to shiver violently. "N-never b-been there." I needed to reset my air conditioning. On the other hand, he should have dried off before getting dressed and not have expected me to look out for him. I wasn't his fucking father.

"Never been there?" I said more tersely than I meant to.

"N-new doctor. Miss J-Jackson set it up."

"New doc— Was her name Kate?" He nodded. I wasn't surprised. Over the years I had sent Angelica many juveniles to defend. More often than not, she put them in therapy with Kate Sherman. I took a seat beside Cai, making sure to give him space while I hurriedly stuffed my feet into my shoes. "We'll talk in the car. Okay?"

"I'm f-fine." The boy took a breath, steeling himself, rubbing hard at his face. He plastered on a smile so genuine that I was stunned. After one more shaky breath, the only way anyone could tell he'd been crying was the slight redness around his eyes. He even attempted to control his shivers.

I felt guilty for blaming him for crying. "You don't need to hold it together, Cai. No one is going to mock you for feeling. If anyone has a right to cry, it's you." What happened to making him a man? *Damn kid is getting to you.*

He pulled out a packet of candy and emptied a handful of orange and brown pieces into his mouth. "I'm fine." I was blasted by the scent of peanut butter.

"We *will* talk in the car." After lacing my shoes, I yanked the bag of candy away. "And stop trying to get high off sugar. Fuckssake. Next bill I get for you is probably going to be the dentist bankrupting me." I crushed the packet and tossed it in the trash on my way out.

Halting in the doorway, I twisted to view Cai behind me. He blinked and rubbed his arms, brows rising in question. If I still had the candy, I would have grabbed his hand and jammed the package back in it.

When did I start sounding like a parent?

Arturo Sees More Action Than Reality TV

Peter was waiting on the bottom step. Darryl was leaning on the bannister, looking up at us. I wasn't surprised. I had figured Cai and I wouldn't be going alone to the shrink's office.

The moment the kid appeared behind me, they both started talking at once. I cut them off.

"Let's go." I turned to Rosa who was clanking about in the kitchen, loudly passive-aggressive in every slam of the pot. "They can stay," I told her, "if you want to ride along."

"The fuck we can," Peter said. Darryl snarled at the same time, "No we fucking can't!"

Rosa came out of the kitchen, wiping her hands on her apron. It didn't do any good. She took her son's cheeks in her palms, leaving flour along his temple and near his ear. "You call when finished so I have lunch ready, yes?"

"Sure, mamma." He smiled and kissed her cheek. She waited for the others to follow suit. Darryl gave her a reluctant peck, but Peter stormed out of the house, the door making a splintering sound as it bent on the hinges from the force of his anger. I cringed. Cai flinched. Darryl followed him out. And I'd swear my door whimpered.

"Why must he abuse my door? It's the only fucking piece that isn't suicidal cream or bowel-movement brown."

"He's so mad," Cai said.

"At me, Nikë, not you. He loves you. Go now." Rosa brushed his face free of flour and flitted us out the door.

In the parking lot Darryl stood at the passenger side, waiting with the door open and the seat tilted. Peter was in the back with Cai. I carefully slid into the driver's seat and joined everyone in silence.

Ten minutes into the drive, I started tapping on the steering wheel and shifting off my ass cheek. Darryl flipped through radio stations. Peter stared at Cai. Cai drew breath pictures on the window.

No one would ever mistake this for a joyride. "No, this isn't awkward at all," I mumbled.

The tension shattered with thunder from Darryl. "You can't leave, you ungrateful little dipshit!" He turned partway in his seat.

Cai sighed and continued his mist sketching. My eyes drifted to Peter. I finally got a glimpse of why Cai had nicknamed him Rabbit. He ripped pieces of his bottom lip with his front teeth and stared at my seat. His nose continuously twitched, eyes blinking rapidly. I hadn't seen the manifestation of his Tourette's until now. It was painful to watch him come apart and know there was nothing I could do about it. Legally, Rosa was Cai's mother. If she wanted him with her....

"We'll never see you again, Cai. That's what they do. They take you away and cut off contact with everyone else," Peter murmured.

"It's only for a couple of years, Rabbit. Until I'm eighteen."

"Just...I know things have been...bad the last few months."

"We'll do better, kiddo," Darryl promised vehemently.

Cai said nothing the rest of the drive.

Kate's building took up the entire block at the top of the 16th Street Mall, intersecting with the busiest street in Denver. Businesspeople trickled out the revolving doors, onto the plaza or took seats on the marble single-seat benches near the walkway.

Pulling in front, I turned the car off and watched Peter in the rearview mirror. His hands rubbed up and down his thighs, nose twitching even while he pulled his top lip into his mouth. I rubbed the ache in my chest and checked the time, disappointed that there wasn't enough of it to climb back there to console him. "His appointment is in ten minutes. Let's talk about this when he's done. 18th floor, that building there." I pointed and waited for a nod from the kid that he heard me. I would have missed it if I hadn't been staring intently at him.

No one was talking. No one was moving. I motioned to Darryl. He pinched his lips and threw open the door, yanking the seat up. I resisted petting my poor abused car.

Cai picked a loose thread in his jeans, jaw trembling. "Let me go, Rabbit. I can't live like this," he pleaded. "I can't be your penance anymore."

Peter clasped his hands and viciously rubbed his eyes. "You don't know what you're talking about."

"He's dead, Rabbit. They're both dead. You killed mine," Peter's head shot up, eyes widely staring at his brother, "—and I killed yours, and it's over. They're dead. Don't look at Dare. It was Uncle Nikki who told me. He sat there that night, laughing. *Bragging*. Making his hand into a gun. Laughing about it." Cai's plucking became more intense, until a ribbon of flesh peeked through the cotton.

Eight minutes until his appointment.

Darryl sat on the car edge, head hanging between his slumped shoulders. "What a fucking mess."

Peter's twitching became cataclysmic. He reached for Cai, drew back and gripped his own knees. "He made me. I swear to God, Cai, he made me."

The hole in Cai's jeans grew. "I know he did, Rabbit! That's why you need to let it go."

"It's not that simple." Peter rubbed his forehead raw.

I shifted in my seat in the ensuing uncomfortable silence. Peter's mouth opened and closed randomly like he was searching for something to say. Darryl hadn't moved a muscle. Four minutes until his appointment. Cai had stopped responding, but still hadn't made a move to exit the car. My fingers drummed again while I decided whether to break this up or let them work it out. It was an unbelievably inappropriate time to hash out a really-needed-to-be-hashed-out problem.

Finally, Cai pulled himself out of the car and looked at me briefly before staring at the ground. "Let it go, or I'm leavin', Rabbit," he whispered. "You 'n' Dare gotta just let go. You gotta get your own lives, and you gotta let me have one, too." Slapping away tears, he walked stiffly through the courtyard to the entrance of the building. Peter scooted out after him, stopping him just outside the doorway and pulling him into a hug. Cai's hands hung at his sides for a few seconds and then scrunched into Peter's shirt as he buried his face in his brother's neck.

11:01. The kid was late. And I didn't see this ending soon. If this took much longer, it would be called in to dispatch. Cai would be arrested. Someone had to light a fire under their asses. "You're not going over there?" I asked while hunting through my virtual rolodex for Kate's number and slipping the headset over my ear.

"Right now they need to work it out," Darryl said, flopping in the front seat.

I was going to point out that that wasn't exactly true, but my phone rang. I pushed the button on the steering wheel to answer. "Glass."

"Oz—"

"I was going to call you this morning."

"Shut up, and listen to me. Get the kid out of the building."

"Cai?" I unbuckled my safety belt and leaned forward. I spotted Cai and Peter pushing through revolving doors.

"Yes. I couldn't stop it. They're waiting for him at the shrink's office."

"Who?"

"You want me to explain or you want to get that kid before they take him?"

"What's going on?" Darryl asked. The string to his pink hoodie was wrapped tightly around his finger. He yanked at it.

"Stay in the car," I said. After waiting for a car to pass, I threw open the door and tore out of the seat.

"Hey! What's going on? Is it Peter?"

"Stay with the fucking car! In fact, get in the driver's seat," I yelled as I ran across the plaza, reaching into my back pocket for my phone. The Bluetooth was still streaming our call; I tore off the headset and hung up without a word to Dave. After nearly smacking my face into the revolving door, I stopped, scrolled to find Peter's number and pressed 'call'.

I spun to the right, toward the sound of the first ring. The second ring brought my hand to my right front pocket. By the third ring, I was holding Peter's phone in my palm. *"Borrowed your jeans. Took them off again when I saw your bare ass."*

"Fuck!" I raced to the elevators and machine-gun punched the up arrow until my thumb hurt. "I don't give a damn how low my pants hang on you, Peter, this is the last time you borrow them!" And the phone was locked. I couldn't even use it to call Cai. "Fuck me twice!"

I tossed Peter's phone into my front pocket and used mine to redial Dave's cell. Voice mail. I hung up and redialed, barely resisting slamming the phone against the wall when it clicked to voice mail again. The doors pinged open just as I dialed their home.

In the elevator, my finger rapidly pressed the button for the 18th floor. A business woman stepped in after me. As she reached to press a lower floor, I did the only rational thing. I panicked. Grabbing her briefcase, I tossed it out the door, ignoring her screech as she chased out after it. I squashed the 'close door' button like a dog with an itch. Marta answered the phone just as the woman directed me to the lowest depths of hell. The door closed out her escalating tirade.

Trust Is An Illusion

"Oz? Help. He is crazy!" Marta cried, hysterical with tears.

I quickly summoned an image of a lunatic there to kill her. "Have you called 911?!"

"No. No. It is Dave. He is throw our cloth in bags and saying we fly to Sweden."

I heard a rustling and more angry screams from Marta, then Dave took over the conversation. "Oz? Did you get him?"

The elevator climbed up to the fifth floor and stopped. "In the four minutes since I hung up with you? No, Goddammit. Who's up there?" I pressed 'door closed' before it even opened and kept my finger there. Tucking the phone against my shoulder, I barely contemplated the gender of the person who I pushed out of the elevator.

"Hey!"

"Take the next one," I thundered.

"I tried to stop it all after they killed Alvarado, but..." Dave, said.

The doors closed and the elevator pulled up, but it wasn't moving fast enough.

"Confessions later! Who? How many are there, worst case?"

"They just want the kid. So two, maybe three."

Twelfth floor.

"Guns?"

"Cops, Oz. At least one will be a cop. Probably Mick and Dick, they're always together. So, yeah, three."

"Who's the other one?"

"Leila Alvarado."

Shit. Leila Alvarado was a crack whore with a mean streak as big as her beehive hairdo. Luis and I had presumed that Prisc had killed her. Maybe it was the other way around? Now she was armed and waiting up there for Peter and Cai. And Dave had seen fit to only inform me five minutes ago. Silently I called him every name I could think of, but because I needed him, the words festered in the recesses of my mind. And I had to think rather than give in to the urge to vent.

Fourteenth floor.

Cops involved. Couldn't call 911. Mick and Dick surely had their radios. They'd hear instantly if I called. What would be their reaction if they heard the call? They'd just shoot Peter. Probably shoot them both. "Luis in on it?"

Fifteenth.

"I don't know. Maybe. Probably. I don't know everyone involved. Only a few of the bigger players." Trust Luis or not? *He's always trusted you. He's always stood by you. Risked his career for you.*

So has Dave and look where that got you.

I went with my gut. "Call him. Tell him everything." I hung up.

Eighteenth floor. The ding announcing the floor was like a gong. The doors slid open slowly.

"Go!" Peter screamed somewhere down the corridor furthest from me.

Cai emerged from the left hallway, about forty feet in front of me. He banged his shoulder against the door marked 'STAIRWELL'. Avoiding the stairs, he stepped onto the railing and jumped off. I didn't have time to contemplate where he landed. Peter was four steps behind him.

I propelled forward on autopilot, stopping just as a bullet splintered the doorframe near his head. "Jesus Christ," I whispered, automatically reaching for my nonexistent gun. Shit. Fuck.

Rather than follow Cai down, Peter pulled the door closed, effectively using it and himself as a shield. Two figures barreled down on him. Mick and Dick pushed past without a struggle. When the door swung shut leaving Peter behind them, I saw why.

Peter pulled a hand from his stomach, a patch of red blossoming there as he stared at his fingers. I was a few feet from him when Leila Alvarado put her gun to the back of his head.

"No!" No. No. No.

My shout startled her. Her hand jerked. But I was too late. Peter's forehead disappeared in a mist of red, and Leila's gun lifted and pointed directly at me.

Chapter Twenty-One

Tourette's is Contagious

I barreled on toward Leila. A shot whizzed a foot from my shoulder. I ducked, ran two more steps and plowed my head into her stomach. Her next shot hit the ceiling. A sickening crack filled the corridor as her skull collided with the wall. I didn't bother to watch as she slid to the floor—unconscious or dead. I preferred dead. I snatched the gun from her hand, secured it in my waistband and then crawled to Peter. Sitting back on my heels, I cradled his head in my lap.

He was wheezing each breath, but he was breathing. Streams of blood pumped from his skull and seeped between the fingers he cupped over his stomach. I blinked away sweat and tried to see his head wound while fumbling blindly for my phone. It wasn't beside me.

Until that moment, it hadn't registered that the gunshots had been muffled—since no one heard them, no one was coming to help.

"Peter, don't sleep. Don't stop breathing." I needed a phone. I scanned the area and saw mine down the hall near the elevator. In my haste to get to Peter, it had slipped from my fingers. "Help!" My voice cracked. "Peter?" He whimpered in pain. There was so much blood, leaking into my jeans, stiffening the material. "HELP!" I wiped at his forehead, but his hair was matting into the mess. I couldn't see anything. I pressed my hand over his. At least I could hold one wound closed. "Peter, don't pass out. Don't you dare pass out." *Or die. Don't die.*

Several people peeked into the corridor. Kate and her receptionist Kira were the only ones who didn't hesitate to run to us. Kate immediately began feeling around Peter's head. I tried to judge her reaction through a swath of her silver hair. It was impossible. "If you die on me, so help me, Peter...I swear to you. I fucking swear that I will let Cai rot in jail. I'll pin drugs on Darryl. I'll..."

"Officer Glass," Kate said, "I need you to stop yelling."

Was I yelling? Who gave a shit? "Call a fucking ambulance!"

"I've called 911," she said calmly. "I'm a doctor, Officer Glass. I'm going to take a look at them. Just take a deep breath, and try to focus." She made a move to check Leila whose head was also within reach.

"Not her. You don't fucking look at her!"

Kate hesitated, then nodded. "All right. For now. Kira, get some towels from the bathroom." The younger woman's ponytail bounced as she jogged down the hallway. Kate checked Peter's scalp. "Listen to me," she said, moving my and Peter's hands from his stomach. They were slick with blood. "His head wound is superficial, but he's weak from blood loss. You need to calm him down before he goes into shock. And yelling isn't going to help."

"I'm not yelling!"

Peter choked on a laugh and moaned. "Cai." He reached up and pushed weakly at my shoulder.

"Are you kidding me? You think for one second I'm going after Cai with you like this? You fucker! Asshole. Son of a bitch, whore, jerkoff." Apparently his Tourette's was contagious.

He moved his bloody hand toward my face. I tilted my cheek toward it and closed my eyes. His fingers pinched my lips shut.

I couldn't even summon a smile when his hand fell away. Opening my eyes, I took a moment to adjust to the light blurring my vision. The scent of blood was overwhelming. I grabbed his hand again and held on.

Kate had removed her blazer and was pressing the linen against the stomach wound. Kneeling by Peter's head, Kira offered Kate a stack of paper towels.

"Kira, take over here." They switched places, Kate taking the paper towels and pushing them up against Peter's head. He groaned, and his breathing grew shallow. Kate caught my attention with a deliberate snap of her fingers. "Listen, I don't think the bullet breached his skull. For now it looks like the scalp is torn apart. Head wounds bleed excessively even when they're not serious."

I knew that already, but hearing it gave me an emotional shake. "Wake up, you fucker." Peter's eyes fluttered but remained closed. I slapped his chest gently with our joined hands. "Wake. Up!"

"Stop. Whining." He cringed.

"I'm not whining. I'm yelling. And Christ, can't you stop giving orders even while shot? Domineering prick."

He choked a laugh again. I could barely make out his pink skin through the caul of blood on his face. The smile in the midst of that red mask was macabre even while uplifting. "Cold," he wheezed.

"You fucking cliché. Don't say shit like that!" I gave a panicked look around for something warm to put over him.

"It's the air conditioning and the blood soaking his clothes," Kate assured me. "He's not going into shock yet. Someone have a blanket?"

"How do you know? How fucking long is it going to take them?" I watched the elevator doors, blinking only when sweat dripped into my eyes. I was being unreasonable. It couldn't have been more than ten minutes since I stepped off the elevator, more like five.

"They'll be here soon. And I know because he's laughing and talking to you and because you're shivering too." Kate lifted Peter's lids. Was I imagining the murkiness clouding the blue of his eyes? "Peter, how old are you?"

"Twe-twenty."

She looked to me for confirmation. I nodded. She was checking for signs of shock. "Ask him something useful," I said. "Like does he love me not?"

"Soon," he breathed.

"Smartass."

"Ro...mantic."

Romantic? What the fuck? Since when was Peter romantic? "Should he be talking this much?"

Kate nodded. "There doesn't appear to be damage to his lungs or throat. His breathing is most likely labored due to pain. Keeping him talk—"

The elevator dinged. We collectively inhaled, watching the doors slowly open.

The Things I Do For You

I counted four cops. Two gurneys. Four paramedics. The EMTs stayed behind while the uniformed officers assessed the scene. I yelled out my name, rank and badge number and told them the scene was secure. The number of people standing inertly in the hallway must have convinced them. They motioned the EMTs forward.

The paramedics quickly push-pulled a gurney down the hall. Without being asked, the gawkers parted to allow them through. Though I regretted releasing of Peter's hand, I was finally in my right head enough to let them do their work. I let go, stood and took a few shaky steps backward.

Two officers checked the stairwell. Another checked the hallways then backtracked to where I was standing.

"Detective Glass?"

I nodded.

"You don't remember me, do you? James Hutcherson…"

My mind couldn't focus on his face. I stared at Officer Hutcherson blankly. He was a blur of black hair and brown eyes. "Sorry."

"We went to the Academy together."

"Ah, yeah." He seemed to be waiting for more. "Hey."

He smiled with warmth. "So, want to tell me what happened?"

My voice was monotone, explaining what I saw without embellishment. Strictly the facts, Jack—or James in this case. I didn't mention Mick's and Dick's names until the very end.

"Sir?"

"Officers Kelly Fitzpatrick and Jason Dillon."

"Yes, sir, about that, you said Mr. Dyachenko was blocking their path?"

I met his eyes. "I said Peter was unarmed and standing in the doorway."

"You are sure he was unarmed?"

"His hands were braced against the doorframe. I saw his entire body. A second later they converged on him. I didn't see which one shot him. They ran past him. He started bleeding. The second shooter, who I identified as Leila Alvarado, came down the same hallway and shot him in the head. The whole thing took maybe a few seconds." I lifted my shirt, showed the gun and waited. He got the clue, retrieving it from my jeans.

"She got off two more shots before I tackled her." I nodded to Leila. One of the paramedics was examining her. Another had cleaned Peter's head wound and was bandaging it up. Hovering against the wall, I tried to assess the wounds as they cleaned them.

The EMTs were working quickly, but I saw enough of Peter's injuries to clench my fists.

The second bullet had ripped through his scalp from the side of his head to his temple. I thought I saw bone peeping through before the white linen hid the gash. It looked worse than it was. They'd probably shave his head and stitch it up.

If he lived.

If? If he lived?

A pair of scissors sliced through Peter's shirt. The wound to the right of his belly button was only a small round hole. It looked innocuous, but I knew there was carnage below the surface.

Watching the latex-covered hands work all over his body brought my own hands up. They were gloved in blood. My heart tripped in its beat. I wanted to take back that gun and shoot Leila in the face until she was unrecognizable.

"Could Mr. Dyachenko have been shot before he blocked the doorway?" Hutcherson asked.

I glared at him. For the briefest of seconds, I considered punching him in the gut and asking him to run down the hallway. I chose the diplomatic route instead. "Are you an idiot?"

"I have to ask—"

"Have you ever been shot?" He shook his head. "Give me your baton and let me jam it into your stomach."

"Point taken, sir."

People had better quit calling me sir.

My pocket began to ring again, pulling me out of disturbing images. This time a classical ringtone played. Rachmaninoff maybe. It just had to be Cai.

Peter's hand twitched and pointed at my pocket. I shook my head. "No you can't fucking talk to Cai." *I should answer it, though.* But not while cops were here. I wasn't trusting anyone on the force right now.

"Code," Peter rasped though his oxygen mask. I waited until the ring had stopped; then I crouched and handed him the phone. He punched in the code and folded my fingers around the plastic. "Please."

"Even if I wanted to, I can't leave. I'm a witness."

"It's okay, Detective Glass, I think we have everything for now," Hutcherson said.

Bigmouthed asshole.

Down the hall Dave's ringtone brought my phone to life. My attention was splitting in too many directions. I didn't feel like a cop right then. I had zero interest in pursuing leads or hearing evidence from suspects or chasing teenagers. Peter was my only concern. "All right. I *can* go. But I *don't* want to." I looked at our hands, caked and coated in red, but entwined. The pristine moment when they were clasped like that earlier in the day seemed weeks ago.

"Clean." Peter said.

"Can I get a water bottle or something to clean his hands?" I scanned the crowd. He drew my attention back to him with a pull of my hand.

"No," Peter said. "I'm...clean."

I had missed who Peter was until that very moment.

I had called him names and treated him callously. I had read every micro expression in a vacuum of how it related to Austin Glass. And in return Peter had cared for my wounds, treated me tenderly and assured me that he was HIV negative while bleeding out in a hallway of strangers.

I broke. It wasn't a visible fracture. I didn't sob or explode into anguish. I didn't give in to my vomitus urge that came from the burst of self-loathing. But I shattered nonetheless.

"Well, you look filthy," I said, hitting redial on his phone and jamming it to my ear. "I'll find him."

Can't Anything Just Be Easy?

Cai's voicemail clicked on immediately. His phone was either turned off or dead. Mine began ringing again. Letting go of Peter's hand again was difficult, but I had to. I dodged the other gurney, snatching my cell off the floor before the wheels could roll over it. I didn't have to see the caller ID to know it was Luis.

"Guess what I found," I said with fake cheer while staring at Leila's unconscious form.

"Your career?"

"Is everyone getting wittier, or am I getting more stupid?"

"I'm here with the captain."

"Great. You can both guess! I'll give you a hint. It has big hair and a bad attitude."

"Leila."

"Ding. Ding. Ding! Wait, were you really guessing?"

"Buchanan called, gave a few names."

"And then poofed?"

"That kind of thinking proves you're not getting stupider. I was just explaining to the captain how this case needed two detectives not one. And how there's only one I know who's not part of this shit."

I backed out of the way as the paramedics raised the gurney. Peter's eyes were fighting to stay open, but in the end they fluttered closed and stayed that way. He looked paler than usual against the dark grey blanket.

"I might actually hump you next Wednesday, Luis. Were Mick and Dick among those names he gave you?"

"Yup. Top of the list. You all right?"

"I'm covered in blood. I watched Peter get shot in the stomach and then the head. Mick and Dick probably have his brother and are torturing or murdering him as we speak. I don't have my gun or badge, and my best friend is a criminal. Sure. I'm doing great. Thanks for asking."

"The boy okay?"

"If you mean Peter, I don't know. They're getting ready to wheel him out now. I can't even go to the hospital with him because he's an asshole and insisting I have to find his brother—his probably dead brother. And I have no badge and no gun. I mentioned that, didn't I?"

"The brother isn't dead. Mick and Dick just put a BOLO out on him."

I covered the mouthpiece and tapped Hutcherson on the shoulder, pointing at Peter. "You with him. No one, not even other cops, get to him without you watching. Leave his side and you'll have to repatriate to Canada to avoid me. Got it?"

He nodded and gave me a wry grin. I really didn't have the authority to order him anywhere. I went back to my call.

"They haven't caught him then?" I said it loudly for Peter's benefit. His eyes were closed, but I sensed he was listening—or trying to listen between all the chatter from the paramedics and the people around us. His body relaxed, and he attempted a deep breath. I lowered my voice. "Oh, good. Now every dirty cop can Be On The Lookout, armed and ready. He doesn't stand a chance."

"Thought the kid was a genius?"

"He is. But he's also having issues with his medication. I don't know if he functions well without it."

"We'll find him."

"Before they do?"

"It's what we do best."

"Finding people is what you do best. Interrogating them is what I do best. And I may have mentioned that *I have no badge or gun!*"

"You do now. I'm on my way there with them. Captain is reinstating you. Give me your loc."

Stepping into the elevator with Peter and the paramedics, I looked down at my clothes and sighed while considering my options. If I stopped at a store I'd have to deal with checkout lines. If I went home, it'd be fifteen minutes out of the way. Jeffrey's was two minutes from me. I rattled off the address of my tailor.

"You're buying suits?"

"I can't even see the color of my shirt through the blood. Press is at my house, it's lunch hour downtown, tailor's less than two minutes from here with my wedding suits. You have a better idea?"

"I'll be there in ten."

Never had I been so grateful for Angelica's fastidious wedding choices.

Peter was out cold by the time the elevator hit the lobby. We all rushed out when the doors opened. Another elevator opened, more paramedics sped by me. On the gurney was, unfortunately, a still-breathing Leila.

Officer Hutcherson and I jogged close behind. Digging into my pocket I fished out my wallet and gave him a business card. "You call me with news. Leave a message if I don't answer. Do not leave him," I repeated. We split up. He followed Peter out the regular doors, and I veered right, pushing through the revolving ones, running for my car.

Would Penis Bullets Hurt?

Darryl was sitting in the driver's seat, phone against his ear. I tapped the glass, heard the door unlock and climbed in. Darryl's jaw dropped when he saw me. My pocket rang again. His eyes flashed to my pants. "Where's Peter? Where's Cai? Whose blood is that? Why do you have Peter's phone? Was that them with the ambulances?" I yanked the back of his pink hoodie as he tried to open the door.

"Drive. I'll—"

"Drive? *Drive?* That's your explanation? Peter would never give you his phone unless... Two people wheeled out of there, and you think I'm just going to leave without Peter and Cai? Where are they taking them?"

"I'd boot you out of this fucking car if I didn't need you. Get in and drive. Stop arguing with me. Cai is on the run. We need to find him before they do. And by they, I mean the bad guys. And *they* have the advantage of the GPS on his ankle bracelet, whereas I just have you." That shut him up. He took another look at the ambulance as it drove off. "Three blocks down make a right."

He started the car. "That's a one-way. You can't turn right."

My God I hated this area. "Get me to 16th and Market." He threw the car into drive and pealed out. I winced and stroked the dashboard lovingly. "Drop me off and go park the car. Text Peter's phone with where you are, and stand by the curb." I started to pull everything from my pockets: wallet, a yellow bandana, the phones. Darryl glared at me between each stop light and pedestrian walkway.

"Whose blood is that?"

"If Cai calls you, tell him to keep moving."

"Whose. Blood. Is—"

"And to get rid of the anklet however he can."

He jerked to a stop. I braced against the dash, this time protecting myself from going through the windshield. "Two seconds to answer, or I will beat you until you do."

"Peter's. Don't!" I jerked up the emergency brake before he could turn the car around. "You can't do him any good pacing a hospital waiting room. He's probably in surgery. I need you to help me find Cai."

"Did you shoot him?"

"With what? The bullets in my penis?" I was shouting again. "Just get me to 16th and Market and do what I said."

"We're here already, dickwad!"

Oh.

I scrambled out.

Breathe and think—(Of 1001 Ways to Shut Darryl Up)

Besides distance, convenience, and a large bathroom where I could clean up, there was another reason I chose Jeffrey's shop. It was isolated enough that if Luis was part of the conspiracy, the little tailor shop would be a perfect place to ambush me. My plan was to take some time in the bathroom and see if someone showed up. It wasn't the most foolproof of experiments, but I wasn't in a position to be picky. When an impatient Luis called after waiting a few minutes, I knew my gut instinct about him had been correct.

"You got blood on your neck," Luis said as I filled the passenger seat of the unmarked car.

I flipped the visor and tilted my head, rubbing at the spot. "Thanks, dad. We're picking up a third party." I told him where to get Darryl. He handed me my badge and gun, then hung a U-turn. "We need to find the kid, "I said. "He has something they're after."

"Any idea what?"

"Whatever is in that safety deposit box."

"Nope. Box contained only the clothes he was assaulted in."

"They got into the box?"

"Nah, they used x-ray vision."

I ignored his sarcasm. Angelica's quash hearing hadn't gone her way, apparently. That explained the sudden rush to get Cai. Whatever they needed was probably in the box. "He left the clothes there as a message," I ventured.

Luis pursed his lips and leaned against his door, thumb tapping the steering wheel. "Makes sense. 'I was here. I have what's in the box.' Regular dicks would assume he was keeping it as evidence. Anyone involved in the wrong end of the case would wonder what he may have taken from it. Now the why?" I pointed, and he pulled over. Darryl plopped in the back seat with a glare, crossing his arms.

"I've been waiting here forever. You didn't answer any of my texts, dickwad."

"Your texts were all the same damn question, the answer being: I don't know how Peter is. When I hear, you'll hear."

"Glass?"

I glanced at Luis. "Yeah?"

"What the fuck are you wearing?"

"The only thing he had hemmed," I said, looking down at my tuxedo. "Subject at hand, please. Cai put the clothes in the box—"

"What clothes? What box? Who is after him? Which hospital is Peter at?"

"Darryl, open your mouth again, and I'll cuff and gag you. He obviously—"

"Go on and try, dickwad. We'll see who ends up on top."

Luis rubbed his forehead and the bridge of his nose. "The clothes are an interesting choice to leave in there."

"Yeah," I said. "He knew it'd be cops, Peter or his lawyers getting in that box." I tapped my finger against my knee. "Whoever the clothes were a message for knew that whatever he took from that box, he took *after* he was assaulted. It wasn't Peter, wasn't Angelica and it wasn't Mick because he drove Cai to the house and installed the bracelet. Cai would have panicked back then. We have more dirty cops out there."

"*Raped!*" Darryl kicked the back of my seat. "Assaulted makes it sound like he got hit. That's not what happened. Don't dumb it down. So cops knew he was *raped.*"

I wasn't going to argue with Darryl. He was stressed and worried, not to mention bitter and angry. "The only time he would have been able to put the clothes in the box was Saturday morning."

"Our bank is open until four on Saturdays," Darryl said.

"Okay, but when I picked up Peter at three, Cai was there. Actually he was upbeat. Maybe he thought he was free and clear?"

"Sugar and his meds. He gets like that when he's high, too."

I turned around and stared at Darryl. "Cai does drugs?"

"What do you think? His best friend is a smack addict. He's bipolar, and his meds rarely work right. He's sixteen. He self-medicates."

"How bad is his habit?"

"He doesn't have a habit yet. He mostly scores uppers and downers."

"Smack?"

"Not a chance. And before you get all high and mighty deciding that addicts will use anything," he rolled up his sleeves, "Cai's the one who got me off it. He wouldn't touch it."

The information put a perspective on where he might be. "You know his dealers?"

Darryl's face didn't even flicker when he answered, "If I did, they'd have a bullet between the eyes. I know someone who can help. I called a few minutes ago, and she was there. She said cops already called asking if she knew where Cai was."

"Did she?"

"She told them she didn't."

I didn't miss his careful wording. "She told *them* she didn't. What'd she tell you?"

"I'm supposed to trust you two?"

"Who else you got?" Luis asked.

He stared out the window. Luis and I waited while he decided. "Goth Nation. On 14th Street."

Cai is Going To Military School When This is Done

We drove to Capitol Hill and illegally parked in front of the shop. Goth Nation was squashed in the middle of the street between empty buildings and a corner beauty salon. A rent-a-bike kiosk stood on one corner. An Indie record shop on another. And on the last corner, a coin laundry/convenience store. Most of the people milling about were twenty-somethings with band t-shirts, wide studded belts and jeans tight enough to outline tattoos. We followed two of them into the shop.

Tiny, dusty, dark and moody was how I would describe the place. The shelves were black. The small square counter was black. So were the carpet, the clothes; the walls; the shoes; the door to the backroom—all black. The only spots of color were the "Legalize It" stickers haphazardly posted everywhere and the gold knob on the door behind the counter. Oh, and the pink-haired girl and blue-haired guy standing in front of us. The shop was also empty of salespeople.

"Beat it," Luis said, then flashed his badge at the teens. They shrugged and walked out. A tinkling bell signaled their exit. We all looked at the door behind the counter.

"Stay here," I whispered to Darryl while Luis and I pulled our guns and leaned against the door frame. He motioned me to turn the knob, signaling that he would follow me in. I nodded and signed a countdown from three. I twisted the knob, and we filed through the door as quickly and quietly as possible.

Moving silently, we stopped at each row to check down the narrow walkways. We crouched and peered through shoeboxes and stacks of t-shirts in each before moving on to the next. Over a pair of four-inch platform boots, I spotted a figure. Luis motioned me forward. I darted across the row to the last shelving unit and pressed my back against the wall. Peeking briefly around the corner, I signed that I saw one person. I pressed my hand flat, then took a longer look from a crouched position.

The girl, or rather her breathing, talking skeletal remains, was splayed on the ground, her neck propped by a metal shelf and the far wall. She was babbling incoherently. A puddle formed between the v of her legs. The stench of urine filtered through my adrenalin. I didn't see a weapon.

I heard Luis calling for an ambulance as I approached her. She wore black holey tights and a micro plaid skirt. Her mesh, long-sleeved shirt was pulled up on one side, revealing a piece of black rubber loosely ribboned around her arm. A syringe was pushed into a large angry red and bruised lump at the inside corner of her elbow. The t-shirt over the black mesh read 'Daddy'z Gurl' in neon pink.

"Hey." I squatted next to her and checked her eyes. Her pupils were pinhead small in the midst of brown. "She's wasted. Darryl, come here!" I took off my jacket and folded it behind her head. I didn't smell or see vomit, and her airway remained clear. I checked her pulse and breathing. Shallow.

She dribbled spit as she slurred, "Cai, dun."

"Rachel?" Darryl rushed over. He bumped my hand out of the way and attempted to take out the needle himself.

"Don't," I cautioned. "You might poke through skin."

"I know how to take out a needle." He gently removed it and checked the plunger. "Rachel?" He tapped her face a few times and blew out a breath. "She's no fucking use."

Luis checked his watch. "Forty minutes since the BOLO was called in. How long since you talked to her?"

"Right after I parked the car. Maybe five minutes before you picked me up."

"Fuck." I stood up and kicked the nearest object. Several boxes flew off the bottom shelf on the other side of us. My phone vibrated, bringing my tantrum to a halt. I looked at the screen. Text message from an unrecognized number.

—Still in surgery. Waiting 4 updates. Will txt when no more.—
Thank you officer Hutcherson. "You didn't talk to Cai?" I asked
Darryl.

"She said Cai was in back, trying to get the anklet off."

It took one minute to locate the anklet resting on the shelf by
Rachel's legs. "Call his cell."

"We need—"

"Quiet," Darryl waved his hand rapidly at Luis as he pressed
his phone to his ear and looked at the floor.

Nearby, a cell phone began to play. We all began the mad
scramble for the phone. It was Luis who thought to check under
Rachel's back.

"That's Cai's phone." Darryl grabbed it. "Weird. That's not his
ringtone." He pressed some buttons on the cell and frowned,
mumbling, "Thought he'd leave a text or something."

Luis held up something when Darryl turned around to
concentrate on the phone.

Shit. I started to adjust my thinking to the significance of the
other syringe my partner found. "So he changed his ringtone?" I
asked.

"Yeah, but…it's weird. Cai wouldn't ever have that ringtone.
He has this thing about how classical music expands the brain
blah blah blah. And the only way Rabbit and I will listen to it is if
he plays it on our phones."

"I'm going to wait by the door for the bus. You two can argue
the semantics of fairy music." Luis walked off.

The ringtone. A thread of thought pulled. I tugged at it. Cai
was smart. Too smart. His message would be obscure but seem
perfectly reasonable in his mind. I walked to the end of the row
and did what always worked when threads of thought were stuck.
I worked it out aloud. "The ringtone. What's that song?"

"You got that look, Glass. You think it means something?"

"Of course it means something. Idiots," Darryl muttered.

"Ambulance is here." Luis walked out to meet them. My
thread went with him. It was hard to concentrate with so much
going on an so much weighing on me.

We all moved out of the way while the EMTs worked on
Rachel. I tried tugging my thread from new angles while they all
tried getting some sense from her.

I almost had something, but I lost it as they wheeled out the girl and I caught Darryl's expression. His face was white, his eyes watering. "What?" I asked.

"She— Lying bitch."

Whoa. "You got some sense out of her?"

"No. She's a liar. Just babbling."

"Darryl, if she said something about the—"

"She lied. I told you. It's bullshit. And it—"

"She said the kid shot her up," Luis provided.

"What?" I repeated. That idea was more ridiculous than... Than what? Darryl admitted Cai did drugs. The kid obviously wasn't the marshmallow I thought he was. And he was smart. Logical. And fucked up without effective meds.

Luis and Darryl began arguing. I tuned it out. Think like Cai. You're on the run. He's smart enough to know the anklet was going to be traced. Maybe even he expected to be caught at any second. How fast was he? I remembered Peter dodging me when I ran after him. That was fast. Not just fast. Efficient. He ran efficiently. He'd be ahead of the cops, but not by much. And Peter ran just like him. He'd wait, expecting Peter, but as time ticked by... "Darryl—" The bickering continued.

"You asshole cops always think the worst. He's a kid."

"Who self-medicates and shot up his junkie friend with a heavy dose of—."

"She's lying. I told you." Darryl cracked his knuckles into a fist.

"Shut up. Both of you. Shut the fuck up! This isn't helping." Their mouths clamped shut. "I need to concentrate." My fingers tapped. "He expected Peter to get here eventually. He doesn't know he's hurt. He'd leave a message."

"Cai didn't leave a text message," Darryl said.

I nodded my agreement. "Which leaves the ringtone. What is that fucking song?" I hummed a few bars. "Call it again."

Darryl picked up the phone and shook his head. "Or I could just look it up. Idiot," he said quietly. He flipped through the phone, finger sliding across the screen until he looked up at me with his nose scrunched. "Last ringtone he added was Come Home."

I didn't have to hear Darryl say where he was going to understand he was off to Joe's. His eyes blew wide as he tried to run past me. I grabbed his hood again. He made a choking sound and twisted sideways, his foot arcing to connect with my stomach.

I coughed, jerked the hood and pushed him into a shelving unit. It took Luis's gun to get him under control while I doubled over and tried to get my breath back.

"Calm down," my partner growled.

"I need to get to—"

"You need to calm the fuck down."

"Wait" I tried to breathe, speaking between huffs. "Just think a moment."

"You're going to get him killed. He's there and waiting for us. Why are you still here? Call the damn cavalry!"

"He's not there!" I finally had a voice, even with the after effects of what felt like a baseball bat to the belly by a major leaguer.

"You don't know that."

"Think." Luis thumped him in the back of the head. He almost got a punch to the face in response. Darryl pulled his fist back at the last second and hit a nearby box with enough force to send it and several others flying off the shelf. They landed on my earlier pile.

"He didn't leave his phone so Peter could find him," I said. "He did it so Peter would find some*thing*."

"How do you know that?"

"Because he's too high to make it to Joe's." I lifted a hand at Luis. "Show him."

Luis held up the second syringe. "Kid gave her one shot, took the other one."

"That's the stupidest thing I've ever heard. You two are idiots. Cai would never tell her to shoot up. And he'd never touch the stuff."

"Darryl, he saved her life by giving her that," I explained. "He waited here for Peter too long. He needed to be incoherent when they got to him. He needed to make sure they couldn't question him even if they wanted to. And he made sure Rachel was a useless witness so it would be pointless to kill her."

Chapter Twenty-Two

Maybe I Should Remove the Cummerbund

We left Goth Nation arguing, and we continued doing so while we waited to hit Joe's place. It was Luis who suggested we avoid Joe's townhome until we had everything in place. I had a procedural suggestion of my own: throw Darryl out of the still-moving car. It had been five minutes since we exited the shop, and he hadn't stopped complaining and ordering us around.

"You don't even know for sure they have him. I told you like twelve places we could look."

I grabbed the home-monitoring anklet we had found and twisted in the seat to show him it. "Do you see this cut here?"

"So?"

"See how he didn't cut all the way through?"

"He could have scooted his foot out after he got partway," Darryl rationalized.

I knew he was upset. He wasn't thinking right. I was familiar with denial. But that didn't stop me from getting irritated. "And then he took the time to unlock the anklet properly? After it was removed?"

"Maybe it unlocked after his foot was out. Or maybe he cut a wire and—"

"They don't work like that," I tried to explain.

"You want the kid to live?" Luis asked.

"Just when I thought cops couldn't get more stupid."

Luis and I simultaneously leaned our heads back on our seats and exhaled. If we didn't need Darryl, I might have flipped Luis for who got to shoot him. Luis must have read my thoughts. "You're a lousy shot," he said. "You'd miss, and we'd have to listen to his whining." He pulled over and flipped off the air-conditioning.

"Find him first. Not the stupid evidence! You're more concerned with that than my brother."

"We are concerned about the kid," Luis said. "And we'll find him. But we're doing it in a way that doesn't endanger him. What do you think they'll do to him if they know we're close? Listen, kid—"

"I'm twenty-two," Darryl sneered.

"Act like it," I said. "And think. Where would Cai have hidden something?"

"I already said that I don't know!"

"How long do we have?" I asked Luis.

"Maybe an hour until he's lucid enough to answer questions."

My phone rang. I answered it immediately in order to avoid popping Darryl in the face. "Glass."

"Canada is cold, but this lady says she's his mother," Officer Hutcherson said.

I covered the mouthpiece. "Did you tell Rosa about Peter?"

"Of course I did. While you were getting spiffy for your job as a waiter—"

"It was the only suit he had hemmed." *Maybe I should remove the cummerbund?*

"—I was calling hospitals and Rosa! And you look idiotic."

I shrugged off the insult and moved my hand off the mouthpiece. "Describe her."

"Which one?"

"There's more than one?"

"Yup. One says she's Rosafa Strakosha. No ID." Of course Rosa had a WitSec name that she was not going to flash to random cops. I didn't interrupt with that information though. "5'9 or 5'10. Black hair, brown eyes. Early forties. 115 lbs. The other has I.D. Zhavra Dyachenko..." He paused. "Sir, the FBI is with them. I may have to let them through when he's out of surgery."

My head was spinning. Peter's mother? "Go ahead and—"

"Mister Glass," a heavily accented, stern voice said into the phone.

I hung up in horror. The phone rang again a moment later. I turned it off. "So...we were...the drugs..." I cleared my throat. "An hour until they find a way to get the info out of him. Will we be ready?"

Luis nodded and gave me a sideways squint. "We'll be ready. Are you flaking out?"

"Detective," Darryl said gently.

I avoided Luis by turning to Darryl. "What?"

"I know where he hid it."

Never Ending Story

"You know?" I asked. "Or you think you know? Because if you're wrong…"

"I'm pretty sure." He nodded. "No, I'm positive. Last year Joe found an X tab. He went ballistic and searched Cai's room. I mean seriously searched. Cai comes in right in the middle of it, and then they have a blowout. Cai takes off."

"Does this story end?" I asked. "Ever?"

"I'm explaining so maybe you can make up your mind, dickwad! Rabbit had to skip classes to find him. Cai finally picks up his cell phone after forever, and Rabbit said that they'd work out a lock for his room. Because Rabbit felt guilty 'cause the tab was his."

"That's it? In his room? I need more than—"

"My point, dickwad, was that Rabbit couldn't get Joe to agree to a lock on his door. So he bought this crappy little safe where Cai could hide—well, whatever he was hiding."

How I went from prettyboy to dickwad in a week was a mystery. "Where?" I asked, leaving out the obvious question of why Peter would give a kid who was using drugs, a place to hide them.

Darryl shrugged. "His room somewhere."

"Which is toast," Luis pointed out. "Metal?"

"Yeah. With one of those dial thingies."

"Not a lot to hang our hopes on, Glass."

I thought about fire and water damage. "If it's a weapon in there, we're good. I should have taken Cai up on the tour of his room so we'd know where to find this thing."

"Cai invited you to his room?" Darryl asked.

"Yeah. He said he had some painting he wanted to show me."

"Weird."

"Second time you've used that today with regards to the kid. Not that I'm disagreeing. Weird doesn't begin to describe him."

"Cai's pretty shy. Plus, you're a cop. It's weird."

"Cai was not shy that day. I guarantee you. And this might be a shocker, but some people like me."

"Who?" Luis asked.

"Cats, or mangy creatures formally known as cats."

"That's about right," Luis said, lifting his phone to his ear.

Popularity is Overrated

Luis and I both checked our guns while we waited near the burnt wreckage of Joe's townhome. Waiting was always the hardest part of being a cop. Waiting for warrants. Waiting for information. Waiting for unobserved access. Waiting for fire marshals.

"Hey, Luis?"

"What?" He switched his badge to a neck chain and fitted it over his bulletproof vest.

"I'll take the bullet this time."

Luis sat back and put his elbow over the center of our seat, his finger pointing directly at me. "Remember a few months back, when we stopped at that bodega—"

"Never mind. Forget I said anything." I interrupted, quickly trying to fix my badge to my neck chain and tuck it into my shirt.

"—and you bought the coffee—"

"We should get going."

"—but the lid popped off and you spilled it?"

"Have you called the captain again?"

"You jumped around in the car and unbuckled your pants. "Screaming to get you to the emergency room."

"You were really reckless, by the way."

"Only it turned out they mistakenly gave you ice coffee."

"Ice can burn, Luis."

"Hey!" Darryl said. "Remember that time," he kicked my seat, "two asshole cops sat in their car telling stories while more asshole cops tortured my—" he nearly knocked my seat out of its bucket with the next kick, "brother?"

Luis and I both looked at Darryl then each other. My partner jerked his thumb at the back seat and pursed his lips. "I like him."

"More than me?"

"I like everyone more than you."

"Why do people keep saying that to me?"

"Want a list?" Darryl said.

"Why is he still here?" Luis asked.

"Because, Luis, if we don't keep him in the car behind locked doors, he'll do something stupid. Like wade through the wreckage of Joe's house before the fire marshal has declared it safe. Then he'd probably do something even more stupid, like bargain with the kidnappers."

"Too damn right I will. It's more than what you're doing."

"What he doesn't realize is that once they have the items, they have no use for witnesses. Plus, and this is why cops are better at kidnapping cases than, say, *bartenders*—cops realize that bad guys might be watching the house, waiting for an unprotected Tinkerbelle wearing a glow-in-the-dark, neon pink hoodie to lead them directly to what they want."

"Do you know what I did to the last guy that called me Tinkerbelle?"

"Slept with him?"

Darryl was silent for a second. "After that."

My lips pulled up in the first real smile since this day started. Because he was behind me, I wasn't sure if Darryl's did, too. I didn't get a chance to look. Luis's phone rang with the call we had been waiting for.

I Love You, Man

"Fire Inspector just finished. We're a go," Luis said. "CSU will be here in thirty."

"Can you see my vest?"

"No."

"Luis?"

He grunted a, "What?"

"If I don't have a job after this—"

"You will."

"—I want you to know—"

"I know, kid." He shifted and stared out the window.

"—that I masturbated to images of you in a thong and corset."

"Dios Mio, give me strength."

"I'm going to check it out," I nodded to the townhome.

"I'll brief CSU. Inspector said to stay off the second floor."

I twisted to look at Darryl. "Cai's room is on the first floor?"

He jerked a nod. "I'll go with you. You won't recognize anything."

"No can do," I said. "You're a civilian, that's a crime scene, and I'm in enough shit without having a beam fall on your head and the Department getting sued."

"You're not going to know what to look for."

He was right. How was I going to recognize anything in Cai's room if the safe wasn't out in the open? Which it wouldn't be, because Cai wasn't an idiot. I tossed Darryl my cell phone. "I'll video it. Sync our phones. That's as close as you're getting." He rolled his eyes, typed into my phone, and threw it back at me. I smiled brightly at Luis as I tucked the phone into my pocket. "Kiss me goodbye?" He whacked me in the back of the head.

"Get out, and don't get dead."

"Ditto," I replied, climbing out of the car and jerking a thumb to Darryl. "And give him to one of the uniforms when CSU gets here or he'll follow you." I remembered what Peter told me about Darryl. "Actually make it two uniforms. With Tasers." I started to shut the door.

"Austin," Darryl said. I stuck my head back in, expecting to be told to get bent. "Don't let a beam fall on your head or nothin'."

"Worried about your meal ticket?"

"And that would top the list of reasons no one likes you." He glared.

"Sorry. Listen, if you promise not to double back and do something stupid, we can have someone drive you to the hospital."

"Nah. I'll stay."

I nodded, then slammed the door.

I understood Darryl wanting to stay. At the hospital he'd be climbing the walls, pestering nurses, taking care of Rosa and...the other one. I knew that was how I'd be. Focusing on work gave me a brief reprieve from my worry. Peter's name alone brought the image of him looking at his bloody hand in confusion and Leila's gun pressed against his head. Better to not think about him at all. Better to not wonder if later, when all was said and done, I might never again feel him lying against me.

If I thought about that. If I believed that. Would I try very hard to avoid a bullet?

True Irony Is Lost on the Idiots

I wasn't looking forward to seeing Peter's life reduced to piles of black dust. Just outside the door, I paused and took a breath. The fire marshal jogged up to greet me. I flashed both my badge and a forced smile at her. Her serious eyes were framed by a surgical mask and a bright yellow hard hat. She carried an extra of each in her weathered hands. "They told you not to go upstairs?"

I nodded, and she held out the mask and helmet to me. "Can I see something in a red? Yellow isn't my best color." My joke fell as flat as my smile.

"Can't let you in there without them."

"Are you coming in with me?"

"I'll be inspecting next door if you need me. The homeowners are anxious to check for recoverable items." She nodded to the townhome on the right.

"What about here? Are there recoverable items?"

"Nothing salvageable in the main room. Further to the back of the house, soot, ash and water damage are the most concerning. Upstairs it's mostly water damage. Fortunately, the firehouse was close." She gave me a quick rundown of safety measures and turned to leave. Her sneakers squeaked as she crossed the lawn. The sound faded as I stepped inside Joe's front door.

The smell hit me first. A mixture of chemicals and the acrid stench of smoke. The air was also moist and more than a little suffocating. My mouth opened to draw in sufficient air where my nostrils failed. It only grew worse from the living room to the back bedrooms.

Along the hallway the drywall had burned, leaving exposed wires, cross beams and pipes. The remaining walls and furniture were black with soot. What wasn't black was grey with ash. All of the painted memories were gone. The loss of those missing portraits and murals weighed on my soul. Images of Peter in his youth gone forever. It was heartbreaking.

I turned away from the walls and took a step past Peter's room, only to backtrack and push open what was left of the door. Maybe something was salvageable in this disaster.

The carpet squished under my shoes, but the water wasn't deep enough to wash Peter's blood off the tips. It was just deep enough to make me grimace. Light from the broken window gave me more information about the destruction of Peter's life than I could ever want. My grimace expanded.

His bookshelf had imploded like a well-timed demolition. The bed's wire frame survived, but the mattress was basically carbon. The computer desk had split; it and the monitor were now propped by what was left of a cat carrier that had been sitting underneath. Books, papers, bits of ceiling were strewn across the floor. Everything was wet and reeked. I turned my back on it all and prayed that behind the blackened closet doors, something was left.

Tentatively, I slid the door open. My eyes rolled up to make sure the ceiling wasn't going to crack and fall on my head. Satisfied that asbestos and stucco weren't going to rain down, I crouched, examining the pile of shoes scattered at the bottom of the closet.

I found the bunny slippers in the corner under a pair of canvas high tops and another pair of slippers I hadn't seen before. The rubber from the high tops melted to the fuzzy brown toe of one slipper. It took a few minutes, but I pried the sneaker free and squeezed the water from the slippers. My phone rang as I hunted for something to wrap them in.

I tucked the slippers under my arm and dug for the phone. "Glass." Water soaked through my jacket and trickled down my ribs.

"I thought you were going to send a video? How long does it take?" Darryl demanded angrily.

"Wanna see what I see? Here!" I turned his volume down, pressed the video button and then put the phone back in my pocket. He could hear me, but I didn't want him to see my attachment to the fucking slippers.

Footsteps along the hallway caught my attention. "Hey, do you have a baggie or something?" I asked the inspector as I rounded the corner directly into the barrel of a gun.

"Whoa, hello." My hands jumped to my gun reflexively.

"Don't," Detective Frank Marco ordered. "I got nothing to lose here, Glass."

I brought my palms up in front of my stomach. The slippers splatted to the floor. "Hey, Frank. What's up?"

Sweat dripped from his forehead. He blinked excessively and wiped at it with his arm, but another drop followed the same path. The hand holding the gun shook. "Where are they?" The tip of the barrel jammed hard into my forehead.

"Ow. Where's what?" I took a step back, using considerable effort not to raise my hands higher and rub the pain away. Any sudden movements could set him off.

"Don't fuck with me. Where are they?"

"Look, Frank, man, I came in here to see if I could salvage some clothes."

"Don't talk like we're friends, Glass. You ain't got friends. I count myself lucky that it's you in here because anyone else would be hard to shoot. But not you. Give me what I want, and I'm outta here. Don't, and I'll find ways to encourage you to give it to me."

Ouch. Don't argue with the desperate. "I haven't found anything," I said honestly.

"This is the wrong room." Frank squinted and tilted to look past me. "This is the other one's room."

"Frank?" A voice called from what sounded like the entrance of the house.

"Back here, Del." Frank's eyes never left me.

A second later, Detective Max Delmonico's movie star smile beamed behind Frank. "Martinez and the fairy are sitting in the car playing with their cell phones. Captain thinks we're here to oversee CSU and this faggot. We're good to go."

"Get his gun."

Del reached across and slipped my gun from the holster, tucking it in his jacket pocket. "Why are we in this room?"

"Found him here." They both glanced around the room. "Are they here, Glass?"

I only hoped Darryl was still recording. I needed to buy time. "I don't know." I turned slowly toward the room. "I haven't had a chance to look thoroughly. I've only been here once." *On Wednesday when one of you assholes tried to set me on fire.* Wednesday. Why was I in Peter's room on Wednesday? On Saturday, Cai had tried to lure me to his own room. On Wednesday Cai had pointed me to Peter's. Cai had directed me here. It *was* in Peter's room. The safe was in this room. "CSU will be here soon, and Luis is bound to get suspicious if I don't check in."

"You'd better find it two minutes before 'soon' then, because a minute before that and there will be one less faggot rich boy staining the uniform." Del stuck his gun against my nose and ripped off my face mask.

"Did the irony in that statement make you laugh just a little?" My eyes crossed to look at the gun.

"Fucking find them, Glass. We ain't interested in your smartass remarks," Frank said and pushed Del's arm away.

Del and Marco weren't the brightest of pairs, but desperate, stupid men were more dangerous than the smart ones. The stupid ones acted first. I was just as likely to get shot in the head as I was to have a kneecap blown off. I decided to obey and scanned the room, turning slowly. What had I missed?

One of them poked the back of my head with a gun. Why the head every time? Couldn't they poke my ribs? My back? It was hard to concentrate with the headache starting to form. It was even harder to focus with fear punching my heart and crushing my lungs. But that was when things usually got worse for me. When fear controlled my mouth. *For once, Austin, just keep your mouth shut. Don't poke bears.*

What had Cai said? Where was he directing me? He had said I didn't know who Peter was. He sent me to this room to learn about Peter. I went back to the crispy remains of the bookshelf.

Too obvious.

"Get moving," Frank poked again.

"I'm thinking. Let me think!" The one thing I was good at. The one thing every detective knew I was good at.

What was the one thing here? The thing that Cai knew I wouldn't miss in this room? The one thing he knew I wouldn't leave without?

"I'm going into Strakosha's room," Frank said. "Keep an eye on him."

"We already searched that room."

I turned a full circle.

Don't look for Peter in this room. Look for Cai.

"I'm searchin' again," Frank said. "Just watch him. And see if you can get Dillon and Fitzpatrick on the line. They were supposed to check in twenty minutes ago."

The moment I saw it, I knew. And apparently I gave myself away.

"Wait," Del ordered. Frank halted and flipped around. "He's got something."

"I hope it's not crabs," Dave said, grinning as he stood in the doorway.

And All I Got Was This Stupid Cat

My gun was in Del's pocket. Del's gun was on me. Frank's gun was on Dave. And Dave carried no gun at all that I could see. This was not a good day for Austin Glass. If I had one more surprise, there was a distinct possibility my heart was going to bounce right out of my chest and plop into the mush at Frank's feet.

"What the fuck you doing here, Buchanan?" Frank's gun changed target from me to my best friend. "I told you to stay outside when you got here! How the fuck are we supposed to know who's coming if you're in here?"

"Crotch stains are always a good indicator." I couldn't help myself. Fear brought out the smartass.

Dave pinched his brows and lifted his lip, which told me that he was two seconds from a facepalm at my stupidity. "Frank, is that anyway to greet someone who came to give you good news?"

"You," Frank said, waving the gun at me. "Get—"

"They found the Strakosha boy," Dave interrupted. "And Mick and Dick. Just came over the radio."

"Fuck!" Del wiped his mouth frantically. "Marco, if they're talking…"

"Hard to talk with a bullet to the head." Dave inched inside.

"We gotta get outta here." Frank stuck the gun to my forehead again and pushed me back against the wall. I threw my hands up against it and tried to look nonthreatening. It wasn't difficult. I was scared shitless. The other men in the room were one tick away from trigger happy. Sweat rolled off Frank in rivers. Between that smell and the soot, I gagged. "Where. Is. It?" He jammed the gun into my head to emphasize each word. The fear, pain and fumes were making me dizzy. I couldn't think clearly. I couldn't decide what was in my best interest.

If I told him, I was dead. If I didn't, I was dead. I looked from Dave's calm face to Frank's sweaty one, to Del tapping his gun against his chin and muttering while he paced. These were not just worried cops, they were terrified. Something worse than the threat of jail time caused that kind of terror.

Dave laid a hand on Frank's shoulder. "Yo, man, that gun goes off and they'll be in here in seconds. That doesn't help any of us. We destroy the passports, and we take him with us."

Frank's gun still imprinted on my skin. I tried to look anywhere but on his shaking trigger finger. Nothing Dave said seemed to placate Frank. And Del was hyping himself up. "Shoot that faggot in the balls! Press it close. They won't hear a thing from way back here. He'll fucking talk then." My dread reached an insane peak.

"Del, you're not thinking clearly. Go watch the door," Dave said quietly. When Frank didn't contradict him, Del opened his mouth to argue.

"Do it," Frank said. Del lowered his gun and squished out of the room.

"Okay, man, he's not going to tell you anything with a gun to his forehead." We all heard a door close. That's when Dave brought his gun out and pressed it against Frank's temple. "It's over, Frank. I'm not going to let you shoot him."

Frank's mouth slowly opened. A battering of breaths escaping in a wheeze. "Del?" He called out loudly.

"Martinez has him now, Frank. It's over. No one else dies. Give me the gun."

"You know I gotta get them papers, Buchanan." The twitch of Frank's finger caught my breath. "Bullet to the head is better than what they're gonna do to me. To all of us."

"You and me, Frank, we can get protection. We'll go in together. It's the only way."

"Nah. Nah. There won't be anywhere to hide if they find out what happened to that girl, Buchanan. I told you that. What they do to snitches ain't half of what they'll do to us. To everyone in our families. Marta? Your girls? We're all dead. Destroy them papers and I'll drop the gun. Turn myself in."

"Oz, man, where are they?"

What the fuck was in that safe?

Was I going to trust Dave? Maybe this was some kind of ruse to get me to give up the location. Then he shoots me and they grab the safe. Only three things wrong with that line of thought. First, he'd warned me they were after Cai. Second, he'd come in here rather than just calling Frank's cell phone. Third, I was just as dead if Frank and Dave were working together, but if they weren't? "The cat carrier. It's in the cat carrier."

Frank's breath eased out, his gun moving off my face. "Get it." Neither he nor Dave lowered their weapons when I pushed off the wall and kneeled in the muck to get at the cage door.

"The plastic's melted around it. I need a knife or something."

"Is it in there?" Frank stepped forward, leaning in to look, his gun gliding across my vision. I grabbed his wrist and jerked down.

A bullet fired into the floor, near enough to my knee that it frayed the fabric of my pant leg. I pulled his arm down further, trying to shove his hand under that knee. Frank's fist slammed into my nose. I grunted as pain shot through my forehead and partially lost my grip. He leaned into me for leverage. We toppled over, both of us now locked in a struggle under the desk face-to-face. A piece of wood scraped through my jacket, my stitches ripped open, and my nose ached and bled; but I wasn't letting go of Frank's wrist.

Another bullet fired. Behind me, someone grunted and fell with a muffled 'thump'. Dave? Shit! I started to twist and roll my shoulder over Frank's arm, but he jerked at my grip and pulled backward. I wound up half on top of him chest-to-chest, two hands around his wrist, gun flailing above our heads. Through blood, ashy water and sweat, I couldn't see where Dave was in the room.

Over all our grunting and swearing, several sets of feet sloshed down the hall. There was shouting, but with the blood pounding in my ears and my rough panting, I couldn't decipher what they were yelling. I was too petrified to let go of the gun. With my nose already weeping blood and broken, I cringed in anticipation, right before I cocked my head back and slammed my forehead into Frank's face. My nose gave another crack, pain shot up into my brain, and my vision went black. At the same time another bullet split through the air. Someone cursed in Spanish. I went limp. Lights out, Austin.

Sleep. Sleep Would Be Good Here

I wasn't out long. A minute maybe. Long enough to get pulled off of Frank and jostled outside. The pain turned to an aching throb once I was set on the lawn. By the time the EMTs arrived, I just went with the flow. My eyes were flushed out, my nose and throat checked, butterfly stitches were applied to my lip. Like an intense sugar high, my adrenalin dissipated. The noise and chaos around me faded away. I passed out again in the ambulance.

I was lying on my side. My ass felt like it was on fire. Bright lights and a brown, nearly bare leg greeted my awakening. I followed it up, past a section of bandaged calf, up over a plump belly, to meet Luis's dark glare. He sat on the gurney across from mine.

"What happened?" I asked groggily. My voice sounded nasal. I lifted a hand to my face. Thick bandages covered my cheeks and a metal splint encased my nose.

"I got shot. Because of you. Again."

"Bad?" It came out 'bah'.

He shrugged. "Passed through muscle."

"Can't even get shot right."

"You're paying for my pants."

A hail of painful spikes kept my smile from forming. "Peter?"

"Still in surgery."

"Fran—?" None of my hard consonants were sounding. My tongue refused to contribute to the pain in the roof of my mouth.

"In custody. Del and Buchanan, too."

"Dave shot?"

"Bullet hit his vest. He's bruised, but fine."

"Cai?"

"Last I heard, he was being treated at Mercy General." I already knew what happened to Mick and Dick.

"Where are we?" My lip had split, I felt it tug as my 'w' formed, and a trickle of blood dribbled into my mouth.

"Denver General." Across town. Not too far from Peter.

"The safe? They said passports." I was sore, but not so broken that I needed to continue lying down. It took effort to sit up, however, and to balance on one ass cheek. I figured I should get used to that anyway.

"Just lie down, Glass. Doc has to reset your nose. We can talk about the case when we go in for a briefing."

"Lezgo." Lying here meant thinking. I couldn't think. I couldn't let myself think. There wasn't anything else I cared enough about to stymie the thoughts of Peter. Still in surgery. "Timezit?" I shook my head, thought I could feel my brain rattling around. "Time's it?"

Luis looked at his watch. "Quarter to four. I've been shot, Glass. This is as far as my statement goes tonight."

I nodded and immediately wished I hadn't. This time my brain did rattle in my skull. Nearly five hours since Dave's first phone call. I tried to construct a timeline up until they took Peter to the hospital. According to that timeline, Peter had been in surgery approximately four hours. I patted my pockets. "Where's my cell?"

"Evidence. You forget you recorded everything?"

Shit. "I need to get out of here."

"Tinkerbelle is getting your car."

"Don't call him that." And that defense of Darryl should have convinced anyone that I wasn't in my right mind.

Luis shook his head at me and tossed me a cell. I caught it with one hand and frowned at it. "Strakosha's phone. Haven't had time to hand it in," he explained.

"Come get me tomorrow." I used Cai's cell to text Darryl, ordering him to meet me out front with the car. I handed the phone back to my partner and then I hobbled off the gurney and toward an exit.

I couldn't remember the nurse's name from Wednesday, but I recognized the voice as it chased after me. "Officer Glass? Detective?" She caught me at the automatic doors. They slid open and then closed.

"Got a ride to catch."

"You need your stitches replaced and your nose reset."

"Lady, what I need is a bath, to sleep a year, and about a bottle of Vicodin. What I want, and what I'm going to get, is a ride to St. Mark's hospital."

She looked about to argue and then took a deep breath. "At least let me get you into some scrubs. Your wound is probably going to get infected."

I looked down at my tux. My shirt was grey, the jacket was grey, and everything was damp with blood and ashwater. I laughed. Ow. No laughing. Laughing bad. "Gimme the scrubs."

Chapter Twenty-Three

Thinking About Anything But Peter

"You look like shit," Darryl greeted when I carefully folded into the passenger seat of my car. "We should get you to a hospital."

I stared blankly at his grin. If the smile had actually reached his eyes, I might have been tempted to offer a sarcastic rejoinder. "Just drive." I flipped the visor open and examined my face. I looked like a bruise with three lips. Closing the visor in disgust, I fingered the butterfly stitches holding my bottom lip together.

"Cai's okay," Darryl announced.

"Good." Right then I cared about Peter, not Cai.

"Your cop partner is cool."

"Yeah." I couldn't summon the strength to talk. I wanted to tell him that I needed silence, but I figured he needed to talk. Maybe talking would keep my mind off Peter.

Darryl opened his mouth, took a quick breath and then held it. His mouth closed again. He reopened it and blurted out a quick, "Thank you."

"Don't thank me. I didn't find him. And before you ask, I don't know who did."

"Just take the freakin' gratitude, dickwad."

"You're welcome," I said, fighting a smile.

"They tried to take my cell phone."

"Evidence."

"Fuck them and the evidence they rode in on. Rosa couldn't call me."

"Did she?"

He shook his head. "Zhavra did. Peter's mom," he elaborated at my confused look. "He's out of surgery."

"And?"

"She hung up. She doesn't like me."

"Do you get along with anyone?"

"Men."

"And Peter thinks I'm the misogynist," I muttered. "We'll find out about Peter in a few minutes." I turned off the air conditioning and rolled my window down.

The wind felt good on my face. I tipped my head back and closed my eyes. Images of Peter from this morning flickered against the screen of my lids. His subtle smile. The tease of his ass before he'd shut the bathroom door. A glimpse of the weird flat portion of his hair where he'd slept on it. I was grateful when Darryl turned on the radio and pulled me out of my mental slideshow. We rode the remaining ten minutes with The Who, The Clash and Lynyrd Skynyrd.

Great. Now *I* Hate Hospitals

Darryl turned off the car in the middle of Free Bird's guitar riff. The hospital loomed a half block from our spot in visitor parking. I wasn't looking forward to the trek there, short as it was. Darryl seemed even more reluctant.

He pulled the car keys into his lap and fiddled with them while staring straight ahead at the hospital. "Coming?" I asked. He said nothing. "Poor choice of words."

"I hate hospitals." He brought his thumb up to his mouth and began chewing zealously at the nail.

"It's a building with people. Nothing to be afraid of."

"It's the only place in the world where there's a reminder about what being gay means." He spit out a piece of nail, selecting another digit for oral attack. "You know that super old game show with like doors you get to choose?" He didn't wait for a response. "It's like that. Behind door one, we have people with AIDS. Behind door two, a bunch of babies and married people." He looked at me. "Door three? That's where Nurse Bitch is stationed, programmed to ask, 'Are you a family member?' You know what my favorite is?"

I was too tired to get into what being gay meant. I'd been avoiding this very conversation for weeks. "This is perfect timing for this discussion. No, really. It is. Perfect."

"My favorite is the signs. You know the 'give blood' signs. Except we can't give blood. Because we're gay. And apparently, we're all tainted. Like breeders don't have HIV?"

"Know what else is in there?" I asked when he finally let me get a word in. "Peter. So take your fingers out of your mouth, get your perky ass out of the car and trail your pixie dust through those automatic doors. Okay, Tinkerbelle?"

"If you hadn't said the ass bit, they'd have to reset your nose again."

"They haven't set my nose yet, and why do you think I led with the perky ass part? I can't figure out why everyone unloads on me—everyone except the one person I want to. Christ, if Peter was this forthcoming, we'd probably be arguing a lot less." I got out of the car and slammed the door, limping away without checking if Darryl was following.

He caught up with me a few seconds later. "Honey, I wouldn't worry about Peter opening you up." The gesture he made was so obscene, I barely kept my ass cheeks from clenching.

"Nice. Thanks for that." I rolled my eyes.

He laid another lovely statement on me as the automatic doors opened. "You should know, Peter's mother is an evangelical who thinks I'm going to hell because I suck dick."

"I don't think I count. I've only done it that one time."

Good Doggy

Zhavra Dyachenko's cheeks were flushed, and her mouth was rapidly moving. I couldn't hear through the glass, which probably meant the doors were too thick—or she was whispering irately.

Across from her, Darryl flipped up his middle finger and shoved it close to her nose.

Between them both, Peter rested silently on his hospital bed. Though they definitely shared the same DNA—red hair, fair skin, pointed features—today it would be difficult to tell that Zhavra was his mother from Peter's drawn face and sallow coloring.

"Would you like some coffee, Glass?"

I didn't look at Officer Hutcherson. My attention was riveted to the ICU room, where Peter slept off his anesthesia. "Given up calling me 'sir'?"

"I'm off duty."

I couldn't look away. If I did, Peter would die. I was suddenly sure of it. Even blinking seemed a betrayal. It was useless to try to stop the inevitable. Bodies don't respond to superstitions. Bodies work on automation. My eyes watered from the strain. Finally, my lids ticked down, pushing the tears out.

"Were you there when he was brought out of surgery?" I asked.

"Haven't left his side. As instructed. Canadian citizenry would only be interesting for a few days."

My smile was feeble. "The doctors wouldn't give information to a nonfamily member. Other than twenty-four to forty-eight hours. Did you hear anything?" Zhavra had been less than helpful.

I registered the sound of paper rustling and imagined Hutcherson was reading from his notebook. "Bullet went through bowel. They repaired the damage, but there's a high risk of infection." He paused. "Someone'd better go break them up before the blond pops her one."

"Thanks. For everything. You should head home."

"I have some paperwork to do at the station." It was an offer more than a statement. The implied 'if you need me' eliciting a nod from me.

"I might take you up on that," I murmured, then opened the sliding glass door and stepped inside the ICU room.

Peter's mother turned on me before the door closed. "You are not welcome here."

"You said that the first time you kicked me out. So I thought I'd give you some time to reconsider." I took a seat near the bed. Her seat. It was petty. I was petty. "Then, while I was having my nose set, I thought to myself, 'what a great hospital. I bet they could use a million dollars.' Guess what? They did!"

Darryl laughed and flopped in a nearby chair.

"I am still his mother," she said staunchly.

"Yeah? Good luck with that. I'm still rich."

Until he took my hand, I hadn't realized Peter had woken up. We all went silent. He opened his eyes slowly and met mine.

"Your nose," he whispered.

"Petya. Sweet boy." His mother combed her fingers through his hair as she kissed his forehead.

From the corner of my eye, I saw Darryl squeeze Peter's knee.

Peter's eyes never moved from mine. I couldn't speak. "Hey, mamma," he said with a barely there smile. My throat closed on an emotional swallow. His lids fluttered, then lowered and his breathing once again slowed.

For the next seven hours, we sat in silence. The nurses came and went way too often. Darryl occasionally left to call and update Cai and Rosa. Not that there was much to update. Peter woke up three times besides the nurses visits. The longest was two minutes. Each time he asked for water. We gave him ice shavings, and he slipped into sleep again. So did I at some point.

I awoke to a tingling sensation spilling over my scalp. Peeling my eyes open, I blinked a few times at the blur of shadows. Fingers spread into my hair, curled up and then radiated outward again. I tilted my face from my crossed-arms pillow and gave Peter a bleary smile. His hand slipped along my cheek and fell to the bed softly.

"They broke your nose?"

"It might be an improvement." I stretched and yawned. "Been awake long?"

"Few minutes." He turned his head. I twisted mine to follow his stare. Darryl was curled and snoring on the floor. Zhavra was missing.

I took his hand and brought his attention back to me while I played with his fingers. "Cai's safe."

"I know. Darryl told me a while ago."

"How do you feel?"

"Sleepy."

"Sleep helps with that."

"Going to sleep in a second." His turn to yawn, though he winced at the end of it. There was a long pause after I threaded our fingers together. "Austin?"

"Yeah, Peter Rabbit?"

"Kiss me goodnight?"

"No," I said, studying our joined hands.

"C'mon."

The strange foreboding crept over me again. That a kiss was his way of saying goodbye. And if I pressed my lips against his, I'd catch his last breath. I pushed the selfish thoughts away. Leaning up, I braced my hands near his shoulders and let the heat of him draw me close.

He smelled of antiseptic and sweat, and the weird hospital scent that clung to the sick. "Your breath reeks." I grazed his lips with mine. His fingers touched my thigh. My heart wrecked into my ribcage. I dusted his mouth with another kiss and felt him sigh against me.

"I'm not dying." He wet his lips, his tongue inadvertently brushing against my mouth.

"Oh, good, because I'm not into necrophilia, but all that could change." I tugged the hair over his forehead and licked the taste of him off my upper lip. "Want me to go get your mother?"

"Stay."

"Arf," I said softly. He fell asleep with a smile. I was sure that was the most useful thing I'd done all day.

Running On Empty

I was pulled out of my vigil a few hours later and taken to the station to give my recorded statement. There, I learned Frank, Del and Dave were exchanging information for protective custody. After leaving the interview room, a crutch-wielding Luis filled me in on the details that Internal Affairs had refused to divulge to me.

"You look like you're on your last leg, partner."

"Get it all out, Glass." He sat his butt on the corner of my desk, leaned his crutches against the arm of my chair and exhaled with an almost pleading look to the ceiling.

"I'm done," I said, resting back in my chair. I wasn't feeling very witty. What I did feel was conflicted between wanting to be with Peter and resolving the case.

Luis tossed a paper-stuffed file on the desk. "The plastic melted around everything like a seal. Some smoke and water damage, but the passport numbers were salvageable."

"Nothing but passports?" Frowning, I waded through the stack of photocopies from the files.

"Just passports," Luis confirmed.

I drew one of the papers from the pile. A pretty girl with shiny lips and glossy hair stared back at me. "Catarina Perez? I know that name."

"That's because she's Carlos Jiménez's niece. The one who went missing and started that war I mentioned."

"Oh, shit, yeah. I thought it was a rival cartel that took her." The Jiménez cartel was relatively new, making a name for itself quickly. Too quickly to suit the older cartels. The logical leap was that a rival cartel snatched the girl. The war that ensued made headlines even up here in Colorado. "So what? Alvarado took her?"

"Alvarado, Joe and Leila were bringing in cash and drugs for the Jiménez cartel. The money was being laundered through various hands, each taking a percentage. The illegals were the side business."

"Alvarado figured while he was making trips to Mexico, he'd pad his pockets."

"You must be loads of fun with twenty questions. Go ahead if you got all the answers."

"I have been told it's annoying to play it with me." I checked the other papers, no other names jumped out at me. "Okay, I'm stumped. They're bringing in illegals as a side business. How does she fit in?"

"Alvarado was bringing in five, six illegals a month. Each paid five thousand dollars—one way or another—for forged green cards."

"Dench handled forging papers," I guessed.

"With help from an ex-cop who worked in immigration. He was picked up last night."

"Twenty-five grand a month isn't much when split up."

"Which is why Alvarado got even greedier, making more trips. Too many for the immigration connection to keep up with. Alvarado set up a safe house for those waiting for papers—the ones that couldn't pay up front went to work for him or were sold."

"Or their kids were sold," I added. I turned the sheet of paper with Catarina's picture to him. "She paid up front?"

"Partially. Ran away three days after her Quinceañera with a boyfriend the father didn't approve of. Used three grand in gifts from family to pay her and the boyfriend's way across. They all found out who she was later. After."

"After what?"

"After she was raped and murdered in the whorehouse Alvarado put her in."

"Jesus," I whispered. "No wonder they needed that paper trail destroyed. Jiménez would do worse than kill them when he found out. Why the hell didn't they get rid of the papers?"

He pointed to the folder. "Dench handled all the paperwork. Leila Alvarado found out about the girl's death. She started killing everyone who could link the missing girl with their operation. The other seven people in that file are buried somewhere unknown, along with the girl. Dench had a strike of conscience. He tucked evidence in two safety deposit boxes. If he handed over Peter's box it meant jail time. The second kid's box was a death sentence for everyone involved. Buchanan thinks he keeled over from the stress. By then he had hidden both sets of passports."

"Until Peter dredges some of them up, minus the most important evidence."

Luis grunted his agreement. "Del and Frank see Alvarado in custody, they watch the interview tape and see that he's ready to deal."

"They had to get rid of him," I finished. "So how'd they set up Cai?"

"They went after Alvarado. In an effort to save himself, he tells them that your boy has the passports."

"Peter, not boy," I corrected offhandedly. It was getting uncomfortable that people were describing him as a boy. Even if to Luis I was a kid.

"Leila offs Alvarado, and that's when Nikolaj comes back to the house. Probably to off Alvarado himself. Now they have a witness, but the boy takes off before they can take care of him."

"They don't know who he is and can't ask Alvarado because he's dead," I guessed.

"Yep. Nikolaj ran out of the house, so he was nice and visible to all the neighborhood, but none of them recognized him. Then you come into the station and ID him. They know who the kid is now, but they also know you're involved with Peter. So, instead of going after Peter directly, they decide they do two things. Get you off the case somehow and then use Nikolaj as leverage. They arrest the kid. Then comes a second problem"

"Cai's figured out that there's one more safety deposit box that no one knows about but him." If I wasn't so anxious to get out of there, at this point I could have made a crack about how good things do come from fucking with witnesses. But I was tired and all I wanted to do was go back to the hospital.

"Nikolaj tells them he has the evidence," Luis continued, "But he's in custody. And then Peter goes straight to you when the kid is arrested. Next thing they know, the kid is at your house and guarded by the FBI. They can't get to him. They can't get to the brother. Until the kid leaves to see his shrink."

I knew the rest. "Were all of them involved?" I didn't want to hear that Dave had been involved in this disgusting event. Everything I believed in the world would have come crashing down on me if I learned he was capable of this monstrousness.

"You want to know about Buchanan?" Luis asked. I kept eye contact and waited, angrily contorting a paperclip during the interim. Luis pulled a package of Mexican taffy out of his pocket and offered it to me. I chose a green one and stabbed the pointy end of the paper clip viciously into it. "Haven't heard his whole story," my partner continued. "From what I hear, he was funneling money only. They didn't tell him about the girl's death or the illegals until after you got suspended."

At which point Dave came to spy on me. Although it was good to know he wasn't the worst of the worst, I was ashamed to admit I might have stood by my best friend even if he'd been more involved. I had my limits, but did they stop at cover-ups? Which made me consider something more relevant to my future. Could I ever be a good cop after this?

52:14

Fifty-two hours, fourteen minutes. That was how long it took for the doctors to move Peter from ICU to his own room. Of those hours, I spent less than thirty minutes alone with him. Alone meaning Zhavra and Darryl were either asleep, home or down in the cafeteria.

We spoke very little. Peter was tired, and the times where he stayed awake for extended periods, I gave to his mother. In return she gave me dirty looks and informed me I would not be "dragging her son with me to hell."

I responded in my typical mature and professional manner. "Surely not for just the one blow job. I don't even think I was that good. It's because I swallowed, isn't it?"

She spat something in Russian at me. It only made me flash her every tooth in my head.

"Austin," Peter warned. I winced, refusing to turn around to look at him until Zhavra brushed by me with her arms open.

"Petya, you are awake." She kissed his forehead. I'd seen him do that exact same thing to Cai. The memory made my heart contract.

"I'll go hang out in the waiting room." I worried that Peter was listening to her about going to hell. Was he rethinking the last two weeks now that things had settled? Was I? And what did it say about my current mental state that 'settled' was the term I used to define where we were now?

"Wait, Austin. Mamma, it's nearly ten and you've been here all day. Go get some sleep."

"I do not think you should be alone with this man, Petya."

"I'm twenty years old, mamma," was all Peter said. I wasn't sure why I was on the receiving end of her glare that time.

"I see you early tomorrow." She kissed him again, her lips lingering on his cheek and her eyes closing. A wave of guilt passed over me when her hand slipped into his and squeezed. The other hand shook slightly as she swept it over his forehead.

"I can take you to your hotel, Mrs. Dyachenko," I offered.

She considered me with a hard look, then her wrinkles smoothed. "Thank you, but Petya wishes to speak with you. I will have a cab." Gently taking her purse from the side table, she headed for the door, stopping next to me. Without turning, she said, "You may pick me up. Early. Do you understand early?"

"Between noon and one?" I grinned.

"He's kidding, mamma," Peter interrupted and sighed at me after she had left. "Do you have to antagonize her?"

"I'm an ass. It's what I do. Does she have to act like I'm going to toss you on your stomach and assrape you in front of her?" I sat to his side and dragged a finger over his hand.

"Pretending you're not thinking about it?"

"You look like shit. Fucking you is not in the cards. I was thinking blow jobs."

"Can you sit on the other side?" He moved his hand away.

"Why?"

"You know why. Can you just do it?"

"I don't give a fuck about the colostomy bag, Peter. It's temporary anyway."

"What if it's not temporary?"

"Then I guess the rest of my life will be resigned to doggy style sex." The words were out of my mouth before I could think about them. "I mean however long...when we're...that wasn't a fucking proposal."

"Okay."

"Don't smile like that. Smugness doesn't become you."

"Okay."

"Scoot the fuck over. You're hogging the bed."

"I can't move myself. I'll split my stitches."

After some maneuvering, I lay down next to him and used my arm as a pillow. The other hand was firmly attached to the remote control. I flipped to baseball. "Do you even like sports?"

"Hockey." He took the remote and replaced it with his hand. We watched most of the third inning before he spoke again. "Austin, about being exclusive." My stomach tied itself into knots.

"Yeah?"

"It's not the end of the world if you want to change that."

"That what you want?" *What the fuck?*

"You are just out. It's too soon for you to be exclusive."

Because he sounded so tired, I held my anger in check. "Is that so?"

He blew out roughly. "You're angry. Again."

"You're telling me how I feel. Again."

"Just think about it."

"Think about fucking anything that moves until I can decide if I want to be exclusive to someone? How many dicks do I have to suck to get to the center of my gayness?"

"Or dating or just being with men like you. It doesn't have to be reduced to fucking. But yeah, you're going from gay to relationship in two weeks." His heart monitor accelerated. I needed to control my anger and not perpetuate or escalate the argument.

I squeezed his hand and scooted until on my side, facing him. "Listen to me, because this is about as serious as I get." His nose twitched, nostrils flaring. I forgot what I was going to say when the epiphany hit. "Your Tourette's," I said, smiling in wonder.

His face became icy still. "Fuck off."

I laughed and kissed his nose. "That's why you give those glacial looks. You're controlling your twitches."

"Not just twitches, Austin. You have this idealism that's just not realistic when it comes to me. My nose twitches. My nostrils flare. I clear my throat twenty or thirty times an hour. I get facial ticks. Sometimes I bark. Still think it's so cute?" The monitor ticked louder.

I did think it was cute. To me, everything about Peter was cute. But my nose was broken and that was his go-to appendage when he was pissed off. I decided to ignore his question for now.

"When I was sixteen my grandfather told me he'd cut me out of his will if I saw my faggot friend ever again. I think he and my dad knew what I hadn't admitted to myself." The burrow of Peter's brows amused me. "I didn't care. Not about the money. Not ever about the money." I dragged my arm from under my head and smoothed out his brow with my thumb, willing him to relax. "It wasn't until after Jesse died, when I was vulnerable, that he struck.

"He was astute. A genius lawyer. He figured me out and how to get to me. 'Just you remember, boy, fags live alone and die alone. And anyone associated with them. Do you want a family? Don't you want a normal life? Or do you want to die alone? Hear me, boy?'"

It hurt when Peter pulled back from my hand, turning his face to the ceiling. I guess I had my answer, but maybe I needed the nail driven in further to fully appreciate how much I was alienating him with my commitment issues. Which were less issues than needs. "He knew what I was, and he knew that I needed to be part of a family more than I needed to be myself."

"Austin—"

"So I really don't need to fuck a bunch of men to figure out who I am and what I want, Peter. I just need to fuck one."

"Okay."

I exhaled at Peter's universal word for an excited yes. "Okay," I said.

"I come with a lot of baggage."

"And a colostomy bag." He gaped at me. I lifted his sheet and looked at his stomach. "Seriously, that's gross."

He reached up and flicked me on the nose. "Ow! Christ!" My eyes were watering, and my nose throbbing, but I was smiling as I leaned in and kissed him.

"God, you're an ass." He laughed.

I Might As Well Grow a Vagina with All This Sharing

Nurses awakened us at four to check his abdomen for infection, and I decided to stay awake so I could pick up his mother at six. The nurse lifted his gown and prodded his stomach. The small bullet hole was patched, but the slash from sternum to below his belly button was panic inducing. I avoided looking at his wounds and used the time to catch him up on the case.

"So all of those people are dead?" Peter asked.

"The seven women and men who shared the safe house with the girl were killed, along with four more at the whorehouse, they think. None of the cops was part of that, so they say, and Leila isn't talking anytime soon. They haven't found the bodies yet."

"Joe?"

"We think the stress of keeping the secret caused his heart failure. He had called Ron several times to intimate he had evidence but wasn't sure what to do with it."

"He died protecting Iss." He smiled a little, but it was melancholic. I hadn't destroyed his cop-hero completely. He wasn't the good man Peter had thought, but he wasn't a monster. "Romantic in a bizarre way."

"Since when are you romantic?"

"You've known me two weeks, Detective Glass. I know how to cook, I like beer, I want to stick my tongue in your ass, I secretly love that disgusting cat Cai brought home and I'm *romantic*. Still so sure about me?"

"I'll rethink the exclusive nature of our relationship if you bring home another cat. Or another brother. You can have all the beer you want. It's not detective any longer. I'm unsure about the tongue in ass. I'm equally disgusted and intrigued." Obviously, I wasn't that disgusted. I was also hard.

He took a deep breath. "They fired you?"

"They were probably going to, but I quit."

"Aren't you some kind of hero or something?"

"Who announced he's gay to the stationhouse, slept with a suspect, concealed evidence of his lover's crime, housed a murderer and is best friends with a crook?"

He relaxed into the pillow and yawned. It set off a chain event. I yawned. The nurse checking his vitals yawned. She also loitered a little too long during our conversation. "What are you going to do now?"

"Devote a few months to learning about gay sex." I bit his nose gently and cradled his jaw in my hand. "After that? Maybe I'll try private investigation."

"Cool. I can be your man Friday." My brows popped up at the reference. He smiled and shook his head, then turned to the television. With a touch of his hand, the screen flickered on. "I like that I can surprise you." Suddenly, he turned off the television and cocked his head. "How'd Cai get free?"

"The FBI. They tracked him down. Rosa is a pretty important witness. Her son demanded full attention."

"Is Cai still in trouble?"

I shook my head. "Angelica is fighting to get him released. They have to formally drop the charges. He'll probably be free tomorrow." I raised my brows at the nurse who was eyeing us sideways and pretending to write things down on the chart. Who was she trying to fool? Her pencil wasn't even touching the paper.

"What happens to Detective Buchanan now?" Peter asked, taking a deep breath and sinking into the pillows.

"Dave? He made a deal. Three years federal prison for his testimony, and then he's going to split to Sweden. His wife and kids are there now." I took the remote and flipped the TV back on.

"Austin?"

"Hmm?"

"Thanks."

"Shut the fuck up. I'm trying to watch the game."

Chapter Twenty-Four

Checking Out

In the aftermath, the sprint into my relationship with Peter was marked by blips of volatility during the intervening quiet.

Four days after Peter's room change, we learned that Leila had succumbed to her head trauma. I didn't mourn her loss; nor did I think about the fact that I had caused her death. I had more important things to do. I spent that evening fighting with Peter over the remote control.

"I'm sick," he protested when I flipped the channel to sports.

"Anyone who doesn't like baseball is sick."

"Were you always this boring?"

"I'm boring because I don't watch political shows? There are millions of people around the world who would disagree."

"What kind of man takes the remote from an invalid?"

"The kind who is enlightening his man to the beauty of baseball." I said it to shut him up. It worked, but it equally shut me up. I ended up missing the entire game because I was busy thinking about the implications of that statement. I didn't even notice when Peter took the remote.

The next night I brought in my laptop so he could watch his cable news channels and I couldn't say stupid things like 'my man'. Propping my feet on his bed, I watched the game. Neither of us, thankfully, brought up my slip of the tongue. And every once in a while, Peter's finger would trail along the arch of my foot propped on the bed near his hip. I would shiver and shift in my seat. He would smile.

The charges against Cai were dropped, with a signed witness statement from Frank Marco on how Leila—now conveniently dead—pulled the trigger on her husband. Who knew if that was the truth. Cai refused to talk about it. Not long after his release, Luis brought Cai to the hospital along with Rosafa; and we left Peter alone with them to catch up.

"Looks like I owe you again," Luis said as I filled the vending machine with quarters.

"For what?" I knew he was talking about my having taken full blame for concealing Peter's crime. At the same time, I had handed in my resignation.

"Don't play idiot."

"You tried to stop me."

"I didn't stop you, is the point."

I smiled, handing him a cup of coffee and got a second cup for myself. We sat in the waiting room, side-by-side, studying the opposite wall.

"I was quitting anyway. After all the mistakes, figured I might as well do something right on my way out."

"The captain didn't buy that I was clueless."

"Internal Affairs did. That's what matters."

"I.A. isn't interested in what was pled down to a misdemeanor."

"We're even, Luis. You don't owe me anything."

"How you figure?"

"You never trusted Peter. You always thought Cai was guilty. You held back because you trusted me."

He pointed his cup at me. "In that case, you're right, you owe me."

"I'll send you a gift next hump day." My grin widened.

"If I even see your face on a Wednesday from here on out, I'll shoot first and ask questions later."

"Luis, only Peter can shoot on my face."

"I'm outta here." He hustled out of his chair with more grace than a man his size should have.

I finished my coffee with a lighter heart, knowing my friendship with Luis wasn't lost.

On the way back to Peter's room, I found Angelica gracefully parked in a plastic hospital chair. She pressed her lips together when we made eye contact, took a deep breath and relaxed her mouth into a smile.

"I miss you," she said with a shrug.

Maybe one more friendship could be salvaged.

Picking Up The Peace

"I miss you, too," I replied. I slid into the chair beside her. She laid her hand on my arm.

A nurse passed by and smiled at us both. Me in my jeans and sneakers, Angelica in her favorite navy skirt suit. We were mismatched, but we looked like a couple. What would be the nurse's reaction if Peter was next to me? If I held his hand? If I kissed him? It didn't seem fair to wonder about things like that for the rest of my life.

"I can't stop thinking about it."

Once again, I didn't have to ask what. "Me either. Especially now that I have so much free time to think."

"I have gay friends. One of the firm's lawyers is gay, and we hang out."

"I know a lesbian," I offered.

"I'm not counting coup, Austin. I just don't understand. I never had a question about homosexuality being something you're born with. Unchangeable. But you're twenty-six. I'm trying to get it through my head because of every man I know, you're the least likely person to ever *choose* to be gay. But just suddenly…"

I leaned my head back against the wall and shut my eyes. "I hope you're not asking me to explain it. I've been gay for ten minutes. I don't know how it works. Last night I asked Peter if I had to like the Village People and wear leather chaps."

Her musical laugh danced along the hall. Then she rested her cheek against my shoulder. "He's nice, your," she hesitated, "Peter?"

"He's snarky and vindictive, and romantic," I shuddered, "and yeah, he's nice." Too nice for me. Much too good for me.

"Romantic?"

"I don't think he expects flowers, but he doesn't gag when I call him my boyfriend."

"That is probably too romantic for you."

"Luckily he makes up for it with a mouth that could suck a ping pong ball through a Twizzler." Her upper lip drew up to reveal her teeth. "Too soon?"

Her laughter shook my body as she hid her face in my shoulder. "I love you, Austin."

"Me, too." I took her hand. "Me too, Angel."

"I have this crazy idea."

"Yeah?"

"Why don't you wait until this one proposes to you?"

Don't Look At Me, I'm Not Even Here

A fight about Cai staying with us was in full swing in Peter's room. I sat in a corner chair and buried my nose in a celebrity magazine like it was ESPN porn.

"He is my son, Petya. You cannot expect me to leave him behind forever."

"I'm sorry, Rosa, but it's what's best for Cai. It's not fair, and I'm a terrible person for having taken him from you. But we're all he knows."

"Rosa, if there were any other way." Darryl said.

"This is not right. He belongs with his mother." Rosafa watched her son with tearful eyes.

While they argued, I tried not to look up. When I did, I caught Cai staring at me while playing with the beaded black necklace around his neck.

"Do you want me to stay?" He asked.

Everyone turned to me and waited for an answer. I, of course, responded with my clever and insightful, "Huh?"

"Do you want me to stay with you?" Cai repeated.

I thought about how he must be feeling right now. How difficult it must be to choose between his mother and the only people who never failed him. I hoped to hell he wasn't hinging his decision on me. I wasn't exactly impartial. "Yes. I want you to stay. I think it would be best if you stayed. No one could love you as much as Peter, not even your mother. But I'm biased when it comes to mothers." I went back to reading my magazine. "And…I like you, too," I grumbled.

He kissed my cheek, and I felt the wetness on his lips. First thing I was teaching him was how to not cry all the goddamn time. I didn't look up when he made his announcement. "I'm sorry, mamma."

"No. I will not allow it."

"Let me know when you're done with this conversation. Peter needs his tongue bath. I mean sponge bath."

"Austin, Dammit!" Peter rubbed his face.

Cai hiccupped a giggle. Everyone else was silent as I licked a finger and turned another page.

"You see? He is an animal. You want my son to be with an animal? Sex. All he thinks of is sex. He does not even have a table for a family meal."

"Aaaand we're back to that," I said, flipping another page. I opened my mouth to say exactly what I'd do to Peter on a dining table, but Peter must have read my mind.

"Not helping, Austin." he took a deep breath. "I promise I'll buy a table. We'll eat dinner as a family. I'll even take Cai to the mosque."

"But...um...I don't believe in," Cai meekly trailed off, "God."

The argument waged on for an hour. Cai pulled up a chair next to me and watched them like a home movie, cringing in parts, crying in others, sometimes burying his face in his knees.

"It shouldn't be this easy to say goodbye to her," Cai said for my ears only.

"It shouldn't," I agreed, "But it's not your fault, kid. You don't know her. And staying is what's best for you. She'll realize that before she goes." In retrospect I shouldn't have been the one comforting Cai about his mother leaving. My interest lay in his feelings. I had little sympathy for her. Or mothers in general.

In the end, Rosafa did realize what was best for Cai was staying with Peter and Darryl. I had to give her credit for that. Later, I would find that my behavior with Rosa that day incited Peter to insist I resolve things with my own mother.

Questioning the Gay

Angelica had me thinking about proposals and the future. Gay. It changed everything. But then, it always had. Being gay had defined my whole life, and I hadn't even been aware of it.

Gay was the reason I had no close male friends after high school. Except for Dave. Because I was never attracted to him. Dave was safe. Other men weren't.

Gay was the reason I quit playing football with the guys. After a few boners in the middle of a game, I gradually became busy on Sundays so I could spend them with Luis, with Dave and Marta, with Angelica. Excuses so I could avoid my reactions to sweaty male bodies.

Gay was the reason I hopped from one woman to the next. The reason I never held onto a relationship. If I dug deep enough,

I could probably find a host of other ways that being closeted had impacted my life. But what was important now, what I couldn't stop thinking about was: Would my outlook change now that I had accepted I was gay? Would my moral views change? Did I believe the same things? Monogamy? Marriage? Kids? Peter seemed to think I shouldn't.

"I'm just sayin' it's not realistic," he said, placing his foot on my chair between my legs.

"You and your realism." I lifted it and pulled his sock on, then forced his foot into his shoe. "Because I'm gay I'll suddenly change?"

"Because you're just out. You're going to find a lot of things change. Starting a relationship with the same mentality isn't realistic."

I finished tying his sneaker and motioned for his other foot. He complied, smiling as I rubbed the arch before shoving his foot in the other sneaker. "What about you?"

"It's different for me."

"Because you're not gay?"

"Because I've sucked and fucked enough to figure out that one dick is just like another, one vagina isn't any more special than another, and I've got more important things to do than looking for a new trick every night." He winced and rubbed his abdomen. "I already found out that marriage isn't what holds people together, Austin. And infidelity isn't what tears them apart. We're going to be together on our own terms."

He pulled off his shirt and immediately my questions took a backseat. His abdomen was a patchwork of scars, from the surgical one running straight down his torso to the smaller ones from his colostomy bag and the bullet wound. Their red raw nature reminded me that Peter was still in pain. That his wounds itched and burned so badly he slept in fits. Not a good time for me to start an argument.

As he pulled on a fresh t-shirt, I determined not to give in to the heart pounding fear that was tying knots in my throat. My hands shook as I secured his other shoe. The fight wasn't worth the heartache. "We can talk later."

"I thought we worked this all out?"

"We worked out that I forced monogamy on you when I didn't really figure out if that's what you wanted. Or even if I could be."

"You think I feel obligated to be with you on your terms?" He smiled, tossing me an empty gym bag. I started to pile in the clothes that Darryl and I had bought for him.

"Your mother thinks you're indebted to me because you owe me money. Darryl thinks you owe me because of Cai. And Rosafa thinks you're with me because Cai is choosing to stay here after you decided to move in with me. Yeah, I think you might feel obligated."

"Overthinking. It's like a disease with you. They should make pills for it."

"They do. Little blue ones that drive the blood from the brain straight to the cock."

"Hard-ons don't make you think less. They make you think stupid. Which makes me think you must have one 24/7."

"Ouch."

"Austin." He propped back on his hands, his t-shirt sliding up to reveal a portion of the scar on his abdomen. My stomach contracted in empathy. "For the record, I want to be exclusive."

He had carefully avoided my question. "Do you feel obligated to me or not?"

"Of course I do. I told you that before. But it's not why I want to be with you." He zipped up the bag and picked up the newspaper-wrapped gift I'd given him an hour earlier. Instead of opening it, he'd set it on the side table and ignored it while he got dressed. In the wake of this discussion, I had forgotten it. Now it rested ominously in Peter's lap. Like he expected it to hold some clue to our future.

"I'll get the release forms," I said, standing up.

He ripped open the package before I could escape. "This is why I want to be with you, Austin. Not because of money or emotional debt." He fingered one dingy ear of the slippers I had rescued, his smile taking my breath.

My stomach flipped a few times. "Because I dry cleaned your slippers?"

"Because you value what's really important." He inhaled and exhaled loudly and set the slippers on the bed beside him. "Now I have to ask you for one more thing."

"If it's a three-way with Darryl, I am not going to be the girl."

The severity of his gaze made me glad my nose wasn't within flicking range. But, since his tongue could be just as sharp as his fingers, my ears were already preparing for his barb. "I think you should go see your mother before she dies."

There was no preparing for that.

Whatever It Takes

"No," I said, keeping the rage out of my voice with herculean effort. "Are you ready to go?" I held out my hand. He passed me the gym bag, keeping hold of the handles as I grabbed it. I couldn't jerk it away without jarring him. I let go. "I don't have a mother."

"Not for me. Not for her. For you."

This could be an argument by being stubborn, or I could convince him how bad an idea it was. I sat next to him, staring out the window. "You want me to tell off a dying woman?"

"If that's what it takes," he said. "You've been here six weeks, every day, and didn't even visit when you tested to donate your liver to her! She's one floor up."

"There are a lot of strangers one floor up. Am I supposed to visit them, too?"

"You walked right past her room."

"We should talk about something more important. Like who is supplying your information." There was only one person who could have told Peter I had been upstairs. "You know what I find ironic? My homophobic father has spoken to my male lover more times in two months than he has to me my entire life."

"You know what I find ironic? My homophobic mother offers you her cabbage rolls as a truce and you respond by asking her if it was 'tacit approval' to suck my cock."

"She shoved a phallic symbol my way and told me to eat it."

"If your idea of a cock is a stuffed green leaf covered in red sauce, we have more to discuss than monogamy."

"You used ironic incorrectly."

"Shit happens!" He spat. Oops. I had hit the Peter-thinks-I-think-he's-stupid button.

"Then again, so did I."

He narrowed his gaze and blew out a breath. Our relationship was a series of volatile reactions. With the rollercoaster ride my pulse was on, I could honestly say that I liked it that way. These days our arguments were heated, but not cruel. Our makeups were even better.

He chewed his inner lip. A sign I always took as him figuring out how to get me to do something. "I think you should see your mother. Something is making your dad get involved with all of this."

"You're a manipulative asshole, you know that?"

"You love it."

"Only when your manipulations are to get into my pants."

"Yes, my so clever manipulations to get into your pants. What were those again?"

"Breathing. Talking. Existing." Snagging his suitcase, I swung off the bed and hid his shaved head with my baseball cap. As I fit it over his brow, I made him laugh with a wiggle of my brows.

He straightened the cap and tucked his hands into his pockets. "Well?"

"Yes, you're still hot. Too tall. A little too skinny now. I miss your hair. But the scars are sexy." I feigned innocence with a grin while he stood there, waiting. My hand dropped, the bag bouncing heavily against my leg. "Let it go, Peter."

He looked away and nodded. "Okay."

Releasing the bag, I leaned in, tucked my hands behind his neck and pressed my mouth next to his ear. "Let it go." He turned and caught my lips with his. A second later, the ground tilted and I was wrapped in him.

I never tired of kissing Peter. His myriad of tastes and scents, of touches and sounds overwhelmed the senses. I sometimes felt the strange sensation of levitating when I tried to take in everything. Erotic meditation I called it.

His rough hands gripped my arms, pressing me closer. He smelled of hospital soap and over-the-counter lotion. He gasped, and his breath excitedly exhaled, heating my lips. He tasted of lime Jell-O. I considered buying cases of it just to relive this kiss. But the next kiss he would smell of lemon or cinnamon or aftershave, and he would moan, or whisper my name instead of gasping; and he would taste of mouthwash or the Pixie Stix he shared with Cai or whatever soda he was drinking. And then I'd want a case of those.

I was still in that dazed, erotic meditation, freefalling when Cai interrupted. "Oh. Um. Sorry." He scratched his head and bounced up to his toes. "I just...Darryl and your mom...I think he might, um...hit her."

Peter looked from Cai to me. His laughter trailing to a knowing smile. "Breathe, Austin."

I tossed Cai the keys to Arturo. They bounced off his chest and fumbled into his hands by accident rather than design. "See if Darryl will let you drive home. We have something to do."

Peter stuffed his hands back into his pocket, laughing at the speed of Cai's departure. "Your mother?"

I nodded.

"What changed your mind?"

I traced his lips with my thumb. "Erotic meditation."

"It's a little sad that after making out for five minutes, you're ready to do anything for me," Peter teased.

"I haven't had sex in six weeks. My erections are boring holes through my pants. Pulling up your sleeve at the right moment might convince me to sign over my checking accounts."

"Good to know."

"But I'm not doing this for you." I turned his hat backward and trailed my fingers lightly down his neck. "We have enough baggage without my mother."

"Okay. I mean...good. Yeah. Whatever. Okay." He bit his lip.

Jesus, he was cute. "Speaking of sex, how about a hand job in the elevator?"

He dragged his fingers through my hair and pushed down. "How about you suck my cock right now?"

Are You My Mother?

My father stood when I entered the room. I used that excuse to avoid looking at the bed and concentrated on his wary head tilt. His eyes floated past me to the doorway where Peter leaned casually with his hands in his pockets.

"Son, I do not think it is appropriate for you to bring—"

"My faggot boyfriend in here to flaunt my faggot lifestyle?" Crossing my arms over my chest, I leaned back against the wall furthest from them both. "You should thank him. He's the reason I'm here."

"It is inappropriate to bring a stranger into her room without her permission," he ground out.

"Desmond, would you fetch a nurse?" My mother laid a hand on his arm. I willed her gnarled fingers to wither and crumble under my glare.

My father barely hesitated before striding out the door.

Peter caught my eye. I looked down and gave him a slight nod to indicate he could leave me alone with her. He slipped backwards out of the room. When the tip of his sneaker vanished around the corner, I finally allowed my eyes to rest on her.

She wasn't the beautiful, composed woman who graced my father's arm at charity functions so long ago. Her eyes were hazel baubles surrounded by a brownish-yellow sea. Her skin had a taint of jaundice, and deep lines burrowed into her forehead and at the corners of her eyes. Botox must not be a good mix with liver failure.

My analysis complete, I kept my neutral expression and waited. I wasn't going to give her the upper hand by speaking first. I would not reveal the depth of my rage; it was so profound, my upper lip twitched with the urge to sneer. I would not give her a goddamned thing.

"You look like my brother," she said.

"That's..." Interesting? Who gives a crap? About twenty-six years too late?

"Neither here nor there, I know." She waved a hand blithely and took another sip. "You don't want to hear about Denny or me. You're pissed off, and you want to let me have it. Probably with buckshot."

"Mother's intuition?" I said coldly.

She barked a laugh and took a long gulp from a pink plastic cup when the coughing fit started. The soft color was striking against her pale lips. "Sound like Denny, too." She put the cup down and closed her eyes. "He was a homosexual. Died of AIDS in...'88? '89?"

Her words were a rain of stunning blows. I couldn't speak. I wanted to ask about Denny, about her family, but my tongue was glued to the roof of my mouth. My fingers bit into my palm and arm.

"If you come back, I'll show you some pictures. Tell you what I remember about my folks and Denny."

"I won't be coming back," I said stubbornly, even while another part of me longed for knowledge.

"Suit yourself. You got some cousins and an aunt. I'll just leave you notes with the albums." She pursed her lips and shrugged delicately.

Her fingers swished around in the cup. I heard ice click against the sides. It was the only sound in the room. My rage magnified with each clack.

"Are you human?"

"You think I should be groveling for your forgiveness and giving you a list of excuses about why I abandoned my family. That isn't going to happen. I didn't want to be a mother."

"No shit."

She fished into the cup and popped a few slivers of ice into her mouth. The crunching sound raked along my spine. "That's as much of an explanation as you're going to get."

"I'm so glad we settled this." I pushed off the wall, determined to get out of there before I strangled her. Before I could open the door, she hit me with another stunner.

"Don't you want to know about your brother?"

Baggage for Two, Please

"How old is he?" Peter asked.

The restaurant we stopped at on the way home was filled with family units. My eyes settled on a nearby couple with two rambunctious children. "Six."

"How old is your mother?"

"Forty-five." One of the boys tipped sideways and held onto his seat while looking upside down under his chair. The mother, a woman not much bigger than her child, leaned over and blew a raspberry on the boy's back. He giggled and nearly fell off.

While observing the little kid, all I kept thinking about was Peter. Peter and me. After all the shit we'd gone through, was there even a Peter and me now? I couldn't look at him. So I watched the little boy's antics. Until Peter forced my attention back to him with a gentle tap of my hand.

"Earth to Austin."

"I agreed to take him."

"Tell me something I don't know," Peter replied. "What's his name?"

"Stuart."

"Your father agreed to your having custody?"

"He didn't have a choice. She's got maybe a few days left since my liver wasn't a match. If she dies—when she dies—she threatened to leave her half of the practice to me if he didn't sign over his parental rights."

"Sounds like she's trying to make things right for at least one of her kids."

"Yeah. Hard to stay angry with her after that," I agreed. Actually, it was hard to stay angry with her at all. It wasn't her fault she was fertile.

"Where is he now?"

"Boarding school in the UK. She said he knows about me."

"I don't get someone who doesn't want kids having a second one."

"She was nineteen when she had me. Married to a man who worked ninety hours a week. She said she was star struck by my father and his money and position. Then they tried reconciling a few years ago. She said he just wanted her half of the business." I told him about my uncle.

"That explains her being okay with your being gay." He was smiling, but the way he pushed his French fries around the plate, I knew the smile was for show.

Looking down at my plate of lasagna, I felt queasy. "Which of us is going to address the elephant in the room?"

"Which one? I see a dozen elephants."

I picked the first one to come. "We can still…"

"There it is." He shoved his plate away roughly and picked up his phone. I blocked his screen with my hand.

"Don't."

"Don't what? Be angry you're breaking up with me? Think I'm going to beg you, Austin?"

"I'm not breaking up with you. I— Jesus Christ, I found out an hour ago that I have a six-year-old brother and ten minutes after that I was getting custody. Can you cut me some slack if I don't want you to feel obligated to—"

"I don't feel obligated to be with you, Austin Glass. How many times do I have to say it, you fucking moron!"

The hush that fell over the restaurant had me looking sideways and lowering my voice. "You're twenty years old. I can't expect you to be prepared to raise a six-year-old boy with me."

"Yes, absolutely. Because my track record proves that I have a problem parenting, and I so dislike the idea of children altogether. By any chance was that degree you keep bragging about *honorary*?"

"Touché and ouch."

"You can break up with me because you think we won't last and you don't want to subject a six-year-old to that. Or you can break up with me because you can't handle being gay and raising a six-year-old. Or that you can't handle a relationship at all. But don't blame *me*! I'm twenty, Austin, but I've lived more in my twenty years than you have in your thirty."

"Twenty-six! I'm twenty-fucking-six."

"You're exhausting me. I'm worn out fighting for this relationship. You need to fight for it. It's your turn."

"I worry we won't last, and I have no idea what being gay means or raising a kid or if two men can do it—or should. I feel selfish for even thinking of trying to make a relationship work with all that."

He looked everywhere but at me. Then he pulled his fingernails into his palms and stared at his fists. "Be selfish, Austin. That's the only begging I can do. Be selfish."

There was a stutter of my breath as my heart sped up. The noise around us seemed to dim as I asked the one question that was vital to my decision. "Can you tell me you love me, Peter?"

He spread his fingers. His hands shook so hard they drummed against the table, vibrating the silverware. "Do you think I'd be this terrified if I didn't?"

I put my hands over his. It wasn't much of a help, mine were shaking just as much. "Wanna raise a six-year-old with me?"

He exhaled slowly, each second marked by the tick in his breath. "I think I owe it to humanity to undo whatever influence you have on him."

"Hey, Peter Rabbit."

"What?" He looked up, his hands flipping to take mine.

"Don't you want to ask?"

"If you're ready for anal?"

Maybe we would make it after all.

Epilogue

Ass Hair Spawns the Weirdest Discussions

Peter sat on the bed, leaning back on his hands provocatively. I ignored him as best I could. I needed to get out of the house, and sometimes that wasn't feasible when Peter looked like he did. "I can do it for you really fast before you go," he offered when I turned my back.

"No you can't."

"I've done it before."

"No. You shaved *half* of my ass before. Then you buried your tongue in it for twenty minutes and your cock for another half hour. After that, you fell asleep. I walked around with ass itch for a week from having stubble on one side and hair on the other."

He bit his lip which did nothing to hide the grin. "You weren't complaining at the time."

I finished buttoning my shirt and began tucking it in. I was doing my best not to focus on his lips or the way his jeans molded against his legs. "Your 'come hither' thing," I pointed at the way he'd leaned back on his elbows and spread his thighs, "isn't going to work."

"No?"

Yes. "No."

"Why are you unbuttoning your shirt then?"

I looked down and quickly re-buttoned the tail end of my shirt. When did I untuck it? "Fucker."

"We have," he looked at the clock, "twenty minutes."

"Which I'm going to use to eat before my two-hour ride to the penitentiary." Every fourth Sunday I visited Dave in prison. He was to be released next month. After that he was off to Sweden. "I can't miss today."

"I could eat you now, and you could eat a hamburger on the way."

Damn his smile. I hesitated while buckling my belt. My eyes floated to his crotch. "Tonight," I said breathily. "Cai will be home tonight. He can babysit."

"He's getting in from Europe. Twelve hours of flights and airports. I don't think he'll be into much more than sleeping."

I gave up and went over, pressing our hips together as I lay atop him. "Then Darryl can babysit."

He locked his legs around my waist and slid his hands up my sides. "Did I say happy birthday?"

I scowled. "I thought we decided we weren't mentioning it?"

"Twenty-nine. A year from thirty. Maybe we shouldn't have sex. We have to start thinking about your heart."

"If I didn't have to go, I'd show you exactly how virile I can be."

He leaned up and whispered into my ear. "You could spend that two-hour ride with my come inside you."

"You're killing me," I groaned, inhaling raggedly.

Peter and I had finally settled the monogamy argument. We didn't choose it because of society; or because we needed to be faithful to prove anything. We chose to be monogamous because we didn't want to worry about condoms and HIV. It was hedonistic, really. But it worked for us. Which is why Peter surprised me with his next statement.

"Marry me."

My head jerked up from the crook of his neck. I stared into the depths of his eyes. "What?"

"Deaf in your old age?"

"Marry you?"

His hand rested on my chest. "Your heart is beating really fast. Is that fear or excitement?"

"It's both. And confusion." When Peter said he was romantic, it was in the way that I was romantic. A blow job and an "I love you" before rolling over and falling asleep. 'Marry me' was definitely outside our normal routine.

"Stuart asked…he asked if I wanted to adopt him."

"Oh." I climbed off him to think. I needed to get my head in gear. The other one.

"Do you not want me to?"

I smiled and laughed, shaking my head. "I brought it up with him last week."

"Okay."

Inscrutable bastard. "Okay?"

His nose twitched. "I want to adopt him. Legally, marriage makes sense."

That was the Peter I knew. "That settles that then."

"Okay." He smiled and bit his lip. That was when I knew it meant more to him than a legal issue.

"How do you manipulate me after three years?"

He pushed to his knees and wrapped himself around me from behind. "Because you love me."

"I love your cock."

DWS—Driving While Stunned

By the time Cai turned seventeen, he was six foot two inches tall. He seemed to tower over me even back then. I thought he was well over that when I picked him up at the airport.

"I thought teenagers stopped growing at eighteen?" I hauled his bags into the trunk. He must have brought half of Europe with him.

"It's only an inch and half?" He opened his winter coat and looked down at his, in my opinion, too tight jeans. "Am I too tall?"

"No," I assured him. "But did you eat in Europe? You're a stick with a head."

"Oh. Um. There wasn't a lot of time for food."

I took off his hat and mussed his hair. The snow looked strikingly white against the black sheen. "You look great."

"Peter couldn't come?" He checked the front seat and scrunched into my Aston Martin.

I shut the door after joining him in the car. My new baby purred to life. "He has finals. We were expecting your flight later tonight. How did you get here two hours ahead of schedule?"

"Money?"

"You had money left after you bought most of Europe?" I pulled onto the highway.

He laughed. "Most are presents for Stu."

The thing about Cai was that his moods were unstable. I never knew what his reactions would be to something. The roads were icy and the weather snowy and cold. I was reluctant to upset him while driving in sleet. But Stuart was excited about the adoption, and it was likely the first thing he'd hit Cai with.

"We have news about Stuart."

"I already know. Stuart texted me. I think it's cool." He blew steam on my window and drew a skewed heart.

"It doesn't mean…"

"Austin," he said, smiling at me, "Peter loves me. You love me. We all love Stuart. I'm not threatened."

"Peter is it? That's new." The new, adult Cai apparently had decided 'Rabbit' was juvenile.

"I have news, too."

The heart. "You met someone?" Thank God. The reason we had sent him to Europe for a year was to get him over Agent Riley Cordova. Maybe that was why he seemed so grown up, despite the innocence and sweetness of his smile.

"No," he said quietly. "You and Peter never did understand. I belong to Riley."

Christ. "Cai, he's my age. He's rejected you three times. You need to get over it." I didn't mean to be harsh, but those rejections had nearly broken Cai. And dealing with a depressed, suicidal teenager was not fun.

"I was underage. Now I'm nineteen."

"And he's thirty. That didn't change."

"I never told you. I never told anyone." He pulled out a beaded black necklace from beneath the neck of his sweater. I'd never seen him take it off. "He kissed me."

I nearly ran us off the road. "What?"

"He kissed me?" Cai looked sideways at me while grabbing the dashboard for dear life. "Just a kiss."

"I think you'd better tell me your news before I drive us into a ditch."

"Oh. Um. Maybe I should…so you don't…I don't want to die."

"Cai," I warned.

"Pull over?"

I took the next exit and stopped in a motel parking lot. "Please tell me you didn't shoot anyone."

"Shoot? Oh. No, I didn't shoot anyone." He scraped his teeth along his upper lip. "But um. I'm um… kind of in… not trouble. Not really. Maybe a little. But…Well. Interpol has a file…"

I gaped at him. There weren't words enough to describe how utterly devastated I felt. "Now is where you tell me you're innocent."

"Oh, well, Um. I'd like to tell you that. I really would. But if they question you…" He lifted his shoulders and winced a smile with raised brows. "Plausible deniability and all that."

About the Author

Dani Alexander is an American living way out in the boonies of Scandinavia. Dani has long since terrified all the introverted neighbors with bright smiles and the American Ways of bringing cookies and muffins over to their house. Sometimes they run when they smell baking. The neighbors find respite often, as Dani is almost always cloistered away in the computer room, fiendishly typing up new characters and figuring ways to torture them. Oh yeah, there's also two cats, a dog and a put-upon husband. For news and information visit Dani's website at http://slashfiction.org.

16510882R00208

Made in the USA
Lexington, KY
29 July 2012